Walter's Odyssey

The long walk.

A Conversation Recorded in 1986.

Published by New Generation Publishing in 2024

Copyright © Tony Mead 2024

Cover Photo - Martin J. Gabanski.

First Edition

The author asserts the moral right under the Copyright, Designs and Patents Act 1988 to be identified as the author of this work.

All Rights reserved. No part of this publication may be reproduced, stored in a retrieval system or transmitted, in any form or by any means without the prior consent of the author, nor be otherwise circulated in any form of binding or cover other than that which it is published and without a similar condition being imposed on the subsequent purchaser.

All characters are fictitious.

Paperback ISBN: 978-1-83563-219-2
Hardback ISBN: 978-1-83563-220-8
eBook ISBN: 978-1-83563-221-5

www.newgeneration-publishing.com

New Generation Publishing

Contents

Chapter One 1
Chapter Two 14
Chapter Three 26
Chapter Four 30
Chapter Five 46
Chapter Six 55
Chapter Seven 62
Chapter Eight: 69
Chapter Nine 76
Chapter Ten 88
Chapter Eleven 95
Chapter Twelve 100
Chapter Thirteen 107
Chapter Fourteen 112
Chapter Fifteen 115
Chapter Sixteen 121
Chapter Seventeen 126
Chapter Eighteen 131
Chapter Nineteen 137
Chapter Twenty 141
Chapter Twenty-One 147
Chapter Twenty-Two 150
Chapter Twenty-Three 155
Chapter Twenty-Four 159
Chapter Twenty-Five 171
Chapter Twenty-Six 177
Chapter Twenty-Seven 185
Chapter Twenty-Eight 197

Chapter Twenty-Nine 205
Chapter Thirty... 210
Chapter Thirty-One... 218
Chapter Thirty-Two... 223
Chapter Thirty-Three... 228

Chapter One.
Walter's Odyssey.

As the rain drummed a soft melody against the window of number 28 Almond Terrace, Walter Middlebrough sat in his weathered chair, his gaze fixed on the outside world. In his stillness, he is a silent witness to the passing of the seasons, the changing of generations, and the ebb and flow of life's journey. The droplets formed intricate patterns on the glass, each rivulet a reflection of his thoughts, stories of laughter, tears, victories, and struggles etched into every line of his weathered face. Clad in a worn jumper and slippers, Walter cradled an old photo frame, his fingertips tracing the edges with a tenderness that betrayed his solitude.

'It's just another day, much like all the others,' he whispered to the photo, weariness tinged his voice. 'Wish we could catch up later, my dear. Feels like an eternity since we last met… we had some good times.'

With gentle care, Walter placed the cherished photo frame on the mantelshelf, its spot among the other tokens of memory. Settling back into his chair by the window, the partially drawn curtains allow him to watch the raindrop rivulets that cascade down the glass, casting wavering shadows in the dimly lit room.

A car pulled up outside, its engine's hum faintly audible through the rain's pitter-patter. Walter paid it no mind until a faint tap on the front door disturbed his solitude.

'Hello, Mr Middlebrough, are you in?' called a voice through the letterbox. 'It's Joe Dobson from social services.'

Walter, his scepticism evident, cautiously inspected Joe's identification badge before unhooking the safety chain.

"What's this about?" His tone remained guarded.

"Just a quick chat, nothing to worry about," Joe reassured.

"Come in then. Don't want folks thinking you're the tallyman."

As Joe, armed with a bulging briefcase, stepped inside, he felt the familiar nervousness of meeting a new client. He wondered about their preferences and whether they would accept him. His imposing presence softened as he offered a reassuring smile.

"I can put the kettle on if you fancy," Walter offered. He was glad to have someone to talk to.

"Oh no, don't trouble, Mr Middlebrough."

"You'd better come in and sit down." He ushered Joe into the cosy living room, illuminated by soft natural light seeping through the curtains. The room seemed frozen in time, filled with sturdy yet enduring furniture, and weathered photographs capturing moments of the past, evoking a strong sense of nostalgia. A lingering aroma of tea hinted at the countless conversations held within these walls.

"Right, I'll just move my chair a little bit, so that I can see you better." As he pushes the chair he smiles down at it. "This blooming chair's needed recovering for at least ten years; mind you, I've sat in it for the last twenty. It's a bit like that Tardis machine, it transports me back to happier times." He chuckles to himself. Joe helps him turn the chair around.

"I'm here to talk about you going into care. Can we talk about that, Mr Middlebrough?"

As Joe gingerly approaches the topic, countless emotions play across Walter's face caught between the desire for independence and fear of change.

"You can call me Walter," he says, as he studies his visitor, a young man with neatly parted blonde hair.

Joe realised that it had been a mistake to open with the remark about Walter going into care and that there was a slight tension lingering in the air, the weight of his initial statement hanging uncomfortably between them. He needed to redirect the conversation swiftly.

Glancing at the faded photo on the mantel, Joe shifted gears, eager to steer the dialogue away from the uncomfortable territory they had unwittingly entered.

"I'll bet that everything here," Joe gestured around the room, "Is filled with stories, isn't it?"

Walter's expression softened, and his guarded manner eased. "Aye, you could say that. I suppose they've all got their own tale to tell."

With cautious steps, Joe ventured further, "I've always been fascinated by the stories that people's belongings hold. They're like whispers from the past."

Walter's eyes sparkled with a hint of intrigue. "Indeed, they are. Like this old photograph," he gestured toward the cherished frame. "It's more than just a picture; it's a sort of gateway to memories."

A flicker of understanding passed between them as Joe nodded in agreement. "Precisely. It's like every object has its own unique history, carrying within it moments that shape our lives."

A warmth spread through the room as they found common ground in their appreciation for the narratives embedded within everyday objects. Joe's careful redirection seemed to ease the earlier tension, inviting a more relaxed atmosphere.

"You have quite the collection," Joe remarked, gesturing toward a vintage record player resting on a side table.

Walter's face lit up, pleased to share. "Ah, that's been with me for years. Still plays a good tune, despite its age."

Their conversation drifted from one relic to another, each holding a cherished memory or a forgotten tale. The weight of the initial discomfort dissipated, replaced by a shared appreciation for the stories woven into the fabric of Walter's home.

As they explored the story behind each object, an unspoken understanding blossomed between them, bridging the gap that had initially stood between Walter and Joe.

Their shared fascination with the narratives of life infused the room with a newfound ease, fostering a connection that transcended the discomfort of the earlier conversation.

"It reminds me of my Nan's room, in a nice way, with the glazed tile fireplace and the obligatory 'Gas Miser heater'."

"We all got them when they stopped us burning coal. I didn't much like coke, it didn't burn the same."

Joe smiled, pointing to the side of the fireplace, "And she had the horse brasses on a strap like that."

Walter's mood seemed to lift as a distant memory surfaced. "Them's proper brasses."

Joe shared his own nostalgia, "My Nan polished hers until there were hardly any details left. Her whole mantelpiece was filled with brass ornaments... there was a swan that held matches between its wings."

Walter chuckled softly, the corners of his eyes crinkling with the memory. "Ah, the swan match holder! I remember them. Seems like every family had its own collection of brass treasures back then. It's a shame how these things have faded away with time."

Joe nodded in agreement, observing the old clock on the mantelpiece ticking away. "I suppose people don't hold onto these traditions much anymore. Everything's so different now."

"It is," Walter concurred, his gaze wandering to the old clock. "Sometimes I wonder if the world my generation knew will only survive in memories. You know, it's strange. In some ways, I've been living in the past, surrounded by the echoes of bygone days. It's been my way to keep those memories alive, to remember the world as it was."

Joe leaned forward slightly, intrigued. "Is that what keeps you going, Walter? The past?"

Walter nodded slowly, his voice filled with a sense of reflection.

"Partly, yes. Those memories are like old friends, reminding me of a time when life was so different. It's comforting, in a way, to hold onto the past. "It would be nice to have someone to share them with."

Joe smiled warmly. "I'd be glad to be that someone, Walter."

As Walter contemplated Joe's words about becoming his confidant, a quiet warmth settled within him. The prospect of sharing his treasured memories felt like a fragile gift after years of solitude.

The room lingered in a thoughtful silence, memories creating an invisible bridge between them. Joe glanced at the large bookcase, its shelves groaning under the weight of time-worn volumes, their spines a mosaic of adventures waiting to be unfurled.

"You must have journeyed through countless stories," Joe remarked, trying to steer their conversation to a lighter note.

"Aye," Walter replied, his gaze fondly caressing the spines of the books. "These books have been my comfort. Each one holds within its pages a world of its own."

Joe's eyes gleamed with curiosity, eager to unravel Walter's literary companions. "Do you have a favourite among them?"

Walter's eyes twinkled with reminiscent delight. "Ah, that's like asking a father to choose his favourite child. Each book has its own charm and wisdom, guiding me through uncharted landscapes."

As Joe leaned forward, an air of shared fascination enveloped them. "It's fascinating how stories transcend time, offering solace and knowledge."

"Aye, they do," Walter concurred. "In this room, I've travelled far and wide without leaving my chair. Through wars and peace, love and loss, these books have been my faithful companions."

Their shared appreciation for literature dissolved the lingering weight of their earlier conversation, infusing the room with a newfound lightness. Their bond, woven from shared memories and a love for stories, seemed to grow stronger with each exchanged word.

Joe's gaze wandered to the window, where raindrops danced in a fleeting ballet. "The rain's easing up now. Perhaps, Walter, you'd allow me the privilege of sharing one of your stories?"

Walter's eyes sparkled with unexpected joy, his smile warm and genuine. "Aye, I'd like that very much."

Their conversation shifted, weaving between the anecdotes and musings of a life lived and stories absorbed through pages worn by time.

"I understand that the nurse called last week after you'd had a fall," Joe said sympathetically.

Walter sighed, his voice carrying the nonchalance of someone accustomed to life's mishaps. "It were nowt... I caught my leg on summat in't yard and I fell ower. She bandaged it up for me. I've had a lot worse than that."

"Is it all right now?" Joe asked, concern evident in his voice.

"Bit sore, but it'll be fine," Walter assured him.

Joe was curious about the photograph, he nodded towards it, "Who's that in the photo?"

Walter's gaze softened as he looked at the photo of his late wife. "My wife: Alice, we were married... fifty-two years."

"Gosh, that's a long time," Joe remarked.

"It doesn't seem it now... I don't know where the years went." Walter's voice carried a tinge of nostalgia. "What about you, are you married?"

Joe's lips twitched, revealing a touch of vulnerability. "Six years... we've hit a bit of a rough patch lately," he admitted, the confession slipping out before he could hold it back.

Walter's eyes met Joe's, understanding passing between them.

"Life's too short for rough patches," Walter said, his tone maintaining a hint of reserve, but his underlying nature remained warm and welcoming.

In that shared glance and brief exchange, a silent understanding passed between the two men, acknowledging the complexities of life. Joe observed Walter's reactions keenly, an instinct ingrained from years of working in social services. He saw more than just Walter's surface reactions; he glimpsed the nuances in the old man's eyes, the subtle twitches at the corners of his lips, the tales hidden behind every wrinkle.

As the shared silence settled, bridging the gap between the generations, Joe's thoughts drifted. His gaze fell upon the well-thumbed books lining Walter's shelves, each title a clue to the man seated before him. Joe understood the solace found in the pages of a well-loved book, the comfort drawn from cherished memories, just as Walter found in his weathered photographs and the quietude of his home.

A passing neighbour caught Walter's attention.

"Oh, there goes Mrs Gardener from forty-two… I never had much time for her, but Alice used to chat with her a bit. She used to say 'Poor Mrs Gardener, her husband knocks her about you know,' and then when he died, she used to say 'Poor Mrs Gardener, she must miss her Harold.' She probably poisoned him if you ask me, I couldn't stand him either."

While Walter's gaze wandered to the window, observing the passing neighbour, Joe absorbed the scene around him. He noticed the small intricacies that made up Walter's world, the familiar but worn armchair, the antique clock with its steady ticking, and the faded rug that seemed to have weathered time itself.

With a quick glance at Walter, Joe recognised the man's longing and the wealth of untold stories locked away in the recesses of his mind. It stirred a sense of respect and empathy within Joe, reaffirming his commitment to understanding Walter's story beyond the surface.

Walter's reminiscence about Mrs Gardener from number forty-two caught Joe's attention. He noticed the subtle shift in Walter's tone, a blend of nostalgia and detachment in his words.

"Mrs Gardener, eh?" Joe nodded, gesturing towards the passing figure outside. "Seems like everyone's got a story around here. It's curious how the lives of neighbours weave together over the years, isn't it?"

Joe seized the opportunity, his curiosity is eager for more glimpses into Walter's life.

"It's fascinating how places like this, and the people in them, hold a wealth of memories. Speaking of which, Walter, forgive me if it's too personal, but what brought you to this part of Yorkshire? Your accent says one thing, but there's a richness to your words that speaks something else."

"It's a hell of a long story, lad," Walter replied wistfully.

Joe's inquiry held a blend of respect and genuine interest, hoping to uncover more layers of Walter's life story and the experiences that shaped the man sitting before him. He decided to inquire further, wanting to learn more about the older man's daily routine and what brought him joy.

"Walter," Joe began, "I'm curious about your daily life here. What do you enjoy doing? Are there any particular routines or hobbies that keep you busy and content?"

Walter's eyes twinkled with a hint of amusement as if he hadn't expected such questions.

"Well, lad," he said with a hint of Yorkshire pride, "Routines... I do have routines. The morning starts with a cup of strong tea, and then, aches and pains permitting, I tend to my little garden, right there by the window. Flowers, mostly. Roses and dahlias, they bring a bit of colour into my world."

He paused, his thoughts drifting to the past. "In the afternoons, I enjoy my books. It's my me time, and when I enjoy a good read." He points toward his bookcase. "And sometimes, if the weather's fair and my old legs will let me, I take a slow walk down to the towpath but that's a bit of a rarity these days. The canal has been a constant companion for years, always something to see or remember along its banks."

Joe listened intently, captivated by the glimpses into Walter's daily rituals. He admired the simplicity and richness woven into the fabric of the older man's routine.

"That sounds lovely, Walter," Joe remarked, a genuine smile curving his lips. "The dedication to your garden and the comfort found in books and the towpath, it's a beautiful rhythm."

Walter's eyes crinkled at the corners, a subtle acknowledgement of Joe's understanding. "Aye, lad, there's a certain peace in these simple things."

A comfortable silence settled between them, the ticking of the clock providing a gentle rhythm to their conversation.

"Tell me more about the canal," Joe prompted, genuinely intrigued by the picturesque setting Walter described. "It sounds like you've spent quite a bit of time there."

Walter's face brightened, the memories rushing in like a cherished flood. "Ah, the canal! I've seen it change over the years, witnessed the boats come and go. It's where I've found solace, where the reflections on the water seem to mirror the stories of the past."

Joe leaned forward, his interest piqued. "It must hold so many tales within its waters."

"Aye, it does," Walter agreed, lost momentarily in his recollections.

"There was the summer of '72 when the swans nested near Lock fourteen. People used to come from miles around to see those elegant creatures make their home."

A reminiscent smile graced Walter's face as he continued, "Or the day when the old barge, The Lady of Lea, got stuck near the bridge. Took 'em hours to free her, but the friendship of the folks gathered that day, helping out, it's a memory etched in my mind."

Joe marvelled at the vividness of Walter's stories, feeling transported to that canal, witnessing the vibrant scenes through the older man's eyes.

"It's as if the canal holds a map of life itself," Joe remarked, his voice filled with admiration.

Walter nodded in agreement. "Aye, lad, that's the beauty of it. Every ripple, every passing barge, they're like pages in a never-ending storybook."

And what about your interests, Walter? Any particular subjects or hobbies that you're passionate about?"

Walter leaned back in his chair, a wistful smile playing on his lips. "Ah, lad, I've always had a soft spot for history. The stories of the past, the tales of people who've lived and loved in these parts, it's like uncovering hidden treasures. And I've a knack for tinkering with old things, fixing them up good as new. Last winter I fixed Geoff's lawnmower."

"Geoff?" Joe enquired.

"Old lad that's down t'road, he got it all jammed up wi' a length of string, but I got it as good as new for him."

"Is Geoff a friend?"

"Not really, I've not seen him since I fixed it for him."

Joe leaned in, curious about Walter's interactions with his neighbours. "So, you just helped him out with the lawnmower, and that was it?"

Walter nodded, a hint of melancholy in his eyes. "Aye, just a small gesture. You know, it's the little things we do for each other that make a community. We might not be close friends, but we look out for one another when needed."

Joe smiled, appreciating the sentiment. "That's a good way to live, looking out for your neighbours."

Walter nodded in agreement. "It is. In this fast-paced world, we often forget the importance of simple kindness."

As they continued their conversation, Joe realized that Walter's life, while seemingly quiet and uneventful to some, was rich with the warmth of community and the satisfaction of helping others, one lawnmower at a time.

Joe felt a deepening connection with Walter, a sense of shared appreciation for life's simple pleasures and the intricate tapestry of memories and routines that made each day unique. He remembered that when he first arrived, he only saw an old man at the door, hunched and weathered by time. But now, as they shared stories beneath the warm glow of the living room's antique lamp, Joe realized that there was far more to this man than met the eye.

Their conversation meandered through the worlds of art, music, and literature. Joe discovered that Walter was not just a casual admirer but a connoisseur of fine art, a dedicated collector of vinyl records, and a voracious reader of classic novels. It was in these moments that Joe realized he had underestimated Walter's depth of knowledge and passion for the finer things in life.

As the morning progressed, Joe couldn't help but smile at the realisation that beneath the wrinkles and the frailty of age, Walter was a treasure trove of wisdom, experiences, and a zest for life that was truly infectious. Their friendship, which had started with a simple conversation, had blossomed into something profound, reminding Joe that sometimes the most remarkable people are the ones you least expect.

Walter rose with effort and shuffled to the kitchen. Joe's offer of help was met with a gentle refusal, a testament to Walter's determination. He returned, a battered cake tin cradled in his arms, a relic of nostalgia and sustenance.

"It's my lunchtime, Joe," he said with a kind grin. As he unwrapped the package, memories spilt out onto the faded paper, and he offered Joe a sandwich.

"Ham and cheese... would you like one? Please, will you share with me?"

Joe accepted with gratitude, a simple act of communion binding them closer.

"That's very generous, thank you. I didn't have time for breakfast."

Walter's eyes twinkled, his voice carrying the weight of shared experience.

"I've not bothered with any breakfast either this morning; doesn't seem any point." He studied his sandwich box a moment. "I allus still make more than I need, maybe I still make Alice's too."

As they savoured the sandwiches, a camaraderie blossomed, born from vulnerability and the willingness to share fragments of their lives. Their conversation flowed like a gentle stream, weaving together the threads of past and present, fears and hopes.

Joe's lips curved into a warm smile. "Shall I make us a cuppa? I'm ready for one."

Walter nodded appreciatively. "Sounds like a sterling idea, coffee... milk, no sugar, please."

As Joe rose to fulfil the simple request, the room hummed with the resonance of connection. In this space of shared moments, two lives, distinct yet intertwined, found solace in each other's presence.

Walter's gaze lingered on the ornate silver clock, its glass dome reflecting the soft glow of the room. "It's an ornate thing," he muttered, his eyes tracing the intricate swirls and plant-like motifs adorning the clock's face. "Silver Wedding gift from Alice's friends. Those spinning balls drive me mad."

Joe returned with the coffee, concern evident in his eyes. "Do you eat sandwiches every day, Walter?"

Walter's lips curled into a wry smile. "Can't be bothered with cooking anymore. Council used to send meals, Betty was a nice lass who'd bring them and she always had time for a chat. Then the council cut its services as if that fixed anything. The young lad next door fetches me chips sometimes when he goes for his mum. I give him a couple of bob for his trouble."

Joe's gaze turned thoughtful. "Any other relatives?"

Walter's gaze shifted to a far-off place. "Might have some, haven't seen 'em in so long, could all be dead for all I know. I can't actually remember the last time I saw any of them, I'd like to know what happened to them."

As Walter rummaged in his biscuit tin, two small packages emerged, wrapped in foil. Joe eyed them curiously. Walter grinned and extended them.

"Fruitcake and Wensleydale cheese. Old Yorkshire tradition... cheese and Christmas cake. Reminds me of Christmas every time."

They both took a bite, savouring the unique combination. Walter's eyes danced with a fleeting sadness before he brushed it away.

"I'm hoping someone will show up one day and take me for a picnic. Been wrapping sandwiches like this for years."

Joe leaned back, intrigued. "First time I've had them together... I like it. You know, Walter, you seem like you hold a lot of knowledge."

Walter's voice softened, carrying the experience of a long life. "See, lad, life's a blend. You savour the good moments and endure the bad because both will shift as time slips by. Took me years to figure that out."

Joe smiled and added good-humouredly, "It seems that you are a bit of a philosopher too."

Walter's gaze held a hint of surprise. "Well, I've learned to accept things. Enjoy the good, wait for the bad to pass. Both change as time goes by."

Joe leant closer, absorbing Walter's words. "It's an interesting philosophy. Acceptance is the key, I suppose."

A hint of a smile tugged at the corner of Walter's mouth. "Exactly, lad. Life's a bit like that clock, spinning orbs and all. You make your peace with the spinning, and the ticks don't seem so loud."

Joe's nod held a newfound appreciation. "I'll remember that, Walter. Thanks for sharing."

In the quiet interlude that followed, the clock's rhythmic ticks seemed to echo Walter's philosophy, a reminder that time marched on, carrying wisdom and connection in its wake.

Walter folded the sandwich paper meticulously and replaced the lid on the tin with care. He resumed, his eyes distant as he spoke. "At times, our expectations of dread can yield surprising outcomes. What seems grim, might turn out not so bad, or even unexpectedly delightful."

Joe responded with a knowing smile and a nod. "Well, my aim is to become a journalist, though luck hasn't favoured me so far. With a growing family, I need to look for a better wage. Don't mistake me… I do find satisfaction in this work, I've met interesting characters along the way. Julie believes I should have it all figured out at my age."

A sigh escaped Walter's lips before he enquired, "And what does Julie do?"

"She's a science teacher at the local grammar school," Joe explained. "Apparently, female science teachers are a rarity, and as soon as she finished university she found a job. The school where she works now welcomed her eagerly. She nags me because I'm undecided but I don't think that I'm any different to most people. Who does know what they want to do?"

Walter pondered momentarily, then shared, "I've never been one for cards, but an old song's lyrics resonate: knowing when to fold and when to play when to depart and when to stay."

Joe's smile reflected genuine understanding. "Yes, maybe we burden ourselves with matters beyond our control."

Walter's nod held wisdom. "Precisely. You don't reach my age without learning a few things. Above all, know when to worry and when to let something go."

Leaning back, Walter settled into his seat and relaxed. "You know, sitting by the window staring out... it gives me great comfort to know that the world still keeps spinning." Walter searched Joe's face. "You might think that's childish, perhaps it is, it's certainly peaceful."

A look of boredom almost despair crossed Walter's face, "I'm fed up with being cooped up. This street has been my home, save for the wandering years." He stood up to look out of the window. "Do you see that house, number twenty-three? That's where I was born."

Joe's curiosity surfaced. "Wandering? What's that about?"

A hint of mystery played across Walter's expression. "Ah, a lengthy tale. You might not think that I have got very far in life… being that I live opposite where I was born… but you'd be mistaken."

Walter stared at the small notebook Joe had taken out of his case and placed it on the table.

"Why don't you tell me about it?" Joe said, his journalistic curiosity coming to the fore. "Maybe it could make for an interesting article." He looked enthusiastic. "The editor of the local paper mentioned that if I could bring him a compelling story, he might consider offering me a part-time position. Come on, Walter. Something tells me that your story could be something of a little gem."

Walter leaned back in his chair, a distant look in his eyes. "I've often thought about all the people who've entered and exited my life but sadly now they've faded away… like footprints in the sand. Perhaps another time, Joe. Let me ponder it. I'm not up for it right now."

Joe nodded, understanding. "I didn't mean to push. Enthusiasm isn't a bad thing. I'll bet that you used to have it, didn't you?"

Walter's gaze dropped to his hands, weathered by time. Joe's mention of lost enthusiasm struck a chord within him, but he remained silent.

With a kind smile, Joe pulled out a couple of official-looking forms from his bag.

"When you're ready, take a look at these papers. They're about considering care options. If you remember, that's why I came."

Walter took the forms, examining them closely. "Yes, I'll go over them after I've finished my tea."

Joe offers a reassuring smile. "You know, Mr… Walter, social services are here to support individuals like yourself. We can help arrange regular check-ins, and maybe even connect you with some local community groups. It's important to have some social interaction and support, especially in times like these."

Walter considered Joe's words. "I appreciate the offer, lad. But sometimes, it's just hard to let new people into your life, you know? I've got used to things being a certain way."

Joe nods in understanding. "Change can be difficult, that's for sure. But sometimes, a small change can make a big difference. Just having someone to talk to, to share a cup of tea with, can brighten up the days."

Walter's gaze softens, and he looks out at the rain again, lost in thought. "You might be onto something there."

Joe closes his notepad, sensing a connection. "Well, I'm here to help. If you're open to it, we can work together to make things a bit less lonely, a bit brighter."

Walter smiles, a glimmer of hope in his eyes. "Maybe you're right, lad. Maybe it's time for a change."

As the rain continues its gentle rhythm against the windows, two lives converge – one filled with memories of the past, the other with a determination to bring some light into the present.

"Perfect. I'll come back tomorrow." Joe rose from his seat, and Walter held the door open for him. As Joe's car pulled away, Walter's eyes followed him up the street.

Turning to the photograph on the shelf, Walter whispered, "It was nice to have someone to talk to, Alice. I hope he comes back tomorrow."

He sighed, a mixture of hope and loneliness flooded into his heart. With a determined expression, he picked up the forms and began to read through them. The television droned in the background, but he soon nodded off. The papers fluttered from his knee to the carpet.

Joe switched on his car radio as he set off for home, seeking to break the oppressive silence that had settled within. The familiar tunes played, yet they felt intrusive, muffling the echoes of his recent conversation with Walter. He sighed and turned the radio off, inviting the night's quietness to envelop him.

Navigating the familiar, dimly lit streets of his home town, Joe's thoughts lingered on the unexpected bond he'd formed with Walter. Initially seen as someone he was simply tasked to assist, Walter had evolved into something more—a person with a narrative, passions, and a life that transcended the circumstances that had brought them together.

Julie greeted him at the door, her face etched with signs of stress.

"Hey, how's everything?" Joe observed the strain in Julie's expression.

"I'm alright, but Debbie's been a handful since I picked her up."

"Sorry to hear that. Was she okay at your Mum's?"

"You know my Mum, always on Debbie's side." Julie shrugged and planted a quick kiss on Joe's cheek. "How about you? How was your day?" Her interest was sincere, a hopeful distraction from her own worries.

"My day has been very interesting, I've got a new client, an old chap on the far side of Huddersfield. We chatted for quite a while he'd made sandwiches and he shared them with me it was quite a surprise but I felt some sort of connection with him I can't put my finger on just what it was."

Inside Debbie sat on the sofa playing her favourite video game. "You alright sweetheart?" Joe asked. She just briefly looked up and nodded knowing that she had been a bit of a handful.

Joe and Julie sat at the kitchen table to share their evening meal.

"You look like you want to share something with me," Julie said pausing between bits of her meal.

"Well, this may seem a bit profound but something struck me like a revelation and I realise that I've been guilty of reducing people I encountered as a social worker to mere case numbers… anonymous individuals, defined by their problems and challenges. Walter today has shattered that perception, he has reminded me that each of them has a past, a history, and a unique journey that has brought them to where they are."

"Oh my, something has really hit home, I can see that," Julie whispered softly to him.

The weight of this realization nagged at Joe throughout the evening. It was as if a veil had been lifted, allowing him to see the humanity in the people he helped.

"To say I want to be a journalist, I've been blind. I realise now the number of stories I must have walked right past. People's lives and their untold stories, the dreams they once harboured, and the resilience they carried in the face of adversity... I missed it all."

This newfound perspective left Joe both humbled and inspired, knowing that his role wasn't just about solving problems but also about recognizing the inherent dignity and complexity of the individuals he encountered. He knew that his journey as a social worker had taken an unexpected turn, one that would forever change the way he approached his work and the lives of those he sought to help.

Chapter Two.
A time for reflection.

Walter glanced outside from his usual spot by the window and noticed the tell-tale signs of winter's arrival. The air held a crispness that tingled with the threat of colder days ahead. A delicate ground frost had painted the world outside with a glimmering sheen, adding a quiet beauty to the otherwise familiar landscape.

His thoughts, still consumed by the previous day's conversation with Joe Dobson, momentarily paused as he glimpsed the empty milk bottle on the kitchen counter. An exasperated sigh escaped his lips.

Contemplating the empty milk bottle, he cast a longing gaze at the busy frost-laden street. He imagined the short journey to the corner shop, it had at one time been effortless, a simple task but now it was beyond his reach reminding him of the life he had once led.

Walter's day had become a dance of observation and reflection. He observed the neighbours bustling about, children rushing off to school, and the occasional passers-by wrapped in their winter coats, their breath visible in the cold air. These sights, while familiar, only served to highlight the distance between him and the bustling life outside.

Returning his attention to the kitchen, Walter sighed once more, resigned to the reality that he couldn't fetch the milk himself. Instead, he made a mental note to call the local store for a delivery. As he settled back into his armchair, the view from his window remained his connection to the world outside, it was a world he could observe but not physically engage with.

"Ah, damn it," he muttered, glancing at the biscuit tin on the counter. "Digestives for breakfast, Alice."

Just as his disappointment began to settle, a tap echoed from the door. Walter's weathered features brightened, and he hurried to open it.

"It's me again, Walter," Joe announced, a hint of a smile tugging at his lips.

A surge of gratitude washed over Walter as he welcomed Joe inside.

"Come in, lad, it's freezing out there."

"I brought some milk and bread," Joe offered, raising a carrier bag. "Noticed you were running low."

A genuine smile played on Walter's lips. "Proper thoughtful of you. Almost had to settle for a digestive for my breakfast."

As they settled at the worn kitchen table, Joe's gaze fell on the paperwork left hardly touched from the previous day. "Did you read the forms?"

"Sorry, I did try but I fell asleep."

Joe's reassuring nod brushed off the apology. "No worries, we can go through them whenever you feel up to it."

Walter leaned back, his eyes lingering on Joe. "I was wondering… if you're still interested in my story?" he said trying to put off facing the form filling.

Joe's enthusiasm was obvious. "Absolutely. I found our conversation yesterday quite fascinating.

Walter's chuckle held a hint of modesty. "Oh, but I don't know if my tale will interest you. If you're planning to write it down, you'll need more than a little book."

With a notebook poised, Joe was eager to make a start. "Whenever you're ready."

Clearing his throat, Walter's voice trembled slightly as he began, memories of a distant past flooding back.

'I was born in 1896 – just across the road at 23, I think I mentioned it before."

He gestures toward the window, eyes reminiscing through the glass.

"I was the sixth member of a bustling brood. My siblings' watchful eyes often cast me in the role of the family's perpetual baby. A charming position, yet it came with its own peculiar downsides… I was the continuous endpoint in the line for hand-me-downs and sundries. Thankfully, not to the extent of girls' frocks," he chuckles, a wistful smile gracing his lips.

"Tilly, the eldest; was followed by Joyce, Jack, Elsie, Claire, and finally, me.

In those days, life was lived within the stark confines of a mill house, the same as this. A stone-built privy stood in the backyard which served as a witness to our humble existence. The yard was a multi-purpose space which doubled as my Mum's laundry room in summer and our playground most days. There were days," Walter continued, "When we'd play in the yard, creating our own adventures out of nothing. Mum used to hang the laundry, and we'd imagine those sheets as sails on great ships, or the stone privy became our fortress against imaginary foes. It was a simple time, with few joys but plenty of imagination."

Mum and Dad worked in the local mill as weavers, we hardly ever saw Dad, because he worked extra shifts if he could. I suppose money was tight but we were no different to the rest of the street. The one thing we had in common with the rest of our community was that we were all short of brass."

Walter's recollections of his family's life in the local mill painted a picture of hardworking parents who struggled to make ends meet. Joe listened with a growing understanding of the modest circumstances Walter had originated from.

"That must have been quite tough for your parents," Joe remarked, offering a compassionate response to Walter's narrative. "I suppose you found ways to make the best of what you had."

Walter nodded, a faint smile touching his lips. "Aye, lad, we did what we could with what little we had. It was a different world back then. Money was scarce, but the warmth of family and the creativity of childhood filled the gaps."

Walter nodded, his eyes reflecting a blend of nostalgia and melancholy.

"Aye, it was a different world back then. The millwork was gruelling, but it put food on the table, just about."

Joe leaned forward, genuinely intrigued. "What was life in the mill like, Walter?"

Walter leaned back in his chair as if transporting himself back in time. "Well, of what I saw of it, it was a world of its own. dusty, noisy, and monotonous. Rows and rows of clattering looms, spools spinning, and the rhythmic thumping of machinery. And in that never-ending dance of threads, my parents toiled hard to look after us. Some mornings, the smog from coal fires and furnaces was so dense that you could hardly see your own hand in front of you. Mind there was very little traffic to worry about and most of that was horses."

Joe tried to visualize the scene, "It must have been a tough way to make a living."

Walter nodded solemnly. "It was. The hours were long, the work was hard, and the pay was meagre. But that was our lives." Walter shrugs his shoulders. "We didn't know any different."

Joe's curiosity didn't wane. "As a child did you ever visit the mill?"

A hint of humour touched Walter's lips. "Oh, yes. When I was a lad, I'd sometimes sneak in after school. I was fascinated by the machines and their relentless motion. I used to watch the massive spools spin and the fabrics take shape. The workers knew me because Mum and Dad were there, so they'd give me odd jobs to do or a bit of thread to play with. It was my little escape."

Joe smiled at the thought of young Walter exploring the mill with wide-eyed wonder. "It sounds like you found some solace in that chaotic world."

Walter nodded. "Aye, I did. The mill, the streets, it all shaped who I became."

Joe leaned forward, genuinely interested. "It's remarkable, Walter. Your early years, they've woven the fabric of your life so intricately."

Walter acknowledged this with a thoughtful smile. "Aye, and like those looms in the mill, my life's been a weaving of stories, each thread connecting to the next."

There was a long pause and then suddenly Walter's mind threw him another memory.

"Monday never wavered as wash day... a ritual I'll not forget. All of us would fetch buckets of water from the standpipe at the corner. We didn't have running water then. A grey Peggy tub made from corrugated metal and a posser that danced in a soapy rhythm was the only equipment needed, Our Jack usually did the possing and after a while, he'd check his arm muscles to see if his biceps had increased in size." A smile curled Walter's lip.

"Looking Back, everyday life carried quite unique experiences, they seem like snapshots from another era now. For instance, the privy in the yard wasn't ours alone; it was shared with neighbouring houses, and it somehow forged an unusual connection between our lives.

I recall that the door went from the top to about six inches off the floor. To make sure the privy was vacant, it was the custom to peer under the door to check for legs or feet and to see if anyone was in residence. As a child, my feet dangled well above the floor while I was seated on the 'throne,' so my feet couldn't be seen and there were a few embarrassing moments when next door tried to get in while I was there.

My Grandma, wise and imaginative, pinned handwritten psalm verses on the walls and although I couldn't read I was told to keep singing to warn everyone of my presence.

Grandma was an important part of my life in those years. She made us our tea and tended to our yard, scrubbing the flags with the determination of someone possessed. When she went out to the front steps, the whole street seemed to follow her lead. They formed a line of apron-clad women, each of them armed with a bucket and a donkey stone. Beneath their headscarves, curlers tightly shaped their hair ready for that night's Bingo session at the working men's club.

Summers brought outdoor baths for us kids. It was a communal affair except for Tilly, who clung to notions of modesty."

"What about privacy?" Joe asked.

"Privacy? Nah, that was like some fancy thing we couldn't even dream of. We were all crammed up in that one bed, just huddled together. The most valuable thing we had was innocence it was worth more than gold? Innocence, plain and simple. All year round the yard transformed into realms of adventure, evolving from castles to farms with our ever-changing moods.

At this time of year, we huddle around the living room fire to get dressed. We didn't have central heating and that meant on a morning the house was so cold that we could write in the ice on the insides of frosty windows.

"That sounds tough," Joe added, he tried to imagine waking up and trying to get dressed in such conditions. "What about school?" Joe asked as he felt himself being drawn into this bygone time.

"School days, oh, well we only went part-time and they were a mix of fleeting joy and misadventures under the watchful eye of Miss Foster, who wielded her slipper with painful precision. She took great pleasure in dusting the back of my pants with her slipper; it hurt like hell, but I didn't dare tell when I got home.

Joe gives him a questioning look. "Why was that?" He asks.

Walter smiles and shakes his head.

'Cos, Dad would have taken his belt to me for being in trouble again.'

'Did he do that a lot?' Joe asks.

'No, not really… anyway, nobody thought owt about it in those days and getting a clip around yer lugholes was normal. Such was our lives, we followed a predictable path, all except for clever Tilly, who tiptoed into secondary school full-time. Looking back, life seemed pretty straightforward," Walter chuckled throwing his hands open. "It's a stark contrast to the complications of today."

"Yes, I know what you mean, things have changed even in my lifetime. So, moving on, what do you remember about the turn of the century?' Joe had been thinking of subjects to ask about in case Walter ran out of ideas.

Walter paused with a distant look in his eyes.

"What about a coffee… it might help jog my memory." He gave Joe a cheeky wink.

Joe retreated to the kitchen and set the kettle on the stove, he couldn't help but notice the near-empty fridge. He soon returned with two steaming mugs. The room felt oddly quiet as if the memories were settling around them like dust.

Joe took a moment to observe his car parked outside the window, then turned his attention back to Walter. "I hope it doesn't snow' he said 'I hate driving in snow.'

"You know, Walter, I've just realized that you're in your nineties. I would've never guessed."

Walter offered a shy smile, "Well, my joints can testify to my age… you should see me first thing in the morning."

His mind was racing as memories flooded back.

"You asked about the turn of the century… I recall a grand celebration down the street, with bunting and flags hanging off every corner. They set a long table up and filled it wi'buns an' all kinds of treats. There was a feeling of change in the air, folk felt a sense of excitement and promise. It was a welcome splash of colour in a very drab world."

Walter accepted the coffee with a grateful nod, wrapping his hands around the warm mug. The fragrant aroma filled the air, lending a sense of comfort to the room.

"So, tell me," Joe began gently, trying to steer the conversation back to the topic at hand, "What was life like during that time? What stands out to you?"

Walter took a slow sip of his coffee, his eyes fixed on some distant point as if he were peering into the past.

"Don't forget I was nowt but a bairn when the century turned. But my thoughts were that it was an era of change; traditions held on but everywhere there were signs of progress. The streets, once cobbled lanes, now began to hum with traffic. Every morning, the town awakened to a symphony of footsteps as workers streamed towards Bentley's weaving sheds at the end of the road." Walter paused as he thought about the mill. "It's long gone now, they knocked it down I'll bet it was over twenty years ago. There was the clatter of hooves that mingled with the occasional chugging of early automobiles, a sight that still bewildered many. It was a time when the rhythmic clatter of machinery began to dominate the town's soundscape, weaving its industrial melody into the fabric of daily life.

Amidst the industrial clamour, the town's essence lingered in the air, a heady mix of coal smoke from the houses and factories and the irresistible aroma of freshly baked bread wafting from the nearby bakeries." Walter couldn't suppress a smile as he moved on. "But it was the fragrant whispers of a hidden pork pie maker that I remember best as a cherished memory. Somewhere nestled in the back alley, an artisan sculpted culinary delights that filled my days with interest. The mere scent of those pies with their harmonious blend of spices and succulent meat was an invitation to indulgence."

Walter's gaze softened as he continued, "I remember the excitement in the air, a sense of anticipation for what the new century might bring. The world felt smaller, yet vast with possibilities. We were on the cusp of something, though none of us quite knew what."

He looked back at Joe, his eyes now reflecting a blend of curiosity and longing. "As I said, I was just a lad then, but I could sense the change, the energy of progress. It was both thrilling and daunting, like stepping into a new, uncharted chapter of history."

Joe listened intently, captivated by Walter's ability to transport them both to a bygone era. The room seemed to fade away, replaced by the bustling streets of history. Walter's memories, like flickering candlelight, illuminated the corners of their conversation, casting shadows of a world long gone.

"Even at such a young age, little changes mattered. Not world-shattering events but little things… for instance, I remember my sister, Joyce, falling ill with mumps. When she recovered, they bought her a new whip and top. I seem to remember thinking that I wished I could catch a similar ailment so they'd buy me a new toy, but fate had other plans and I remained stubbornly healthy."

Walter couldn't help but keep his eyes fixed outside, "It was a right shame because the next year, we lost the Queen, God rest her soul. She'd been reigning for over six decades, a time that folks thought would never end.

Elsie caught, Scarlet Fever, and she'd to spend a couple of weeks in a quarantine hospital. But much worse was to come, a few years later when I was just eight, I lost my Mum and my Grandma, both of 'em within the same week." Walter stopped to clear his throat, this resurfaced memory had a painful edge to it.

"I knew both Mum and Grandma were poorly but I never realised how bad until one morning I caught my dad with his head in his hands sobbing bitterly. As the sombre day of the burial approached, our small family was swathed in a cloud of gloom. The air was thick with grief and a heavy silence loomed over our home. My father, usually as tough as a rock, was shattered by the loss of his beloved wife and mother, and I couldn't comprehend the depths of his despair. He often sat in the quiet corner of our dimly lit kitchen, head buried in his hands, tears streaming silently down his weathered face. It's an image that's etched in my memory, a heart-breaking witness to the cruel hand life had dealt us." Walter drained the last of his coffee and then closed his eyes to help his memory.

Joe put his pen down a moment. "I'm so sorry, losing Grandma and your Mum together like that, I don't know how you coped."

Walter slowly replied as he felt the pain with every word, "As a young lad, the weight of grief was an unfathomable burden, a sorrow too immense for my tender heart to bear. The days that followed were shrouded in a veil of mourning, each passing moment was a reminder of the void left by them. Our humble home, which was once a haven of warmth and laughter, now echoed with the haunting silence of their absence. Their familiar presence lingered in every corner, in the scent of Mum's favourite flowers and the echoes of Grandma's gentle lullabies that used to lull us to sleep.

The funeral, as you might expect was a sombre affair. The sky mirrored our misery, a leaden veil of sorrow wrapped around us as we gathered at the cemetery. Neighbours, companions in our past joy, now united in shared grief. Without the brass for a proper funeral, they were consigned to a pauper's grave, tucked away in a forsaken corner, a resting place for forgotten souls. Standing amidst the hushed whispers and tear-streaked faces of those who had gathered to bid farewell, I found myself gazing skywards and wondering about where they had gone. The earth reclaimed their mortal remains, one casket at a time, which was a profound reminder of life's briefness. It was as if each shovel of soil that settled over them carried away a piece of our family's heart.

In the aftermath, our house was filled with silent sorrow. Father, grappling with his own anguish, shouldered the responsibility of nurturing our fractured family. His attempts to fill the void left by Mum and Grandma were valiant but rendered bittersweet by the painful absence that lingered in every room. His stories, a poignant tapestry woven from cherished memories, brought fleeting moments of solace amidst the unrelenting ache of their loss. Yet, despite his efforts, our family portrait was irrevocably altered, the absence of two beloved women leaving an unfillable chasm in our lives." Walter leaned back and ran his fingers through his grey hair. "Each day was a reminder of their absence, and the void they left in our lives was palpable. But Dad tried to be strong for us, telling us stories to make us smile and laugh. Among these stories was the one about rainbows. He'd often say, 'If you ever spot a rainbow in the sky, that's Grandma watching over you from up in heaven.'"

It was a tale that gave me comfort, even in the darkest of times. Whenever the rain fell and the sun broke through, painting the sky with vibrant colours, I would run outside, searching for that magnificent arc in the sky. Each time I found one, I couldn't help but believe that it was Grandma sending me a sign, letting me know that she was there, watching over me and keeping me safe.

But, in the quiet moments when I lay in bed, I missed Grandma the most. She had been my sanctuary, the warm knee I would sit on when life got tough. Her voice was a soothing lullaby that could chase away any fear, and her arms offered a reassuring embrace that could mend any hurt. I remembered the comforting hug and tender kiss she gave me, regardless of whatever mischievous adventures I'd been up to that day. Her love had been a constant presence, and without her, I felt a void in my heart that nothing could quite fill.

Those early years without Mum and Grandma were difficult, and our small family clung to one another as we tried to carry on without them. Yet, in Dad's stories and the occasional appearance of a rainbow, we found moments of solace and a connection to the loving souls we had lost."

The dark memories showed in Walter's eyes as he delved deeper into the past. "Losing them really reshaped our lives," he said, his voice soft with emotion.

"It meant that Tilly was forced to leave school to take care of us. It was a burden she carried, and she bore it with resentment." Walter paused, reflecting on those tumultuous times.

"She was as mad as a hatter and didn't hide it. You never knew what would set her off, and she always had a word on the tip of her tongue, sharp as a blade. After she had to take care of us, she was in a perpetual storm of frustration, especially when Dad had to work those long overtime hours. Bossy and impatient, she was always angry." Walter's eyes glistened with memories of his older sister, a complex mix of love and exasperation.

He chuckled, offering a hint of warmth amid the sombre recollections. "And, well, her cooking was dreadful. The less said about that, the better." A soft, nostalgic smile crossed his lips. "Although to be fair, looking back, I suppose she did the best she could with our meagre rations. Times were tough, you know."

Joe sat on the edge of his seat, drawn into the narrative as if by an invisible thread, every word painted a vivid stroke in his imagination. The pen in his hand trembled, as he struggled to capture the depth and emotion of Walter's story.

Walter's conversation changed direction and caught Joe off guard. "Were you a good student?" Walter's voice cut through the nostalgia, snapping Joe back to the present.

Joe chuckled, rubbing the back of his neck. "Not exactly. I went to the local grammar school and scraped through five O levels but then I ditched school to help out a friend's dad in the market. That didn't pan out too well, which led me to this job."

Walter's eyes twinkled with interest. "What kind of job was it at the market?"

Joe leaned back, a casual grin on his face. "It was a bit of everything, really. Selling fruits and vegetables, helping out with deliveries, and even working at the butcher's stall. It was tough work, but when I got to know a lot of the regulars it was fun too and it taught me the value of hard graft."

Walter seemed to appreciate the sentiment. "Sounds like you've had your share of life experiences, just like the rest of us."

Joe nodded. "Absolutely. Life has its own way of shaping us, doesn't it?"

Walter raised an eyebrow. "Speaking of life experiences, were you any good at sports back in the day?"

Joe chuckled a hint of mischief in his eyes. "You know, I wasn't too bad. Football was my game. I played for our school team and even for a local club. Those were the days, running around the pitch with my mates."

Walter's interest was piqued. "You played football? What position?"

"Mainly midfield," Joe replied. "I wasn't the best, but I could hold my own."

Walter smiled a touch of nostalgia in his gaze. "It's funny, you know. Even though our lives took different paths, it seems we've both held onto pieces of our youth."

Joe nodded, understanding the bittersweet nature of memories. "That's the beauty of memories, Walter. They're like fragments of a past life that we carry with us, reminding us of who we used to be."

Walter's gaze turned wistful, and he spoke softly, revealing the ache hidden beneath the nostalgia. "I find there is a downside to them too… sometimes I want to relive them so much that it bloody well hurts. I yearn to be back there, warm in Alice's arms, touching her hand, kissing her lips."

His voice quivered as he continued, the words escaping from a place deep within.

"But worse, much worse… there is so much I want to tell her and share with her. There's an ache in my heart, Joe. It's as if every memory I have is laced with a longing so profound that it's almost unbearable."

A tear welled up in the corner of his eye, his voice trembling. "I hurt, Joe, I hurt every day because I can't be with her. I hurt because I can't make up for all the lost time, all the things I didn't say or do." The vulnerability etched in every line of his face was laid bare, his love for Alice and the haunting sense of missed opportunities more profound than ever.

Joe pondered Walter's words for a moment before expressing a profound thought, "History is often portrayed through grand events, the wars, the rulers, the monumental changes. But the essence of history lies in the stories of ordinary people, their daily lives, struggles, and triumphs. It's the ordinary and the mundane that holds the true essence of our collective history. Each person's story, their daily routines, and experiences, that's what weaves the tapestry of our past."

The clock's sudden chime startled them both, a harsh reminder of time's relentless march.

"Good heavens, look at the time. I'm sorry, Walter, but I must run. Can I come back tomorrow?" Joe said as he shuffled his notes together.

Walter's eyes twinkled with a faint smile. "Of course. I'll rustle up a few sandwiches. Mr Singh from the corner shop drops off a few odds and ends for me every week; I'll ask him for a loaf."

"I'll be looking forward to it, Walter. Take care."

Joe hurriedly headed to his Ford Escort, the engine coughed to life as he drove away. Walter settled back into his chair, his eyelids heavy.

As the room's silence enveloped him, Walter's memories danced around his mind. He felt warmed by the sense of nostalgia that hung in the air, and soon, his eyes closed, inviting slumber to wrap him in its embrace.

Joe heads home

Joe's heart raced with anticipation as he rushed home through the bustling streets.

It was raining hard and the rhythm of his wiper blades set the tempo of racing thoughts. It wasn't often that he stumbled upon such a remarkable story, and the anticipation of sharing it with Julie added an extra skip to his heartbeat. The discoveries he had made that day had ignited a fire of excitement within him.

He dashed into the house his mind still racing. After draping his coat over the chair, he dashed up to the spare room with a mission on his mind. He rummaged on the top shelf of his wardrobe and retrieved from its resting place his handy-sized tape recorder which he had not used for months.

"Ah, that's what I need, taking notes is fine but I need Walter's emotions too." He flicked the recorder open to make sure there was a tape installed. 'I need to be ready to capture every detail, every nuance of the story.' He thought his enthusiasm bursting within his brain. He rummaged through his cupboards for spare tapes. The thought ran through his mind that the local newspaper would be the perfect platform to share this newfound treasure trove of history with the world. He imagined the headlines, the intrigue it would generate among their readers, and the possibility of unearthing even more hidden stories.

The notes he had diligently scribbled throughout the day he transferred to a larger, more organized notebook. He wanted to be able to provide a clear and concise narrative, a compelling tale that would transport his readers to those moments lost over time.

With meticulous care, he ensured that the batteries in the tape recorder were new. As he tested the recorder, the sound of his voice filled the room, a preview of the words that would soon grace the pages of the local newspaper.

Everything was in place ready for the following day neatly tucked away in his old sports bag. Joe couldn't help but rub his hands together in glee. It was a rare and exhilarating feeling, knowing that he held the key to a story that he hoped would captivate their town, perhaps even the world.

Downstairs again he filled his time setting the table for dinner, he just hoped that Julie had bought something simple so that he could share his story with her. The rain outside drummed a soothing melody against the windows, adding a cosy ambience to the scene. He couldn't help but glance at the clock every few minutes, counting down the moments until Julie's return. Anticipation swirled within him like a tempest, his mind consumed by the urgency of sharing this newfound revelation.

Joe's thoughts raced and he tried to rehearse the perfect story, one that would captivate Julie's imagination and convey the depth of his discovery.

The clattering sound of the front door signalled Julie's arrival.

"Hi honey, I'm home." He heard her call.

They embraced and exchanged a loving kiss that held comfort, passion, and joy.

"How's your new guy been today?" she asked as she placed her shopping bag on the kitchen table. She rummaged in the bag and finally produced a paper-wrapped package. "I called in at the butchers, some lovely big fat sausages for tea."

Joe was rather subdued during the meal, his mind was slightly overwhelmed by how he should tackle this new adventure.

"Penny for your thoughts," Julie offered.

Joe pushed his notebook across the table to her. "Read that, I've had a real roller coaster of an emotional day."

He watched her expressions as she flipped the pages of his notebook. She blew a heavy sigh. Wow, that's developing into a real story. His mind must be alert enough despite his age."

"Oh yes," Joe gave her a knowing wink. "This guy has all his marbles at home."

Chapter Three.
A Neighbours Concern.

Early the next morning, just before dawn, Walter was also bubbling with excitement.

As he dressed he mused, "I wonder what time Joe'll be here?"

The joy of yesterday's chat was still in his mind, "I didn't realise how much I've missed being wi'folk," he whispered to the kettle. Although the memories had been bittersweet he felt better for the chance to share them.

In the kitchen, he hummed a little melody as he neatly prepared sandwiches, his fingers were moving with newfound energy. Unusually, he felt a pang of hunger and decided to indulge in a proper breakfast.

There was a rapid knock on his door, at first, he thought it would be the anticipated arrival of his new friend. So, he was surprised when it was his old friend Mr Singh from the local shop who stood on the step with a beaming smile.

"Good morning Mr Walter," Mr Singh brought his palms together in a prayer-like position. "I was just passing and I have some beautiful fresh bread, so I thought I would bring one for you and make sure that you were alright."

Walter gratefully accepted the fresh bread, his eyes shimmering with appreciation. "That's very kind, Mr Singh. I appreciate your thoughtfulness." He held it to his nose to enjoy the unique smell of freshly baked bread. "Oh, lovely, it smells wonderful. "Walter smiled gratefully, "That's so kind. Thank you."

"I saw a young man enter your house yesterday, are you sure everything is fine?"

"Oh, that was Joe, yes I'm fine. He's my new social worker, but he wants to write a story about me and my life experiences. He seems a nice lad. Just here to learn about an old codger's life. No need to worry."

"I'm sure it will be a fascinating story. Well, as long as you are alright."

"Yes, thank you for your concern. Give my respects to your lovely lady wife."

The local shopkeeper's concern wasn't missed by Walter, and he nodded warmly

Mr Singh's smile widened. "It's always good to have someone interested in your stories, Mr. Walter. And thank you, I'll be sure to pass on your regards to my dear wife. You have a good day."

With a final nod, Mr Singh continued on his way, leaving Walter with the simple yet heart-warming gesture of a fresh loaf of bread and a genuine check on his well-being.

The clock ticked past ten o'clock when a gentle tap echoed at the door, announcing Joe's arrival.

"It's me, Walter... Joe," his voice carried warmth and familiarity.

Walter swung the door open, a genuine smile stretching across his face as they exchanged a firm handshake, a bond already forming.

"How's your morning, Walter?" Joe inquired.

"I'm well, thank you, I'm glad to see you," Walter replied, a genuine appreciation lacing his words. "Mr Singh from the local shop has just popped in with a loaf to check up on me."

"Oh, that was kind of him. I've taken the day off work. A well-deserved break, I reckon," Joe remarked.

"Come in, come in. The kettle's already humming a sweet melody," Walter gestured, inviting Joe into his cosy haven.

As they settled at the table, Joe's unexpected statement hung in the air, "I hope you don't mind, but I brought a tape recorder."

Walter raised his eyebrows, "Music, perhaps?"

Joe chuckled softly, "No, my friend. It's here to record your story."

Steam rose from their mugs as Walter poured the hot water and immediately the air filled with the rich aroma of coffee.

"How's your little one this morning?" Walter enquired, his eyes brimming with genuine concern.

"Fairly well, thank you for asking," Joe replied, a hint of fatigue tugging at his voice.

"And Julie?" Walter probed gently.

Joe's expression shifted, a mixture of fondness and frustration. "Ah, you know... I told her all about your story, and she was really interested. She was tired and fell asleep during the film we had planned to watch, I think it was even before the credits rolled."

Walter chuckled, his eyes sparkling, "Cherish the moments, my friend. Now, what about your girl... you said there were a few problems."

Joe's sigh held the weight of unspoken words, "She's been diagnosed with autism. But that can mean all kinds of things... mostly she's just hard to reach. It's very trying at times."

Understanding dawned in Walter's eyes, "Patience will be your greatest ally."

Walter carried his mug into the living room and before he sat in his chair he peeped out of the window, "The road seems a bit busy this morning." He observed and then sat down.

With a determined motion, Joe placed his tape recorder on the table using it as a distraction.

"Alright, where shall we begin?" Joe asked. "We delved into the turn of the century yesterday. What about your siblings? Were you close?"

There was a thoughtful pause, and then Walter's eyes softened with reminiscence.

"Were we close? Jack and I were the best of buddies. I always looked up to him; he was my big brother. I tagged along after him despite the age difference, and we had plenty of adventures together. Tilly, on the other hand, always seemed a bit distant. She was almost ten years older than me and had a quiet manner but like I said when she was forced out of school to be our new Mum, she was angry and took it out on me. Joyce, well, she liked school, but she only went part-time before she went into Barkers Mill as a spinner, I didn't really get to know her much as a kid. She had her interests, and I had mine. Elsie and Claire were twins, although Elsie claimed to be the oldest. Elsie had this nurturing side, wanting to take care of everyone. After Grandma and Mum passed away, she became my rock, providing comfort when I needed it the most."

Walter stopped to smile as his other sister came to mind. "Claire, if she were alive today, she'd be a free spirit, a hippy for sure. I can just imagine her driving a VW camper called Boris or some such name, covered in bright-coloured flowers. She was immensely creative, always fashioning intricate patterns and crafting pictures out of the simplest of things. I recall her creating a whole family of pebbles, each adorned with a unique face, carefully arranged by size. She'd play with them and enact all kinds of dramas. Her sweet, soothing voice had this magical, ethereal quality that could calm even the most troubled souls. When she sang it was heavenly, she often sang special solos down at the chapel. As a child, I often imagined she might be descended from the Fairies that were rumoured to inhabit the nearby woods. We all got on pretty well, I suppose, but things were about to change."

Joe stopped the tape, "And you've no idea what happened to any of them?"

"Be patient, my young friend, all will be revealed," Walter said with a hint of mystery.

"My Dad's invitation to take a peculiar outing remains fixed in my memory, it was like a piece of a puzzle that just didn't fit."

Walter settled down in his chair with his drink and prepared to continue his story.

"One crisp morning in the early light of dawn, Dad seemed in a funny mood, he seemed preoccupied and distant. I could tell that something was nagging at him. Our small dining area, which usually felt cold and lifeless in the mornings, now held a strained atmosphere. The fact that he hadn't already left for work was peculiar in itself. For the first time in my memory, he was lingering around the table while I tried to choke down some of Tilly's gruel." He pulled a face at the thought of it.

"As I watched him, I couldn't help but wonder why he was home at that hour. My older sister, Tilly, didn't give away any clues as to what was going on, she busied herself at the sink with her back toward me. Dad's presence was a mystery, and I longed to ask him what was going on, but something in his solemn expression told me that this wasn't the time for questions. He had a small sack, I think it was an old pillowcase with him, and he kept glancing at it as if checking to ensure its contents remained undisturbed. The silence was heavy in the room, the only sounds were the occasional clinking of cutlery on plates. I couldn't help but feel a sense of unease that I couldn't quite explain. I cast a questioning look at Tilly, my only sibling who could perhaps offer some insight. However, she remained immersed in her work, her disinterest in my concerns as consistent as ever.

Eventually, Dad seemed to find the resolve he needed. With one last lingering look in my direction, he rose from the table, lifting the small sack in his hand. His eyes held a mix of determination and a tinge of sadness. The seconds ticked away and I instinctively knew something was wrong.

As he headed for the door, the tension remained. I could feel that something significant was about to happen, something that would change the course of my life, but I had no way of knowing just what lay ahead. The house, once a place of familiarity and comfort, now held the echoes of secrets, secrets that slowly began to cast long shadows over my life.

'How about a walk, lad?" he suddenly asked. "Let's go for a stroll,' he said, the words tinged with an unusual enthusiasm. He gestured to me to put my coat on, stressing, 'You love walking, don't you? We're heading to see a friend of mine who owns a barge.'

Back then, I found the prospect strange. Why just me? Why did Dad wear a sad look and what was in the sack? However, the thought of a barge intrigued me; I often watched them loading and unloading at the wharves. Little did I know what the journey's extent would be.

Chapter Four
The long walk begins.

As Dad and I silently walked by the canal, our destination unveiled itself… it was a wide-beamed canal barge, with a black hull and a dull green cabin. It looked quite homely with a full clothesline above the cargo hold. The shirts fluttered in the breeze and their empty arms seemed to wave a silent welcome.

The bargee, a stout man with grey sideburns and a boisterous smile, greeted us and then led us aboard. After a few minutes, a buxom woman appeared, she reminded me a little bit of my Gran. She had a broad, warm smile and carried a tea tray piled high with homemade biscuits.

"This is our Walter." My Dad proudly announced, guiding me to a small buffet in the corner of the cabin. He dropped the sack beside me.

Jos, a broad smile lighting up his weathered face, extended his hand in a warm greeting.

"Pleasure to meet you, Walter," he said, his voice filled with genuine friendliness. Then, with a mischievous twinkle in his eye, he turned towards the woman beside him. "And this 'ere is Dolly, the queen of the kitchen. If it weren't for her, I'd probably starve!"

My dad let out a hearty laugh, somehow it seemed a little bit forced.

Dad suddenly explained, "Ah, Jos and me, go back a while, we do. We were schoolmates, would you believe it? Even way back then, we used to call him Owd Jos. He always had this air of wisdom about him, like an old sage.'

'More like an old sack if you ask me,' Dolly joked and almost seemed to explode with laughter at her own comment.

I was wide-eyed… not afraid but very wary of what was happening.

The room filled with warm laughter, and the air was thick with friendship. It was a simple introduction and at that moment I didn't understand its importance, however, I was still suspicious that something was going on. I sat on my buffet eating biscuits and studying the unusual array of ornaments that filled every nook and cranny of the cabin. There was a potbellied stove with a pile of firewood beside it and I watched a huge spider crawling in and out of the logs.

The banter that was going on between the adults was friendly and yet I sensed an underlying tension, a bit like when your parents are taking you to the dentist and they don't want you to know. After a couple of hours, Dad got up to go and I expected to leave with him, but his words shattered that notion.

"You stay here with Owd Jos, my lad. You'll be fine. There's some of your clothes in the sack."

I don't know why I asked, "What about school?" It was the first thing that entered my slightly bewildered mind.

Dad just smiled and gave my shoulder a friendly punch. "Don't worry about that… you weren't very good at it anyway."

I could see that he was unhappy, his face was flushed and he looked sad but away he went without a backward glance. I waved him off and wondered when I would see him again."

His unexpected departure left me with a sense of abandonment. Dolly put her arm around my shoulder, 'Here, have a ginger snap, it'll make things seem better.'

Joe clicks his tape machine. "Oh, sorry about that, I need to change the tape."

He changes the tape and then writes on the little label something to identify it.

'All right Walter let's carry on. What did you think about what had just happened to you?'

Joe's tape machine clicked, interrupting Walter's train of thought.

"Well… my first thought was one of dread, I wondered if my siblings would forget me. My second thought was a bit brighter when I realised that at least Tilly wouldn't be able to spank me anymore. So, life took off in a rather unexpected way and it was the beginning of what I like to call 'My Long Walk'.

That evening, the reality of Dad's decision settled in and I couldn't help but feel a sense of relief… I could see the upside of it… the prospect of skipping school and no more dreaded spankings from Miss Foster or Tilly's watchful eyes, ready to report any mischief. It felt like a moment of rebellion, a daring escape from the constraints of my daily routine.

In those bewildering moments, after Dad left the barge, a flurry of thoughts raced through my young mind. I couldn't help but wonder if he had taken the others, Tilly and maybe my brother Jack, to different places. The idea that our family might be split up was incomprehensible, but I was too young, too naive to truly understand the gravity of the situation.

Fear had not yet set in, for the innocence of youth shielded me from the full weight of the possibilities. Instead, curiosity and a sense of trust in my father's actions prevailed. I chose to believe that whatever was happening, Dad had a plan, and it was for our family's betterment.

The feeling of uncertainty, however, lingered in the background. It was like a faint whisper, a nudge in the subconscious that something unusual was afoot.

I soon found out that Dolly was an outstanding cook and made heavenly pasties, those delectable pockets of savoury delight that she somehow conjured up in her little galley kitchen were to die for. Their appearance was a rare treat for me; something out of the ordinary. As I took that first bite, my taste buds danced in newfound ecstasy. The flavours unfurled like a symphony, and for the first time in a long time, the world seemed like a far better place.

That evening, in the company of Dolly and Jos, I enjoyed my first supper. At the outset, an undeniable apprehension lingered within me. But as we gathered around the makeshift table, sharing not only the meal but stories and laughter, my initial fears began to dissipate like morning mist yielding to the sun's warm embrace.

Dolly and Jos were welcoming, their warm smiles and friendly conversation soon put me at ease. As the meal went on, the fears that had initially clung to me began to slip away. It was as if I had found two new allies in this unexpected adventure. We talked about the barge, about the canal, and about the journey we were embarking upon. Their laughter and friendship soon made me feel like I belonged.

In the company of these newfound friends, the barge ceased to be a place of uncertainty and became an exciting part of our shared journey. The world outside was vast, and the canal, though filled with unknown challenges, held the promise of adventure.

That first supper with Dolly and Jos marked the beginning of my life on the barge, a life that would be filled with experiences and stories that would shape me in ways I could never have imagined.

Once supper was over, Dolly told me to follow her. She showed me a makeshift bed constructed from piled-up sacks in the cargo hold. The darkness of the hold was enveloping, and the roof was barely ten inches above my head, leaving me with just enough room to lie down. It was a stark contrast to my shared family bed.

As I lay there, my young mind began to wander. I couldn't help but reflect on the events that had led me to this point. The image of my Dad walking away, leaving me behind, still stung. It was a bitter pill to swallow, but even at that tender age, I understood that things were different since the passing of Mum and Grandma. Life had taken a difficult turn, and I guess with one wage less coming in, Dad was faced with the harsh reality of struggling to make ends meet.

In the quiet of my new bedroom, I became determined to make the most of my new circumstances and to try and see it as an adventure. It was a chance to break away because if I had stayed then I knew that my future lay in one of the textile mills that dominated the town.

The following morning, Dolly presented me with a bowl of porridge, but this was no ordinary porridge. She had prepared it with milk, a luxury beyond our reach at home where we typically made do with water.

Jos popped his head around the door to make sure I was finished and then led me up onto the towpath, 'Come on lad I've someone I want you to meet.'

This was when I first met Troy, Jos's majestic horse that tirelessly towed the barge. I gently patted Troy's velvety nose, and in response, the magnificent creature extended his long, warm tongue to give my hand an affectionate lick. He had a wonderful smell about him, a mixture of straw and his own unique aroma.

"He's quite fond of the occasional sugar lump and a few carrots," Jos shared with a fond smile.

I was utterly captivated by the animal. Troy's coat gleamed in the sunlight, and his powerful muscles rippled beneath it, a testament to his strength. I couldn't help but admire the magnificent animal from every angle, and Troy, the ever-patient and friendly giant, stood still, allowing me to take in his grandeur. I was supposed to help with his harness and halter, but it was too heavy and anyway, he was far too tall for me to reach.

"You'll grow," Jos assured me."

Walter took a moment to compose himself, his weathered hands smoothing down the fabric of his trousers. As he shifted in his seat, he couldn't help but wince at the stiffness in his ageing legs. The years had taken their toll, but his spirit remained undiminished, ready to continue the journey through his memories. Joe was speechless, he was totally wrapped up in this turn of events and oddly he could empathise with him and understand the pain Walter had felt.

Walter continued his narrative, his voice filled with nostalgia.

"Standing on that wet and windy towpath," he recounted, "There was an instant bond formed between us all. As I took the first of a great many steps on that long walk, it didn't take me long, even at that tender age, to realise that my Dad had done me a great favour when he introduced me to barge life. I had seen it at first as an act of betrayal, but then I knew that it was an act of love."

Walter's eyes glistened as he spoke, and his weathered face held a mixture of emotions, from the pain of separation to the warmth of understanding. Joe listened intently, captivated by the unfolding story of a young boy's journey into the world of barge life.

"Getting away from the smoke and the noise of the weaving sheds was a gift like no other. With Troy beside me, his gentle warmth radiating, I felt to be the luckiest lad in all of Yorkshire. The rain, which had been falling persistently, seemed inconsequential now, as if it couldn't dampen my newfound sense of contentment however hard it tried. The towpath stretched ahead, a path to a different life, where each step carried the promise of adventure and a unique kind of freedom.

Jos and Dolly, my surrogate family, looked on with affectionate smiles, understanding the significance of that moment. Troy, the magnificent steed, with his kind eyes, seemed to nod in approval as if welcoming me into the close-knit circle that was our barge family.

The very next morning we were off. I took up my new position next to Troy and we boldly stepped out into the unknown. I held his reins loosely in my hand. We walked alongside the barge, and the regular tempo of my steps matched the rhythmic clip-clop of his hooves on the towpath. Quite soon we left the industrial scenery with its towering factories and sooty chimneys behind. The rain washed away the residue of the industrial city, leaving me feeling cleansed, renewed, and ready to embrace the unknown. Troy was more than just a horse; he was a symbol of this extraordinary life journey that awaited me, and I was grateful for the privilege of experiencing it. I felt as if I was setting sail on a pirate ship to find buried treasure on a far-off island.

I suppose in a way I did find treasure maybe not gold and gems but something much more valuable, love and friendship. Over the next few weeks, Owd Jos shared tales, he was a treasure trove of anecdotes. Dolly, intrigued me, her cooking was a newfound delight but she was like every lovely mum rolled into one.

One story stood out… a clever duck escapade. He told me a tale about selling a dozen Muscovy ducks to a fellow from Ipswich… Jos had looked after them since they were ducklings and they followed him wherever he went. He clipped their wings so that they wouldn't fly off… but he forgot to tell their new owner to do the same and sure enough a month or so after they were sold, they all came home to him, the crafty old devil sold them again to someone else."

Walter paused and his gaze drifted beyond the windowpane, a subtle smile gracing his lips as sunlight burst through the clouds, bathing the room in warmth.

Taking advantage of the pause, Joe seized the opportunity to stretch his legs. He went to the kitchen to put the kettle to work. His thoughts were deeply entwined with the unfolding tale. A quick glance at his watch betrayed his anticipation.

Resuming their conversation after the caffeine infusion, Joe's fingers deftly flicked the switch of the tape recorder. Walter's eyes wandered as he embarked on the next chapter of his reminiscences.

"I settled in quickly… mostly because I'd never eaten so well in all my life and I had my own bed… well, it was more of a cot really… the sacks had been replaced with a well-padded mattress. I thought about my family now and again but... they seemed a long way off. I just hoped that they had not forgotten me.

Owd Jos was something of a mentor, and as we walked we talked. He showed me how to catch rabbits... and while we were going from one place to another along the towpaths he used to show me which herbs and roots were good to eat. He even shared his somewhat unusual philosophy about life with me. Occasionally Dolly would dash off returning with her apron filled with Elderflowers, chestnuts or whatever she knew was waiting. It was as though the whole world was her larder, she knew when everything was ready for her to harvest.

Life on the barge, with only Jos, and Dolly aboard, created an intimate sense of family. It wasn't that I had forgotten my own family, but somehow, this new chapter in my life seemed to compensate for the irreplaceable losses I had endured.

As the days passed on the barge, Jos and Dolly became more than just my employers; they became my closest companions. We shared stories of our pasts, dreams for the future, and the simple yet profound moments that life on the barge offered. I have to say as a boy I had very few ambitions, I knew nothing of the world or what it could offer, and I knew that I didn't want to end up in a weaving shed like the rest of the family. The close quarters and the tranquil beauty of the surroundings fostered a unique bond between us. I found solace and a renewed sense of belonging.

When I first joined the barge, I was a scrawny and undersized individual. The new life was demanding and filled with hard work and challenges. However, it was also a transformative experience in many ways. The combination of plentiful food and constant physical exertion wrought a remarkable change in my physique.

Day by day, the rigours of life on the barge sculpted my body, gradually replacing frailty with strength. The hearty meals provided by Dolly, coupled with the ceaseless tasks that came with barge life, brought about a remarkable transformation. The once scrawny figure that I had been, began to fill out, my muscles grew firmer, and my endurance increased.

It was as if the barge itself infused me with its vitality. The repetitive tasks of tending to the barge, loading, and unloading cargo, and navigating the waterways moulded me into a robust and capable individual. Each day brought a new challenge, and with it, an opportunity for personal growth.

The shared meals, the laughter, and the moments of quiet reflection as we navigated the canal all contributed to the feeling that, aboard this barge, I had found not just a new chapter but a new family to cherish and call my own.

Our barge was a broad-beamed vessel with a gaping storage hold and so we usually carried bulk loads of coal or iron ore, it was pretty mucky work and the canal was too dirty to bathe in, but every so often we'd come across a natural beck or stream where we could top up our drinking water and have a wash. They taught me how to swim and one hot summer we had a great old-time swimming and picnicking miles away from anywhere in what seemed like our very own private, secretive pool."

Walter suddenly looked up with a real glint in his eye.

"And then there was Autumn, ah, Autumn was a feast," Walter's voice grew animated. "Hazelnuts, sweet chestnuts by the bucketful and an orchestra of berries, fruits, and nuts all ripe for picking. Dolly, a galley genius, transformed nature's bounty into jams and pickles, her bubbling copper cauldron infusing the barge with a sweet fragrance."

A shadow danced across Walter's face as his narrative deepened.

"Yet, beneath the idyllic facade, an enigma thrived. Some evenings after we had moored for the night; lone men sought refuge within the cabin's confines. Dolly's laughter like a siren's call could be heard loud and clear. Jos and I would sit on the bow of the barge until the visitor had left.

"Jos insisted these clandestine callers were just old friends, a notion I held onto as my innocence navigated these murky waters. Quite often, there was an improvement in our meals, and I guessed that the caller the previous night had been a local butcher or baker. Their visits always seemed to bring a touch of comfort and an extra bit of warmth to our lives, both in the form of their presence and the delectable treats they left behind. It was as if these secret friendships added a layer of richness to our otherwise humble existence, and I clung to the idea that they were just kind-hearted souls who cared about our little family."

Walter briefly paused, "Troy, was a steadfast companion and he became my confidant as our friendship blossomed. Our conversations, even though they were a little one-sided, forged a bond of unspoken understanding as we journeyed together."

As Walter's gaze settled on his cup, the residue of memories lingered.

"Whenever possible we had to put Troy in a stable for the night. Sometimes, our search for shelter would lead us to a rustic barn where Troy and I could take refuge amidst the soft, fragrant straw. On one occasion, Troy's colossal frame unknowingly rolled on top of me, his weight threatening to crush me, yet it provided an unexpected warmth in the chilly surroundings.

Maintaining the horses that pulled our barges was a vital responsibility. Along our journey, dedicated stables catered specifically to these dependable animals. These places weren't merely stopovers; they excelled in ensuring the utmost comfort for our equine companions. With skilled blacksmiths at hand, any hoof-related issues were promptly addressed. Ensuring their shelter, sustenance, and rest was paramount. They were the powerhouse of our voyage, hence their welfare took precedence.

Every morning, as dawn broke, I diligently attended to Troy's box, ensuring immaculate cleanliness. The next traveller and their horse needed to commence on a pristine slate. Neglecting this task wasn't an option; any oversight could lead to consequences or fines imposed by the stable proprietors. I approached this responsibility with the utmost seriousness, as our reputation as conscientious canal travellers hinged upon it. These horses weren't just colleagues; they were our comrades on this aquatic expedition, and their well-being mirrored our own significance.

Me and Troy, we travelled miles together. Sometimes, I got to ride on his big back, I needed a hand getting up 'cause he was the height of a tram! Or so it seemed. The scenery changed constantly under our feet... from the bustle of Manchester to the calm hug of the Aire Gap in the Dales. The Five Rise Locks were tough, really hard work. Every step was sweaty and hard, but it made me and Troy even closer, working together like that.

Exploring the waterways allowed us to witness an incredible array of wildlife. On stretches where there were few locks to manage, we moved steadily and silently along the water and it seemed to lull the creatures into a sense of calm. Kingfishers, with their vibrant colours, would perch on overhanging branches, undisturbed by our passage. Deer, graceful and elegant, would graze by the water's edge, acknowledging our presence with a watchful eye. Herons, tall and regal, stood still as statues, waiting patiently for their next meal.

Jos, our captain, knew all the best spots to see animals in their natural homes. He guided us to rivers with lots of tasty trout, so our meals were always fresh and delicious.

In those moments, surrounded by nature's beauty, I felt a strong bond with the world around me. The calm canals and the wildlife made each day feel like a thrilling adventure. I was thankful for every moment I got to experience it all."

Walter paused for a moment, his mind filled with memories and feelings. He knew there was more to share, more of his life to tell. With a deep breath, he kept going.

"It wasn't all work, there were lulls, like when we were waiting for our next cargo or to go through a set of locks. Troy and I would take leisurely strolls or indulge in grooming sessions that he visibly relished. I had a set of combs and brushes for him and he would patiently stand as I worked around him removing mud or loose hair. He'd make funny noises in his throat in appreciation. Sundays provided a welcomed breather and it was the one day that we refrained from walking. Jos, unfailingly led us to a chapel wherever we were and we'd lend our voices to the local congregation. Usually in the afternoon, I'd attend Sunday School, a sanctuary I cherished, unlike the conventional classrooms. Here, the dust of academia was replaced by an acceptance that resonated with my soul, allowing me to embrace learning without the confines of discomfort. The people were kind too and there were a few places along the way where we were offered the chance to take a hot bath. That really was a luxury… quite often Dolly would repay them with pots of her jams or pickles. Other times Jos and I would mend a fence or restack a drywall. Jos taught me another valuable lesson here, he said, 'Make sure that you do a good job, give folk value for money and then they'll welcome you back.'

The diverse landscapes that we passed through such as the picturesque Yorkshire Dales were a stark contrast to the sooty urban air I'd left behind. Though I missed my siblings dearly, the decision of my Dad to send me on this unique journey was a pearl of wisdom I couldn't deny. The lush expanse of nature became my refuge and a lasting love, it's a joy I still have to this day and it anchored my heart away from the clamour of the town.

Our journeys, at times, extended beyond a month and were marked by the different cargoes that we carried."

Joe suddenly raised his hand, interrupting Walter mid-sentence.

"Oh, sorry, Walter. Can I pause you for a moment? My tape needs changing… luckily, I've got plenty with me," he chuckled while deftly swapping out the cassette. After a quick adjustment to his tape recorder and a rummage in his bag for another cassette, he announced with a grin, "Okay, we're ready to roll again."

This minor intermission prompted Walter to shift slightly in his chair as he prepared to resume his narration.

"Sunday school opened up a new world for me because they taught me how to read and write, something I'd not really mastered at regular school. The teachers there were kind and helpful and I never got my pant's seat dusted. Once I'd got the hang of reading, Jos would hand me a newspaper, and in an evening, I'd read the news aloud to them, sharing all the latest happenings. The only hitch was that the newspapers were sometimes weeks old, not that it seemed to matter much. If I stumbled upon unfamiliar words, I'd simply conjure up something plausible. The stories about royalty always delighted them the most. Jos would turn to Dolly and say, 'You're my queen, lass, none finer anywhere.' Their affectionate exchange would be punctuated by a kiss and a playful slap, accompanied by Dolly's retort, 'You'll blurt out whatever nonsense crosses your daft head.'"

Joe suddenly interrupted, interested in Walter's new family he asked, "Were they a close couple, a loving couple?"

Walter leaned forward, his eyes sparkling with the memories of his newfound family. "Well, I'd say so. They both seemed kind and generous, but it was more than that. It was in the little things they did for each other. The way they'd hold hands when they thought no one was watching, the knowing glances they exchanged across the table. You could tell there was a deep, unspoken connection between them."

Joe leaned in, genuinely intrigued. "What do you mean, Walter? Could you share an example?"

Walter nodded, his voice carrying the weight of a cherished memory. "Certainly. There was this one time, when we were having a day off, probably a Sunday, and we went for a picnic near the river. Dolly, as usual, had made all kinds of treats. But, when it started raining, she insisted on sharing her coat with Jos. I found shelter under a sprawling oak tree but they happily squeezed together under the coat eating the remnants of the picnic. They looked cosy together and it spoke volumes about their love."

Joe was moved by the depth of Walter's recollections. "It sounds like they had a remarkable bond."

Walter smiled, the wrinkles at the corners of his eyes deepening. "Remarkable is the word, lad. They were best friends and soulmates. And even after all these years, thinking about them brings warmth to my heart. If there's one thing I've learned in my long life, it's that love is the most precious thing we have."

"Another remarkable memory stands out… we'd often call at the Methodist chapel in Skipton so I could go to school there. A generous lady from there gave me a bundle of clothes. She mentioned that her son had outgrown them, and I was welcome to them. Among the treasures were a proper shirt and a warm vest… quite valuable with the cold weather on its way. But the pièce de résistance was a pair of long trousers. Until then, I had only ever worn shorts, which meant chapped legs on a frosty morning. Dolly had to use one of her special creams on the inside of my thighs to ease the sting of chapped legs.

To go back to her kindness on that occasion, Dolly surprised me with genuine leather clogs from the market. Though second-hand, they were my pride and joy… akin to golden slippers. They initially chafed and blistered my heels but Dolly knitted me some socks and treated them with soap to prevent further discomfort. I'd been barefoot for months. My clogs were fitted with metal segs on the soles and heels, they became my ticket to dance, I would scrape sparks from the cobblestones… kicking and stamping like a clog dancer which was a source of endless amusement."

Joe glanced up from his notes, seeking clarification. "You mentioned going barefoot. Did you not have shoes before the clogs?"

"I did have a pair of Jack's old shoes," Walter reminisced, his voice tinged with a hint of nostalgia, "but they wore down within a few months. You see, the majority of towpaths are made of gravel or crushed cinders, and they're so abrasive that they gradually wear away everything that uses them. It was no different for Troy. In fact," Walter continued, his tone filled with admiration, "We had to pay a visit to the farrier every so often for Troy to have his shoes repaired. He was a fine fellow, that farrier, skilled in his craft. And Troy, well, he was always the height of bravery. He'd stand stock-still as the farrier rasped his hooves and then held those hot irons onto his feet to make sure the shoes fit. It smelt awful but it was necessary.

The journey along the towpaths remained relatively flat until we reached a lock. At this point, Troy and I would chart an alternative course around it, reuniting once the barge emerged. Certain stretches of the canal demanded frequent unhooking and manoeuvring. Troy's familiarity with the route proved invaluable… without his guidance, we might have lost our way. Complications arose when we encountered another barge heading in the opposite direction. One of the barges had to slacken its line to allow it to pass beneath the other barge, enabling their horse to step over. Indeed, those encounters along the tranquil waterways often opened doors to new friendships and conversations. As the barge glided through the picturesque countryside, I found myself engaged in discussions with fellow travellers, curious locals, and occasional passersby. These interactions, often initiated by a shared admiration for the beauty of nature or a common fascination with the bargeman's way of life, blossomed into genuine friendships.

The slow pace of the barge allowed for unhurried conversations. Tales of distant towns, folklore of the countryside, and the shared appreciation for the simple joys of life wove a sense of camaraderie among those whom we met along the water's edge.

Occasionally, these encounters led to impromptu gatherings. Beneath the starlit sky, by the gentle glow of lanterns or campfire, stories were swapped, laughter echoed across the water, and friendships deepened."

I cherished these moments, finding comfort in the connections forged amidst the stillness of the water and the rustle of leaves in the wind." As he shared these experiences, a warm smile crossed Walter's lips, and his eyes sparkled with the fondness of cherished memories. "In those chance meetings, we found not just companionship but also a profound sense of belonging in the vast tapestry of the English countryside.

English weather, unlike Troy was far from reliable. Each day, we had to confront the elements head-on. Rain and, at times, even snow would assail us and so, to combat these conditions, a tarpaulin was used as a makeshift cover for Troy's back, while I wore a few worn-out sacks. Regardless of the weather's temperament, the towpath always beckoned us on. There was no respite for inclement weather; we differed from cricketers who at the first sight of rain head for cover."

Walter's reminiscences sent an involuntary shiver coursing down his spine.

"There was one particular winter, a Christmas season that stands out above the rest. The weather forecast, which you can't always trust, had issued a dire warning of an impending cold snap.

We were moored in Dewsbury Marina, and as the days passed, the temperature plummeted with a swiftness that caught us all off guard. It was so bitterly cold that Dolly, concerned for my welfare invited me into their cosy cabin on a night. We huddled together, seeking warmth and comfort from the biting cold that raged outside. The wind howled relentlessly around us, a constant reminder of the harsh winter's grip.

Inside the cabin, the potbelly stove crackled and emitted a comforting warmth, casting a soft, flickering glow across our faces. The hypnotic dance of the flames provided a sense of security amidst the winter's fury. For those few comforting nights, I lay there, listening to the rhythmic melody of Dolly's peaceful slumber, her soft breaths a soothing counterpoint to the storm outside.

When morning broke, we were greeted with an amazing sight. Overnight, the world had been transformed. A severe blizzard had dumped a ton of snow, blanketing everything in a pristine white quilt. Snowdrifts had piled up so high that the canal, along with the neighbouring barges, had vanished from view. Some folk had to dig their way out of their barges. The waterway had frozen solid, and the icy grip of winter threatened the hulls of the other boats. It had happened in the past that as the ice expanded hulls were put under such pressure that they sprung a leak.

Jos had positioned our barge wisely. He'd sandwiched us between another vessel and a sturdy jetty so that as the ice expanded we were safely bracketed between the other objects. This strategic mooring had shielded us from the encroaching mass of ice, sparing us from the potential damage that others might incur. As I gazed upon the frozen landscape outside, I couldn't help but marvel at the way Jos's experience and foresight had protected us from the harshest of winters.

During those tough weeks when no money was flowing in, and bills loomed over us like a relentless storm, Jos had to reach into his money belt to keep us afloat. Getting money out was worse than having teeth pulled for Jos.

Typically, in years past the bargees would come together to celebrate Christmas with a grand feast, roasting geese, rabbits, and, of course, venison on outdoor spits. However, the unyielding weather that particular year made it impossible to forage for wood or stand outside in the biting cold. Luckily, we had been hauling coal, and that old pot-bellied stove remained a source of comforting warmth, its fiery heart blazing red.

As soon as it was fit to get out, Jos did some trading with other bargees in the marina ... he'd swap coal for flour or anything else he could trade, it was trade by barter and Jos was a master at haggling a good deal.

Dolly possessed a heavy cast iron pan with a fitted lid, affectionately referred to as a Dutch oven. In it, she baked bread and crafted hearty stews, turning the day before Christmas day into a symphony of kneading dough and baking loaves.

As soon as possible I trudged through the snow using a plank of wood nailed to an old broom handle as a snow shovel to reach Troy's stable. I was worried about him and I needed to check on him and ensure his warmth and well-being. I had to dig the snow away from the stable door which meant no one else had managed to get in. Toby was definitely pleased to see me. The icy grasp of winter had frozen the water in his trough solid. So, I wielded a hammer, commandeered from a nearby windowsill, to shatter the ice. In the stable, where about ten horses stood, I made rounds to ensure each had access to water. I reckoned that some of the owners might be snowed in and unable to tend to their beloved animals. Before I left I made sure they all had water and feed. It was hard work, but at least it warmed me up." Walter chuckled at the memory.

"That afternoon, we gathered to sing carols, our voices rising to fill the cabin with warmth and joy. Then, in a heartfelt gesture, Dolly handed me a present. It was a moment of profound emotion, for up until then, I'd received very few gifts in my life. When I was at home we rarely got a gift, Dad would walk us around the shops that were closed for the holiday and we'd peer in.

'It's a pity the shop's closed lad,' he'd say regretfully. 'I'd have bought you that if it were open.' I did get wise to this ruse eventually.

Dolly's gift was wrapped in plain brown paper, I eagerly tore it open, revealing its contents: six biscuits, a pair of hand-knitted gloves, and a book. It was my first-ever book, and you'll never guess its title," Walter smiled and rushed forward not allowing Joe a chance to guess.

"Lorna Doone."

Overwhelmed by this unexpected gift, I found myself moved to tears, my emotions flowing freely like a river finally breaking free from its icy confines. It was as though a dam within me had burst, releasing a torrent of feelings I had long held back. Dolly, with her heart-warming gesture, had created a crack in the emotional ice that had surrounded my soul for some while. I couldn't hold back the surge of gratitude and tenderness that washed over me.

Dolly, ever the warm and caring motherly figure, gave me a hug that felt like a sanctuary, a refuge from the storms of life. I held her close, tears of joy and heartfelt appreciation trickling down my cheeks. In that embrace, I could feel the love and kindness that had become a steadfast companion on my journey along the canals.

Unable to find the right words to express my feelings, I leaned in and gently kissed Dolly's cheek. It was a silent but profound "thank you" for the warmth and compassion she had showered upon me. At that moment, I realized how much I missed my own Grandma, who had been a source of comfort and affection during my early childhood.

The memory of my Grandma's loving hugs and tender kisses resurfaced, mingling with the present. It was as if Dolly's embrace had bridged the gap between past and present, allowing me to feel the warmth of both women's love simultaneously. The tears that fell were not just tears of gratitude for Dolly but also tears of remembrance for the love that had once surrounded me.

As I stood there, enveloped in Dolly's hug, I felt an unspoken understanding pass between us. It was a connection forged through kindness, shared loss, and the enduring power of love. In that timeless moment, as the river of emotions flowed, I found solace in the arms of the woman who had become like a mother to me, and in the cherished memories of my dear Grandma."

Walter's eyes sparkled with the fond memories, but he moved on slightly embarrassed by his emotions.

"Lorna Doone, a life-saver of a book. I'll explain more later," he said mysteriously. "Every night, by the light of a single candle, I would immerse myself in the adventures of Doone Valley." He shared a knowing look with Joe, his mind already drifting back to those thrilling pages.

"I was drawn into the story, and before long, I was sneaking away for secret trysts with the alluring Lorna." A wistful smile played on his lips. "I think I might have fallen in love with her as well. I rode with John Ridd through that mysterious valley, hiding from Carver Doone and his gang but prepared to fight for my true love." Walter leaned forward in his chair, speaking in a hushed tone. "It took me more than a month to finish it. I was still reading it when I moved back to my own cabin after the cold spell."

Walter's expression turned somewhat sombre as he continued, "It was a bit advanced for me at the time. I didn't understand some of the words, but I was determined to learn their meanings. I'd write down the words that I didn't know and, whenever we were near a library, I'd go in and ask about them or find a dictionary to look them up."

Walter's eyes sparkled with a glint of youth. "It was as if I embarked on a journey, just like John Ridd. Learning those words became a mission, a quest for knowledge. I wanted to read it to Dolly and Jos, but I wanted to fully grasp it first."

He fondly recalled his interactions with the librarians. "Most of the librarians were intrigued when I showed up with my list of words, asking for their meanings. One or two of them got to know me and would say, 'Oh, here he is again with his twenty questions.' I don't think they minded, really. If they weren't too busy, they'd read a passage with me and explain the plot. One lady even found a map of Devon and showed me the wild Exmoor locations in the story. She told me stories about other places, like Cornwall, where King Arthur's castle was located, and other points of interest. I knew which days she worked, and if I was in the area, I'd visit the library to see her. I think she was always glad to see me; sometimes she had a few boiled sweets and we'd share them."

The friendship Walter shared with the librarians seemed to delight him. Joe couldn't help but smile at the thought of a young Walter venturing into libraries, eager to decode the book's mysteries.

Joe looked up from his notes and added, "It sounds like you built your own little book club within those library walls. The librarians, they became your mentors of sorts."

Walter nodded with a hint of pride. "They were like my guides through a world of words and ideas. It was more than just reading; it was discovering something new every time I turned a page. The other librarians used to tease us, saying 'she's with her fancy man again,' because they'd find us in a secluded nook shoulder to shoulder immersed in our literary adventures."

Walter's story took a touching turn as he recounted the gift from Jos.

"Jos gave me a tin box with a hinged lid to keep my book in. 'Here, lad, this will protect your book and all those notes you're making about it.' Sometimes I was tempted to... well, to call him Dad. I don't think he would have minded. He and Dolly were always kind to me, and it felt like the right thing to do." The unspoken emotions beneath his words painted a poignant picture of the deep connection he had found with this surrogate family.

Joe attempted to fathom the many contrasts in Walter's life. On one hand, the harshness of working at such a young age and the exposure to the fickle changes in the weather and the complex mixture of love and life, pondered aloud, "I wonder how you all didn't come down with all sorts of ailments."

Walter chuckled under his breath before responding, "If ever a chesty cough or other ailment took hold, Dolly always had a concoction as a remedy."

As the reminiscing continued, Walter's gaze turned inward, lost within his memories. Abruptly, he veered onto an unrelated train of thought, 'Dolly said I had a fine voice. Thus, as twilight draped the day and Troy was settled in the stable, Jos would draw melodies from his weathered squeezebox, and I'd join in, giving voice to the evening's serenade."

Walter's contemplation wavered, a weariness settling in his expression. His advancing years seemed to drape on him heavily, and as memories surged forth, it was as if he had stirred the ashes of a fire long extinguished. Despite the weariness, he forged ahead, resolute in his endeavour to share his life's journey.

Recollections flowed in a gentle stream, and Walter's voice regained a trace of vitality.

"There was this particular instance, an unpleasant memory that has stuck from when I was around fourteen years of age. A span of about three or four years had already passed since I first set foot on the barge and I was feeling quite at home. Jos declared that our barge required attention in a drydock at

Mirfield. The hull needed some maintenance and it needed to go into the drydock for inspection.

'I'll have to rent you and Troy out for a while. I've heard through the grapevine that there's a narrow boat waiting for a tow to Manchester, it'll earn us a bob or two if we help out. There is also one to bring back to a place outside Halifax called Sowerby Bridge. You'll go on the narrow canal and come back on the broad."

A flicker of discomfort swept across Walter's face, a signal that beneath the words lay a reservoir of disagreeable memories. Joe sensed that his friend was digging deep into his emotions to recount the tale.

"There was no point in arguing. I unhitched Troy when we reached the dry dock and set off for Huddersfield's marina. Jos had drawn me a vague map and given me plenty of directions. I could see that Dolly was not very happy with this decision either, but we both understood that Jos was making this choice for the best.

Dolly, always the caring soul, prepared a knapsack for me, filled with a few of her special delights. Jos covered Troy with a blanket, creating a makeshift saddle so that I could ride him. The sense of bittersweet anticipation hung heavy in the air. We knew this journey would take me away from the life I had grown so accustomed to on their barge, but it was a necessary step to keep money coming into our venture.

As I mounted Troy, I felt the powerful muscles beneath me, and the horse, sensing the weight of responsibility on his back, stood tall and proud. Dolly hugged me tightly, and Jos slapped me on the shoulder, his silent way of conveying his faith in my ability to handle this new challenge.

With the knapsack slung over my shoulder and the reins in my hands, I set off towards the marina. The world ahead was uncertain, and my heart was heavy with a mixture of nervousness and determination. This was the path Jos had set before me, a path filled with new experiences and a chance to learn to be more independent. But at least the weather was fine.

Separated from the warm embrace of Dolly and my friendship with Jos,' I confess, that Troy and I felt akin to driftwood as we embraced this unfamiliar endeavour. I suppose that I was a bit hurt that he should rent out our services as though we were just another commodity.

Chapter Five.
A new Boss.

We had to walk from Mirfield into Huddersfield to find our new barge. I thought about visiting my family but I think I was still sulking over being sent away from home.

Our barge was too wide to sail this route and so everything was new for me, even the pick-up point.

My new boss was named, Harry King, and he immediately struck me as a miserable soul. In stark contrast to the welcoming and supportive environment I had grown accustomed to, the aura that Harry brought with him seeped with discomfort and unrest. His manner was consistently etched with bitterness and it rubbed off and made me feel sad too. The new barge offered no solace; my bunk was a chaotic mound of sacks tucked within the bow locker, I was sharing the cramped quarters with coils of rope and sundry other equipment. The air had an acrid tang; cobwebs dangled and dust covered everything."

Joe realised that this part of Walter's expedition was definitely not a happy one. He sipped his lukewarm coffee and waited for the story to continue.

Walter smiled as though he had lost the thread of his story for a moment.

"We left Huddersfield along the narrow canal, and if truth be told, there was nowt different for Troy and me, we trudged ahead of the barge as usual. The vessel was a true narrowboat with a beam of just over six feet almost four feet narrower than ours. It was a lot lighter than ours too.

The canal, as always, was flat between the locks which meant that when we began our slow ascent of the ancient Pennine hills we went through a series of them. It was demanding relentless work. However, our most formidable challenge lay ahead as we approached Marsden the highest point on the canal. Here, the canal had to penetrate the very heart of the mountain. While the barge would navigate through this monumental tunnel, Troy and I had a different task we had to undertake a challenging climb over the hills to meet the barge at the other end in Lancashire.

As we approached the tunnel entrance, we had to moor up and wait for the team of men that were on hand to move barges through its dark depths. The leggers, a tough and gritty gang of men who powered the barge by lying on their backs and walking along the tunnel's ceiling and walls, were crucial to our passage through the mountain. However, from the very beginning, it seemed that Harry was caught up in disputes with them, setting a tense atmosphere for the journey through the tunnel."

After I'd disconnected Troy, we stood watching the barge until it disappeared into the dark, forbidding tunnel. We took directions from a helpful local. It was a tough climb, there was a track but it was in bad repair and not easy to follow. I found comfort in the thought that it was a one-time ordeal. The weather was clear which helped our climb. As we reached the top there was a strong crosswind that made me catch my breath and stop for a moment. After the exertion of the climb, we had spectacular views of the hills around us. They looked quite formidable and even on a sunny day, they looked bleak and dangerous. It was a place of rare beauty but it held dark secrets of the past. I sang aloud, which curiously brought memories of my Grandma to mind. I hoped that the verses would shield us from fear. Even Troy, despite his size, displayed a certain unease and I could sense that he too was nervous. Somewhere on the hilltop, we found a patch of lush grass. We stopped and Troy tucked in and enjoyed a moment of contentment. I sat on a rough bolder to absorb the symphony of the moors. At first, I could only hear the wind but then other sounds came into play. Jos had shared his wisdom with me regarding identifying various birdsongs, and so, I immersed myself in the melodic names of nature's performers. In those moments, the effort of the climb felt justified.

I'd kept the contents of my knapsack secret, I suppose I should have shared but my new family seemed very mean and I guessed that there was not going to be much joy on this trip. After I'd eaten the last of my biscuits we carried on along a well-trodden path, one that Troy seemed to welcome as eagerly as I did. After what felt like an eternity, we finally descended back down to re-joined the towpath beside the barge. Harry's booming voice shattered the relative calm as we took our place again in front of the barge. "Where have you been?" he barked, his impatience palpable. "Time's money, you know."

I ignored him and reconnected our towline to Troy's harness. Mrs King gave me a half-hearted smile. I pitied her and wondered how long she had been forced to suffer her husband.

The leggers gathered around Mr King and I thought that there was going to be a fight. The atmosphere became charged, not only because of Harry's brashness but also due to an ongoing dispute with the leggers' boss. They were arguing over their fees, I thought that they deserved every shilling. However, Harry's stubborn nature meant he was unwilling to part with his money, setting the stage for a heated confrontation. I thought they were going to come to blows but eventually, Harry gave way and paid them.

 Another memory has just surfaced… one night I had to turn Troy out into a field due to the absence of a nearby barn. The sight of him joyfully galloping about like a new foul was a remarkable sight. Rather than going back to the barge, I fashioned a makeshift refuge using tarpaulin and an ancient Beech tree and then wrapped Troy's blanket over his broad back along with another piece of tarpaulin.

I gathered together some loose dried twigs and made a fire. It crackled away as I prepared a rabbit I'd shot with my catapult, another art taught by Jos. Armed with the knowledge of how to butcher it and a pocket knife given to me by Jos, I transformed the catch into a tasty meal. It smelt wonderful, infused with the aroma of wild sorrel leaves. However, before I could savour the meal, Harry appeared and claimed it for himself and his wife.

"You ungrateful sod," he snapped at me. "Don't you ever hold out on me again or you'll know what for."

Only after asking them for some back was I granted a portion, it certainly taught me a lesson. The next time, I waited until Harry was sound asleep before indulging in my meal."

A look of satisfaction crossed Walter's face as he gave Joe a knowing nod.

"They were strangers to the church, and so I had to miss Sunday School for the first time in months. I was disappointed but they insisted that we keep moving even on a Sunday and it was non-negotiable. I was worried that Troy would get tired, he needed his day of rest but I consoled myself that at least we would reach our destination quicker.

We finally reached Manchester's bustling wharf, a juncture that held the promise of a change of barge. Once I was ready to leave, I requested my wage from Harry. He turned on me and gave me a harsh slap across my face.

'Don't be insolent, young lad,' his words stung as much as the back of his hand.

I held my cheek; his assault had split the skin just below my eye. There was a slow trickle of blood. Knowing that I was in the right gave me the courage to stand up to him.

In retort, I stated, 'I'll not work for you again and Jos will surely deal with you for violating your agreement. When he discovers my unpaid dues, he'll be as mad as hell.'

He dug in his pocket and begrudgingly gave me a couple of bob, it was still short by six and a half pence.

King snorted at me, 'I paid that thieving sod Jos for the loan of horse and driver. I docked your wage for the food we gave you.'

I wasn't happy but I just wanted to get away. As I prepared Troy, Mrs King touched my shoulder, she cleaned the blood from my cheek in a motherly way, it was our only interaction of that whole journey.

'I'm sorry he hurt you… you've worked very hard… thank you.'

I had a feeling that Harry maybe used his fists on her too.

The wharves were a hubbub of activity, they also harboured danger… shadowy figures engaging in unsavoury dealings lurked in the shadows. Jos had somehow arranged for me to return with another barge and before I left Mirfield he handed me a slip of paper with the second barge's mark on it. I searched for the next barge marked with two diamonds and two hearts, a visual language enabling even the illiterate to discern one vessel from another."

"I need a little rest," Walter sighed, his voice weary. "I can pick up the story later if you're still interested."

"Absolutely, you take a little rest. I'll get more coffee, and lunchtime isn't far away," Joe responded, determined to hear more.

Walter's curiosity about Joe's daughter led to a deeper conversation about their respective family experiences. The homely surroundings of Walter's living room seemed to invite the sharing of personal stories, and they spoke with a sense of understanding that transcended words.

Walter enquired, his voice gentle, "Does your daughter attend a regular school?"

Joe's response held a mixture of hope and concern. "No, there's a special unit for her," he explained. "Maybe in a year or two, she'll be able to, but for now, she needs a lot of attention. The local infant's school couldn't accommodate her, which was disappointing. Thankfully, Julie's mother helps look after her at times."

The conversation naturally shifted to Joe's own family, and Walter's curiosity led him to ask about Joe's parents. As Joe shared, a shadow passed over Walter's face, his own childhood memories resurfacing.

"I haven't seen them since I was eleven," Joe admitted, his voice tinged with a mixture of pain and acceptance. "They dropped me at my aunt's, claiming they were too busy to look after me and embarked on a spiritual pilgrimage. My aunt later said they'd likely joined a commune; they were both addicts."

Walter felt uneasy realizing that he had steered the conversation onto sensitive ground. He offered an apology, but Joe's response was marked by a sense of resignation. "They made their choices," Joe said, his voice carrying the weight of years of coping. "Anyway, my aunt was a true blessing. I still call her Mum. We take her shopping every Wednesday, and she gets along well with our daughter, Debbie."

During their shared history, Walter found a strange sense of comfort in their conversation. "You see," Walter mused, "We are kindred spirits in a way."

Joe considered Walter's words, a thoughtful expression on his face. He chuckled as he commented, "Yes, I suppose you're right. I'd not thought of it in that way. I was luckier, where I went to live they looked after me and loved me, and they made sure I had a good education."

Walter smiled, a rare expression of contentment. "Well, I think that I had a good education too, not the usual sort but one that helped me survive."

Joe chuckled softly. "There is something in that, I must say. I wouldn't know where to start if I had to survive living off the land."

As they both fell into a contemplative silence, the room seemed to hold the weight of their experiences, the joys and challenges, the resilience, and the blessings. In the quietude of the moment, their shared journey, though different in its details, forged a connection between them, one that transcended the boundaries of time and circumstance.

Returning to the story, Joe eagerly asked, "So, about your journey? You'd just reached Manchester. I must say Walter I find aspects of your world quite alien."

Walter leaned back, recalling the stark differences between his past and the present. "Aye well, what about this, I'd never been to the cinema or picture house as we later called them, never spoken on a telephone or heard one for that matter, never been transported by anything other than my feet or a horse, the only tram that I'd ridden on was horsedrawn."

Joe considered his words for a moment. "Wow, we take so much for granted these days."

Walter's expression shifted, struggling to recall. Joe assisted with a prompt.

"Manchester, you'd just completed one barge delivery and were on the lookout for the next."

"Aha, yes, sorry I'd forgotten where I was. Looking back, it was a miracle that I made it safely to my new barge.

Walter's recollections continued to flow as he recounted the risky journey.

"So, there I was a young lad with only a faithful horse as my companion. The bustling wharf was a world of its own, teeming with all sorts of people from different walks of life. It was a place where one could easily get lost, and not just physically. Some were there for legitimate business, loading and unloading cargo, while others, shadier characters, loitered away from the light, looking for opportunities to exploit young lads like me. A young lad with a fine horse must have looked an easy target for any wrong 'uns that were hanging about, and there were plenty of unsavoury characters hanging around the wharf.

Young lads were targeted and often pressed into service on ocean-going ships. I saw one or two eye-me-up but there was no threat and I wondered if Jos's influence stretched further than I thought. I passed by groups of lads my age who were mostly working as barrow boys and who seemed lost, caught in the whirlwind of the bustling marina, their eyes revealing a mixture of longing and apprehension. I wondered about their stories, their destinies.

It was a stark reminder of how easily I could have been swept into a different, less fortunate path.

I remember that the cobblestone streets were uneven and the carts that were drawn over them made a dreadful racket, adding to the chaotic symphony of life around me. The air was thick with the scent of adventure and danger. What lay ahead was a complete mystery."

Joe listened intently, captivated by the unfolding narrative. Walter's ability to paint vivid pictures with words was nothing short of remarkable. He wore a smile of admiration.

"You were very brave to take that chance alone."

Walter returned a smile, "I'd no choice… anyway, I wasn't alone, I'd Troy with me. We sort of gave each other strength."

Walter took a swig of his cold coffee before he settled down to carry forward his story.

"I found the barge and when I first met my new boss, Mr Kendrick, he was pleased to see me and made a fuss of us both when we arrived, he was obviously in need of help to get his load home and he was very impressed with Troy. He walked around him like folk do these days when they are buying a second-hand car, luckily, he didn't kick his tyres or legs.

He asked me; "Are you a fighter?" he turned my face with his hand and looked at the cut and bruise on my cheek from the slap I'd received from Mr King.

"No sir, my last boss was a bully and didn't want to pay me. I'm sure Jos will make sure he changes his ways," I answered with a wry smile. When I think about Owd Jos in those days I can't help but draw a parallel with Dicken's character, Fagin." Walter laughed.

"And were you the Artful Dodger?" Joe added.

"Maybe." Walter laughed.

Kendrick kept hold of my cheek. 'Well you'd best not give me any trouble or I'll more than slap yer face," he warned.

Kendrick, my new boss, blended in seamlessly with the rugged world around us. He was a man of the canals, dressed in the typical attire that defined his profession. His waistcoat was worn and a patchwork of muted colours that had seen many days under the sun's harsh rays. Atop his head sat a hat they affectionately called a 'Billy Cock,' a sturdy bowler hat that completed his workman's ensemble.

Kendrick's face bore the marks of countless hours spent outdoors, etched with lines that told stories of wind, rain, and sun. His eyes, though weathered, held a shrewd and knowing look, a testament to the years of experience on the waterways.

He was a man of few words, preferring to let his actions speak for him. I quickly learned that Kendrick's knowledge of the canals was as deep as the water that flowed beneath us. Underneath the rough exterior was a seasoned bargee who had seen it all. I felt confident as we embarked on this new chapter of my life.

His barge was loaded with great slabs of salt, and we were to deliver them to a place called, Sowerby Bridge near Halifax, it had a salt warehouse on the wharf.

I'd reached Manchester on the Huddersfield Canal and now we were going to go back on the Rochdale Canal, a very different route. They reckon that there were 91 locks, so, as you can imagine it was a lot of work but at least there wasn't a tunnel.

Kendrick's family was an integral part of the barge's daily life. Mary Kendrick was like no woman I had ever come across, I can recall every feature."

Joe dived in, "Steady on, Walter, you'll send your blood pressure soaring."

Walter could not be put off as the memories of the woman danced seductively through his mind. "She was striking… and there was a mysterious charm about her, her raven-black hair flowed in untamed waves around a face reminiscent of a free-spirited gipsy girl. There was a longing in her eyes, a yearning for more from life and the intensity of those dark amber eyes was mesmerising, pulling you in like swirling whirlpools. I have to confess that I was overawed by her, I suppose these days you'd say, I fancied her despite our age difference. When we first met I was speechless and she must have thought that I was some sort of simpleton unable to put a sentence together.

But she was like a heroine from an old Valentino film. And oh, her complexion boasted a sun-kissed glow and a sprinkle of freckles across her cheeks added to her natural charm. Her features, marked by high cheekbones and a gently curved jawline, carried an exotic beauty that hinted at a heritage wrapped in mysteries. Her voice, smooth and alluring, held a certain seductive quality, almost like a purr."

Walter's emotions were riding high on these sensuous memories. "Mary's attire often reflected her free-spirited nature. She wore flowing, earth-toned skirts that danced around her ankles, adorned with vibrant patterns and loose-fitting blouses with plunging necklines that often revealed more than was proper. Around her neck, she wore trinkets and talismans, evoking an air of mystique and folklore."

"Blimey Walter, I think she had a remarkable effect on you," Joe chuckled.

Walter's expression softened, memories flooding back. "I'll say she had, I was infatuated by her. It was like something I'd never felt before, Joe. I found myself looking for excuses to be near her, drawn inexplicably to her presence whenever she was around. There was a charm about her that gripped me, you know? Her laughter was like music, and every word she spoke felt like a verse of poetry. I was utterly smitten, I tell you, Joe. It was like being caught in the current of a river, unable to resist its pull."

The barge was a playground for their three pint-sized children. It was as if the cargo hold, concealed by canvas sheets, transformed into a labyrinth of adventure for them. Laughter and youthful energy filled the air as they navigated the maze of crates and bundles, their small feet barely making a sound on the wooden deck.

In the close confines of a canal barge, Kendrick's family added a touch of warmth and vitality, a reminder that even while demanding work tired the body, life continued to thrive.

Nights on the barge were curiously silent. Even the children, usually the harbingers of youthful laughter, seldom made a sound. It was as if the very essence of the place had swallowed their joy, leaving only a quiet, solemn existence in its wake.

The flamboyant Mary was a quiet soul, who bore the weight of her responsibilities with good grace. Her hands were constantly full with the needs of her little ones. However, one day, the children's playful antics took a worrisome turn. A tumble led to one of them slipping into the water. Panic swept over the mother as she retrieved her child, and in a flurry of maternal instinct, she washed him down with clean water. The waterway we travelled was perilous, not deep, but stagnant and polluted by industrial runoff. As Josh once remarked, the waterway held more diseases than the jungles of far-off Borneo, an exotic and mysterious place that I couldn't quite pinpoint on a map at that time but it sounded dangerous.

"After that fright, she made sure they stayed away from the deck for the rest of the journey. One evening, as we sat around a crackling campfire, which we had used to cook our evening meal, she shared with me that living on the barge wasn't her first choice. But, she explained, difficult times sometimes necessitated making the most of the hand you were dealt. I hung onto her every word, as though absorbing wisdom from a sage. I found the motion of her lips as she spoke utterly captivating. We got on well together and she seemed pleased with my company and shared valuable knowledge, teaching me the art of roasting chestnuts. With a short-handled spade held over a wood fire, she demonstrated how to place the chestnuts just right, ensuring they cooked evenly until they popped, ready to be savoured. They were a rare treat, a taste of heaven to enjoy on a cold evening.

In addition to chestnuts, she cooked copious amounts of acorns collected along the way. Whenever we encountered an old oak tree, she would send me scaling its branches to gather nature's bounty. Boiled and transformed into a paste with the addition of herbs for flavour, it wasn't the most delightful of dishes, but it filled our bellies and served as a seasonal bonus.

As our journey continued along the tranquil waterway, the barge became a peculiar blend of toil and moments of shared warmth. Amidst the trials and tribulations of our unique lifestyle, her nurturing instincts and remarkable resourcefulness brought a sense of solace to our unconventional existence. Looking back, I reckon that perhaps, in my adolescent heart, there existed a fondness, a deep admiration that might have echoed the tendrils of young love."

Chapter Six.
Manchester to Sowerby Bridge.

After a long climb through countless locks up the Lancashire side of the Pennines, we reached a place called, Summit."

Walter took a moment and chuckled heartily to himself, "I'm sorry, but this next section of this journey will amuse you I'm sure. The new boss said; come on, me lad, we can mek a bit o'brass today. We went to a nearby inn, around the back was a meeting of some sort, the air was filled with tobacco smoke and it seemed a jolly gathering. Groups of men drinking ale were standing around upturned barrels using them as tables. There had been some cock fighting and some of the results were still being disputed. Suddenly, Kendrick took hold of my collar and marched me through the crowd.

The air was thick with tension as Kendrick bellowed to the gathering crowd, "I've got a lad here who'll fight anyone!" The words sent a chill down my spine, and fear gripped me like a vice. I'd tussled with my siblings before, but this felt altogether different… more serious, more menacing. I had a sinking feeling that this was not going to be a pleasant experience and that I might come out of it a bit damaged.

From the midst of the spectators, a figure emerged accompanied by a colossal lad who looked like he could bench-press a cow. His father stepped forward confidently, proclaiming, "My lad'll see to him." My heart raced as I took in the sight of my opponent. He was a monster, and my anxiety grew with each passing second and I looked for an escape route. He strode confidently into the middle of the ring to a great amount of applause.

Amidst the chaos, Kendrick, my mentor of sorts, leaned in and whispered in my ear, "Don't let me down, kid. Take off your jacket and earn some pocket money. I've seen this lad before; he's big and likes to throw his weight around. But stand up to him, and he'll crumble." I hesitated, thinking, "Yes, he'll crumble me if I'm not careful."

Joe laughed at Walter's humour. "Your boss was way out of order putting you in such a predicament."

"I suppose so, well, I had no formal training in fighting, so I relied on instincts sharpened through rough-and-tumble bouts with my brother, Jack. Without a second thought, I charged straight at my formidable opponent, hurling myself at his midsection before he could react. Despite his immense size, he folded like a half-filled sack, and we crashed to the ground, the crowd erupting in a thunderous cheer.

Now, I resorted to my tried-and-true tactic: running for my life. My opponent chased me, around the ring swinging his meaty fists, but I stayed just out of his reach, dodging his punches with agile footwork.

During the chaotic chase, I caught a glimpse of Kendrick, who flashed a thumbs-up, momentarily diverting my attention. In that brief moment of distraction, I saw stars as my opponent caught up to me and landed a punch on the side of my face. I hit the ground hard, but instinct took over, and I rolled away just in time to evade a potentially devastating kick. I kept rolling and rolling, much to the crowd's amusement, until I was safely out of harm's way. After dusting myself off, I stood ready, realizing that a direct charge wouldn't work again.

Suddenly, I recalled the advice Owd Jos had once given me about fighting. "Don't aim for their head," he had said, "they can see that coming, and you might break your hand. Hit them low and hard, there's not a man in the land who can stand that."

With newfound determination and a strategy in mind, I waited for my opponent to approach. His face contorted with rage, and he huffed like an enraged bull. I could tell he wasn't pleased and hadn't appreciated my earlier antics. Timing it just right, I dashed toward him. Just as he prepared to throw his next punch, I ducked low and delivered a powerful uppercut right into his groin, it was a lower shot than I intended, but the effect was immediate.

The lad doubled over in excruciating pain, sinking to his knees, and clutching his injured groin. The crowd's reaction was mixed, with some booing and others cheering, but most seemed content with the outcome. I extended a hand to help him up and offered an apology. The lad, still wincing, managed a feeble assurance not to worry before issuing a chilling warning that he'd seek revenge and probably kill me if our paths crossed again.

I understood his sentiment, and though his handler seethed with anger, he did nothing more than curse Kendrick. The lad's father begrudgingly handed over a sum of cash, likely the result of bets placed on the fight, with most favouring my opponent to win.

Kendrick, his face a mix of pride and gratitude, patted me on the back and reached into his pocket, slipping me a tanner, six old pence, at the time I thought that it was more than fair compensation for my efforts. Despite the shiner I'd received from the lad's punch, my spirits soared as Mary served me an extra helping at dinner that night. I was left with a sense of triumph, having faced a formidable challenge head-on and come out on top in this rough-and-tumble encounter.

That night, in the dim glow of our campfire, Mary knelt closely in front of me and held my gaze as she carefully applied a thick, sticky lotion to my cheek, her touch, gentle yet firm, worked wonders. I winced slightly at her first touch but she parted her soft lips and made a gentle sound 'tush, tush' which instantly eased the pain. Her focused attention and the intimate proximity stirred an unexpected sensation within me. With every gentle dab on my face, a subtle curl danced on her lips, hinting at a hidden amusement or perhaps a shared moment that only she seemed to understand.

In that pivotal moment, I felt the transition from boy to man. Her presence felt almost electric, stirring an unfamiliar unease in my breathing, making it stagger and falter. I couldn't help but notice the irregularity of my breath, a rhythm disrupted by her presence. The softness of her touch, coupled with the way she held my gaze, created an unspoken connection. There was something in her expression, an unspoken language that spoke volumes, leaving me strangely captivated and breathless in her company. It was an intense moment, one that lingered in the air, leaving me caught in a whirlwind of emotions and unspoken feelings."

That moment seemed to hang heavily in the air as Walter reclined and fixed his gaze into the distance. It was evident that the memory had ensnared him, transporting him back to a time when the weight of that particular experience was palpable. The room fell silent as the memory settled upon him, a poignant reminder of a time long past.

"Blimey Walter, you are a dark horse," Joe added playfully.

Walter just nodded in reply still unable to shake off that memory.

He smiled and nodded to Joe indicating that he was ready to proceed.

"Navigating the canal network was a constant adventure, filled with challenges and unexpected moments. As the barge descended from Summit, the journey was indeed downhill, but it was far from easy. The path ahead was marked by numerous locks, each one a hurdle to overcome. The canal, bustling with activity, posed its own set of difficulties.

"As we navigated along the canal, the towns appeared to merge seamlessly, a tapestry of quaint settlements nestled amidst the green valley. Every mile unfurled a new scene, yet a curious sense of Deja vu lingered as if caught in an eternal loop of picturesque familiarity. The architecture varied subtly, each town boasting its unique steeple or a quaint marketplace, yet the essence remained familiar, creating an intriguing labyrinth of similar yet distinct places.

Amidst this rhythmic parade of towns, the changing seasons painted a vibrant picture. Spring's arrival heralded the golden procession of daffodils blanketing the hillside, their sunny hues a beacon of optimism and promise. The air carried the sweet scent of growing life, a hopeful symphony amid the ever-changing panorama. It was as if each cluster of daffodils whispered tales of rejuvenation, infusing the journey with an undeniable sense of anticipation for the unfolding future.   The width of the Rochdale Canal provided a bit more room for manoeuvring. Yet, even on these wider waters, there was always something to keep us on our toes. One vivid memory stands out: a heavily laden barge, burdened with steel, threatened to lose control. As the barge passed us on the way into a lock, a powerful nudge from the steel-loaded vessel tested our skills and our hull. Miraculously, disaster was averted, and we remained afloat.

I was pleased when the journey finally ended, and the cargo could be safely unloaded. The town was new to me. I was impressed by the huge salt warehouse and other wharf buildings. I collected my wages, unhooked Troy, and left after we'd rested for a couple of hours.

I said goodbye to the children and then Mary lightly touched my arm. "Look after yourself young man," she whispered softly, "Have a good life."

Kendrick shouted after me "I hope we see you again soon."

I just nodded and waved and tried not to look back.

I was surprised to see Jos at a lock called Salterhebble near Halifax. He had been waiting for me and we walked over the hills and back to the dockyard in Mirfield. He asked how the journeys had been and I told him most of the story but not about the fight at Summit… I did tell him about his so-called friend not wanting to pay and slapping me.

"Don't worry I'll not rent you out again, we need to earn as much as we can. If I catch him, I'll teach him a lesson for slapping you."

Dolly was delighted to see me after she'd inspected the scar on my cheek she gave me a huge hug, which felt a little bit like when Troy had sat on me in the barn. She'd made some sort of stew and dumplings which I was very pleased to eat."

Walter sank back into the old armchair, his eyes now lost in the depths of the past.

"That long walk to Manchester and back, it took me almost three months. By the end of it, every muscle in my body was aching, and I yearned for a good, long sit-down. Jos mentioned that we'd have to wait for two days before our next cargo, which suited me just fine. During that brief respite, I brought up the topic of acorns to Dolly. At first, she seemed hesitant, fearing they might be poisonous. But curiosity, as it so often does, got the better of us, and we decided to try them later on. Some years later a learned chap told me that oaks were not really a native species of Britain, after the Ice Age, the first settlers who arrived in Britain brought them as a reliable source of food. I'm full of useless knowledge… it's probably what I'm best at.' He laughs.

"Would you like a break, Walter?" Joe asks, giving his friend some space to collect his thoughts.

Walter, with a hint of weariness in his eyes, rubs his temples as if to conjure up the next thread of his life's story. "Aye, Joe, a breather might be in order. It's been a long trip down memory lane today."

"Let's get a breath of fresh air."

Joe hands Walter his coat from behind the door.

"I think you'd best put this on… I don't want you catching a cold," Joe smiles and helps Walter slip his arms into the well-worn sleeves.

Walter chuckles as he slides into the coat, feeling a sense of care and warmth in Joe's gestures. "You're looking out for me like a mother hen, Joe."

Joe grins mischievously, his eyes twinkling with humour. "Well, we can't have the man with all these stories and memories catching a cold and leaving me hanging, now can we?"

Walter laughs. "You've got a point there. I'd better stay in good health to keep the tales flowing."

As they step out onto the porch, the golden hues of the late afternoon sun bathe the terraced houses in a warm, nostalgic glow. Joe takes a deep breath, the crisp air tingling in his lungs. He gazes at the row of houses, the Yorkshire stone is blackened with years of industrial smog but each has its unique character and history, just like the man beside him.

There's a lull in the traffic and the distant chatter of children playing in the streets fills the air. Joe turns to Walter with a smile. "You know, Walter, these houses might look worn and weary, but they're like the pages of a book, each one holding its unique story. And you, my friend, you're the master storyteller who's bringing these pages to life again."

Walter's eyes twinkle with a mixture of pride and humility. "Ah, Joe, it's not just me. It's the memories that keep these old stones alive. And I'm just the one lucky enough to share them."

With a contemplative look, Joe considers the uncharted territory of Walter's life that still awaits them.

"Well I feel lucky to have met you," Joe adds with a smile. "I hate rushing you, but I know there are so many more stories to tell."

Amid this tranquil moment, an ambulance tears past, its siren wailing and its blue lights painting streaks of urgency in the fading light. The sharp contrast between the past and the present couldn't be more evident. Joe and Walter stand there, temporarily swept away by the urgency of the present-day world.

Walter breaks the silence with a wistful reflection, his voice carrying the weight of time. "Some poor sod's having a bad day." His gaze follows the ambulance as it tries to negotiate the congested traffic. "It's a noisy world these days. I remember when it was mostly the clip-clop of horse's hooves or the occasional rumble of a car. Back then, you could hear yourself think, and life had a different rhythm. Now, there's so much noise, hustle, and bustle that it's hard to find a quiet corner for your thoughts."

Nodding, Joe's gaze swept the bustling street, a stark contrast to the tranquil world Walter reminisced about. The cacophony of honking cars and hurried footsteps underscored the pulsating rhythm of modern existence.

"Yes, you're right, the world's a different place now. It's so much louder, faster, and busier. Sometimes it feels like we're all just racing to keep up."

They both stand there for a moment, letting the blaring ambulance pass by. It's a stark reminder of the modern age they're living in. But in that shared silence, it's as if they're bridging the gap between two different eras, where the past and the present intersect, and their shared journey through Walter's remarkable life continues.

"I don't fancy going too far today, it's blooming chaos out here." Walter looked uncomfortable in his wheelchair.

Back indoors, Joe carefully stows away his tape recorder, he can't help but chuckle. "I think we'll call it a day," he says, suppressing a grin. "What's for your tea... not more sandwiches?"

Walter raises an eyebrow, his face a picture of faux indignation.

"Sandwiches are a perfectly valid meal choice, you know," he retorts, his voice filled with mock seriousness. "Especially when they're filled with... well, whatever I happen to find in the fridge. Anyway, Mr Singh dropped a fresh loaf off for me and I've a large tin of chunky soup."

Joe can't help but laugh. "Fair point, Walter. Those chunky soups you mentioned, are quite a culinary masterpiece."

Walter nods with a sly grin. "Oh, indeed. I like to consider myself a gourmet chef when it comes to microwaveable cuisine."

Joe can't help but laugh at Walter's self-proclaimed culinary expertise. "Alright, Walter, enjoy your gourmet meal. I'll be back tomorrow to hear more of your tales."

With a wave and a shared chuckle, Joe heads out, leaving Walter to his chunky soup adventure.

As Joe arrived home, he was greeted by his mother-in-law. "Oh, hi," he said with a warm smile. "Where's Julie? Is everything alright?"

His mother-in-law returned the smile. "No problems, dear. They've just gone into town to do some shopping. I think they were after some new shoes. Debbie goes through them so quickly; it must cost a fortune to keep her shod."

Joe nodded in understanding. "It can't be helped, I suppose."

His mother-in-law leaned in with curiosity. "Julie tells me you've got an interesting new case."

Joe's eyes lit up with enthusiasm. "Yes, that's right. I'm hoping to do an article in the local paper. I've only just got to his teen years, and already, I could write a book. It's certainly opened my eyes for when I visit somebody new. It's so easy to see them as just another case."

Just then, Julie and Debbie rushed in, full of excitement. Debbie ran straight at Joe, her eyes shining. "Look, Daddy, new shoes."

Joe knelt down to her level and admired the shoes. "Oh, they're lovely, just like you, my little pumpkin."

They had a leisurely evening watching TV, but even as they enjoyed their family time, Joe's mind was still on the memories Walter had shared with him earlier. The intriguing life story had taken root in his thoughts, and he was eager to explore it further.

Chapter Seven.
Florence.

When Joe arrived the next morning, he found Walter sitting in his chair, looking a bit under the weather. Concern crossed Joe's face as he asked, "Do you feel alright? You look a bit pale."

Walter, appreciating Joe's genuine worry, offered a reassuring smile. "Don't fuss, lad. It's just old age. I ache everywhere this morning. Some mornings it takes longer than others to get going."

Joe's concern remained evident as he persisted, "Shall I call the doctor for you? We've got to look after you."

Walter let out a hearty chuckle, though it was accompanied by a wheeze. "No, don't be daft. It's winter, and my body seems to remember every knock it's taken over the years."

Realising Walter might not have had breakfast yet, Joe asked, "Have you had your breakfast? I'll put the kettle on, and we can have a nice cuppa. I've brought some coffee and milk with me."

Walter's eyes twinkled with gratitude. "You're a good lad, Joe."

Joe's voice held a hint of guilt. "Nay, Walter, I should be looking after you better. I'm so keen to get your story down that I forget to look after you."

Walter's response was filled with warmth. "You're the best tonic I've had in years."

The room seemed to cocoon them in a warm embrace, the rich aroma of coffee mingling with the echoes of stories shared. Their shared quiet spoke volumes, affirming their strengthening bond. The sunlight streamed in through the lace curtains, casting delicate patterns on the worn carpet, as if nature itself acknowledged the significance of this moment.

The only sounds to be heard were the gentle clinks of their mugs as they took sips, the constant hum of traffic out on the street and the ancient clock on the mantelpiece that maintained its steady tick-tock, a comforting background rhythm to their contemplative thoughts.

In that tranquil moment, it was as if the weight of the years had lifted, allowing them to sit in shared solitude, each aware of the other's presence, the unspoken understanding, and the beauty of simple moments that transcended the constraints of time.

After a while, Joe gently broached a sensitive topic. "My boss asked if you've had any thoughts on us getting you into a care facility. I know you're not keen, but I think maybe you should consider it. I can even take you to one and show you what's on offer."

Walter's gaze remained steady, fixed on Joe, the years etched into the lines on his face. It was a poignant moment, filled with unspoken sentiments. His home was more than just bricks and mortar; it was a sanctuary of memories, a living archive of his life. He had grown old in its familiar embrace, and every creaking floorboard and peeling wallpaper told a story.

Finally, Walter's voice emerged, gravelly but resolute. "Joe, I appreciate your concern. But this place... it's not just a house to me. It's a keeper of my history. Every creak, every crack, they're reminders of all that's come before. My Alice's laughter... it's real here... the shape of her nose and the curl of her lips are all real here. It's hard to explain, but this place, it's like a part of me."

Joe nodded in understanding, realizing that the home was as much a part of Walter as he was of it. The care facility was a practical suggestion, but it couldn't replace the irreplaceable. "I get it, Walter. We'll explore all the options, but we'll do it on your terms."

Walter managed a faint but appreciative smile. "Thank you, Joe. That means more than you know."

They sat there, sharing not only coffee but a silent agreement to tackle the future together, as friends who had uncovered a trove of memories and were now navigating the uncharted territories of the present and the unknown roads of the future.

"How are you feeling now?" Joe asked.

"I'm fine, what about doing some recording?" Walter seemed to perk up a little at the thought of telling more of his story.

Walter's memories, began to unfurl, like a tattered map showing the twists and turns of his life's journey and echoes of the past came back as Walter continued, "Our next venture took us on a long path, all the way from Huddersfield to Goole, a trek we'd to tread again to get home. We took huge bales of wool to Castleford, then we picked up coal and took that to Goole, and then back we'd go, lugging salt and iron to Leeds. At least as we headed east, the land started to level, easing some of the toil as the locks grew fewer."

Walter's eyes lingered on the mantlepiece as if he were grappling with the memories that lay there, waiting to be unveiled.

"On our return journey as we approached Castleford, an unfamiliar barge pulled up beside us," Walter recollected, his eyes drifting into the past. "The owner, a man who greeted Jos as if they were lifelong pals, stepped onto our deck. His demeanour was grave," Walter continued, immersed in the memory. Then he asked for 'Walter Middlebrough.'

Jos's response held a hint of suspicion as he acknowledged, "Why, what's to do?"

"I'm afraid I'm the bearer of some sad news." The man seemed to have to steady himself before continuing. "I bear sad tidings," he said with a sympathetic tone. "Both your sister Joyce and your father, John

Middlebrough, have passed away, the cause is due to pneumonia." He nodded towards me, acknowledging the weight of the news, before tipping his hat respectfully and returning to his barge.

Walter's voice trembled with the emotions of that distant moment. "I struggled to hold back tears, feeling utterly helpless. I was far from home, unable to comfort my grieving family. The burden of guilt settled heavily upon me," he confessed, turning his gaze towards Joe, revealing the enduring guilt that had stayed with him.

"Dolly and Jos did their best to console me, but I couldn't shake the feeling of guilt for not being there when my family needed me most."

Joe listened in silence, aware that this was a pivotal moment in Walter's life, a time when he'd been torn between his newfound surrogate family on the barge and the heart-wrenching news from his own blood. It was a decision that had no easy answers and a choice made out of necessity rather than desire.

As Walter's voice trailed off, he took a deep breath, composing himself. "It was a difficult time," he continued, his tone heavy with the weight of the past. "I was grateful for Jos and Dolly's support, but it was impossible not to feel the guilt, the helplessness of being so far away when my family needed me. I wanted to be there with them, to provide some comfort, but life had its own course, and I was just a passenger."

Joe nodded in understanding, knowing that sometimes life's currents were beyond anyone's control. "It must have been a tough choice, Walter, but you did what you had to do with the circumstances you were given."

Walter offered a weary smile. "Aye, that's the truth of it, lad. We don't always get to choose our paths, but we make the best of the journey nonetheless."

They sat in thoughtful silence, Walter suddenly carried on his tale.

"It seemed a long journey back to Huddersfield but somehow Troy seemed to sense my sadness and he kept nudging me as if to say he was sad too. Finally, we reached home, and I went to see my family. When I got there, Tilly was still in charge but Jack had left home. I was sorry not to see him. I'm not all that sure that Tilly was pleased to see me at first. 'Look at you, Walter, in your good clothes and my words you must be getting plenty of grub.' Her tone was sarcastic, almost bitter.

I'd taken a couple of rabbits with me… and that made her happy. My other sisters, Claire and Elsie were just happy to see me. We hugged and danced around the kitchen table. They took me to where Joyce and Dad were buried… there was just a stark wooden cross with a little brass plaque to mark the place. I never knew his first name until the bargee said it was John…. he was always just Dad.

During those precious days, we spent together, we tried to catch up on all our news. Jos had entrusted me with some money to purchase gifts for everyone. I decided to secretly pass the funds to Elsie, knowing her responsible nature would ensure wise spending.

As we gathered around the table for dinner, Claire's words hung heavy in the air. "We don't know where Jack's gone," she said with concern in her voice. "He talked about running away to sea, but... you know what he was like. He's probably down a coal mine somewhere."

Tilly, with her culinary skills, prepared a hearty meal from the rabbits, a few potatoes, and a Yorkshire pudding. It felt like a reunion, and in no time, we were all immersed in laughter and lively banter, reminiscent of our childhood days.

Before leaving, I handed Tilly the last two shillings I had, a gesture of gratitude for the wonderful meal and the warmth of their company. She kissed me in a motherly manner and expressed her thanks. Little did I know it would be the last time I'd see her. Because, when I returned home, perhaps the following year, they had all vanished without a trace. The search for their whereabouts proved fruitless, and it was a hurtful shock for me.

I stood across the road, near that lamppost, and tears welled up in my eyes like a helpless child. The emptiness and sense of loss were overwhelming. It was fortunate that I had my new family to lean on during those trying moments."

Walter paused and looked sad but he soon rallied and continued his tale. A wry chortle escaped from him as yet another memory from that time resurfaced in his mind.

"I was about fifteen at the time, though I can't say I knew my exact birthday. Josh suggested we use the date I joined him as my birthday. It was on that special day that I received an unforgettable gift. Dolly, with her mischievous grin, pulled me into her cabin and slammed the door behind me, 'I've got a special gift for you,' she said with a mischievous grin and it was then that I finally understood what all that giggling and secrecy had been about.

When I emerged from that cabin, my face was probably as red as a tomato, and I couldn't help but chuckle at the situation. Jos, the ever-jovial soul, gave me a hearty slap on the shoulder and let out a booming laugh. 'No charge for your first voyage on the good ship Dolly,' he said with a wink, 'but remember, any more journeys come out of your wages." Walter looked embarrassed and said; 'I think that's all I need to say about that matter.'

The window seemed to hold Walter's gaze, a portal to his memories of a time when life was a different kind of journey. "The next two years were a proper marathon," he began a hint of nostalgia in his voice, "Mostly we hauled coal and iron. Jos had his eye on the brewing conflict with Germany, so business boomed as the different nations began building battleships and weapons. Those long walks tested my mettle and my resolve to keep going."

A warm smile crossed Walter's face and his eyes lit up with his next thought.

"Florence," he said, it was as though he had picked a name out of the air. Yet, her name was a whisper that held a world of emotions, "She was a lass I met on the barges. She was about the same age as me, and she had auburn hair hanging over her shoulders usually in pigtails that glinted in the sunlight. She was carrying a couple of buckets of water back to her barge and because I'm such a gallant chap," Walter quipped, "I asked her if I could help and carry one for her. Back at her barge, her father gave me a very disapproving glare as he snatched his bucket from me. From behind his back, she signalled me to meet her on the far side of a hump-backed bridge further along the canal. I winked to say I'd understood the message.

I set off and hid behind the stonework. Her father mumbled something as I left but it was lost on the wind. The heavy Yorkshire stone of the bridge made it a perfect place to be out of view. I sat on a stone ledge and watched the water. She turned up ten minutes later obviously excited by our secret triste. We held hands and for the first time, I looked at her as though I was in the presence of an angel. It was her eyes that struck me first. They were such a soft almost misty blue and I felt that it was like looking at distant mountains, they drew me in and I felt that I could fall right into them. After that whenever we could we walked out but always in secret. We were young and innocent and not aware of the dangers that could lurk in the shadows when young couples were in love. We'd been out a few times but one day she suddenly kissed me. 'I think you're very handsome Walter,' she whispered. She took my heart with that quick kiss. One afternoon out walking, we carved our initials into the bark of an ancient oak. She carved a love heart around our names and love bloomed amidst the coal dust and the canal's gentle whispers, but it was never meant to be. Her father was a stern and unyielding man who kept a tight rein on her."

Walter paused, his mind drifting back to those stolen moments. "Whenever our paths crossed, we'd sneak off together, cherishing every stolen moment. Sometimes, we'd go gathering nuts, fruits, herbs… anything really, just to pass the time. And then, the very next day, she would vanish from my life, like a ship disappearing over the horizon. Our love was like the ebb and flow of the tides, an on-off relationship shaped by the fickle demands of our separate schedules."

Joe observed Walter thoughtfully, his keen eyes tracing the lines of experience etched into the older man's face. In those lines, Joe saw the story of a man who had weathered storms, embraced joys, and carried the weight of memories. In his youth, before time had woven its tapestry of wrinkles,

Walter might have been leaner and more muscular, undoubtedly a strikingly handsome young man. Yet, even in the present, with a slightly arched back and weathered skin that bore the marks of a life well-lived, Walter possessed an undeniable presence. Walter's presence, far from being diminished by time, seemed to have ripened, like a fine wine gaining complexity and richness with every passing year.

"I lost touch with her during that busy time but sometime later I heard she was married, to another bargee, of course. It was constant hard graft but we were all in the same boat, if you'll pardon the pun and we just accepted it. We didn't have many holidays," Walter reminisced "But Easter, Whitsunday, and Christmas were always sacred. And so, when those days came around, the barges would moor up, and there would be a celebration that could rival any on land."

A spark of excitement flickered in his eyes as he continued, "You see, despite the fierce rivalry between the boats, woe betide any outsider who dared threaten one of us, bargees. We were a close-knit family on those waterways, bound by the shared experience of life on the canals."

He leaned in a bit closer, as if sharing a secret, "Now, certain areas we frequented had these deer parks. Officially, it was illegal to hunt the deer within them, but every now and then, we'd have a special gathering meal, and the main course would be venison. You might wonder how we managed that with the threat of long custodial sentences for poaching hanging over us."

Walter let out a hearty chuckle, the lines on his face deepening with mirth.

"It was a rare day when the coppers came knocking. We had our ways, you see." Walter gave Joe a sly wink. "We knew every nook and cranny, every secluded spot where the law seldom ventured. We knew the best rivers to catch trout and pike, and where to find hares and wild deer that could be caught without any questions being asked."

He leaned back, his face a mask of contentment. "Funny thing was, if anyone did happen to notice that there had been a bit of poaching going on, the gipsies usually got the blame. Our little world on the canals was a dance of secrecy and we bargees were the masters of it.

However, it was a time when our everyday concerns were about to be swallowed by the looming phantom of something much larger. The world seemed to be in a strange whirl, and despite what people might have hoped for the future, the shadows of war were once again creeping closer. Newspapers nervously warned of the state of affairs in Europe and about the assassination attempt on Roosevelt in the States. Public unrest was everywhere: A National Miners' strike, the tragic news of the Titanic sinking dominating the papers, although many found it hard to believe. Ireland simmered with trouble, and the suffragettes caused upheaval, demanding women's rights here in England.

The smoke had barely cleared from the Crimean War and the Boer War, yet a confrontation with Germany seemed unavoidable. The world stood on the edge, bracing itself for what appeared to be an inevitable clash.

'I think we'll take a break there, Walter,' Joe said and clicked off his tape recorder he was afraid that Walter was getting too tired.

Walter looked slightly confused for a moment. 'I've made a selection of sandwiches today, I asked Mr Singh at the shop if he had any Cornish pasties... I like a pasty now and again.'

'And did he... have any pasties I mean?'

'No, said he had only a few samosas.'

'I'll bring some pasties next time,' Joe said. He opened the pack of sandwiches Walter handed him.

Walter smiled at him and said rather sheepishly' 'Crab paste... it's all I had left in the cupboard.'

Joe sniffed them and closed his eyes as his own memories came back. 'Smashing... it reminds me of picnics with my grandad. It's years since I had any.'

Joe caught up in his own memories, opened his eyes and looked at Walter with a softened expression.

"Thank you, Walter. These sandwiches have brought back some wonderful memories."

Walter nodded knowingly. "Sometimes, the simplest things hold the most significant meaning."

Chapter Eight:
War looms.

After their lunch break, Joe tinkered with his recorder, ensuring it was ready for the next session. Walter adjusted the heating to combat the falling temperature outside.

"Do you mind if I let Julie listen to your story? We've been talking about you. She was wondering if she might come and visit you and bring Debbie to see you. She likes meeting new people," Joe asked, his tone infused with warmth and genuine interest.

Walter's eyes lit up with gratitude. "That'd be grand. I don't often have visitors. We'd have to conjure up some special sandwiches for that day," he gave a lively chuckle and then, his expression turned slightly concerned. "Is my room too messy? I never bother doing much cleaning these days. I'd be embarrassed if you thought it was a mess."

Joe responded reassuringly, "Don't worry about that. I can help you dust and vacuum if you like. I don't mind; I have plenty of that to do at home."

Once the lunch dishes were cleared, Walter and Joe settled back into their seats, ready to delve into the conversation once more.

"I remember vividly the day war was declared," Walter began, a touch of nostalgia colouring his voice. "It was August fourth. The papers were bursting with the news. Tensions had been building for weeks since the assassination of some Duke and his wife in a place I'd never even heard of. And then, the bombshell dropped… Germany invaded Belgium, and that was the moment when we all realized, war had truly begun." His tone carried a hint of sorrow as he continued.

"The war ignited fervour among the young men; they were eager to escape the daily grind of mills and mines. Government propaganda fuelled the fire, compelling us to 'Teach the Hun a lesson and fight for our country.' Old Jos assured me that my role contributed to the war effort and spared me from the front line." There was a mixture of memories and emotions playing across Walter's weathered face as he recalled those significant times.

Walter smiled knowingly, a subtle acknowledgement of the gravity of the situation.

"They assured us it would all be over by Christmas," he remarked, his tone laced with a touch of irony, "but as the old joke goes, they forgot to specify which Christmas. The headlines of that era were nothing short of sensational. The newspapers fed us a constant diet of propaganda. We were constantly informed about newly appointed admirals and generals, none of which most folks had ever heard. World order dominated the newspaper pages, highlighting the looming storm of war. It was a time when the call to arms was more than just a local matter; it held the potential to affect the entire world.

Walter looked serious and his memories came easily. "As days turned into weeks and months, the global landscape began to shift. Countries across the globe declared their intentions, alliances were forged and contested, and the fate of nations hung in the balance. Politicians engaged in impassioned debates, their voices resonating over the violation of Belgium and the encroachment into France. The world was gradually awakening to the fact that it was being inexorably drawn into a conflict of unprecedented scale and consequence. The calm before the storm was marked by a palpable tension, as the world held its collective breath, aware that the course of history was being irrevocably altered.

Urgency enveloped us, tasks intensified, and goods were transported relentlessly. Thirty tons at a time was the norm. Coal, timber, and iron ore flowed along the canals, and even nocturnal journeys became a necessity. Nights were illuminated by the lamps on the barges, a stark departure from the familiar. Troy's rest periods were calculated so that he was not overworked, which meant he still had to have his regular stable breaks even during our relentless endeavours. With Dolly's ingeniously crafted harness and cable, Jos and I helped manoeuvre the barge and we employed a small sail when wind and bridges permitted. While Troy was resting we'd break our backs and keep the barge moving. Then I needed a swift jog back to fetch Troy."

However, Jos was very pleased with the extra work, he said that we were getting paid a much higher rate than before the war, and he even gave me a pay rise of four pence.

In the beginning, there was a prevailing sense of optimism surrounding the campaign. People rallied behind the cause, believing it to be a noble endeavour. However, as time wore on and the casualties mounted, a sombre realization began to dawn upon all. It became evident that this was a disaster unlike any seen before.

The most confounding aspect was the sudden and widespread disillusionment with those in positions of authority. Politicians, members of the royal family, and almost everyone in power were viewed with growing scepticism and distrust. The early enthusiasm for the war faded, replaced by a stark and harsh reality. People lost faith in the reports they read in newspapers because what was printed on those pages did not align with the grim toll of injured and deceased soldiers returning from the front lines in France.

As this disillusionment deepened, the voices of socialists and communists found fertile ground for their dissent. They seized the opportunity to air their grievances and gained followers among those who had lost faith in the established institutions. The aftermath of the war would be marked not only by its physical devastation but also by a profound transformation in the public's perception of authority, truth, and the state of the world.

The military seemed to have a plan and across the country, they formed what was referred to as the Pals battalions and lads from the same streets or same industry were banded together to form battalions and regiments.

In 1916, two years into the war, this policy led to an even bigger catastrophe when the Manchester pals were fighting in a place they called, The Somme. They fell by the thousands, and soon they were followed by the regiments from Bradford and Halifax, uniting cities in grief. Streets filled with tears, and a collective mood shift swept the land. People were angry and wherever we went, folk were out in the streets and most of 'em were crying. That same year Bradford had its own disaster at home when the munitions factory in Low Moor exploded and devastated the area.

The Toffs didn't care really, it was their war but they just sat and watched while everyone else bled, they made more money and everyone else got killed… same as usual. Any remaining support for the war waned with food shortages and as the mounting deaths in the trenches became known. Political unrest gripped society, reshaping its foundations.

Joe interrupted, teasing out a smile. "You were a budding socialist, it seems."

Walter laughed softly, unaware of the term at the time. "I'd not even a clue what a socialist was then. But the actions of Russia's Trotskyites in 1917 resonated with me. However, their withdrawal from the war shifted the tide against us."

"The sight of women weeping spurred my decision to enlist. Not to slay Germans, but to challenge the likes of Field Marshal Haigh, whose decisions left mothers and wives mourning. Finally, I'd seen enough and I knew I had to lend a hand and join up. When I told Dolly, she cried, she went and sat in her favourite corner and mopped her tears with the tea towel, which started Jos off too; so, it was a rather wet send-off, I promised to write and not to get shot. With a heavy heart and a final slap on Troy's great neck, I set off. I was about to go on another long walk.'

Suddenly, letters cascaded through the letterbox, slapping the kitchen floor with a force that startled Walter. 'Bloody hell! That made me jump,' he confessed, laughter rippling around him. "It'll be nothing but junk mail. I seem to be on every list in the country."

"I'll pick it up, you have a little break," Joe offered, eager to be helpful. As he fetched the mail, the tape continued rolling, capturing every moment. And as he returned, Walter's narrative seamlessly continued.

"Where was I? Ah yes, I'd just enlisted," Walter reflected, a mixture of nostalgia and a hint of apprehension colouring his words.

"I was sent off for some basic training near York, mostly keep-fit exercises and endless marching. They didn't have to show me how to walk a long way; it was almost second nature. But there was one redeeming feature, we were fed pretty well. The barracks were crowded with only very basic conditions, bunk beds mostly or a camp bed if you were lucky. For me it was alright, but there were lads there who had only been used to a comfy house with their own bedroom and they complained constantly. I did enjoy being able to take a shower, that seemed a real luxury to me back then.

"I made new friends for the first time since leaving home, finally finding companions my own age. And for the first time in my life, I had new clothing, even if it was just a khaki uniform. I felt a surge of pride wearing it. We were issued rifles, and spent hours lying on coconut mats, honing our skills by shooting at targets. Otherwise, we busied ourselves polishing our boots until they shone like mirrors as if the glint might scare the Hun upon seeing his own reflection."

Strangely, I had a natural aptitude for it, shooting, not shinning and I emerged at the top of my class in terms of accuracy. One day, the sergeant singled me out. 'Come here, lad. We have a task for you.' The sergeant had a rugged countenance with a square-shaped head and eyes as unyielding as steel.

I assumed they intended to assign me the task of caring for the officers' horses, considering I had shared stories of my previous job and my experiences with Troy. Guided by this presumption, I followed the sergeant who had beckoned me, eventually arriving in front of our captain, a man in his early thirties. His most distinctive feature was a broad handlebar moustache that sat above his top lip, he had quite a fair complexion, obviously, he was not much of an outdoor person.

'Good morning,' he greeted me with a certain cunning, much like a spider luring an unsuspecting fly. 'I've heard that you possess skills in surviving off the land and navigating on your own. Is that an accurate assessment?'

Yes, sir, I've—" I began, only to be cut off abruptly by the sergeant's thunderous voice, which rang uncomfortably close to my ear.

'Quiet, lad!' he barked.

The Captain, with an air of finality, continued, 'Excellent, we require individuals with your unique talents. You'll be reassigned to a specialized unit. Dismissed, Private.'

That was the extent of the information provided, and before I could fully grasp the situation, I found myself transported to a location in Kent, designated for specialised training. And to my surprise, I learned that I was being groomed to become, of all things, a sniper."

Joe couldn't contain his astonishment. "What?"

"A sniper! I had no idea what that entailed, but they provided me with a new rifle equipped with a telescopic sight. Every day, I fired that weapon until the barrel glowed red-hot. They despatched me on solitary missions for days... sometimes on the moors, other times in woods and forests. I was convinced the war would be over before they were done with me.

Eventually, I received a distinctive badge to sew onto my tunic. Alongside that, I enjoyed an increase in pay by eight pence per week. When I re-joined my regiment, it was just as they were preparing to set sail for France.

The lads were all in high spirits about going abroad, but none of us realised the harsh reality that lay ahead... a journey into the depths of hell."

Walter sighed heavily, it was obvious that these recollections were taxing for him. Realising this, Joe halted the recording and carefully organised his notes as if he were tucking away a piece of their shared history.

"Let's wrap it up for today," Joe said, his voice holding a hint of reluctance. He placed the recording device gently on the table and looked up at Walter, his eyes filled with a mixture of admiration and compassion.

Walter, sitting across from him, felt a twinge of melancholy. He was growing accustomed to these sessions, he had long wanted to share his memories with someone who not only listened but was really interested. The past was a cavern of secrets, and with Joe, he was slowly illuminating its depths.

"Alreight," Walter agreed, nodding thoughtfully. "When can I expect your call again? I wouldn't want to lose track of where we left off."

Joe considered for a moment, his fingers idly tapping on the table's weathered surface. The weight of these stories, a lifetime of experiences and emotions, hung in the air.

"Most likely tomorrow, if that suits you," Joe replied, his commitment unwavering. He knew that every conversation with Walter was a journey into a bygone era, and he wouldn't leave it unfinished.

Joe's decision made, he briskly headed off to the local Coop for a swift errand. Inside the supermarket, he wandered amidst the neatly arranged aisles, initially meandering without purpose. His gaze flickered over assorted goods until the sight of the pasties ignited a sense of direction, and he moved with intent. As he went about gathering his items, the process of bagging his groceries acted as a brief interlude, a moment of pause that momentarily anchored him in the present.

He left the shop and was greeted by the outside world's buzz of activity. It only took a few minutes before he stepped back into the familiar embrace of his home, an unexpected tension hung thick in the air. It was as though the very atmosphere had shifted. Julie, usually radiant with warmth, now wore an expression that blended weariness and unmistakable concern. Joe immediately sensed the shift, a ripple in the usual rhythm of their home, prompting him to tread cautiously.

"Hi, love. What's up?" Joe asked gently, his voice a soothing balm.

Julie sighed, her shoulders slumping as if to shed the weight of the world. She swept her long, dark hair back out of her face, her gaze fixed on the upstairs bedroom where their daughter often grappled with her inner demons.

"I don't know how much longer I can handle her," she admitted, her voice heavy with the burden they carried.

Joe nodded in understanding. Their daughter's struggles had brought a torrent of challenges into their lives, challenges they were trying to face together.

"It's quite a challenge, I know," he said, his voice filled with empathy. "But what other choices do we have? Her therapies do seem to help, even though it can be uncertain at times."

Julie nodded in agreement, her eyes reflecting both frustration and unwavering love. "I try," she said, her voice tinged with helplessness. "But sometimes... I feel so powerless. She's so intelligent in many ways, but she just loses control, and I can't seem to reach her at all."

Joe embraced her and felt her relax in his arms. They shared a moment's peace.

"So, what can we do?" Joe whispered sympathetically. He couldn't help but feel a profound sense of responsibility and empathy. Their bond, forged through the ups and downs of life, had only grown stronger over the years, but occasionally, it was stretched to its limits.

"What's she up to right now?" Joe asked, eager to understand the current situation and offer his support.

"Sleeping, I hope," Julie replied, her voice filled with emotion.

Julie shared the details of their daughter's day, including a minor setback that had added to the mounting challenges. Joe listened attentively, offering comfort, and understanding where he could.

Feeling the weight of the day's emotions, Joe decided to shift the conversation to something more manageable, an attempt to provide a sense of normality in their lives.

"What's for dinner?" he asked expectantly, looking for a small comfort they could enjoy together.

Julie met his gaze, her eyes filled with a mix of weariness and gratitude for his unwavering support. With a weary sigh, she confessed, "I'm sorry, love. I haven't made anything yet. I just don't have the energy."

Joe tightened his embrace, enveloping her in a reassuring hug. "Don't worry," he said softly. "Why don't we order a takeaway? I'll call the local pizza parlour; you like their Hawaiian special."

In that moment, their shared understanding and love provided a sanctuary from the storms of life. They held each other, finding solace in their connection and the simple pleasure of a shared meal. Julie went to change as Joe phoned the takeaway.

Chapter Nine.
On the Docks.

The next day, as Walter sat down to tuck into his breakfast Joe knocked on the door and walked in.

"Perfect timing for a cuppa, kettle's nearly boiled," Walter said with a grin. "You're quite talented at turning up when there's a brew on offer."

"No worries, I'll make it. You finish up your brekkie. I've brought some fresh milk, a few teacakes, and a damn good cheese. I remembered that you're fond of that white stilton? Julie managed to snag some for you. I'll pop it in the fridge," Joe said.

"The milkman used to call but I don't get enough to make it worth his while. It used to come in gills, but now it's all pints. I'll square up with you once I dig out my purse," Walter replied.

Joe grinned back, his bond with his new friend deepening.

"Talked about you and your story to the newspaper editor this morning. He was chuffed and reckoned I should stick with it... might just land me that job after all," Joe shared.

"Well, that's good news. How's Julie holding up today? And Debbie, of course? Pass on my thanks for the cheese," Walter said. "You seem a little bit quiet this morning, it's my turn to ask now, are you alright?"

"Debbie went a bit mental last night, all 'cause the bus was the wrong colour. Julie seems like she's at her wit's end," Joe said.

"Tell me, what happened?" Walter prodded.

Eventually, the right-coloured bus showed up," Joe recounted with a look of relief.

"And she calmed down after that?" Walter prodded further.

"Yes, she quieted down and hit the sack straight after. She gets tired easily," Joe explained.

Walter cracked a smile, saying, "Actually, I did a bit of tidying last night, just in case Julie tagged along today."

"Wasn't needed, Walter," Joe reassured.

"Needed doing, and I feel better for it. Are we recording today?" Walter asked.

"Yes, if you're feeling up for it," Joe confirmed.

The air filled with the aroma of their coffee, and when it was ready, they took their usual seats in the cosy sitting room. Walter picked up the thread.

"I remember where I left off. We were ship-bound, it was a bitterly cold day as we stood on the docks... one by one, we climbed onto that grey battleship. I'd written a letter to Dolly and Jos and managed to post it to them from the dock. It was a nightmare, hauling ourselves up the gangplank, our heavy studded boots rattling on the woodwork as we lugged all our gear, rifles, and whatnot.

I saw an aeroplane for the first time that day; it flew over, spluttering and belching black smoke from its engine. On the second pass over us, the pilot was waving... showing off, I reckon. My mate asked me, 'Do you ever think about taking a spin in one of them contraptions?' 'Nah, not for me,' I said. 'I'd rather keep my feet planted on solid ground.'"

Once we were all on the deck of that ship, we were packed like sardines... barely space to breathe. Then the rain started again, it was more like sleet and bitterly cold. Thunder and lightning, like nothin' I'd seen before, it went on for what felt like ages. By the time we all got on board, we were soaked through," Walter continued.

"I'd only been on deck just a few minutes when someone shouted my name. I could see a sailor bouncing about on the deck, signalling me. Even after all them years, we knew each other straight off, it was my brother, Jack. We pushed through the crowd and then we finally embraced. In the middle of all that ruckus, we managed to exchange a few words. We wished each other well, and then he had to go 'cause the ship was ready to set sail. He looked fit, so navy life must've suited him," Walter shared as he took another sip of coffee.

Walter took a pause, clearly lost in thought, before he continued, "I'd never seen the sea before, except for that time we went to Liverpool and the estuaries in Hull and Goole, but that's not proper open sea. Suddenly, the ship's crew were bustling about, throwing lines and cables in all directions to release us from the dock. The ship's horn blasted, nearly deafening us, and we were pulling out of the harbour. Somewhere on the docks, a band struck up, and people were waving flags and banners, blowing us kisses and cheering us off.

We had hardly left port when some of the blokes started throwing up; the sea was rough, waves splashing over the bow, soaking us like we were swimming there. As we rode the swell, the throb of the ship's mighty engines gave us a feeling of security. Three more planes, like the fabled albatross, circled above us, then vanished. There were battle sounds already in the air, massive guns barking away. It was probably the worst journey of my life, and it felt like a lifetime before we hit land. And then, as we jumped ashore, it hit me, I was in a foreign place."

It was a foul day, the rain beat down on the war-torn landscape, transforming the roads into meandering streams of mud. If the opportunity to retreat had presented itself, I believe a fair number of us would have taken it. The inclement weather took its toll on many, leading them to fall ill, but I was hardened by previous ordeals and not easily deterred. As water dripped from the brims of our tin hats we pressed on, our figures were shrouded in the protective embrace of our oilskin capes. We could not only hear the heavy guns but we could also feel the vibrations beneath our feet.

I don't think at that point I was afraid, but later when we had time to consider our position we became wearier. Our first encampment was a makeshift affair, hastily erected near a muddied road in a field that bore the scars of countless bomb craters. It was there, amidst the desolation, that our Captain, a young officer hailing from Surrey, summoned me. Despite his youth, his countenance was etched with worry, it was as if he carried not only the responsibility of command but also the burden of the entire world on his shoulders. With a sense of urgency, he delivered his orders.

"There's a sniper perched in a bell tower near the village, he's wreaking havoc. Your mission is to eliminate him," he said, his tone betraying the gravity of the situation, his words enunciated in what we colloquially called a 'BBC voice,' a polished accent that marked him as one of the toffs.

So, I found myself venturing out once more, trudging along the rain-soaked ground, armed not only with my rifle but also a rudimentary sketch of the village. Most of the old town lay within the perilous expanse known as 'no man's land.' The trenches, those lifelines and death traps in equal measure, snaked through gardens, roads, and even the sacred grounds of the churchyard. As I navigated the treacherous terrain, there was the acrid smell of burnt cordite and death in the air. It was a smell I would soon become very accustomed to. The rain mingled with the tension in the air. Every step taken was laden with the knowledge that each move could be my last, yet duty and a profound sense of purpose propelled me forward.

A few shattered buildings emerged before me, a ghostly silhouette amidst the downpour. The bell tower stuck out above the ground mist. Was this the sniper's perch from where havoc had rained upon our ranks? With every nerve on edge and senses heightened, I inched closer, my heart pounding in my chest, drowned out only by the drumming of the raindrops on my helmet. The village, once a place of serenity, now exuded an eerie silence, broken only by occasional distant echoes of gunfire. I scuttled forward finding shelter wherever I could.

During this perilous task, I found myself contemplating the nature of warfare, the futility of violence contrasted against the courage of those who trudged on despite the odds. Each step forward carried not only the weight of my own survival but also the hopes and fears of my comrades. The landscape, marred by the scars of conflict, served as a stark reminder of the sacrifices made in the name of duty and honour.

I found a garden shed for shelter and even though it had two walls missing and most of the roof was gone, it felt cosy in there, safe. I sat in the corner and by way of a distraction, I cleaned my rifle. I was proud of that weapon, it might sound strange, but the polished wooden stock and gun-metal barrel looked impressive. Part of me did think of just staying put in the hope that it would soon be over. However, my sense of duty got in the way of me just staying there. Later, I moved to a ridge behind a wall, trying to spot their sniper. The rain kept coming, so I placed my cape over me, and with my rifle tucked safely out of the wet I patiently waited.

We were told by our sergeant, back when we were training, to never take up a spot like a church or a bell tower. He said it might give us a good view, but if the Hun managed to overrun the place, we'd be stuck up there like rats in a trap. Only one way down, and that'd be covered by the enemy guns.

So, there I was, waiting and squinting through my field glasses, trying to spot that other sniper. The rain finally stopped about mid-afternoon. And there he was, that sneaky fellow, takin' shots at our boys in the trenches. It was ironic. He must've had the same trainer as me because he'd taken a spot on the roof instead of up the tower. I reckon that it must've still given him a good view.

The exchange of gunfire continued into the evening, our lads firing off rounds in the direction of that ominous bell tower. You could see the stonework taking the impact as dust puffed up from the hits. As nightfall blanketed the war-torn landscape, I moved cautiously through the gardens, seeking any shelter I could find. Among the rubble and debris, I discovered refuge beneath a heap of fallen trees. Our sergeant had sent me off with a ration pack, which was a meagre pack of essentials. I was starving and so, I eagerly unpacked the contents: a tin of bully beef, but no tin opener, a few morsels of chocolate, some ship's biscuits, and a solitary piece of toffee. It wasn't a feast by any means, but it was sustenance.

As I savoured the meagre meal, my eyes were drawn to a rather peculiar sight in the garden. There was a child's swing hanging from a bright green frame with an orange seat and remarkably it was still intact amidst the chaos around us. It swayed gently in the breeze as if beckoning the return of its young owner, a haunting reminder of the innocence shattered by the relentless conflict. I found myself fixated on it for a while, I could almost hear the excited laughter of children playing on that swing and then maybe a shout from their mother calling them in for tea.

As the light faded, I wrapped myself in my trusty cape, a futile attempt to ward off the bone-chilling cold that seemed to seep into my very soul. The air was heavy with the pungent scent of burning wood, a stark contrast to the innocence embodied by the empty swing. I clung to my rifle, although it brought little solace in the face of the looming darkness and the uncertainty of the nights that lay ahead.

Daybreak arrived, it was cold and dank, I don't think that I'd managed very much sleep and I felt grumpy, and annoyed with the world and everything in it. There was the constant rumble of heavy gunfire, occasionally a wayward shell would screech overhead and hit somewhere behind our lines. I could hear the chatter of machine guns and I wondered who was being attacked by whom.

I had to use my bayonet to open the bully beef and I scraped the fatty contents out with my blade, although it was nice, it left a very salty aftertaste. I needed a swig from my water bottle.

When I looked about I realised I was in a better spot than I had thought. But now I had to be careful with the field glasses, the sun was shining right at me and if it reflected off the lenses it could give away my hideout to anyone across the valley.

"Boom…!" Walter shouts and ducks to his left. Joe looks confused and startled by Walter's sudden outburst. The room remained still, and there were no apparent signs of danger.

"Walter! Joe exclaims, his concern evident in his voice. "You frightened me to death!"

Walter, now composed, gave a wry smile. "Sorry, lad. Just a bit of a flashback. That's how it was. There would be an explosion and all you could do was dive for cover."

Joe listened intently as Walter continued his account of that fateful day. The weight of the past seemed to press down on them both.

Walter's voice was steady as he recounted, "It was like that the whole time, sudden loud bursts that scared you half to death. A series of loud explosions quite near me shook the ground, it was something I wasn't used to, and I was still shaking after the sound had faded. I rolled under a fallen tree, gathering my thoughts and my courage. I was really scared; my hands were shaking, and I doubted that I could fire my rifle even if I could see their sniper."

Joe could sense the fear and uncertainty that Walter had felt on that day. As they continued their conversation, Joe couldn't help but wonder how those wartime memories had affected Walter's perspective on the world and his daily life.

"When things settled, I peeked out again, looking for that sniper. I felt a huge weight of responsibility, I had to stop him from taking more of my mates' lives. I knew he'd been firing; his rifle had a very distinctive sound that stood out above the rest."

Walter stopped and studied a moment it was as if he could still hear those frightful explosions. Slowly his mind cleared.

"I was out on the flank of our line and I figured that maybe the enemy sniper wouldn't look my way. It took me a while to spot him again, but there he was, stretched out on that church roof, he was cleverly hidden by the fancy stonework. He must've moved in the night 'cause now I had a clear sight of him. There was a real gunfight going on, machine guns were rattling and there were explosions and the screech of heavy shells going back and forth. Sometimes, I can still hear them in my sleep.

I'd never aimed at a live target before, it made my gut churn. A pang of conscience bit me... takin' a man's life is no light matter. But I pretended he was just another target from training, one of the many I'd shot at. But like the sergeant said, it was him or me. I'd a gadget they'd given me which was something that used triangulation, to figure out the distance. I realised that I might be too far away for a clean shot; I didn't wanna miss or let him know where I was."

Joe could feel his own pulse rate increase, and the tension in Walter's words was making it hard to take notes. Walter was in full flow, and nothing could have stopped him. Walter's narrative had an unyielding grip on him, and it was as if he could smell the stench of the battlefield and feel the muck and filth of the trenches under his own boots.

"I crawled forward again and lost sight of him for a spell. I popped up again near a stinking ditch. The smell was so bad it turned my stomach and I thought I was going to be sick... I soon realised that the ditch was half-filled with bits of corpses. Torn rags that had once been proud uniforms now lay in soggy tatters but sadly there were personal bits too. I fished a faded photograph from someone's backpack and wondered if their loved ones knew of their fate. I felt a little bit like a vulture because I also took any spare rations that I could find in their packs.

I took another sighting and now I was close enough. I had him in my sights, but I still tried not to think about the man in my crosshairs. I took a deep breath, released the safety catch and then held my breath as I slowly squeezed that trigger, the gun jumped but the sound was lost in bigger blasts from the front line. The sniper lay still, I knew that I'd got him."

Walter's voice quivered with the weight of recollection, and his words, like artillery fire, reverberated through the room. Joe, in turn, was both horrified and sympathetic, his emotions mirroring the intensity of the story being shared.

The room seemed to shrink as Walter recounted these experiences. Each word added another layer of dread and heartache, and Joe could feel the shadows of the past encroaching on the present.

It was a tale that held Joe in its grip, and as Walter's narrative unfolded, he couldn't help but wonder how these memories had shaped the man before him. The past and present intertwined in a haunting symphony of emotions, and it was a performance that left Joe breathless.

"Rat-a-tat-tat... rata-tat-tat," Walter became quite animated and Joe was pegged back in his chair. "Mud started dancin', bullets sprayed and flung debris in all directions, a machine gunner had spotted me. 'Rat-a-tat-tat' and then silence, I guessed he was fitting another ammunition belt. I waited and then peeked through field glasses and saw where he was shooting from. He and his armourer were in a dugout with sandbags to protect them. When they fired my way, they had to lean over and were exposed to me. They'd given me another gadget, a periscope. It let me look over things without sticking my head up, and so, I poked it over a stump and found the gunners.

They fired for a while, and though much of the action was out of sight, the sound of bullets whizzing by me occasionally served as a grim reminder of the danger. Yet, amidst the chaos, there were moments when fate aligned in my favour. As the gunner paused to swap over the ammunition belts, I seized my opportunity. With steady resolve, I aimed at the loader, biding my time until the gunner resumed firing. After he fired another belt of ammo, I made my move, my heart pounding like a war drum. A single shot found its mark, toppling the loader. With lightning speed and practised precision, I worked the bolt action on my rifle. There were no feelings, nothing but concentration, my mind fixed on the deadly task at hand. The gunner's cautious peek to see where the shot had come from was his last.

My hands trembled, the weight of the moment settling in. But truth be told, it didn't bother me much; I was merely carrying out orders, I told myself to shed any guilt for my actions. Survival, they drilled into us, hinged on obedience. The generals in their lofty positions likely followed orders too. The notion of fighting for the King and Country started to feel absurd. If the King had a quarrel with his cousin, the Kaiser, why not settle it like my mates and I did? We'd wrestle or play conkers, simple and honest."

A chuckle escaped Walter's lips, his mind drifting back to those days. The memory held such vivid intensity that he found himself perspiring, momentarily disoriented about his present surroundings.

Clearing his throat, Walter addressed Joe, his eyes pleading for assistance.

"I'd appreciate going for a walk, Joe. You mentioned you might help with that." His gaze conveyed his eagerness to be outdoors. "There's a park just down the street. Why don't we find a spot there? It looks to be nice and sunny, I can't stand being cooped up indoors unless it's pouring rain or freezing cold. Sometimes I drag a kitchen chair to the yard and sit there for a change."

Recognizing that Walter had a lifelong affinity for the outdoors, Joe saw the importance of this opportunity. They unfolded the wheelchair, and Walter eased himself into it, his cautious movements reflecting both anticipation and stiff aching limbs.

In the serene park setting, Walter stared at the trees, soaking up their tranquillity he let out a deep breath. The two friends enjoyed the warmth of the winter morning sunlight as they sat near the worn but enduring old bandstand.

Walter shuddered slightly and pulled his coat around his shoulders.

"Me and Alice often came here on a weekend to listen to the local brass band, in fine weather we'd even bring a picnic. I'm sure those trees will still resound to their sound, I'm sure I can still hear it."

Joe's smile widened as he reminisced about the brass band performance he had once witnessed. The vivid scene played in his mind, and he could almost taste the nostalgia in the air. The crowd's chatter mixed with the joyous melodies, creating a lively atmosphere. Balloons swayed in the breeze, and the sweet scent of ice cream hung in the warm, summer air. Children ran around, their laughter like musical notes in the background, calling to each other in playful excitement.

For Joe, a devotee of rock and roll, the brass band's music had been a delightful change. The harmonious blend of brass instruments had cast a spell, creating a resounding tapestry of sound that was both powerful and invigorating. The trumpets had soared like heralds of jubilation, while the deep resonance of the trombones had rooted the music in the earth.

At that moment, he had found a new appreciation for the versatility of music, as the brass band's performance had transcended his usual preferences, touching his heart and soul with its magnificent sound. The music was a cascade of emotions, at times triumphant and uplifting, causing hearts to swell with pride, and at others, it was tender and reflective, inviting a sense of nostalgia. Each note played with precision, contributed to the grand symphony, carrying the listener on a journey of sound that stirred the soul and left an indelible mark in the heart. The brass band's performance was a true marvel, a testament to the power of music to exceed words and touch the deepest corners of the human spirit.

Walter smiled, he could see that Joe was daydreaming a bit, he smiled and wondered what memories the young man had.

"I've brought some bread for the ducks," Walter said, his voice carrying a sense of nostalgia. His eyes drifted towards a cluster of youngsters joyfully swaying back and forth on the swings, their vibrant scarves, coats, and hats contrasting against the wintry chill. Their laughter intertwined with the distant murmur of grown-ups chatting nearby, creating a harmonious blend of sound that echoed through the crisp air.

"I loved playing on the swings as a kid. If you bring your daughter, perhaps she would like to come here," Walter suggested, his eyes softening as he remembered simpler times.

Joe helped Walter put on the brakes and placed a blanket over his knees. He took out his notebook and enquired eagerly, "Are we good to have a chat here?"

Eventually, Walter nodded a faint smile on his lips.

"Yes, no problem at all. And I've got that memory fresh as a daisy. Ready to go? Is your pencil nice and sharp?

After I'd made it back to my platoon," Walter began, his voice taking on a more serious tone, "I headed to report to the Captain, except, I found that it was a different one; the bloke who'd sent me out had got killed that same day... such a waste," Walter sighed, his gaze briefly shifting to the past.

"I Found a few of me old mates," he continued, his eyes staring off into the distance, "but they looked like they'd seen a ghost; a couple of 'em just shook like leaves, couldn't talk, or move. Huddled in the trench their uniforms wet and splattered with mud, they looked like they wanted the earth to swallow 'em up. I was sorry for 'em, worried too, 'cause if they didn't snap out of it, they'd be shot as cowards, and I knew they weren't that."

Walter's expression turned sombre, and he tossed the last of his bread to a cheeky mallard pecking at his shoe. For a brief moment, his mood seemed to lighten.

"No such thing as shell shock then, just cowardice in the brass's eyes," Walter remarked with a tinge of bitterness. "Most days, they sent me off in a different direction, and I started learning the lay of the land. The front line hadn't budged for months, so when the weather dried up a bit... the army was busy with roads and railways. If they'd had barges, I might've felt at home. What locals were left looked as knackered as the blokes, everyone was worn out and defeated.

I sussed out where the good canteens were and where I could get a proper meal. Some of those cooks worked magic with the rations, but others... their grub was so foul I'd've offered them to the Huns to shoot," he chuckled with a glimmer of humour in his eyes.

I started spending days away from my lads," he continued, "When I'd show up again, there were new faces all 'round, no one knew how long I'd been gone and I doubted that they cared either. Once, when I got back, they slapped cuffs on me and arrested me as a deserter. I panicked and I could already hear the shots of the firing squad as they marched me away. So, desperately I showed 'em me special badge and said I'd been out hunting an enemy sniper. They were happy with that and once it was cleared up, they pointed me toward the canteen.

About that time, I tried taking up smoking, but it choked me, coughed like that spluttering plane," Walter reminisced, his eyes narrowing at the memory. "I figured that there were better things to do with my brass, but I always kept a few ciggies, handy for trading, like for chocolate and bully beef. Now and then, I'd come across a wounded lad who needed a smoke, so I'd hand mine over."

On days when I was cold and soaked," Walter continued, "I'd think of Troy and Dolly and wonder if she still had all her friends calling around. Probably saw it as her part in the war effort, but maybe the war had taken them away too. Owd Jos would still be the same, happy as a pig in muck," Walter mused, a faint smile touching his lips. "There were times, that I wished that I'd never volunteered, but looking back, I reckon it was the right thing to do, to stand by the lads," he added, his voice carrying a mixture of pride and reflection.

Walter pulled out a tarnished pocket watch, observing the time. "I think it's lunchtime."

They strolled back down the street, Joe contentedly pushing his friend's wheelchair. Once inside the house, they unwrapped their sandwiches, and Joe revealed a treat for Walter—a Cornish pasty from the Coop.

"Ooh, lovely. Let's hunt down the brown sauce," Walter chuckled, his face lighting up with anticipation. As they savoured their meal, the conversation between Walter and Joe flowed naturally, like a gentle stream winding through their shared moments. Walter, his eyes filled with curiosity, turned his attention toward Joe.

"So, where do you live?" Walter enquired, his interest aroused about the younger man's life beyond these shared moments.

Joe, always hospitable, extended an invitation. "That new estate by the old market; they call it the Oaks. Maybe you'd fancy a visit sometime?" His warm smile and inviting manner held an unspoken hope that Walter might join him in exploring life beyond these walls.

Walter considered the proposition, and "A day out." A glimmer of longing danced in his eyes. "Even if it's just crossing town, would be nice," he replied, his voice tinged with a hint of nostalgia. "The last place I went to was the clinic for a check-up."

Joe, sensing a deeper layer of Walter's emotions, shifted into a caring mode. He asked gently, "How does it feel, being stuck indoors like this?" His concern was evident in his voice and the way he leaned in to listen.

Walter's gaze fixed on a distant point, his thoughts delving into the recesses of his experience. "Dreadful... if you must know," he began, his words heavy with a mix of frustration and a tinge of bitter acceptance, "It feels like I'm in a queue, waiting for my turn to kick the bucket."

Joe's response was heartfelt, his compassion for his friend's plight evident in his words and interest. "That's rough," he said, his voice conveying empathy for the frustration that came with Walter's confinement.

Walter's thoughts drifted back, and he spoke almost to himself, "Funny thing, I can't recall a thing about last week. But these memories, the ones from back then, they're etched so deep that it feels like only yesterday that I was clambering in and out of trenches."

Joe nodded in understanding, his respect for Walter's lived experiences growing stronger with every word. "I can't even imagine how grim that must have been."

Walter let out a sigh, his voice tinged with both weariness and a sense of accomplishment. "I'm glad about that, no one should have to go through that. You see, Joe, there's nowt much to look forward to at this age. Too late for any grand ambitions, and truth be told, too old for any big plans. As they say, the mind's willing but the body's weak."

The complexities of ageing and the inevitable reflection on the passage of time were etched into each line on Walter's weathered face; he paused, his gaze fixed on a distant point before he continued with a hint of guilt.

"I don't really know how many men I shot. I did keep tally at first but it seemed a morbid pastime and I gave up counting." Walter reflected, his voice carrying the weight of memories forged in the heat of battle. "But one day, fate turned the tables on me and by hell, it hurt."

As he spoke, Walter's eyes seemed to gaze beyond the room, lost in the horrors of the past. "I'd been moving, trying to keep out of view. A ghost amidst the chaos. And then, out of nowhere, searing agony erupted in my arm. It was as if a crocodile had sunk its teeth into me, attempting to drag me over the very wall I had taken refuge behind."

He paused his words a bitter reminder of the brutal randomness of warfare. "That's when it hit me, this time I was the one shot. I could feel the warm blood running down my arm. It's a funny thing but when the blood is inside of you, well then you can't tell its temperature but as soon as it escapes you feel it."

The room seemed to grow tense. "The burn was fierce, a pain that cut through my senses. Fear crept in, a fear I hadn't truly known until that moment... the fear of bleeding to death in that forsaken place."

Walter's voice lowered, mirroring his thoughts from that dire day. "It took a while for me to gather my senses and I was more worried about losing my rifle than about my arm. Crawling back to our lines, I was like a wounded animal seeking sanctuary. A sergeant came to my aid, his hands working quickly to tie a rag tightly around my arm. He ordered me to find a field hospital. At that moment a couple of shells burst in the air above us and we were forced to dive for cover."

Walter closed his eyes momentarily as if summoning the memory of that path even with a bullet lodged in his arm. "I'd passed that field hospital so many times... but I'd never paid it much mind before. But now, with my own blood dripping to the ground, I knew the way even amidst the chaos."

Walter's gaze shifted to Joe, a distant expression lingering in his eyes.

"The hospital was a khaki marquee with a big red cross painted on its side. Inside bustled with soldiers trying to find a camp bed to rest for a while or staff hurrying about carrying bandages and bedpans. In there, the smell of blood mixed with the tang of antiseptic and the cry of injured lads. A friendly nurse, a bonny lass with a Jordy accent, helped me remove my shirt. Her tunic, starched but stained with the blood of countless others, was a sombre testament to the horrors she'd witnessed."

Walter's words hung heavy in the air, a silent tribute to the resilience of those who faced the unrelenting brutality. "She spoke softly, kindness in her eyes, and she assured me she'd send someone to tend to my wound. So, I sat there, one among many wounded souls, waiting to be mended. Most were far worse than me."

Walter's voice took on a reflective tone, "And then a doctor arrived, his demeanour was a blend of urgency and detachment. He handed me a vial of gas to inhale, a fleeting escape from the pain. Then, with methodical precision, he prodded and probed my arm, navigating the wreckage left by that bullet."

Walter's voice grew quieter, "There you are, lad," he imitated the doctor's accent, a touch of nostalgia in his tone. "You're lucky it didn't snap your arm.' He dropped the bullet fragment into my hand as a keepsake.

Walter recalled the moment with vivid clarity and then produced a misshapen bullet from his cardigan pocket that he had kept all those years as a memento. "Kept that bullet to remind me that no matter how bad things get, they could always be worse." He handed the bullet to Joe, a small but tangible piece of his history.

Joe examined the bullet with curiosity, remarking, "It's not as big as I thought it'd be."

"Doctor told me it had split in my arm, the rest of it came out the other side," Walter explained, his voice carrying a mix of amazement and reflection.

Chapter Ten
It's our Elsie

"That war was full of shocks and surprises, none of which were any bigger than when the nurse came to bandage me… it was our Elsie," Walter continued, his voice tinged with emotion. Memories of that incredible moment played vividly in his mind as he recounted the profound reunion with his sister. The rush of tears and embraces that accompanied their meeting seemed to wash over him once more, evoking a mixture of joy and sadness that only wartime could elicit.

"What a reunion that was. She cried and hugged me, she could hardly talk fast enough. I told her about seeing Jack, and she was still crying and hugging me, trying to convey the news about Tilly's marriage and how she had not seen me since Dad and Joyce had passed away." The room seemed to fade away as Walter transported himself back to that tearful encounter.

As Walter delved into the details of those heart-warming moments, his voice grew softer, painting a tender picture of the time he had spent with Elsie during his stay at the hospital.

"We managed to have a couple of meals together. I had to wait until my arm had healed up before I could leave the hospital. She even arranged for me to have a shower," he chuckled, "She looked at me and said, 'You really need it, what have you been rolling in? The warmth of those moments lingered in my memory like a comforting embrace."

The laughter and innocence of their childhood seemed to illuminate his weary eyes, giving a glimpse of the carefree days that had preceded the war.

The bond between Walter and Elsie was evident in his words as he explained his decision to stay near her instead of being sent to the rear.

"I could have been sent back to the rear of our lines out of the way for a while, but now that I knew where Elsie was, I thought that I'd best stay and make sure she was safe." The protective instinct of a younger brother, fuelled by the uncertainty of war, meant that he felt that his place was with his sister for a while at least. Walter's tone shifted slightly as he introduced a new character into the story.

"She introduced me to a friend of hers, a Scots lass called Jane McConkie from Fife. I must say I was rather attracted to her." His voice held a hint of amusement as if he was sharing a personal detail that brought a nostalgic smile to his face.

"Elsie introduced us. 'This is my brother, Walter, we used to share a bath on Friday nights when we were kids.' Jane gave me a saucy glance and nudged Elsie in the ribs and said, 'I wouldn't mind sharing a bath with him.'"

Walter's laughter resonated in the room, a testament to the camaraderie and banter that had emerged even in the darkest times.

"The food in the hospital was pretty good which was another reason for me to stay. When I'd been there a few days, there were two or three of the biggest, loudest bangs I'd heard in my life. Suddenly, a few days later, our line moved forward a little bit for the first time in months. There was a lot of confusion, and a great deal of the top brass was visiting. I think that they were disappointed because I don't think the explosions had really achieved their expected goals."

The atmosphere grew tense as Walter recounted the unsettling aftermath of the explosions, a reminder that the war was a complex web of strategic decisions and unpredictable outcomes.

"My new captain, a Scotsman from Edinburgh with a thunderous voice that could make even the bravest tremble, sent me off on a daring mission. He said, 'Poke into enemy territory while things are still a bit muddled,' he gave me a wry smile that hinted at the uncertainty of my task.

So, off I went on my mission, weaving my way through a labyrinth of ditches and trenches under the shroud of the night. The darkness was thick, almost tangible, broken only by the feeble glimmer of distant stars. Each step I took was a venture into uncertainty. The trenches, some partly filled with foul-smelling water, seemed like gaping jaws ready to swallow any misstep.

There was the occasion exchange of fire and then flares bursting in the dark would slowly drift back to earth. If one glowed near me I kept perfectly still until its light had faded.

As I crept forward, there were tangles of barbed wire, sinister and unforgiving, like the sentinels of a forbidden realm. My uniform snagged on the barbs, a sharp reminder that danger lurked in every shadow. In that solitude, I carried my own confidence as my only companion, a reassuring warmth in the chill of the night. Between the occasional exchange of fire, there was an absolute eerie silence. I've spent many nights out in the countryside but never one as quiet as that, no owls were hooting or nightjars singing, and not even a dog barked and then there would be a shot echoing across the land.

It's hard to believe, but about an hour later, I came to a stark realisation, that I was now behind enemy lines, deep within the heart of their territory. Pride swelled within me, for I had done in a mere two hours what the generals had sought in vain to do for three long years. However, my pride was soon overshadowed by a daunting reality, that I had no clue how to find my way back.

The enemy's sappers and engineers toiled tirelessly, like busy ants in their underground labyrinth. New trenches and fortifications were sprouting up like malignant weeds, rendering the landscape unrecognizable. My return journey was veiled in uncertainty, and I was just a lone figure amidst the ever-shifting puzzle of war.

It's funny what you find in deserted trenches, mostly stuff someone has left behind, perhaps thinking they'd pick it up on the way back... but they never did. I got some top-notch boots, they fitted me like a glove, way better than the standard issue... I think they were German. They did a lot better with their gear than us. It reminded me of Dolly and the boots she bought me in Skipton. Oh, how I longed to be back there in that place and time.

My lonely adventure behind enemy lines continued and I did some spy work, as you might say. I'd scrambled out of the muddy trenches and away from the killing fields into what once must have been a pleasant village full of life, now it was just a collection of bombed-out buildings and scarred roads filled with debris.

It felt like a bit of a holiday, I could hear the hell going on behind me but I seemed to be somehow isolated from it. It was a very good feeling. However, I knew that I had to be very wary, enemy troops could come marching down the road at any time.

The war was relentless, and in the midst of it all, I found myself seeking solace in an abandoned building, an eerie shell of what was once a school. There, amidst the rubble, I stumbled upon a sketchbook and a set of coloured pencils, perhaps a forgotten memento of brighter days. It struck me that maybe this could serve a purpose beyond its intended use.

From then on, whenever I encountered fallen German soldiers, I took to sketching their cap badges. That way my officers could identify who we were fighting. Yet, I knew that this was not my sole purpose and I couldn't escape the grim reality, I was also instructed to wound, not kill, if the situation demanded it. It was a haunting compromise, one of many that war imposes upon the soul.

One time I could hear a young bloke crying, I figured he was hurt quite bad, so I went to see him. I'd hit him in the leg just above the knee and when I saw him he looked like he was in a lot of pain. I felt terrible, he was only a teenager and I scared him to death when I showed up in his trench. I think that he expected me to finish him off but I shared my water and tried to make 'im comfy. Like I said I always had a few ciggies in my kit, so I gave 'im one and said I was sorry for shooting 'im. I think he understood.

Fortunately, I just barely dodged his mates when they showed up and took him off to their hospital. Luckily, he must've appreciated me treating' 'im decent because he never told on me."

The room seemed to hold its breath as Walter's storytelling carried them through moments of connection, camaraderie, and compassion in the midst of war's chaos.

Walter paused but then pushed himself forward to tell more of his story.

Joe could see the determination of his friend but worried that he might be getting tired.

"Take a break if you like, Walter."

But Walter just shook his head and carried on doggedly.

"We'd been shown pictures of their different uniforms, which helped us tell officers from regular infantry. I stayed there near that village for a few days. Things were looking up for me 'cause I'd found some wine, bottled fruit and tinned meat and so, I made myself comfy. There were even some nice paintings on what was left of the walls. I remembered laughing because one was a portrait of a very severe-looking grandma who seemed to be taking stock of what I was taking from the larder.

Then a bunch of horses clattered into the courtyard. With cold hands and sweating like mad, I took a peek. I have to say that I was more interested in their fine mounts than anything else at first. Then I could see one of the riders was a high-up officer, colonel, or something. Risky, but when they turned to leave, I put the crosshairs of my sights on his back and shot him in the back of the neck. The horse went wild, as he slumped over its neck. It began spinning on the spot and the other riders were clueless about where the shot had come from. They were way behind their own lines and it was a complete surprise. They fired their pistols in all directions and a couple shots came near me, but that's all.

They all dismounted and fussed over the colonel. In all the commotion, they forget about me. I shot three other officers, the other low-ranked men grabbed their officers put them over the back of their mounts and rode off. I sketched their badges before they went.

I feared they'd come looking for me, so I slipped off and followed a drainage ditch into a wood,"

Walter's tone was hushed with the shadowy undertones of intrigue. The setting seemed to materialise around his words, the whispering trees, the damp earth underfoot.

"It felt good to see trees with leaves for a change. It poured it down nonstop but then it just stopped and a thick mist rose from the damp earth. I'd been wondering how I could get home, so, when that pea-soup fog rolled in. I didn't waste time and under cover of that mist I slipped back to our lines."

Walter's voice changed tone almost into a secretive whisper. "It was eerie crossin' no man's land, trees like ghostly guards in the mist. When I did finally reach our lines, I was nearly shot by a sentry who thought I was a German trying to infiltrate their lines."

There was a pause and then Walter resumed, his voice carrying an edge of suspense. The tension of that moment was profound, an acute awareness of life hanging in the balance.

"They arrested me again and sent me for interrogation. The guards were pretty rough with me and gave me a good slapping. I shouted at them, 'Do I sound like a bloody Gerry?'

They threw me in the back of a goods wagon, it was dark and smelt as if horses had been recently stabled there. An officer arrived and they lit a couple of paraffin lanterns. I showed him my drawings and said that the officer who sent me out had told me to go and see what I could see.

He took them from me and his face seemed to lighten as he flicked through the pages of my sketch book. I showed him my special badge and that sort of turned the tide. They fed me and brought a doctor to look at my arm and a nurse to redress it."

Later the officer, who had interviewed me came back to see me. He was very interested when I told him about the colonel and officers and how I'd shot them."

Walter smiled he was obviously pleased with the situation.

"I suppose I was one of the first SAS-type units on my own. Covert ops, they call it now," he confided with a wink.

Joe smiled trying to imagine Walter as a commando or a spy.

A softer, reminiscent tone carried his next revelation: "This new Scots Guard officer sat and chatted with me as though we were old friends. I think he was trying to find out if I was genuine. I wasn't sure if he really believed me."

"After a week, banged up in that wagon, I was sent back to my regiment."

Walter continued, his narrative steadily explaining the ever-changing landscape of war. "The front line for once had moved deeper into Belgium. But when I found my old unit, I didn't recognise any of the men. It was sad because once again, they had all been killed or taken away from the front line."

With a pause, his voice carried the heaviness of memory as he sipped his coffee, each sip a moment of reflection… a moment between words to acknowledge the price of survival.

"I never knew that writing an article would consume so much coffee," Walter mused, his humour shining through. Joe's response brought a smile to his lips.

"Don't worry, I'll fetch a new jar the next time I come and see you," Joe reassured him.

"Now then, where was I?" Walter shifted back into his narrative, resuming his account of the war.

"One day, the Germans fired some mustard gas into our lines, and one of the shells hit the hospital where Elsie was working, it caused havoc. When I heard about it, I ran over there, and so, I was relieved to see that she and her friend Jane were all right." His voice carried a mix of relief and concern, underscoring the close connection he shared with his sister. The image of the battlefield and the chaos that ensued came alive in his words.

"It was terrible stuff, it burnt faces and eyes, and a lot of folks were blinded and disfigured by it. I stayed near the hospital so that I could keep an eye on them. No one seemed to know who I was or what I was supposed to be doing which meant I never got any more orders. I'm not sure that they really cared either because, by that time, everyone, including the officers, just wanted to go home. Anyway, I hung about the hospital, helping out where I could. I remember one lad came in with a load of shrapnel in his back, well, it was grit mostly, but he was in real pain. I sat with him and with a pair of tweezers, as we chatted, I picked the bits out of his skin."

"Later that month, Elsie was sent back home," Walter continued, "and so, I decided to go see if there was anything left of my regiment."

His voice carried a sense of determination, the drive to find familiarity amidst the chaos.

"When I managed to find them, there was still not a face I recognized, and even our old sergeant was missing. The new sergeant said that most of the old lads had been wiped out during an attack... another waste of life and the lines were no further east than they had been two years before that. Lord, it made me angry.

Nobody questioned where I'd been, but I was sent off again with orders to make a nuisance of myself somewhere else. The regiment's new captain looked so young... he looked as though he had come straight from school it was no wonder we were losing so many men.

Walter paused, collecting his thoughts, he wandered off to the kitchen and then returned with a packet of biscuits. "Gingernuts... Alice's favourites." The memory of her eating them was so strong that he could almost hear them crunch as she savoured each mouthful.

"Winter was approaching, and for a while, I fell in with some Yanks," Walter continued, his voice resonating with a mix of camaraderie and shared experiences. "They hadn't been there long, and they were already fed up. It seemed that they had crazier generals than we did... if that was possible," Walter mused, his wry humour coming through again. "They did have some good grub, and so I stayed with them for a while and celebrated Thanksgiving with them. In return, I tried to give them tips on how to survive."

"One of their officers began questioning who I was," Walter said with a shrug, "He did thank me for the advice but said I should return to my own unit, and so I left them to it.

I hadn't fired my gun in anger or anything else for two months, and I began to feel guilty about not helping very much."

Walter looked visibly fatigued, he paused and Joe sensed the weight of the memories and the emotional toll they were taking. He gently places a hand on Walter's shoulder and says, "Walter, you don't have to keep going if it's too much. We can take a break, or if you want, we can continue another time. Your story is important, but your well-being matters more."

"Thank you, Joe, I'm all right for a bit."

A sadness almost a chill filled his eyes as he continued.

"I was afraid that I was becoming hardened to it all. Everywhere there were corpses and the stench of death hung like a shroud over the land. Civilians lay bloated and exposed beside the road and… no one thought to move them. There were horses the size of elephants with their legs in the air and dogs were tearing at their flesh. I've seen paintings by that Picasso bloke and I can really relate to them. Those images were indelibly etched in my brain and I can tell you, Joe, that they will go to my grave with me. I pondered what would happen after the war… and if walking along the canal could ever be the same again? I would have given anything to be able to walk a few steps with Troy and feel his strength beside me."

Walter manages a tired smile, appreciating Joe's concern. "Thank you, lad. It's just... it's hard to put it all into words sometimes. But you're right, maybe a break would do me good."

Joe reaches for the biscuit packet and opens it. "How about a gingernut to lift your spirits? And we can just sit here for a while and enjoy the moment."

They each take a biscuit, and enjoy its spicy flavour, as they sit there listening to the sound of the traffic outside. Walter's gaze seems to drift away, lost in his memories. Joe respects his silence, giving him the space, he needs to gather himself. Eventually, Walter takes a deep breath and looks at Joe.

"Thank you, Joe. I know this isn't easy for you either, listening to all this. But it helps to have someone to share these memories with, even if it's just one person."

Joe nods, his genuine empathy evident in his eyes. "Of course, Walter. Whenever you're ready, I'll be here. And remember, you've got a friend in me."

They sit in that moment of understanding, the weight of the past momentarily lifted by their connection. And as the afternoon sun filters through the window, they find solace in each other's company.

Finally, Joe tells Walter that he must head home and packs up the tape and his notebook. Walter looked serious for a moment, "I'd really like to try and find my siblings… will you help?"

Chapter Eleven
Local newspaper office

On his way home, Joe decided that it would be a great gift for his new friend if he could locate some of his missing family. He knew just the place to call where he might get help with this task. And so, he called to see his old friend at the newspaper's office in town.

He had never become so close to any of his contacts nor had he ever felt this bond with them. He sensed that the pieces of Walter's life story held more significance than he initially thought. As he stepped into the newspaper's office, he was greeted by the familiar smell of ink and paper and the clatter of the printing press as it churned out the day's paper.

The editor, Danny Benn, a stout man with an ever-present warm smile, looked up from his desk as Joe entered.

"Hi Joe," Danny greeted, with a friendly grin. "What can we do for you today?"

Joe returned the smile, feeling a mix of nerves and excitement. "Hi, I'm hoping to use your archives. Do you remember I said I was interviewing an old chap who I'm sure has a fascinating life story?"

"Yes, of course, it sounds like a great local interest feature," Danny replied enthusiastically.

"I've decided to try and trace some of his family. I'm thinking there might be something hidden away in your archives that could help," Joe said hopefully.

Danny leaned back in his chair, intrigued. "Well now, that's an interesting thought, Joe. You're welcome to have a look. Most of it's on Microfilm these days, but I warn you, it might take some digging through. We certainly go back to the turn of the twentieth century."

Joe nodded appreciatively. "Well, I know it's a long shot… I'm prepared for that. To be honest I don't even have a clear idea of what I'm looking for. I just have this feeling that there might be some mention of Walter's siblings or relatives buried in these pages. I'm willing to put in the time to unearth whatever I can find."

Danny's eyes sparkled with curiosity. "That's quite a noble pursuit, as well as good journalism my friend. It's amazing how the past can hold the keys to the present. Take a seat over there," he gestured toward a desk with a microfilm reader, "And let me know if you need any assistance. I suppose you might want a coffee?"

As Joe settled in front of the machine, he couldn't help but feel a sense of reverence for the task ahead. The old microfilm reels held stories of the town's history, some stories might intersect with Walter's life in ways Joe could only imagine. He delicately scrolled through the reel, eyes scanning for any titbits that might lead him closer to discovering Walter's family.

Hours passed, and as Joe meticulously went through the records, he was occasionally side-tracked as he stumbled upon small-town news pieces, obituaries, and long-forgotten events. He marvelled at how the past was meticulously preserved on these fragile frames. Occasionally, Danny would stop by, offering encouragement and another cup of coffee.

The light outside faded and Joe knew that he should be making tracks for home. As the noise from the traffic outside reached a crescendo it indicated that it was at its rush hour peak.

After what seemed like an age Joe's perseverance finally bore fruit. Amongst a series of articles chronicling the lives of local families, he found an article that was a great revelation. His heart raced as he jotted down the details, a mix of triumph and anticipation washing over him.

"Eureka! Hey Danny, can I get a printout of this?"

"Yep, no problem there's a switch on the side; run a couple of copies off and one for me."

The printer churned out several sheets and Joe eagerly caught each one as it emerged. The report, long since lost now burst back to life.

Its Headline read: Young Hero's Daring Valour Recognized: Jack Middlebrough has been awarded The Conspicuous Gallantry Medal (C.G.M.) Following HMS Bounty Tragedy.

Sub-headline: Amidst the Chaos of War, Jack's Selfless Act Shines as a Beacon of Courage.

War Correspondent of The Calder Gazette | [1917] Alf Broadhead reports on this act of bravery by a local lad.

[Off the Isle of Wight], [8th day of May 1917]

Amid the relentless turmoil of this conflict, an inspiring tale of valour has emerged that stands as a testament to the undying spirit of heroism. Jack Middlebrough, a lad from our streets, has been awarded the C.G.M. for his extraordinary deeds in the aftermath of the tragic sinking of HMS Bounty off the coast of the Isle of Wight.

The HMS Bounty, which had dutifully undertaken troop movement missions across the perilous waters of the channel, met its tragic fate as it returned homeward. The stark reality of war struck hard as the ship was attacked by torpedoes; it was first paralysed and listed heavily to its port side and then a great explosion marked its descent into the unforgiving depths of the ocean.

Amid the deafening chaos and the sea's treacherous battleground, it was the unyielding valour of young Jack Middlesbrough that emerged as a shining beacon of hope. With no regard for his own safety, Jack's heroic actions transcended his young age, demonstrating a courage that would inspire all who bore witness.

As the ship succumbed to the ravages of battle, the icy waters became a relentless adversary, claiming the lives of many. Yet, amid this dire situation, Jack's resolve remained unshaken. Without hesitation, he plunged into the frigid depths to rescue several of his fellow comrades who found themselves at the mercy of the ocean's grasp.

Despite the numbing cold and the waves of exhaustion that must have swept over him, Jack pressed on. He continued his valiant efforts, hauling his mates to safety until his own strength waned, and he succumbed to the unforgiving grasp of exhaustion.

It is the selflessness exhibited by young Jack Middlebrough that has earned him the prestigious Bravery Medal, a mark of honour that embodies the spirit of those who rise above the call of duty to protect and save their fellow comrades. His actions serve as an inspiring reminder that, even in the face of the darkest adversities, some shine as beacons of hope and valour.

As the world grapples with the heartache of war, Jack's story echoes across the land, reminding soldiers, sailors, and civilians alike that heroism knows no bounds. His courageous dive into the freezing waters to save his comrades stands as a testament to the extraordinary bravery that continues to thrive amidst the perils of battle. The legacy of Jack Middlebrough shall forever be etched in history, inspiring generations to come to uphold the ideals of valour and sacrifice.

The end: Article by Alf Broadhead.

Joe's heart swelled with a mix of emotions as he left the newspaper office, the weight of Jack's story still heavy on his mind. He had embarked on this journey to uncover the secrets of Walter's family history, but he had never anticipated the depth of the emotions and the courage he would encounter along the way.
"Got what you want?" Danny asked over the rim of another coffee.
Joe was so excited that he could hardly speak, "Oh boy, yes… well it's a fantastic start."
He neatly folded the printout and felt to be floating on air. "I must go, Danny, I'm sure I'll be back."
As he walked back to his car through the bustling streets, Joe couldn't help but feel a newfound determination coursing through his veins. Jack's bravery and resilience ignited a fire within him, a burning desire to unearth more of the past and bring to light the untold stories that had shaped Walter's life.
The path ahead was uncertain, and the challenges were bound to be many, but Joe was undeterred. He knew that every secret uncovered, every memory shared, would forge a stronger bond between him and Walter. It was a

journey of discovery, not just of family history but of the enduring power of friendship and the remarkable strength of the human spirit.

With Walter's and now Jack's story as guiding lights, Joe continued down the path, ready to unravel more of Walter's family's past, one thread at a time.

"Hi honey, I'm home," Joe's voice echoed through the doorway as he stepped into the warm embrace of their home. His eyes met hers, a loving smile playing on his lips.

"How's your day been?" he pecked her cheek affectionately.

With a soft sigh, she leaned against the kitchen counter, weariness evident in her eyes.

"Oh, you know, the usual chaos. The kids are practically counting down the seconds until the Christmas holidays. It's getting harder for me to keep my focus when all they can talk about is their break. How's Walter today?"

A sparkle of excitement danced in Joe's eyes as he set his briefcase down. He tried not to barge in with his discovery but the excitement was almost overpowering.

"Well, guess what? My day wasn't exactly typical. I've made quite a discovery." He leaned closer to her with a mysterious glint in his eye.

A quizzical look crossed Julie's face. "Ha-ha. A discovery? Do tell."

She smiled at Joe's eagerness to tell his tale and flicked the switch on the kettle.

Joe couldn't hold back his grin any longer. "I called in to see Danny at the newspaper and delved into their archives, searching for any leads on Walter's family. And guess what I found?" He reached into his pocket and retrieved a folded piece of paper, placing it gently in his partner's hand he stepped back and grinned at her.

She was curious as she unfolded the paper, revealing the carefully preserved newspaper article. As she read the words that detailed the heroic actions of a young Jack Middlebrough following the sinking of HMS Bounty, her eyes widened in amazement.

"Wow, Joe, this is great, Jack Middlebrough," she repeated, her voice a mix of astonishment and curiosity. "Is it the right bloke? Do you think it's Walter's brother?"

Joe nodded, his excitement was contagious. "It seems like there's a connection. I'm sure that this Jack Middlebrough was Walter's elder brother and I know he was in the Navy. This act of bravery is outstanding."

Julia smiled at him. "That's great it's certainly a start to add some background to Walter's family. Well done, Joe."

Joe's smile turned tender as he reached out to gently touch her hand. "This journey means a lot to me. I couldn't rest until I found something meaningful."

She placed the article carefully on the table, with her gaze fixed on Joe.

"I'm sorry if I've not been very supportive of your journalistic endeavours," she said apologetically.

With a loving smile, Joe pulled her into a warm embrace.

"It's okay, you've a lot on, I can tell you need a break. Maybe we could all have a break, and go to your mum's caravan near Filey in the Spring."

As they held each other, the weight of their shared journey seemed to lift, replaced by their shared love of each other.

The article lay on the table, a tangible reminder that history had a way of revealing its secrets to those who dared to seek them.

"Will you tell him?" Julia asked, her gaze thoughtful and concerned.

Joe paused, considering the question. "Do you think I should? Because it could give him such a boost. I'm sure he has a deep-rooted longing to find his siblings again."

Julia nodded, a small smile tugging at the corners of her lips. "Yes, I'm sure it would be good for him and you're right it really would uplift his spirits."

Their voices lowered, and the room filled with a sense of empathy and shared understanding. "But," Julia continued, her brow furrowing slightly, "do you know what happened to Jack after this? I mean, his story here is incredible, but I'm curious about the rest of his life."

Joe sighed, a mixture of intrigue and uncertainty in his expression. "No, there was no follow-up article that I came across. It's as if this snippet of his life was frozen in time. Maybe he continued to serve, or perhaps he returned home after the war. It's hard to say without more information."

Julie leaned back, lost in thought. "It's a shame that we might never know the full story. But who knows? Maybe something else will come up. Old letters, records, or even other historical sources could shed light on what happened to Jack."

Joe nodded in agreement. "You're right. But there are miles of tape in the archives."

Julie smiled as an idea struck her, "Maybe, this next week during the school break I could go do a bit of investigating for you. Mum said she'd look after Debbie for a few hours."

"Well, if you've time, Danny won't mind, in fact, he'll be glad of the company. Thank you, it will be a great help."

As the conversation settled into a reflective silence, the room seemed to echo with the story attached to Jack.

"I'd tell him... even though the story is not complete, I'm sure that he will appreciate your effort," Julia said.

Chapter Twelve.
Promotion.

The following morning, Joe arrived at Walter's house a bit earlier than usual. He knocked and entered and with a cheery smile, he greeted, "Good morning, Walter. Are you up and ready? It's me, Joe. You must be getting tired of my visits by now."

Walter's face lit up with warmth as he replied, "Oh, not at all. I'm always glad to see you." His response conveyed his genuine pleasure in Joe's company.

"What dreadful weather," Joe complained, "I know it's winter, but it's so dark this morning. Are you okay with continuing your story? I don't want to tire you out," Joe asked his concern was genuine.

"Don't worry about me, I'm fine," Walter reassured Joe, a wistful smile tugging at the corners of his lips. "Back to the trenches, I suppose." As he spoke, Walter seemed to drift away momentarily, his mind engulfed by vivid recollections of wartime. His mental imagery transported him back to the days when he wore a khaki uniform, with his knapsack and rifle slung over his shoulder. In the distant echoes of his memory, the constant rumble of artillery fire reverberated, a haunting reminder of the tumultuous times he had endured.

Walter recalled the time he was given a crucial task. "They wanted me to lead a patrol through the enemy territory. I'd navigated the enemy lines successfully and so they thought I could do it again. But this time, it felt different. I was okay on my own, but leading these new lads made me worry. I didn't know if I could keep them safe.

The generals were desperate for a change in the war. With the Russians out, we were up against seasoned soldiers who'd been fighting in the east and were now unleashed against us."

"They were so keen on this idea that they promoted me with three stripes on my sleeve, thinking it would give me authority over the men in the patrol," Walter said, a smirk playing on his lips. "I wasn't convinced it was a smart move, and I voiced my concerns to the captain. But he reckoned it was worth a shot."

"So, under cover of a moonless night, we ventured beyond our defences into the treacherous no man's land. I did my best to prepare the lads. I was granted two days to practice and show them how to move without being seen. We crept, silent as shadows. across the torn landscape, each step fraught with danger but we hadn't gone far when I had to move from the front of the line to somewhere in the middle to assist a couple of lads who were struggling with nerves and the sheer terror of the mission ate at their resolve," Walter recounted, his voice full of tension. "We aimed to navigate the treacherous no man's land, to move swiftly and quietly among the ditches, unseen by the enemy. But the mission quickly ran aground." There was real tension and urgency in his voice as though he was experiencing it all over again.

"In a sudden, blinding flash, a flare tore through the night sky, it emitted a screeching noise more terrifying than the flash itself. Its brightness caused intense discomfort. 'Keep still and shut up,' I hissed under my breath. "Slowly it descended its light casting an eerie glow all around us and then a second flare just as bright illuminated the chaos that ensued. Bullets whizzed by, a cacophony akin to the frenzy of mad wasps. They ricocheted and sliced through the air, kicking up plumes of mud around us. We tried to dance out of their way hopping and leaping for cover, it was a miracle we survived.

Instinctively, I guided my small patrol toward the perceived safety of a nearby bomb crater. I was so intent on keeping my squad safe that just as I ushered the last member to cover and out of sight, a force struck me, hurling me to the ground. The realization hit me in a fraction of a second… I'd been shot again."

The pain and memories were in his voice. "This time, a bullet had hit me in the side, and the pain was excruciating. I had no idea where that bullet had gone. I rolled into the trench to try and find safety. I must give credit to the lads; they worked as a team and somehow managed to get me back to our lines and off to the hospital."

Walter chuckled softly, shaking his head at the memory. "You wouldn't believe the things we had to put up with. There wasn't even a stretcher, so the lads just put me in an old wheelbarrow, and off we went with me looking like a Plot Night Guy, all I was short of was a cardboard sign saying 'Penny for the Guy.' We went in search of the nearest field hospital."

Joe smiled and commented. "You must have looked a right old sight."

Walter responded, "I suppose so."

The narrative shifted once more, "Hello," a friendly voice said to me. It was the Scottish nurse who had been friends with Elsie. 'I thought you would have gone home with Elsie,' I said.

"Elsie hasn't gone home." The surprising revelation about Elsie was rather shocking. "She's moved to Paris to work in a hospital there," Jane told me. "I think it's a certain doctor she's after rather than the location."

I was sad because I thought that at least she was safe at home.

The doctor came over, weariness all over him like an old coat. It seemed to me that he could use a good rest himself. He poked around at the wound and said 'You're a lucky lad the bullet went straight through. But I have to clean it out,' he said, 'the trouble with wounds like this is, the bullet will have carried bits of shirt in with it.' He mentioned giving me some morphine to Jane to ease the pain while he worked.

During my stay, Jane, came around often, checking on my bandages and such. 'You ought to be sent back home with this wound,' she said, her concern clear. She was sitting on the edge of my bunk taking a short rest and I had a chance to study her. I could sense the weariness that enveloped her. Her hair, although it was neatly tucked into her head square was matted with dried blood and looked dull and lifeless. She gave me a brave smile but it did not hide her inner fears.

I replied, 'I'll stick around a bit more. I quite like having you looking out for me.' I was fond of her, and I wished that we could've met in some other place, far from that mess."

An embarrassed smile floated across Walter's face and for a moment he looked fifty years younger as he said, "She stayed overnight occasionally and we were transported far away from that hellhole, just two young people offering comfort and I suppose love. One night, we stood together for ages beneath the pounding water of the shower, its relentless stream sprayed against our skin. Each droplet cascading down felt like a fleeting reprieve, a brief respite from the weight of our troubles. The steam filled the air, cocooning us in a veil of warmth that momentarily dulled the ache of memories and worries. Yet, despite the deluge, the war and its echoes remained, lingering in the recesses of our minds, resilient against the water's cleansing embrace.

It made me feel that getting shot was worth it just to spend time with her. I made the choice to stay put, and after a month's worth of rest, my sense of duty or something made me go back to my battalion and so, much to the surprise of my Captain, I re-joined them. I was a bit taken aback to find he was still around."

Walter shifted slightly in his seat, settling in for the tale he was about to share. "I was moving from one camp to another," he began, his eyes distant as he revisited those memories. "Just after sharing a cuppa with some lads from Bolton, I stood up, and in that one split second, I realised that I'd made a grave mistake. Lucky for me, I had my backpack on."

He shook his head slowly as if still disbelieving what had happened next. "In that very same instant, I felt a forceful blow, like a kick from Troy, my faithful horse." Walter paused, the memory still vivid in his mind. "I was sent sprawling head over heels into a muddy trench, almost drowning in the thick sludge. As I lay there, I had to take a moment to assess whether I was even still alive."

Walter winced and groaned as he got to his feet, the pain in his legs a reminder of those long past days. He shuffled over to a cupboard and retrieved a rolled-up piece of army-issue webbing. Carefully, he unrolled it to reveal a battered tin box, noticeably dented, with a small hole. Walter's hands were surprisingly steady as he eased the lid open, revealing a rather dog-eared copy of the book 'Lorna Doone.' He plucked the book from the tin and opened it to reveal a fragment of a bullet tucked inside. He poked a finger through the hole in the webbing, a wry smile playing on his lips. "You see," he said, "This book saved my life. It really was a lifesaver. The heavy webbing and the tin box took just enough out of the bullet for the book to stop it."

Joe sat there, his jaw slack in amazement. "Wow," he breathed, still trying to fathom the incredible stroke of luck. "That was the third time you were hit!"

Walter laughed heartily, the sound filling the room. "Aye, it was," he said, his eyes twinkling with humour. "But you know, there was this Welsh lad we called the cat. He got hit nine times, and the Captain finally sent him home, saying, 'You've had your nine lives; now, off you go to those Welsh hills.'"

Joe smiled warmly at, Walter, who was sitting in his cosy armchair by the window.

"Hey Walter, how about we take a little break?" he suggested with a glint of excitement in his eyes. "I've got a couple of surprises planned for you."

Walter looked up his eyes twinkling with curiosity. "Surprises, you say? Well now, you've certainly tweaked my interest, young man. I hope that it's more pasties." He said patting his stomach.

Joe chuckled and motioned toward the coat rack by the door.

"Then get your coat on, my friend. We're headed down to the canal wharf. I promise you, it's going to be worth the stroll."

Walter's brows raised in surprise and he began to rise from his chair it took a minute to straighten his legs. With a good-natured sigh, he said, "Okay, well you've certainly got me interested. So, lead the way! I hope you've oiled that left wheel on my chair because it squeaked like Billy Oh, the last time out."

They made their way out of the comfortable living room and into the brisk outdoor air. The roads were busy and the pavement uneven so they bumped along until they reached a new section of the tarmac path. The canal wharf wasn't too far away, and as they walked, the young man couldn't help but share his excitement.

He had almost to shout to be heard over the din of the traffic "I hope that you don't mind, Walter, I've been working on something special, something I want to share with you."

Walter chuckled. "Well, don't keep an old man waiting. What is it?"

Joe grinned and patted Walter's back.

"I did a little bit of digging in the newspaper archives yesterday," Joe began as they paused near the water's edge. He handed the article he had discovered to Walter, who took it suspiciously into his hands.

"Here, let me put your brakes on for you, or we might end up in the canal. I'll tuck this little blanket around your knees too."

Walter was deeply engrossed in the article, his eyes glued to the paper his face showed a mix of anticipation and curiosity. As he dove into the words, it was as if he was transported back in time. Joe could see memories stirring within him, almost like the world around him had faded away. He was really getting emotional, tears streaming down his face. He even had to pull out a handkerchief to mop up.

The article seemed to be a direct link to his brother Jack. It painted such a vivid picture of a bygone era, capturing Jack's personality perfectly. Joe was watching Walter closely, sensing the rollercoaster of emotions he was experiencing with each sentence.

It was like the story was unfolding right in front of Walter's eyes. Every word seemed to connect him more deeply to his brother. His heart was racing as he read about Jack's achievements and the legacy he left behind. Joe watched fascinated as the whirlwind of emotions swirled in Walter's mind, memories flooding back.

On Walter's face, the emotions were crystal clear. His expressions spoke volumes about the love, loss, and experiences he'd lived through. Joe, just being there, was a reassuring presence amidst Walter's emotional storm. And as Walter kept reading, it was like he was reliving their childhood adventures, the fun times they had shared. He could almost hear Jack's laughter echoing in his mind. Those memories, a mix of joy and sadness, really highlighted the deep bond they shared.

As he neared the end of the article, Walter's eyes were filled with tears. It was a mix of pride and sorrow washing over him. This article had opened a door to a cherished part of his past, reminding him how much his brother meant to him.

Joe, watching this entire emotional journey unfold, gently put a hand on Walter's shoulder. You could see the strong bond that had formed between them in such a short time.

Finally, when Walter finished reading, he looked up at Joe, speechless, but his eyes said it all. He grasped Joe's sleeve, silently thanking him. Their unspoken connection spoke volumes about the power of friendship. For a while, they both just sat there, watching the water in silence.

In little more than a whisper Walter shared his thoughts, 'Yes, I can imagine our Jack doing that. He was always brave and caring.'

"Let's walk a while," Joe whispered.

As they ventured along the canal towpath, the air carried a warning that winter was on its way, a breeze rustled the leaves and whispered stories of days gone by. The pale sun painted the world with shades of warmth, and the canal was hidden beneath a grey mist that clung to its surface.

"You know, Joe," Walter began, his voice carrying a touch of reminiscence, "I've walked here countless times. Back in the day, there used to be some fine stables not too far down the path. Troy, my old buddy… always seemed to lighten up as we approached here. That clever lad knew just where he was."

With the gentle swaying of the reeds and the distant calls of birds, the atmosphere seemed to carry the echoes of Troy's hooves and the laughter of days that had once flourished.

"Troy and I had a connection that went beyond words," Walter continued, his gaze fixed on the towpath. "During the war, when I was far from home, memories of him and our walks provided me with comfort during the chaos."

As the canal waters whispered their secrets, a sense of timelessness enveloped them both.

"By this point, he'd have a real spring to his step," Walter recalled, a fond smile tugging at his lips. "He'd pick up his pace, the knowledge of a comfortable rest waiting for him would spur him on."

Joe suddenly recounted a memory of his own. "Animals have an uncanny ability to connect with us, don't they? Their instincts, their understanding… it's truly remarkable. My gran had a little dog that would tell her if someone was at the door and if it was someone safe to let in."

Walter nodded, his expression thoughtful. "That was obviously a clever little soul. Aye, Joe, you're right. Troy taught me much about life. About loyalty, about savouring each step of the journey because in a way it was as important as the destination. Our journeys along these paths were a sanctuary for both of us. Sometimes, even now, I feel his presence beside me, guiding me through life's ebb and flow."

As they continued along the towpath, the past and the present seemed to intertwine, bound by the tales of Troy and his unwavering companionship. At that moment, Joe realised that history wasn't confined to the pages of books; it lived within the stories of those who had experienced it. And, as he listened to Walter, he understood that the echoes of Troy's hooves would forever reverberate in Walter's mind.

Walter gave Joe a quick glance saying, "Let's go home and put the kettle on. It must be nearly time for you to go home. I thank you for letting me see that article about our Jack."

Back home and seated once more, enjoying the comfortable familiarity of their coffee cups, Joe proposed a spontaneous idea. "Hey, how about we go out for a meal? Julie's away at her mum's for some school holiday arrangements and I'm all free. What do you think?"

A mischievous smile slowly spread across Walter's face, a mix of surprise and appreciation.

"Are you sure? That'd be quite the special treat... could we perhaps have a curry?"

"A curry?" Joe's eyebrows lifted, his grin infectious. "Of course. There's a curry joint in town that opens up early. We could head there if you fancy."

"Oh, yes please, curry sounds lovely," Walter replied, his eyes gleaming with the prospect. "It's been ages since I had a proper one."

Chapter Thirteen.
Indian meal.

So, off they went like a couple of old mates. Eagerly anticipating the delights that lay ahead at the curry house.

Joe had to fight with the doors to get Walter's wheelchair in but one of the waiters came to their aid and held the door open. The warm and inviting ambience of the Omar Khayyam embraced them as soon as they entered. Another young man, dressed in traditional Indian attire, guided them to their seats. The air carried a delicate hint of jasmine, and soft sitar music provided a soothing background melody. The young man handed out menus and to Joe's amazement, Walter spoke to the waiter in what he guessed was Urdu. A brief yet friendly exchange transpired, leaving the waiter with a chuckle before he departed. As they waited for their meal, they heartily indulged in a plate of freshly fried poppadums that cracked and crunched with every bite.

With an amused twinkle in his eye, Joe commented, "Now, you never fail to amaze me, that was a real surprise, you spoke like a native."

Walter just smiled, pleased that at his age he could still surprise folk. Throughout the meal, waiters would occasionally pass by their table and engage in light-hearted exchanges with Walter.

Walter leaned back, offering Joe a knowing grin.

"Well, nowadays I only get a chance to practice with Mr Singh and his wife. You know, I once had friends from Kashmir. Good people. Mr Singh was very surprised when I could order a few groceries from them in Urdu. It turns out these lads are from Kashmir too."

"They are treating you like family," Joe said.

Walter proudly smiled saying, "I think it is just mutual respect."

The flavours and aromas of the meal danced on their taste buds, making a delightful symphony of culinary delights. Partway through the meal, they were presented with a huge butter-rich paratha, "On the house for you Mr Walter," the waiter spoke with his hands in a prayer-like position.

"Well, I'm stuffed," Joe said, "I don't think I'll need to eat for a week." He sat back with a broad smile and loosened his jacket.

Walter was savouring the last morsels of the paratha and just smiled at him.

As he too sat back he pulled out his rather dog-eared leather wallet.

"Nay Walter, this is a treat on me, it was my idea and as usual you've provided the entertainment and an extra insight into your world."

"That's kind Joe, but I like to pay my way."

When the waiter brought the bill, a pleasant surprise awaited them: a generous fifteen per cent discount had been taken off the bill total bringing an extra layer of satisfaction to their dining experience. The atmosphere was one of friendship and before they left, both the restaurant's owner and what Joe assumed was the head chef came to speak to Walter. They all shook hands and exchanged smiles.

Joe stood back to watch as they exchanged farewells. 'How many more secrets and layers are there to this man,' he thought.

"Walter bid farewell to his newfound companions with a warm embrace, their faces adorned with contented smiles. Stepping out into the brisk evening air, the town revealed its festive charm; the glow of shop lights and passing traffic cast shimmering reflections upon the wet pavement. A brisk chill embraced them, lending a refreshing tingle to their senses. Their grins widened as they strolled back to the awaiting car, savouring the lingering flavours of the exquisite meal. The memory of this unforgettable evening found a lasting place within their hearts.

Despite the lateness of the hour, Joe felt a sense of kinship and curiosity, wanting to learn more from Walter. Back home in Almond Terrace, Joe made another cup of coffee.

"Walter, if you're up for it, I'd love to hear more of your story. The parts that perhaps aren't so well-known. How on earth did you come to learn Urdu?"

Walter's face lit up as he remembered an unexpected encounter with the Indian infantry.

"Well, it was another strange encounter. I was out on one of my solo missions again when I ended up with a platoon of Indian infantry. They were dug in amongst the rubble of what had once been a school and I pitched into their trench almost by accident. They looked scared to death as I rolled over the broken walls of the building and in amongst them. They were good lads, but they were tired, frightened, and very cold. Their officer, a young man from Croydon who was straight out of RMS Sandhurst was badly wounded and for some reason, he had forbidden them to light a fire to keep warm. I convinced the officer that it would be all right to burn some of the wood that was lying about. Immediately they began preparing what looked like a feast to me at that time.

My rations had been pretty poor in fact I don't think that I had eaten for a couple of days. So, when I ate with the Indian lads I think it was the best meal I'd had in ages," he mused, a fond glint in his eyes. "They made chapatis the size of tea towels on a wheel hub that they heated on the fire and they made a curry that was hotter than anything I'd ever tasted. But you know, it warmed us up, and I suppose it was like a taste of home for them, even in the midst of all that chaos."

He leaned back in his chair, his thoughts drifting back to that moment in the rubble-filled trench. "Some of them could speak English, so, we sat there, sharing stories as the fragrant aroma of the curry filled the air. They told me about their homes, and their families back in India. It was strange, really, how that makeshift meal brought a bit of comfort and camaraderie amid the war."

With a chuckle, Walter continued, "I spent a good while with them, swapping tales and learning a bit of their language. I'm afraid my pronunciation was terrible, but they got a good laugh out of it."

As Walter fell into a brief silence, Joe couldn't help but reflect on the resilience and camaraderie that defined the soldiers' experiences during the war. Walter's stories continued to provide a window into a world filled with both hardship and unexpected connections.

"I do remember that the first morning after that first curry, I felt like I'd taken a bullet in my arse. It burned so bad on the loo, I thought of heading back to the hospital. But I didn't fancy Jane tending to my rear end. The Indians just laughed and fed me more curry. They said it was the best way to cure it. I suppose it's like *the hair of the dog* they say to cure a hangover take another drink. I got them organised, we built some defences and sorted out a rota for guard duty and we made the officer as comfortable as we could. He was badly wounded but there was no way we could get him to the hospital there was fighting going on all around us. The Germans were trying hard to break our lines and they shelled the area non-stop. We'd sit around our little campfire with shrapnel and debris clinking on our tin helmets as though nothing was happening.

One day, another division of commonwealth troops turned up. Their British officers treated their men like they were dimwits. I was actually ashamed of the way they were speaking to them. I stayed long enough to learn a few more words in their language, certainly more than the officers could.

"They questioned me about what I was doin' there and where my regiment was," Walter began, his eyes distant as he delved into his wartime memories. "As usual, I explained that I was a sniper, just followin' orders to make a nuisance of myself."

He paused, taking a deep breath before continuing, his voice heavy with the weight of what he was about to share. "Then one morning, they sent those poor lads over the top. No artillery cover, just a bunch of 'em marchin' proudly with bayonets drawn into certain death and all to take some useless wasteland."

Walter's gaze seemed to pierce through the years, back to that fateful day. "I did what I could. I found a spot on a hilltop, where I had a clear view of the action and provided 'em with some covering fire. But truth be told, it didn't amount to much even though I worked the bolt action of my rifle faster than I had ever done. On that bright sunny afternoon with bullets flyin' and shells explodin' all I could do was watch as they fell, one by one. I felt sick inside even though I had seen it before this time it seemed to make even less sense."

He sighed, his shoulders sagging under the weight of the memory. "That night, under cover of darkness I joined a few others in a grim task. We went out into no man's land, that desolate scary stretch between the trenches, and brought back some of the lads. It was a terrible sight, bodies lying there, lives snuffed out like candles."

Walter's voice trembled with emotion as he concluded, "It was a tragic waste, a heartbreaking way to throw lives away. War does that, you see, takes the young and brave and leaves 'em as nothing but memories in a barren land."

Joe listened intently, captivated by this glimpse into Walter's wartime experiences. "It sounds to be another tragic episode in your adventure, Walter," he commented, his curiosity piqued. "So, what did you do?"

Walter's expression turned a bit more sombre. "Well, I decided that it was time to move on again. The officers asked me to stay, they were raw recruits and I think they respected my experience. But those lads, stuck with me in my memories. I said goodbye to the lads that were left, and I went back to my solo missions, sketching cap badges and trying to stay out of trouble. But that first meal, that evening with those Indian lads, it's one of those moments that stays with me and reminds me that even in the darkest of times we can still find something to make us smile."

Joe glanced at the clock. "Oh, sorry, Walter, it's getting late, and I'd best be heading out before Julie starts organizing a search party for me."

Walter chuckled heartily, "She'll probably blame me for leading you astray."

As Joe put on his coat, he enquired, "So, what are your plans now?"

Walter grinned, "Oh, that's easy. 'Match of the Day' starts in five minutes, so I'll switch the telly on as soon as you leave. Although, I'll likely doze off before it's over. All those experts droning on about who should have passed the ball and scored tends to make me sleepy."

Joe's departure brought with it the soft hum of the television coming to life. The familiar theme music filled the room, signalling the start of the show. Walter settled into his recliner, his eyes fixed on the screen, ready to enjoy another evening of football analysis, even if it meant drifting off to dreamland before the final whistle.

The drive home was accompanied by the lingering taste of the curry he had enjoyed with Walter. Thoughts swirled in Joe's mind as he navigated the familiar streets. He couldn't help but draw a parallel between his interactions with Walter and the few fleeting memories of his own father.

As he reflected on his time with Walter, Joe realised that perhaps, on some level, he had been seeking a father figure. The easy camaraderie, the shared stories, and the warmth of their friendship had filled a void in his life. It was more than just companionship; it was a connection that resonated with his deepest needs and longings. Walter had become not just a friend but a mentor and a guiding presence in his life.

When Joe arrived home, he was greeted by Julie, who had a mischievous twinkle in her eye. She looked pleased with herself. "I'm really pleased, I got some real bargains and best of all I found an overcoat for Debbie that she actually liked without coaxing."

He bent to kiss her, but she pulled away, playfully scolding him.

"Phew, what have you been eating? Curry, you cheeky monkey, going for a curry without me." Julie's playful tone echoed in the room as she entered.

Joe couldn't help but grin, a surge of warmth and anticipation welling up as he pulled her close and planted an insistent kiss. "I've got a real tale to tell you tonight," he said, his eyes dancing with excitement. "Hey, remember our first curry?" Joe's eyes twinkled with amusement.

Julie chuckled at the memory. "That disaster! You were going out with Sylvia, and I was with George Broadbent I never knew what I saw in him. What a strange evening."

"George and I were best buddies, you know, from our scouting days," Joe reminisced, his voice tinged with nostalgia. "Sylvia didn't enjoy a single thing about that night. She didn't like the meal and ended up completely sloshed halfway through."

"Then George decided to air his grievances, about something or other and it turned into a heated argument," Julie added, a hint of lingering frustration in her tone. "George left me stranded in town; I had to grab a taxi," Julie sighed, remembering the inconvenience.

"I'm glad I rang you the next day to apologize. Can't quite recall how I had your number," Joe admitted.

"George actually gave it to you to arrange that disastrous meal," Julie clarified.

"Well, everything turned out fine in the end, didn't it?" Joe smiled, reflecting on the twists that eventually led to their lasting relationship. The room, scented with the aroma of curry, also brimmed with the sweet memories they shared.

"And what's the story tonight?" Julie leaned in with curiosity, eager for the evening's tales.

Chapter Fourteen.
Back to the Hospital.

The following morning Joe arrived at Walter's later than usual, it had been necessary for him to make other calls that day but he was pleased that he had managed to get to Walter's house before lunch. He had no doubts that his new friend would be delighted to see him and he was looking forward to the usual exchange and carrying on with his story.

"So, how did you get on last night? Did you watch all the matches?" Joe enquired, a mischievous wink in his eye.

Walter chuckled in response, "No, as usual, I missed a couple of matches. I awoke at about two a.m. to an Open University program about quantum mathematics, which sent me straight back to sleep."

Their laughter filled the room, a brief respite from the weight of the past. As the mirth subsided, Joe couldn't help but feel a sense of curiosity and respect for his friend. He leaned forward, ready to dive back into the stories of Walter's experiences during the war

"You know, Walter, your stories have me completely hooked… just like all those football matches on TV. Shall we continue, do you remember where we broke off? I can play it back for you if you like."

Walter gave a satisfied sigh, "I know exactly where we were."

They both took up their usual places and Joe switched on the tape recorder.

"My ammo was running low, and I was in dire need of patching up again. The stitches had given way amidst all the chaos, and I was bleeding like a stuck pig. I eventually found myself in another hospital. They fixed me up and doled out some grub. Morale there, I can tell you, was in the gutter. Poor souls hadn't had a rest for over three months, and it was takin' a toll on 'em.

There was one particular nurse, a kind soul, wearing sad bags beneath her eyes who seemed to try to help everyone. She didn't say much, but I managed to ask where she was from. 'Canada,' she muttered, and that was that. The grub there was welcome, a rare treat amid all the madness. So, I stayed put for a few days, but the wandering spirit got the better of me. I couldn't get my mind off where Jack and Elsie were.

Walter's voice grew softer as he recounted a poignant encounter by a canal that was at the rear of the hospital.

"There was a strange surreal moment. I sat by the canal, staring at the water, my mind drifting back to Troy and Owd Jos. I was tired of it all, the lousy conditions the poor food and the constant fear. I glanced across the canal and I saw on the opposite bank, a Jerry, sitting like he's got all the time in the world, he wore a vacant stare and he was dangling his feet just above the water. He looked up at the same moment and gave me a nod of acknowledgement. We didn't exchange words, we didn't need to. It was as if, in that shared nod, we acknowledged the weight of it all... the futility and the madness of war. We were just two ordinary men, caught up in something so much bigger than ourselves."

He paused, his gaze seemingly fixed on a distant point. "You see, Joe, in those moments, you stop seeing the 'enemy' and start seeing another human being, someone who's as weary and lost in this chaos as you are. War has a way of stripping away the labels and revealing the raw truth beneath."

Walter's hand absentmindedly brushed against his chin again, a gesture that had become a part of his storytelling. "I often wonder what became of that Jerry, whether he made it through the war or if it claimed him like it did so many. It's a strange thing, war. It can make enemies out of strangers and strangers out of friends."

Joe, who had been listening intently, nodded in understanding. "I must say, it's moments like these, Walter, that make your story so compelling. It's not just about battles and tactics, but about the shared humanity that persisted even in the mire."

Walter offered a faint smile, appreciating Joe's sentiment. "Aye, lad, that's the heart of it, isn't it? War may have its heroes and its villains, but it's the ordinary folks caught in the middle who often have the most extraordinary stories to tell."

As they sat there, the room seemed to hold the weight of history, and Walter's stories continued to bridge the gap between past and present.

Walter suddenly chimed up, "One mornin' outside that hospital, a troop of Canadians rambled past. I'd seen what rations they had, so I sort of tagged along. I was feelin' a weariness deep in my bones, a longing for home that weighed heavy on my heart. They said they were from Nova Scotia, not quite Canada, they said. Sounded Irish, most of 'em, names like Doyle and O'Hanlon. Young faces lost and far from home, this wasn't the fight they'd signed up for. I still had my stripes, so they followed me.

We joined up with a bunch of Yanks, their officer sported a ten-gallon hat, like that fella John Wayne. Lord, I said a silent prayer for those lads, 'cause that officer, he was full of bravado, the kind that gets his men killed. I was right there when the news came in, that the war was finally ending. An Armistice they called it. But their faces didn't light up, no cheers or whoops of joy. Just empty stares and gazes that had seen too much, they were wearied by the horrors of it all. It was announced that the war would cease on the eleventh of the eleventh, at eleven o'clock. But at a quarter to eleven, that officer led 'em in a charge, and only four of twenty-eight came back. I reckon the devil's wearing his hat and it's still lying in the mud out there.

Chapter Fifteen.
Homeward Bound.

"The armistice was announced and there was a stunned silence; the only sound to be heard was that of weeping. And so, with the end of it all, the question loomed, what next?

There was complete pandemonium and both men and officers dashed about like headless chickens trying to decide what to do next.

I thought I'd head back to the coast, find a ship, and make my way to the barracks. I didn't rightly know where my regiment was, or if anyone was left standing. I guessed that they'd taken such a thrashing, they might've been sent back home already."

A single poignant tear ran down Walter's face but he didn't even notice it.

"It took me days, I trekked slow and weary until I reached the coast. I'd not eaten for almost a week, but I didn't care, the sights along the way, well, they broke my heart. I couldn't wrap my head around how they'd ever be able to mend the towns and the farms, I couldn't understand how civilized folk, so-called Christian people could unleash such destruction. There were bodies everywhere, mostly civilians, bloated, and left to rot filling the air with a foul stench. Those still living, you could see it in their eyes, fear and disbelief at a world gone mad. I remember stopping to lend a hand and help a family fix their cart. It was piled high with what little remained of their world. Furniture, pots and pans, whatever they could grab but fate was against them and the wheel had come off its axle and they were struggling, so I gave 'em a hand. It just seemed like the right thing to do in a world that had seen too much hurt. The woman who I assumed was the mum, offered me some of her bread but I couldn't take it, I guessed they needed it more than I did."

As they sat in the quiet room, the sum of Walter's experiences hung in the air. Joe, now holding back his own tears, couldn't help but admire the man before him. Walter, a survivor in every sense, had faced the horrors of war and the desolation of its aftermath with a spirit unbroken.

"Finally, I found a ship, not Jack's, mind you. I heard his ship got sunk by a U-boat later on." Walter chuckled wryly, his smile tinged with irony. "Obviously, we know now that was true.

The chaos that engulfed the city was unbelievable, I just wandered through the mayhem with no one questioning me. My presence went unnoticed, blending into the throngs of people driven to desperation by the war. Fights broke out as people scrambled for scraps of food or vied for a chance to board a ship and escape from the hell that the war had dumped in our laps. Many years later I passed the abattoir in Bradford and the smell brought back that journey to me." Walter continued, his voice edged by the grim memories.

"Once on the ship, I just kept quiet and ate some watery broth they dished up," he recalled. "As we crossed the channel, the weather was much the same as it was when I left. I disembarked onto another scene of chaos, the bustling docks, seemed to be in a state of anarchy. A copper approached me and I prepared my papers, but he just pushed me into a warehouse they were using to sort the chaos. It was like a cattle shed and smelt like one too. No one pried as to who I was and I slipped in with a group of lads, no words exchanged. As we emerged out of the shed, we were bundled straight onto trains. No one said where the trains were bound."

Joe looked up from his tape, "Weren't you desperate to go home and see your family again?"

Walter's eyes held a distant look as if he were searching for an answer in the past.

"Aye, Joe, that I was, but you see, I was afraid. Afraid of being shot as a deserter. Rumours were swirling that more men were lost to firing squads than to the Germans. I needed to get back to my regiment. It was nice bein' back in England because those foreign places... they're for foreigners."

Joe smiled at Walter's comment. There was a long pause, Walter glanced at Joe.

"Shall I carry on?"

Joe grinned, "Well you can't leave it there, can you?"

Walter's narrative continued, each word etching deeper into the canvas of his wartime experiences.

"The train took us to London, but it was utter chaos on the train. The compartments were standing room only, and I found myself squeezed between weary soldiers and dishevelled civilians. We were all carrying the weight of the war, both in our hearts and in the overpacked carriages. With no available seats, I ended up finding a somewhat uncomfortable perch sitting in the corridor on my rucksack. As the rhythmic clatter of the wheels filled the air, fatigue overcame me, and I somehow managed to fall asleep, lulled by the monotonous sounds of the train.

When I arrived at the London station, I was greeted by a scene of even greater disarray. It was as if the whole city had been thrown into turmoil by the war's relentless grip. The clamour of hurried footsteps, the anxious murmurs of the crowds, and the constant squealing of train brakes followed by the hiss of discharged steam created an atmosphere of mayhem. I realized that, in such circumstances, no one had the time or inclination to inquire about a lone soldier's identity or destination.

I managed to hop aboard a goods train bound for Leeds, determined to continue my journey back to the barracks I clambered on board. The freight wagons weren't luxurious by any means, but they offered the promise of progress. I found an empty one and even though it carried the lingering, unpleasant stink of cargo that had been there before me I settled down. Still, I felt relieved; at least I was on my way.

As the train rumbled northwards, the landscape outside darkened, and I contemplated the long road that had brought me to this point. I thought of the comrades I had left behind and the stories that would forever remain untold. As I snoozed ghosts of my past floated in and out of that smelly wagon.

It was well past dusk when the train eventually came to a halt in a desolate siding somewhere near Leeds, I thought. I climbed down from the wagon, my legs stiff and weary. In the dim light, I looked around, my surroundings unfamiliar. I had no way of knowing exactly where I was, but I knew it wasn't Leeds.

I was ravenous, and I decided to try and find a place to eat. It was then as I climbed up off the siding that I discovered that I was in a small town, not far from Dewsbury, named Horbury. A few lights were showing in the houses but the town appeared almost ghostly.

I stumbled upon a humble workman's café, little more than a shed with a few mismatched tables and chairs. A couple of tilly lamps hung beside the door and a brazier burnt brightly to one side. A couple of old chaps were nursing pint pots of tea as they sat huddled near the flames. The air was thick with the aroma of hot food, and the warmth inside was a stark contrast to the cold uncertainty of the world outside.

'What can I get you, love?' a woman in a bright apron asked with a kind smile.

I looked at her, my face worn and fatigued, and admitted, "I'm on my way back to the barracks. I've only just landed here from France, but I'm afraid I don't have any money to pay for a meal.

The woman's warm smile only grew. 'Don't fret, lad,' she said, her Yorkshire accent ringing clear. 'Sit thee sen' darn. You look like you could do wi' some warm grub in yer belly.'

She brought me a pint pot of steaming hot tea, and I eagerly sipped at it, grateful for the warmth that spread through me. The friendship of the café and the quiet laughter of other patrons, all reminded me that I was returning to the familiar landscapes and accents of home.

As I drained the last drop of tea, the woman returned with a large bowl of porridge.

'I'm sorry, lad,' she said as she set it in front of me. 'We ain't got much grub. Rationing is pretty tough at the minute, but we've got plenty of oats.'

The porridge was quite salty, thick, steaming, and very welcome. I ate it slowly, savouring every spoonful. As I leaned back in my chair, a feeling of contentment washed over me, and for the first time in a long while, I felt like I had truly left the war behind.

A fellow customer, intrigued by my presence, leaned over and asked, 'So, where are you headed, lad?'

I explained that I had been separated from my unit and was making my way back to the barracks near Pudsey. He nodded that he understood. 'Well, you're in luck,' he said, a friendly glint in his eye, 'because I can drop you off if you like. I've got a truck outside, filled with scrap iron, but there's room for one more.'

With a grateful heart and a newfound sense of hope, I agreed. As I left the cafe and stepped into the chilly night, the sound of the truck's engine idling served as a reassuring reminder that I was once again on the journey, and this time, I was not alone.

So, that was it I had my lift back to the old barracks. I had a Jack Russel called Pepper on my knees the whole journey, he was a friendly little dog and belonged to the driver. 'He's a good ratter,' the driver proclaimed as the little dog settled down to snooze on my legs.

He dropped me off right outside the barracks and then drove away in a cloud of exhaust smoke. It was strange, you might say surreal but nothing seemed to have changed when I arrived back. There were still squaddies marchin' up and down, and everywhere was whitewashed and in order."

Walter paused, reflecting on the stark contrast between the polished barracks and the horrors he'd witnessed.

"When I turned up at the gatehouse a sergeant major, armed with a clipboard and yardstick, looked at me like I was a ghost. He fired questions at me, tryin' to make sense of a sergeant who had been reported as dead for two years.

Finally, he decided I should see an officer. So, off I went, feelin' out of place in my soiled and tattered uniform and my body bearin' the scars of war."

Walter's journey continued with an unexpected turn:

"Stand at ease, sergeant," the sergeant major bellowed in my ear. The officer behind the desk sifted through a pile of files and papers, a puzzled frown creasing his brow. He looked at me with suspicion and said, 'Papers.' Nothing else. So, I handed them over.

He searched through a pile of folders tutting the whole while. 'According to our records, you were KIA two years back.'

I couldn't help but exclaim, 'Bloody hell. Will I still get my wages?' I added with a hint of humour, but the sergeant major gave me a shove from behind, a comical mix of surprise and respect.

"Oh, sorry, sir," I stammered, "but that was some surprise."

As it turned out, I did get my wages back paid for two years, and a bit extra for wearing the sergeant stripes. It was a strange kind of fortune, considering the circumstances.

My first night back with the army was spent in a prison cell, of all places. It seemed that was the only free bed available at the time. The following day, they arranged to have me transferred to a hospital in Leeds.

The nurses who greeted me were very kind, and it was clear that they had encountered many veterans in need of their care. One of them smiled and said, "Come on, let's get you out of those dirty old rags and into a warm bath." Her words sounded like heaven to me.

I soaked in that hot bath, the sensation of warm water and soap washing away the grime and weariness of war was indeed heaven. I didn't want to get out; it was the closest thing to comfort I had felt in a long while. My arm and side were infected and in need of redressing, finally, they received the attention they required. It was during this process that I found Elsie again.

Once again, we almost drowned in the tears of joy as we hugged. 'You rascal,' she said, fussing with the bandages. I don't think your Regiment was back yet."

'I was separated and then ordered to get on a ship,' I told her. I kept quiet about it being my choice to come home.

"Anyway, I heard you were in Paris," I chided.

"Well, I was for a bit but then I came back here to help treat lads who finally made it home. Plus a certain doctor was relocated here." She gave me a sly wink.

Elsie's caring touch and her gentle fussing with my bandages became a comforting routine during my early days back home."

In the quiet, comfort of the lounge, Joe leaned forward, his eyes focused on Walter, his curiosity and empathy intense.

"You see lad, that period right after the war was... peculiar. We thought the end of the war would mean coming home to cheers, parades, and celebrations. We were heroes, weren't we? At least, that's what we thought."

He paused, his fingers absently tracing the rim of his coffee cup. "But reality had a different plan. The images of what I'd witnessed in Europe, the destruction, the suffering... they haunted me. The numbness I felt initially was like a dam holding back a flood of emotions. Then, one night, at three in the morning, it all burst out, and I couldn't stop crying for hours. Elsie came and lay by my side all night."

Joe's expression remained attentive, and he nodded in understanding. He knew that what Walter described was a common experience for soldiers returning from the front lines, although it didn't make it any less painful.

Walter continued, "Elsie, bless her heart, was there for me. She did what she could to soothe my troubled mind. But back then, there was very little understanding of what we now call PTSD. They called it shell shock. I read somewhere that as many as three hundred thousand men suffered from it after the war."

Joe contemplated the enormity of that number. Three hundred thousand men, each with their own stories, their own nightmares, their own battles to fight even after the guns had fallen silent.

Walter sighed, the weight of those years was evident in his voice. "It wasn't easy, lad. The nights were the worst. The nightmares... they persisted for years. It took me a long time to sleep through the night without waking up in a cold sweat. At least I had Elsie to help me through those first few months. We spent Christmas together and I met her doctor. They'd got married in Paris and I could tell that they were in love. He was a nice bloke, very devoted. "

As Walter spoke, Joe could see the resilience that had carried him through those dark times. It was clear that while the war had ended, its scars lingered, etched into the minds and hearts of those who had lived through it.

"The army asked me to stay on and train other snipers how to fend for themselves. I told them cynically, that since this had been the war to end all wars, they wouldn't need any more snipers. I wanted out."

Joe was feeling emotional his friend's story had cut deep into his heart and he needed a break more than Walter did.

"We'll pick it up again later Walter… I think we both need a break."

Walter's weary eyes conveyed his agreement. "Yes, we can pick up from where we left off tomorrow."

"Oh, sorry Walter, it'll be a couple of days before I'm back. I need some time with Debbie."

Walter nodded understandingly. "I appreciate your honesty, Joe. I forget. But I'll be honest; it's a bit disheartening to think that this journey through my life might remain incomplete."

Joe, eager to continue documenting Walter's experiences, reassured him, "Oh, no, Walter. There's so much more to your story, and I'm honoured to write it down. We'll find a way to make this work, and your journey will be told in its entirety."

Chapter Sixteen.
A Day of Balance.

As the morning light seeped through the window, Joe lay in bed, hands clasped behind his head, gazing up at the ceiling. A feeling of conflict lingered within him… a tug-of-war between two significant aspects of his life. His connection with Walter had transcended the boundaries of professional duty; they'd grown closer, turning into friends, confidants, and in some ways, surrogate families for each other.

This bond, intricate and meaningful, left Joe feeling torn between his dedication to the old man and his responsibilities towards his own family. Debbie's boundless energy brought a touch of playfulness to the morning, when she suddenly pounced on him, squealing like a banshee, they were soon locked in a tickling match, rolling about the bed, both of them laughing until they were out of breath.

"You little terror," Joe gasped between fits of laughter.

Julie's voice interrupted their playful tussle. She popped her head around the door, her eyes twinkling with amusement. "Are you two kids coming for breakfast?"

Debbie, her eyes shining with excitement, leapt to the floor. "Yes, please, Mummy! Can I have Coco Pops?" The morning had already begun with a dose of joy and laughter, and they were ready to start their day as a family.

Joe got out of bed, showered, and then went down to the kitchen. Debbie was already there and watching her favourite television programme. As they sat and ate their breakfast, Julie could sense the turmoil her husband was feeling. She had always admired her husband's compassionate nature and his unwavering dedication to those in his care. She realised that Joe and Walter had formed a strong bond. She understood the importance of Joe's work and yet, she also knew that they had their own family and responsibilities that required attention.

Today was a special day for the family as they planned to visit Julie's mother, who lived nearby. It was a rare occasion when they could all be together as a family, and Julie looked forward to sharing these moments with Joe.

"You okay, pumpkin," Joe called to Debbie.

Debbie nodded but her eyes were fixed on the cartoon antics flashing before her eyes.

Julie spoke between bites of toast and marmalade, "You do remember that we are going to Mum's today?"

"Oh yes, of course... I'm looking forward to it." He tried to sound as convincing as he could.

"I'm concerned about you. Do you think that you are getting too involved with Walter?"

"It's hard not to. A bond has formed between us, it's as though I have my father back, not that I ever knew much about him. I can't really explain... but it will do me good to have a break for a day or so and put things into perspective."

As they went out to the car, his thoughts remained firmly entrenched with Walter.

"He'll be all right," Julie said reassuringly. She had guessed where his thoughts were.

"I know," he said with a smile.

In the tranquil Yorkshire afternoon, the sun cast its wintery embrace over Julie's mother's house. Debbie's world thrived on routine and familiarity, and her parents knew this well.

They were greeted at the door by Julie's father. A tall strong character who kept himself in shape by playing golf and taking the occasional bike ride.

"Come in, it seems ages since we were all together. Your mum's in the kitchen."

"Where else?" Julie commented.

"We're having a barbecue, I'll meet you outside," he said heading towards the back garden.

The back garden was crafted by Granddad's hands, an Adventureland custom-tailored to Debbie's unique needs. It was a testament to his love for his granddaughter. A trampoline stood tall, defying gravity, inviting Debbie to soar into the sky with boundless giggles. Swings swayed in harmony with her laughter, while a long, winding slide promised adventure with every descent.

But that wasn't all. In one corner, beneath a rustic wooden canopy, lay a whimsical picnic area. It was here despite the winter's chill that the family gathered, sharing stories and laughter as they savoured delicious meals prepared by Grandad.

And when it came to BBQ time, Granddad took centre stage; he was a culinary maestro of his alfresco grill. He danced around the grill decked out in one of his many quirky aprons, metal tongs in hand, clicking them together like castanets, he turned cooking into a lively performance. His antics never failed to bring smiles, especially to Debbie, who watched in awe.

The day had gently given way to evening, and already the sun had set. The delicious aroma of grilled delights filled the air. The garden was adorned with the warm, smoky embrace of Granddad's culinary artistry, a labour of love that had become a cherished part of their family gatherings.

As twilight settled in and the stars above began to twinkle, Joe and Julie wrapped in their warm winter coats exchanged satisfied glances. They had once again created a day filled with cherished memories for their beloved daughter. The garden, illuminated by several strings of lights and where the scent of BBQ smoke mingled with the laughter of a family's joy, felt like a magical place where time seemed to stand still, and life's most precious moments were celebrated.

Debbie, her eyes heavy with the pleasant exhaustion of a day well spent, was already beginning to drift into sleep when Grandma made a suggestion.

"Why don't you leave her with us for the night? There's no school tomorrow. Put her to bed, and we'll drop her off tomorrow afternoon." She gave Julie a sly wink. "You two can have a few hours to yourselves."

With a tender kiss on Debbie's forehead, Joe and Julie agreed, and they headed for home, leaving their daughter asleep in her own bedroom at Grandma's house.

They drove home with a warm satisfied glow around them. Julie hummed a little tune from her childhood. When they reached home, Joe took a can from the fridge and popped its ring-pull. He dropped wearily into his favourite chair.

However, as the evening drew to a close and bed beckoned, Joe found himself wrestling with his own emotions. He couldn't shake the feeling that he was missing something essential, something beyond the responsibilities of his profession.

Julie came and sat on his knee. "Thank you, my love, for your support and understanding," she whispered.

"You don't need to thank me… you know that. We'll get through this together. Our journey is far from straightforward, but we must embrace everything together."

The following morning, Joe awoke with a sense of purpose, eager to tackle a few tasks in his beloved garden. He threw on his work clothes; a pair of jeans and a polo-necked jumper that had definitely seen much better days. They had a faint smell of creosote from the last time he painted the fence despite several washings.

As he ventured into the garden, the rich tapestry of autumn unfolded around him. Vibrant hues of crimson, gold, and amber adorned the scene, a testament to the season's artistic palette. The scattered leaves from the nearby trees lay strewn across the garden, lending an air of untamed charm, though some might view it as disorderly.

Before the gradual transition towards winter, he had meticulously planned the garden to retain pockets of vivid colour even during this time of the year. Amidst the fallen leaves, pockets of life persisted. Delicate hellebores flaunted their soft, pastel hues, adding a touch of ethereal beauty to the subdued landscape. The bright yellow winter jasmine, like beacons of cheerfulness, offered a stark contrast against the autumnal backdrop, infusing corners with a radiant glow that defied the encroaching chill.

In this seasonal tapestry, amidst the autumnal decay, these resilient blooms stood as a piece of evidence of his thoughtful cultivation, brightening the garden and bringing forth moments of joy even during nature's quiet transition. The fresh air filled his lungs with a revitalizing breath, and the chatter of birds in the hedges provided a soothing soundtrack to his morning.

With a determined stride, Joe approached his trusty lawn mower, its weathered frame was a testament to countless hours spent tending to the garden's needs. He suddenly remembered that he had intended to repaint it last winter but he'd not got around to it.

"I think this will be my last cut for this year," he told the mower. As he pushed it over the grass, the world seemed to slow down. Each deliberate pass of the machine was a stroke of mindfulness, and with each hum of its cutters, Joe felt a peculiar peace settle over him. It was as if the machine's mechanical heartbeat synchronized with his own, a rhythm of unity with nature. The scent of freshly mowed grass mingled with the smells of Autumn, creating a fragrant picture of life.

After some while, Julie appeared protected from the cold by a long woollen scarf with a matching bobble hat knitted for her by her Mum. She carried a tray of sandwiches and a flask of hot tea.

"Come on, grub up," she called to Joe.

They found a cosy spot on Debbie's swing, a place that held its own share of cherished memories. The swing, a symbol of childhood innocence and joy, swayed gently as they enjoyed their impromptu picnic.

"I remember when we bought this for Debbie," Julie reminisced. "Once she'd got the hang of it we couldn't get her off again."

Joe nodded, he smiled as he remembered that particular day, it seemed a long time off now.

They sat side by side, savouring the simple pleasure of sandwiches that tasted like home and sunlight filtering through the leafless branches above them, casting dappled patterns on their skin.

"This is heaven," Joe commented between bites.

"No, it's salmon spread," she joked with a smile.

The garden's quiet beauty embraced them. And in that moment, with the taste of homemade sandwiches and the feeling of the swing beneath them, Joe and Julie found contentment in the quiet togetherness of their garden.

Julie felt at peace with everything, a warm glow embraced her as she kicked with her legs to make the swing go higher. It was a morning of serenity, where the world outside their haven seemed to fade away. Julie stood in front of Joe and tenderly kissed his lips.

"What was that for?" Joe asked.

"I love you, Mr Dobson." She buried her head into his shoulder.

The garden, a place of growth and renewal, mirrored the growth of their relationship.

Chapter Seventeen
A New Awakening.

Walter awoke early Saturday morning, a sense of yearning tugging at his heart. The absence of Joe's visit today left him feeling somewhat adrift, yet it also ignited a determination to launch a change. As he got up from the chair where he had spent the night, he stretched his aching back and stood a moment until the pain subsided. Peering out of the window he was pleased that the bad weather had gone and the sun was shining its bright light reflecting off cars as they dashed passed as if they were on some important business. He rinsed his hands and face in the wash bowl, the cold water refreshed him and his mind turned to his breakfast. Glancing at himself in the mirror he was disappointed by his reflection.

"Lord, am I really that old," he sighed and returned to the kitchen in time to catch the bread popping out of the toaster.

After his breakfast of toast and marmite, he squared up to the hallway mirror, examining himself with a critical eye. His grey hair, tousled from sleep, hinted at the passing years. His fingers traced across the rough stubble on his chin and cheeks as he remarked, 'Time to smarten yourself up, Sergeant Middlebrough.'

These words carried more than just a command; they held a promise to himself, a commitment to improve his appearance, even if it was just for his own satisfaction.

In the tranquillity of his room, he recognised that Joe's visits had brought more than pasties; they had delivered hope and a renewed sense of self-esteem. It was as if Joe's casual chats and companionship had breathed life into his days, giving him a reason to take pride in himself, even in the simplest ways.

He decided that a shave might help his look. With the hot water in the kettle left from his coffee, he made room on the countertop for his shaving gear. The soft badger bristled brush was an old companion, he remembered Alice buying it for him one Christmas. Lost in thought he swirled the brush in the water and then dipped it into his favourite shaving cream. The smell of sandalwood was immediately released bringing back more memories of Christmas and gifts from Alice.

The blade of his safety razor scraped the skin of his chin with precision, expertly removing days of stubble and leaving behind a clean, invigorating sensation. The mirror reflected a transformed man, one who seemed to have shed years with each pass of the blade. Walter stood back, his eyes taking in the newfound vitality in his appearance.

"That's better," he grinned as he ran his open palm over the smooth skin of his cheeks. "Cor, I look years younger... watch out, ladies, Walter's on the prowl." He did a little shimmy of a dance and then immediately regretted it as a pain shot up his leg.

He admired his reflection, noting the renewed twinkle in his eyes and the confident set of his jaw. It was as if he had unveiled a hidden part of himself, ready to embrace the world once more.

However, his triumphant moment was interrupted by a sudden bout of coughing, triggered by the sharp, citrusy scent of his aftershave. Walter chuckled as he reached for a handkerchief, a hint of irony in his coughing fit. But beneath the humour, there was a sense of determination and a readiness to step out into the world, for he knew that change was not just about appearance; it was about rekindling the spirit of living, even if it was only one step at a time.

Standing at the bottom of his stairs, he stared upward, reminiscent of a mountain climber at base camp peering up his next ascent. Though not quite the unknown, it was still a daunting task. Several years had passed since he last attempted the climb, not since the council had thoughtfully installed a downstairs toilet for his convenience.

With each creaking step, Walter began the ascent up the wooden stairs, his hands firmly gripping the bannister to help hoist himself to the next step. Finally, with a sigh of relief, he reached the landing. Glancing out of the window at the world below, he couldn't help but smile as he watched people rush past along the pavement.

After catching his breath, he entered the upper rooms that had been locked away for years. The dust had settled, and cobwebs clung to forgotten corners, but today, they bore witness to a reawakening.

He stared at the wardrobes, once filled with his wife's clothing, now standing empty. Their hollowness weighed heavily on him, a poignant reminder of her absence, her presence only lingered in memories. But as he stared, a smile teased his lips; staring down at him from the top of the wardrobe a huge cuddly bear kept its beady eyes on him.

"Are you still here," he called to the bear, "I'd forgotten about you. Don't worry I'm not going to throw you away," he chuckled and made a growling sound at it. "I think that it is time you came out of hibernation."

He slowly prised open the wardrobe doors the aged wood had swollen and they were stiff, he peeped in.

"It was how I dealt with the pain," he whispered as if seeking understanding from the silent, empty void.

A profound sense of regret and guilt washed over him for parting with her belongings. These had been more than mere garments; they were fragments of her identity. Yet, among the barren spaces, a few relics remained… a scarf from their honeymoon hung behind the door, he clutched it and held it to his face, it still held her fragrance. Concealed in a dusty drawer he uncovered handwritten letters, their fragile pages bearing the faded imprints of long-forgotten words.

These discoveries breathed life into long-gone memories, flooding Walter's heart with a tidal wave of emotions. Grief threatened to engulf him, a burden he had carried in silence for too long.

With trembling hands, he picked up a few old photographs that captured their happiness frozen in time. There were even a few old postcards of places they had visited. There was a mix of emotions as he looked through them.

Sitting on the corner of their shared bed amidst echoes of laughter and love, Walter found a renewed sense of purpose. He couldn't bring his wife back, but he could honour her memory by embracing the life she had cherished. As he unfolded the letters, he traced his fingers over the familiar script, his heart aching with bittersweet nostalgia. Memories of their adventures together, the triumphs and tragedies flooded his mind, and for a fleeting moment, he felt her presence beside him, as if she were whispering encouragement in his ear. Like all married couples, their life had not always run smoothly, there were a few thorns amongst the roses but their love and respect for each other had carried them through.

Tears welled up in his eyes, but they were not tears of sorrow alone; they were tears of gratitude for the time they had shared and the love that still connected them. With each word read, he rediscovered his wife's soul and felt their shared love. It gave him the strength to face the future with a mixture of sorrow, joy, and newfound determination.

Delving into his own cupboard drawers, he unearthed a new shirt, still wrapped in its original packaging; there were five others, presents from Alice. Drawer by drawer, he gathered what he needed to usher in the changes he had envisioned. Out of the red velvet box he pulled his gold watch chain with his hunter still attached. He slowly turned the crown and held it to his ear enjoying the steady rhythmic tic of the watch. He smiled at the bear, 'You stay there, I'll be back soon, honest.'

As Walter descended the stairs, clutching a set of fresh clothes to his chest, he felt a profound vitality surging through his veins. It was time to step out into the world, to seek companionship and connection he had long forsaken. The path ahead remained uncertain, but surely it was not too late to enjoy living. Life beckoned, and Walter was ready to embrace it, one step at a time, with the memory of his beloved wife lighting the way.

He felt like the character from a fairy tale as he threw off his old clothes and dressed in the new ones. The old ones were stuffed in a supermarket carrier bag and thrown out next to the dustbin.

"There you are Alice, I told you I would make some changes."

Throughout the day, Walter moved about at a gentle pace, each step deliberate yet relaxed. In the background, the melodic tunes of his cherished music set a soothing atmosphere, wrapping him in a cocoon of creative tranquillity. With care, he sifted through his extensive collection of vinyl records, seeking that one piece that would inspire him. Gently, almost reverently, he extracted a gleaming black record from its protective sleeve. Placing it carefully on the turntable, he tenderly wiped it clean before setting the needle in motion.

As the initial notes of Mendelssohn's Hebridean Overture reverberated through the room, Walter eased his eyes shut, surrendering himself to the music's embrace. A sensation of weightlessness descended upon him, carried aloft by the symphonic harmonies. The melodies, weaving through the space with a gentle insistence, served as a conduit, transcending the boundaries of his home. They became a portal, whisking him away from the present, transporting him to realms beyond, to another time and place.

The stirring notes triggered a flood of memories, transporting him back to a time when he and Alice had embarked on a boat trip to witness the renowned Fingal's Cave. Reminiscing about their idyllic few weeks spent holidaying in the Hebrides, the music conjured vivid landscapes and evoked cherished yet half-forgotten recollections.

Through Mendelssohn's masterpiece, each crescendo and delicate passage painted a canvas of nostalgia, intertwining Walter's present reality with cherished moments from the past. The music was familiar yet each bar sounded new and fresh evoking the movement of the sea, the call of the gulls and the sound of the waves dashing against the rocks. As it drew to a close he felt invigorated. He moved in front of his bookshelf and he felt happy as he straightened up a few volumes and squeezed others back into their place with the music still echoing around his mind. He ran his fingers along the spines of his favourite novels, drawing inspiration from the worlds contained within.

Outside, the world of Yorkshire carried on, oblivious to Walter's inner world. The sunlight streamed through the window, casting warm, shifting patterns of light and shadow on the room's varied decor. The ticking of the clock on the mantlepiece provided a constant reminder that time was passing, inching closer to the moment when Joe would arrive.

His disappointment was genuine when he realised that the football season had ended and that there would be no 'Match of the Day.' He consoled himself and watched snooker until he dozed off. He slept until the first light of a fresh dawn seeped through his curtains. Walter rose from his slumber with a heart brimming with the anticipation of his evolving journey to make the most of the days that lay ahead. The world outside his window seemed to share in his excitement, the sound of the morning traffic filled the air, but somehow it was not as annoying as it had always seemed.

He proudly surveyed his lounge, once cluttered and dishevelled, now stood as a witness to his determination. He had spent hours the previous day meticulously tidying and cleaning every nook and cranny. The transformation was astonishing… the room exuded an air of tranquillity, as the morning light streamed through the curtains, it cast a warm, golden hue over the freshly arranged furniture.

With a sense of accomplishment, Walter moved towards the kitchen, where he couldn't help but marvel at the almost sparkling kitchen units. Each surface gleamed under the soft morning light, a reflection of the care and attention he had poured into this space. The smell of freshly brewed coffee filled the air, promising a comforting start to his day.

But this was more than just a clean house; it was a symbol of his commitment to seizing the moments life had left for him. It was a canvas upon which he would paint new memories and experiences. Walter's smile deepened as he looked around, his heart swelled with gratitude for the opportunity to embark on this profound journey, where every day held the promise of something extraordinary.

Chapter Eighteen
Demob.

At last, there was the awaited tap at the door, a sound that sent a jolt of excitement through Walter. With a sense of anticipation, he moved swiftly to answer it. The door swung open, revealing Joe standing there, a picture of renewed vitality. He wore a sheepskin jacket and a brightly coloured beanie hat to keep the cold out.

Joe's face bore a radiant glow, and his eyes sparkled with a newfound energy that had been absent in recent times. The days off had evidently done wonders for him. He greeted Walter with a warm smile, and there was an unmistakable lightness to his step as he stepped into the house.

"Morning, Walter. You're looking quite dapper today. Got a special date planned?" Joe quipped, a playful smile on his face.

"Only a date with you, my young friend. I reckoned it was time to spruce myself up a bit. The way I've been lately is not much of a tribute to Alice. She'd have been disappointed to see me letting myself go. The house used to be spick and span when she was around. It might not have been much, but it was her pride and joy. She deserved better," Walter replied, his voice tinged with both longing and regret.

Walter couldn't help but notice the change in his friend. He gestured for Joe to come in and take a seat in the newly tidied lounge, which now seemed to offer a sense of calm and comfort. They settled into a pair of inviting armchairs.

Joe took off his jacket and hung it on what he now regarded as his hook in the hall. He looked around the room, "Wow, Walter, what difference you've made in here. I'm really impressed. Did you hire a cleaner?"

"No, don't be daft, lad and I've even been upstairs."

As they began to catch up, the room seemed to resonate with the warmth of their connection, and the air was filled with the echoes of their shared laughter and stories. It was a day that marked the beginning of a new chapter in their friendship, a chapter filled with renewed energy and a determination to make the most of the time they had together.

"I'm glad you decided to venture upstairs. How did you feel about it?"

Walter shifted uncomfortably in his chair; his gaze fixed on a distant memory.

"It was a mix of feelings, really. I stumbled upon a few photos that stirred up old memories," he said, shaking his head with a hint of sadness. "I gave away Alice's clothes almost immediately after she died, thinking they might bring back too many memories and I was angry that she had been taken away from me." Walter blows a sigh of frustration. "Looking back, I wonder if I acted too hastily. Maybe I should've held onto them a bit longer."

"I'll make a fresh brew. Are you ready for one?" Joe poured the coffee and opened a bag of croissants.

"I fancied some of these. Would you like one, Walter?"

Walter's eyes lit up with anticipation. "Yes, please. It's been years since I've had one. Alice used to dunk them in her coffee, but I found them too soggy that way."

Joe smiled, pleased that he'd sparked a happy memory for Walter. "Tell me about Alice," he enquired.

"You're jumping ahead a bit, my friend. We haven't reached her in my story yet," Walter chuckled. "But I can say that she was a wonderful, kind, and loving person. I don't think I appreciated her enough when she was here. Take it as a lesson, Joe. Make the most of your time with your family."

"You're right. I'll wait until it's her time to take centre stage in your story," Joe agreed.

"Julie has invited you to our house, maybe for tea one day. She scolded me for going for a curry without her," Joe mentioned.

"I'd like to try that fried chicken stuff they advertise on TV. You know, that Colonel something fried chicken," Walter replied.

"Oh, KFC! Debbie's a big fan of that," Joe said before taking a sip of his coffee. "I'm a bit disappointed that we haven't found any more about Jack. Maybe he didn't return to this area. There are so many possibilities. Anyway, during the school holiday, Julie is going to spend some time trawling the archives."

Walter smiled as though another thought had come to him… if Elsie got married, she might be hard to trace… I know it sounds daft but I'm sure that she's still alive."

"Do you fancy telling me more today?" Joe asked, he secretly hoped that Walter would say yes.

They sat down and Joe switched on his tape.

"We'd got to you being demobbed from the army," Joe said relishing the next chapters of Walter's story.

"They shipped me back to a camp in Kent, I'm not sure why but the army likes to make things awkward. There was a certain amount of paperwork to fill out. I'd opened an account with the Yorkshire Penny Bank as it was called back then, and the army needed the details for my back pay.

I was sad to lose my uniform; it had become a part of me in a way, something that identified me. In Civvie Street, I was just another out-of-work bloke, a nobody, I suppose. I don't think that I'm a vain person, but it was nice to share the respect of men who fought by my side. So, I left with about the same as I'd joined up with, apart from what I carried in my head, and now, due to the back pay, I had a decent bank balance.

The train heading north was terribly overcrowded, a sea of faces, each one carrying the scars of their wartime experiences. I couldn't help but share the sandwiches I'd made, much like the ones I made you when you first called. It was January and there was no heating in the carriage everyone looked frozen. I sat next to a lad who had lost his arm somewhere in Belgium. The saddest thing was, that he'd been a joiner before the war, but he couldn't see how he could go back to that with just one arm. We exchanged stories, and it struck me how life had changed so drastically for all of us.

A sense of safety settled in as Sheffield faded behind me. The rickety train wheels clacked and clattered on the tracks. Each mile took me away from the war and nearer to my real life. I watched the landscape change, shifting from the industrial city to the green fields and familiar surroundings of Wakefield. It felt like I was on home turf once again even though there was a thin layer of snow on the ground. But the anxiety of returning to civilian life began to creep in. I couldn't help but wonder how different things might be, whether the people I once knew had moved on, and if I would ever truly fit in again. You can't be knee-deep in filth and mutilated bodies one day and walk as though nothing had happened the next.

As I neared Wakefield, I reflected on the years of service, the camaraderie, and the shared experiences with my fellow soldiers. It was a chapter of my life that had ended, and now I had to face the uncertainty of what lay ahead in the world beyond the war.

On the station platform I'd read the newspaper headlines, I was bewildered because the whole world seemed to be in turmoil, spinning out of control. The politicians were powerless in the face of it all. People were dying from hunger and pneumonia everywhere, and the lads like me who were demobbed had nothing... no jobs, no money, and worst of all, no hope. They deserved better after what they'd been through. The elites, of course, still had their plenty. I toyed with the idea of joining the communists, but reality hit me. Who'd listen to me?

I felt claustrophobic in the carriage and I decided to get off the train and walk home. I thought that maybe I should get back into practice in case Jos would employ me again. And so, I walked back from Wakefield to Huddersfield on the towpath, praying to see Owd Jos all the way.

And when I finally laid eyes on him, a numbness swept over me. It was as if I wanted to sit down and let my emotions pour out, but I held back. Instead, I ran towards him, lifted him off his feet, and we tumbled into the bushes, laughing with an intensity I hadn't felt in ages. Dolly emerged to see what the ruckus was about, and she joined the pile, nearly smothering the two of us and bringing even more joy to the reunion.

"I'm cooking your favourite, rabbit pie," she exclaimed with genuine delight. "And then, my lad, it's time for a good laugh or two."

Troy, my old companion, joined in our celebration, his presence a symbol of the past's return. He scraped the ground with his front hoof, snorted, and shook his head… a display of equine contentment. We all trooped to a nearby inn, and I didn't need to spend a penny on drinks. Men from all around came over to shake my hand, treating me like a hero. It felt strange, almost fraudulent. I didn't think I had done anything to merit such attention. They all wanted to see my medal and the healed scar on my arm – a reminder of a bullet's kiss. I kept my side's scar hidden from their curious eyes.

Jos told me that the army had attempted to draft Troy into service. Well, by now, you know what Jos was like… he hid Troy away on a deserted moorland farm. When the army came for him, he claimed that he was already taken. The matter was never raised again.

During an era where railways were rapidly gaining dominance, the canals held on to their timeless allure, continuing to offer a lifeline of work for people like us. The world outside had evolved, but as we strolled alongside Troy, it was as if we had stepped back in time. The absence of modern motorways and the poor state of the roads ensured that canals remained vital for the transportation of bulk commodities.

Walking beside Troy, the sensation was indescribable. It was like turning back the hands of time, a journey through the memories of days long gone. Words could hardly capture the swirling emotions that coursed through me. Occasionally, I'd take a reality check and I'd stare at Troy or hold his huge neck with my face pushed hard against the warmth of his skin. There was an exhilarating elation, a sense of rekindled purpose, and a profound peace that enveloped my very being."

Walter paused as he relived the sensations he felt on the towpath again.

"With each step, I felt a renewed vigour, as if the weight of the modern world had been momentarily lifted from my shoulders. My feet seemed to glide over the well-worn path, and the world around us faded into insignificance, replaced by the timeless beauty of the canal and its enduring history.

In the company of Troy, my trusted friend who had shared countless adventures with me, conversation flowed effortlessly. Of course, it was me who did the chatting, but Troy, ever the steadfast companion, listened and nodded, his presence a comforting reminder of the enduring bonds forged over the years.

I confided in Troy during one of our heart-to-heart conversations. 'I can't put into words what I've witnessed, my old friend. I know you wouldn't have wanted to be there, and if the truth be told, I didn't either. The more I see of the world and its people, the more I cherish our bond.'

We walked the familiar path along the canal, and it was more than a simple journey; it was a journey through time, a reconnection with the past, and a rediscovery of the joys of simpler days. But there was a downside, my sleeping hours were not so peaceful, and flashes of memory collided with everyday thoughts, making a mish-mash of my mind. If I heard a loud bang or noise, I'd duck for cover and reach for my weapon that was no longer beside me.

In those quiet moments, as the echoes of Troy's hooves on the towpath resonated with the whispers of the past, I couldn't help but confront the ghosts that still haunted me. Memories of the front lines and the friends I'd lost, the thunder of artillery, and the cries of comrades were never far from my thoughts. The tranquillity of this place often gave way to the chaos of war that still lingered within me.

Troy, ever watchful, seemed to sense my unease. His nuzzling against my arm, his silent reassurance, reminded me that I was not alone on this journey, even when the weight of my memories threatened to overwhelm me. In his presence, the past and the present blended into a bittersweet tapestry of life's experiences, and I found solace in the unspoken understanding we shared.

As we continued our walk, I couldn't help but wonder if, like Troy, I could find a way to navigate the tangled landscape of my mind, find peace amid the memories, and rekindle the spirit of simpler, brighter days. It was a challenge, but it was a journey worth taking.

Walter sipped his coffee and didn't notice that it had gone cold. His voice was reflective as he recollected that precise time.

"During this period of my life, I immersed myself wholeheartedly in the world of literature. It was a time of profound self-discovery, and I found solace and inspiration in the timeless words of literary masters. Dickens, with his vivid characters and rich narratives, transported me to Victorian London. The Bronte sisters' passionate tales of love and longing amidst the Yorkshire moors stirred my emotions. Sir Walter Scott's historical epics filled my mind with images of proud knights and alluring mysteries.

But it wasn't just fiction that captured my heart; it was poetry too. I delved into the verses of English poets, savouring the beauty of their language. However, one American poetess, Ella Wheeler Wilcox, held a special place in my heart. Her poems had an uncanny ability to articulate the very thoughts and emotions that swirled within me. I found myself returning to her verses time after time as if they were a sanctuary for my soul.

Through the pages of these books and the verses of poets like Wilcox, I discovered a new world… a world that offered respite from the haunting memories of the past. It was a place where I could retreat during the darkest hours, finding solace in the printed word and the power of imagination.

As we continued our journey along the canals, I couldn't resist the temptation to seek out more books. We'd call in at libraries along the way, and I'd scour market stalls in search of literary treasures. Jos, my ever-practical companion, would jest that we might need a bigger barge if my appetite for reading didn't slow down. Yet, I couldn't help myself; there was no television back then, even the radio or wireless as they were referred to was very limited and so literature had become my refuge and my companion on this winding path through life's twists and turns.

But fate had its own script written for us, and one day it unfolded. Our barge sprung a leak, an unexpected blow, we were somewhere between Skipton and the Aire Gap I mentioned earlier. We were at the mercy of the elements. Jos pulled every string he could, he reached out to every connection, but metal was as scarce as hens' teeth, and the price had shot up to the heavens.

It was agonizing to watch as another barge claimed most of our cargo. The damage hid beneath the water's surface so that when we lightened the load we floated higher in the water above where the damage was. And so, on that day, the four of us – Jos, Dolly, Troy, and I – embarked on another long walk. We towed our stricken vessel back to Huddersfield. Jos, who usually exuded confidence, now appeared uncertain about our direction. Along the way, we encountered several barges for sale, but they were fitted with engines that knocked in that typical diesel power way. Jos made up his mind to purchase one of these, he was convinced Troy's services were no longer required." It was a sad memory and the power of it overwhelmed Walter for a moment.

'You can stick around with me,' Jos suggested.

I couldn't believe that he was prepared to cast off Troy after all his years of loyal service. I was very angry with Jos and once again I felt that my world was under attack. Deep down, I knew it wouldn't be the same. Summoning my courage, I asked if I could take Troy. At first, Jos demanded five pounds, but Dolly was having none of it. She wielded her umbrella like Excalibur, both metaphorically and literally, declaring that Troy was mine for the taking."

Chapter Nineteen.
On the Road.

In Walter's living room, there was a long pause and it seemed that that poignant moment hung heavily in the air. Joe let out a deep sigh of relief, exhaustion creeping in.

"I believe we'll wrap things up here for now. That was quite a session. I'm utterly spent. I don't even know what to say."

Walter cleared the lump from his throat and suggested, "We can carry on after lunch… what about visiting the chip shop?"

Walter's desire to visit the chip shop for lunch was driven by newfound energy and the conviction that sharing his story would be a releasing experience, a way to unburden his soul. The anticipation of this narrative journey filled him with a sense of purpose and resolve, much like the feeling he had when embarking on a new adventure along the canals.

"Okay, get your coat on, we'll have a walk out and pick up some chips on the way," Joe said.

"And mushy peas, oh, lovely, Yorkshire caviar."

Joe was still smiling about the caviar joke as they entered the chip shop. The smell was like no other on earth a blend of hot cooking oil and fish.

"Shall we take them back home?" Joe asked.

Walter looked taken aback at the suggestion. "Not on your nelly, we'll go down to the canal and eat 'em out of the paper, proper Yorkshire style."

As he savoured his meal, the familiar tastes and aromas of the food served as a comforting backdrop to the thoughts and memories he was eager to share. With each bite of his meal, Walter felt a renewed sense of energy and determination, ready to continue the narrative and embark on the next chapter of his journey.

With satisfied tummies, they went back to Walter's house.

"I could murder a cuppa," Walter said above the din of the traffic."

"Me too."

Walter's memory was rekindled, and he urged Joe to set up the tape recorder to continue the story.

"To be honest, as I walked away from my friends, I had no idea which way I was going. I had a little bit of money put by, some from my wages with Jos and my army pay. I felt as though I was well on my way to a new chapter in life.

"Let me share a remarkable twist in the tale. I bid farewell to Dolly standing on the towpath; there were tears in her eyes. She hugged me and pulled me tightly to her bosom. I had to smile when I felt that familiar warmth, one I had experienced so many times whenever she comforted me as I grew up. Jos had gone below, also with a tear in his eye, and he was out of sight of my dear friend and surrogate mother. She slipped something into my hand, something that, at first, I mistook for a fat cigar.

She whispered, 'Ere, but don't let him see, you've earned this, make good use of it and have a good life. Open it later.'

In the stress of the moment, I merely dropped it into my pocket without giving it much thought. She kissed me goodbye and held onto me for a long moment.

"I'll come and see you whenever I can," I couldn't say much; the lump in my throat was making it difficult to speak.

And so, that was that, and once again I began another walk, not knowing the direction I was going to take. That evening, with nowhere to go, I found a place in a secluded wood. I made a tent out of tarpaulin as a shelter and covered Troy with his blanket and waterproof coat. I then lit a small fire and cooked a tin of beans. After my war experiences, I was pretty good at living rough.

I reached into my pocket and unrolled Dolly's parting gift. I was astonished. It wasn't tobacco inside; it was a bundle of crisp, white, five-pound notes. Carefully, I counted them; my hands were shaking, and to my disbelief, there was a total sum of one hundred and fifty-five pounds. At that moment, I held an absolute fortune, a sum that could change the course of my life. I just stared at it for I don't know how long.

I decided that the first thing next morning I would head for the Yorkshire Bank. I had no idea how Dolly would have acquired such an amount… and I didn't want to dwell on it.

Back then, that amount was enough to buy a house, a prospect that had seemed distant and unattainable before. Dolly's unexpected act of kindness and generosity left me with a profound sense of gratitude. It was a gift that not only altered my circumstances but also reminded me of the unexpected turns life can take."

Joe stopped the tape. "Blimey Walter, that must have seemed like a gift from heaven."

"With this newfound fortune, the path ahead seemed even more promising, and I was filled with a renewed sense of purpose and determination to shape my destiny. But before I could fully embrace this exciting chapter of my life, there was one amusing incident at the bank that I must share with you.

I tethered Troy to a post in the local park and then set off down the High Street to find the bank. The lady behind the counter gave me a welcoming smile, and in those days, there were no glass partitions separating bank staff from customers. I produced my bank book, which already had the deposit from the war department, and then handed over the parcel containing the one hundred and fifty-five pounds. Her welcoming look quickly changed to one of slight suspicion. I could sense her thoughts, and I'm sure she believed the money had come from some illegal venture. She made an excuse and went to fetch her manager.

The bank manager was a small man with a pencil moustache defining his upper lip, and I could smell the distinct scent of Brylcream in his carefully styled hair, which was very popular at the time.

"Could I invite you into my office?" he said with a rather odd expression, his mouth squeezed into a tight, unconvincing smile.

His office was a display of highly polished dark wood furniture, and the air was filled with the fragrance of furniture polish and roses. A coal fire burned brightly, indicating his preference for comfort.

He offered me a seat and took his place behind the desk.

"So," he began, consulting my name from the bank book, "Mr Middlebrough, with this sort of amount, we often advise our esteemed customers regarding investments, bonds, and such. I see that you are a war veteran, and we offer help where we can." He sat back, appearing somewhat smug.

"That's interesting," I replied. "It would be nice to see some growth, but I'm not entirely sure about my plans yet."

He continued, "Do you have employment?" His question felt rather blunt, almost accusing.

"No," I replied calmly, "I intend to pursue a private venture. You see, I grew up on the canals."

I couldn't help but notice his cheeks twitching as if he had received a slight electric shock. His unease was evident.

"It's embarrassing, but… can I ask how you came about such a sum?" he ventured.

I studied him for a moment and realized that he was in an awkward situation. Although I was slightly insulted, I kept my composure. "Rest assured, it was nothing illegal… if that's what worries you," I reassured him.

"Please don't be offended and accept my reassurance that I will endeavour to make you some profit on your money."

"Very well, I shall leave it in your trusted hands."

He smiled contentedly, "Very well then, I'll make a quick snap decision, leave some cash for everyday use and let me deal with the rest including your army payments."

We shook hands on the deal and I felt quite important.

This incident at the bank, where my sudden wealth raised eyebrows, marked the beginning of a new phase in my life, one where I would have the means to make choices and forge my own path. The unexpected twists and turns that life presented were becoming more apparent, and I was eager to embrace the opportunities that lay ahead.

Troy and I found ourselves in need of shelter, so we needed to find a solution. I remembered a substantial stable near Dewsbury Marina where we had stayed several times before, I knew it could provide us with the protection we needed as the winter months approached. I had previously met the owner and he was delighted to let me long-term lease part of the building.

The proprietor, a middle-aged man, had experienced the profound loss of both his sons during the war in Belgium. His grief and sorrow were unmistakable, etched into every line on his face.

"We aren't receiving as many animals nowadays. Most folks have switched to diesel engines," his voice, devoid of vitality, reflected his inner pain. "You'll have to provide your own bedding and feed," he said.

The barn offered a simple yet practical solution to our problems, it provided the essentials: a hearth, which was usually used by the farrier I used for cooking, ample straw and sacking to create a rudimentary bed for me and plenty of room for Troy. It was simple but adequate accommodation just right for what we needed… a place where the comforting warmth of a crackling fire made it seem like home.

Sitting close to my fire one evening I tried to work out what my future direction should be. Although I had enough money to buy a barge of my own I want to change to find a new direction and to move on with my life. I'd heard about a farm yard sale and out of curiosity I attended. The farmyard was bustling with potential buyers and folk who were there just to be nosey. The items for sale were neatly laid out for inspection… there were ploughs and cultivators on several robust waggons. One of the waggons caught my eye perhaps I could move things on the roads instead of the canals. I patiently waited through the auction until the waggon came up for sale. There wasn't much interest in it and so I think I got it for what you might call a bargain price. I'd taken some cash with me just in case which meant I could instantly conclude the purchase. The waggon shafts were a comfortable fit for Troy and we proudly towed away what I hoped would be a new beginning for us both. The skills we'd honed navigating the canals were transferred to our road haulage business. Loading the wagon meticulously, ensuring the secure fastening of every item, became a practised routine. I transformed our expertise into a service, extending aid to those in need along the way. I suppose I could have looked for another barge… but I felt to have moved on and those days were behind me.

Setting the fee at thirty shillings an hour was a risk, perhaps more than the norm. Yet, through persistence and a stroke of good fortune, enough work flowed our way to meet essential needs… it covered the rent, providing sustenance for both Troy and myself, and secured a modest surplus for unforeseen emergencies."

Chapter Twenty
The Vardo.

One day, as we travelled through the countryside, an interesting sight caught my eye. It was an old gipsy caravan, the kind you often see painted in vibrant green hues and decorated with similar artwork that was popular on the barges. These caravans, known as Vardos, had a real appeal to me. While their exteriors might appear rustic, inside, they were often fitted with the essentials for a cosy nomadic life. I had some romantic notion of travelling the highways in this iconic vehicle.

I couldn't resist the temptation to enquire about its availability. Little did I know that this caravan would become a vehicle to carry me into a new life.

'It needs a fair bit of work doing to it,' the owner honestly admitted as I handed over five pounds for it. It fit nicely into the barn and that following winter I devoted my time customising it and making it my own. I removed all the wheels to grease the axles but one of the wheels was past repair and I had to search out a wheelwright to build me a new one. It took a while to get it into the condition I wanted, inside needed sprucing up."

Their conversation was interrupted by the clock chiming. Joe hurriedly checked his watch.

"Oh hell, sorry, Walter, but I need to be home, we're going to look at a new school for Debbie. Julie will go spare if I'm late again."

"No problem, I hope it is right for you and of course Debbie. We can pick this up later." Walter gave him a warm smile.

Joe arrived home later than he'd promised, and as he entered, he could feel the tension in the room. Julie, stood in the kitchen leaning against the work unit with her arms crossed, clearly upset.

"You're late, Joe," she said, sounding annoyed.

Joe felt a pang of guilt. "I know… sorry," he replied wearily. "Work… you know how demanding it can be."

"Okay, I suppose I ought to be used to your timekeeping by now." She knew Joe worked long hours and she knew he did try to be on time.

"We have that appointment at the new school today, Joe," Julie reminded him, tapping her wristwatch her voice gentler now. "You know how crucial it is for Debbie. We can't afford to be late."

Joe nodded, fully aware of the importance of this appointment.

"Sorry, I know what a game-changer this might be for her. However, the tuition fees are a big concern, considering our already tight finances."

"I did ring and speak to the school today," Joe explained, trying to sound optimistic but feeling the weight of the financial burden. "They seem positive about Debbie joining. But you know our money situation. It worries me how we'll manage it all."

Julie came closer and put her hand on Joe's arm. "We'll figure it out together," she assured him. "Debbie deserves the best chance, and if this school can provide it, we'll make it work somehow."

Joe smiled, grateful for Julie's unwavering support. They knew they had challenges ahead, but their love for Debbie and their determination to give her every opportunity she needed would guide them through.

The new school was a glimmer of hope for Debbie. They had heard promising things about it. It was known for its specialised programs tailored to children like Debbie, who needed extra support and understanding.

Walking into the school's reception area, Joe and Julie were immediately embraced by a vibrant atmosphere. The walls were a gallery of colourful artworks, a testament to the creativity and talent of the students. A friendly receptionist, who exuded warmth despite her apparent physical disabilities, greeted them from her wheelchair with a beaming smile. She handed them beautifully designed brochures that intricately detailed the school's diverse curriculum and an extensive array of enriching activities. They were invited into the headteacher's office which more resembled a cosy sitting room.

The headteacher greeted them, "Hello, I'm Jean Hardy headteacher. Please take a seat."

Julie couldn't help but feel a sense of relief as they spoke with the school's head. She explained how they focused on individualised learning plans, small class sizes, and a team of dedicated teachers and therapists.

Joe's concerns about the school's affordability lingered in the back of his mind, but as he watched Debbie interact with some of the other children in a nearby classroom, he couldn't deny the potential this place held. The children seemed happy and engaged, and it was clear that the staff cared deeply for their well-being.

"We do have some financial aid options," Jean mentioned as if reading Joe's mind. "We believe every child deserves a chance, regardless of their family's financial situation. There are a few available grants and some help from the government."

Julie exchanged a hopeful glance with Joe.

"Look, we are close to the Christmas break, what about her coming into class part-time and seeing how she settles in? There is no charge."

"That would be great, thank you," Julie said gratefully.

They both knew that they would need to make sacrifices and work out a budget, but seeing the positive environment and witnessing the school's commitment to helping children like Debbie filled them with renewed determination.

As they left the school, they knew that this was a significant decision that could affect their family's finances for years to come. Yet, they couldn't help but feel that it was a step in the right direction, a step towards giving Debbie the support and education she needed to thrive.

As they returned home they were both absorbed by their own thoughts and what they had just witnessed. Debbie played in the backseat with her toy puppy.

"Did you like that school?" Julie asked when they were settled in at home.

Debbie looked deep in thought for a moment. "Yes... I'd like to go to school there."

That evening, Joe and Julie decided it was time to take a closer look at their financial situation. Sitting at the kitchen table, they spread out their bank statements, bills, and a notepad for jotting down ideas. The room was filled with the soft glow of a table lamp, creating a cosy atmosphere that encouraged thoughtful conversation.

Julie, with a pen in hand, started by listing their monthly expenses. She meticulously detailed everything, from mortgage payments and utility bills to groceries and entertainment. As she wrote, Joe leaned in, paying close attention to the numbers.

"Seems like our expenses are pretty consistent," Julie remarked. "But we could probably cut back on dining out and those impulse purchases."

Joe nodded in agreement. "You're right, Julie. We need to be more mindful of where our money goes. It's amazing how those little things add up."

With a determined look, Joe took the lead in examining their savings and investments.

"We've been saving steadily," Joe noted, "but maybe we should explore other investment options to make our money work harder for us."

As they continued their financial review, Joe and Julie felt a renewed sense of purpose.

With a shared vision and a commitment to making informed financial decisions, Joe and Julie knew they were ready to embark on this journey toward securing their financial well-being and realising their dreams.

The next morning, Joe returned to Walter's house, as he entered, Walter, in his usual calm manner, greeted him with a nod. Joe felt a sense of comfort in the familiar surroundings and he knew that he could speak openly.

As he settled into the worn armchair, Walter brewed a pot of tea, their conversations flowing easily like old friends.

Joe's voice quivered slightly as he broached the subject that had kept him awake the previous night.

"Walter, we saw the school for Debbie yesterday. It's a good place."

"Oh, that's good I was going to ask you how you'd got on." Walter, his eyes reflecting the wisdom of years, leaned back in his chair and took a thoughtful sip of tea. "These decisions about your child's future, they're never easy, are they? But you see, sometimes life surprises you when you least expect it." He paused a hint of nostalgia in his gaze.

Joe nodded, his eyes reflecting a mix of hope and anxiety.

"We're willing to stretch ourselves thin, but I worry about the strain it might put on us, especially with the other bills and expenses. It's not like a state school the term fees are quite hefty."

Walter's gaze softened, and he reached out to pat Joe's hand reassuringly. "You know, Joe, I wish I could help you more. You and your family have become important to me, and it pains me to see you in this situation. Maybe I could help."

Joe felt a lump in his throat at Walter's concern. He knew that Walter had already been through so much in his life, and the last thing he wanted was to burden his friend with his own problems.

"Thank you, Walter," Joe said, his voice filled with gratitude. "Your willingness to help means more to me than I can express. But, really, we'll manage somehow. We'll find a way. Your friendship and support already mean the world to me, and that's more valuable than any amount of money." He spoke hand on heart.

Walter smiled, his eyes reflecting his understanding.

"I appreciate that, Joe. Just remember, if things ever get too tough, don't hesitate to reach out. Friends look out for each other, no matter what."

As they sat there, the unspoken bond between them grew even stronger, a silent promise of solidarity in the face of life's challenges.

"How about a walk today?" Walter suggested a faint sparkle in his eyes. "The fresh air could work wonders for both of us. We could bring along some of that leftover bread and head down to the park, just like old times, and feed the ducks."

Joe's face brightened with enthusiasm. "That's a great idea. I'll get your wheelchair ready, and we can head to the park. But if you'd prefer, we could stroll along the towpath again and then to the park. I remember it's your favourite route."

Walter's wheelchair rolled smoothly along the familiar path, the weathered towpath they had traversed before. The sun hung lazily behind thin watery clouds and the chill in the air reminded them that Christmas was barely a month away. Birds chattered in the nearby trees, and the sound of the road traffic blurred in the background.

Joe and Walter strolled down memory lane, sharing hearty laughs and quiet moments that held a depth words couldn't capture. As they reached the park, the verdant surroundings beckoned them to pause.

"Let's take a breather," Joe suggested, assisting Walter from his wheelchair. Together, they settled on a bench near the water, breaking bread to share with the ducks swarming nearby.

The park exuded a serene aura, enveloping them in a tranquil embrace. Ducks squabbled over the bread crumbs, their playful antics drawing smiles from Joe and Walter. They sat in peaceful silence, soaking in the sights and sounds of nature.

The calmness of the scene washed over them, momentarily lifting the weight of their everyday concerns. It was a respite from the hustle, a cherished interlude in their journey, reminding them of the beauty found in simple moments shared between friends. Walter took a deep breath, his eyes fixed on the rippling water as he broke the silence.

"You know, Joe, sometimes I think about the past, about how much has changed since those days in the war."

Joe nodded, his gaze also drawn to the water. "Aye, I suppose it's hard not to, Walter. You've seen and been through so much. Two wars really I suppose."

"Three if you include Korea." Walter's voice was tinged with a hint of nostalgia. "I often wonder what happened to the lads from the regiment, the ones who made it back and the others I met along the way."

Joe sighed, his thoughts mirroring Walter's. "I reckon they've scattered to the winds. Some finding their way, others maybe not so lucky."

Walter's eyes met Joe's, he desperately wanted to help him with his financial problems. "You know, Joe, I may not have much to offer these days, but if there's ever a time when you need a hand, don't hesitate to ask."

Joe's heart swelled with gratitude. "I appreciate that, Walter. But like I said, Julie and I will manage."

Walter watched as a squadron of Canada Geese noisily circled the water and then landed on the lake, they splashed and called for a few moments and then once everyone was settled they swam around each other.

"I like feeding the ducks and sharing a chat, it's not all that bad, is it?"

Joe's smile mirrored Walter's as he realized the profound truth in those words.

Later when Joe arrived home he told Julie of Walter's kind offer of help.

"Oh dear, I hope he doesn't think you have told him to try and get some money out of him" Julie was obviously embarrassed and concerned. As they settled into their cosy living room that evening, Joe couldn't help but reflect on the day's events.

"Well, I've signed her up, she starts in the New Year. But she can start visiting their classes whenever she wants… just to get her used to going," Julie said with a nervous smile.

"That's good of them, I'm sure she'll settle easier if she knows the routine better." Joe was determined they would do their utmost to help their little girl.

While sipping a cup of tea, Joe couldn't help but bring up the topic of Walter's offer once more. "You know, Julie, Walter's offer really got me thinking."

Julie looked at him with curiosity. "What do you mean, love?"

Joe explained, "Well, he's been through so much, especially during the war. Yet, here he is, willing to help us in any way he can and yet he hardly knows us. It's made me realise something."

Julie leaned closer, her interest piqued. "What is it, Joe?"

"I think," Joe began, his voice filled with conviction, "that maybe we've been keeping too much to ourselves, especially about Debbie's condition. We've always tried to handle things on our own, but maybe it's time to let our friends in a bit more, to share our challenges and triumphs."

Julie considered Joe's words for a moment. "You might be right, love. We've always been a bit too proud to ask for help, but maybe it's time to lean on our friends when we need them."

Joe nodded, feeling a weight lifting off his shoulders. "Exactly, Julie. And maybe, in doing so, we can also help Walter. He's been lonely for a long time, and our friendship means a lot to him."

Julie smiled, touched by Joe's empathy. "I agree, Joe. Let's not just be recipients of kindness but givers as well. It's the true spirit of friendship."

Chapter Twenty-One.
Another Long Walk.

The sun was at its noontime zenith as Joe arrived at Walter's doorstep.

Joe was in a surprisingly good mood, and a contented smile played on his lips. His late-night conversation with Julie had worked wonders in setting his mind at ease. It was as if her words had cast away the clouds of doubt and uncertainty that had hung over him.

"Sorry I'm late, Walter," Joe said as he stepped into the cosy living room. "I had to call in at my office and check my workload for the upcoming week."

Walter, seated in his favourite armchair, looked up from the book he had been flicking through. "Not to worry," he replied, his voice as warm as the flickering fire in the hearth. "I've been keeping myself occupied, sorting out some of my books."

As Joe settled into the room, he couldn't help but appreciate the simple and tranquil atmosphere that surrounded him. It was moments like these, in the company of his newfound friend that made him realise the beauty of life's quiet moments.

With a sense of purpose and genuine interest, Joe settled into his role as Walter's scribe. He retrieved a notepad and pen from his bag, ready to capture the rich instalments of Walter's experiences.

"So, Walter," Joe began, he flicked the tape recorder's switch, "Where shall we start today? What part of your life's journey would you like to share?"

Walter leaned back in his chair, his eyes distant for a moment as he reminisced.

"Let's see, Joe. How about we start with the years I spent travelling the country? Those were some of the most exhilarating times of my life. I told you yesterday about me buying the caravan."

Joe's pen hovered over the notepad, ready to transcribe the tales that were about to unfold. "Ah yes, the Vardo you called it. Travelling sounds fascinating. Another long walk, I suppose. Please, take me on another journey with your words." Joe smiled at the thought of where they might be heading.

"I set off on a journey that led me through diverse landscapes and experiences. Unbelievably, I had no direction in mind and we sort of headed where the roads seemed to lead. It felt as if we were following some ancient instinct, a northward pull through the dales and along the old A6, a winding road that meandered through Lancaster and followed the Lune valley and eventually unveiled the breathtaking scenery of the Lake District.

One day I even picked up a squaddie who was heading back home from his barracks and gave him a lift. Our pace was not much faster than walking but at least there was no effort involved. It was Autumn, and the fells had already erupted into a riot of colours as if nature herself were celebrating the changing of the seasons. While the rest of the country was succumbing to the encroaching cold, the west coast held onto a milder climate, an opportune discovery that led me to make a decision: I would spend the winter in this enchanting region. I had heard of a small village known as Cartmel, steeped in history, and home to one of the few priories that had survived the tumultuous waves of the Reformation. The allure of such a place was irresistible, and I resolved to pay it a visit.

I rounded Morecambe Bay, passed through Grange over Sands, and headed into the Lake District. Scouring the landscape for a place that seemed both secluded and serene, I eventually found a spot with a sea view to one side and the towering mountains to the other and set up camp. I gave Troy a good brushing and covered his back with a blanket and tarpaulin to keep him warm through the night.

That evening sitting on the shingle I watched the tide flow gently into and around Morecambe Bay. I'd made a small fire, it was just enough to keep out the chill and cook my meal. However, my peace and quiet was soon interrupted by an unexpected visitor. The local constable, with a gruff voice that mirrored his authoritative presence, knocked on the side of my van.

"So, what are you doing around here, lad?" he enquired.

I met his scrutiny with honesty, "I'm simply seeking a place to spend the winter," I replied "I'm still trying to lose the war from my head and cast off a few ghosts."

Although I think he sympathised with me, he responded sternly, "You can't stay here." I took his word for it, but he never offered an explanation.

As his typical interrogation ensued, he probed into my origins, my name, and my intentions and eventually the living space of my Vardo. I think he was looking for any signs of illegal activity.

"Where did you serve?" he asked, "My lad was in the Royal Navy."

"Oh, so was my brother Jack."

He was quite impressed and seemed friendlier. He walked around my Vardo and he seemed to be drawn to Troy. 'Fine looking animal he said' as he slapped Troy's neck. With his hands on his hips, he offered some advice, "I suggest you follow the coast north and ask permission from one of the farmers if you can stay through the winter."

"Thank you for your advice officer," I said and then enquired, "Will it be possible for me to stay here for the night?"

"As long as you are gone first thing and don't leave any mess, it'll be alright."

Chapter Twenty-Two
Farm Hand.

In the thick sea mist of the next morning, I carefully loaded up my belongings, making sure that no traces of my brief visit remained behind. The mist added an ethereal quality to the landscape, shrouding it in a mysterious ambience as I prepared to move on. Even Troy seemed jittery as I secured the traces and backed him in between the shafts of the van.

After some searching and many miles, I eventually stumbled upon a welcoming place to stay. A friendly farmer named: Bill Thomson agreed to let me set up camp on his land for the winter.

"You can stop as long as you want, mind you, I'll expect a bit of a hand when I need it." He said.

"Sounds fine to me, Bill, I'll park the Vardo. This is Troy, my faithful friend," I said introducing him.

"He looks a fine animal, I've a spare loose box for him."

I accepted his terms and found a level spot to park the van. Troy, seemed content with our new home. He had a cosy shelter for the chilly nights and a pleasant pasture to share with two other ponies and a lively flock of native Herdwick sheep. There were plenty of bales of hay and straw for his bedding too.

Bill, welcomed me into his life, he was an enigmatic figure in many ways. He had a quietness about him, a tendency to keep his thoughts and feelings well-guarded. Every action he took seemed to require an extra effort, and there was an undeniable undercurrent of sadness that surrounded him. He told me that he was a widower and still reeling from the loss of his wife who had been taken by a fever only a few years before. He was generous and he possessed a heart of gold. Over time, he allowed me into his world, and the bond of friendship grew stronger with each passing day. It was through our shared labour and the rhythms of farm life that our friendship developed.

The work on the farm was demanding, but it brought a sense of satisfaction. Early mornings became my new normal routine. We'd eat a hearty breakfast and then set off to tackle our daily chores. I must say that he was a pretty good cook and he could make even a basic meal seem special.

We worked well together, herding the cows for milking, and carefully stacking straw and hay to keep the animals going through winter. We had some light moments and shared our laughter too.

He had an old threshing machine that I made into a project and whenever there was a spare moment I'd work on repairing it. We also put Troy to work to earn his keep, I think that he enjoyed towing things around the farm, it was pretty light work compared to what he was used to.

As the days grew shorter and the nights colder, Bill's need for companionship became increasingly evident. I sensed that my presence served as a welcome respite from the isolation that often accompanied the long, wintry evenings.

It reached a point where my van was no longer a suitable shelter against the biting cold. Bill, ever the kind soul, offered me the use of a spare bedroom in his farmhouse. It had not been used for years but with an effort I was able to clear the cobwebs and make it feel like home.

On those chilly evenings, we'd sit by the crackling fire, open a few bottles of a local beer, and listen to the wireless. We exchanged stories, digging into our very different pasts, and sharing moments of joy and sorrow. In these conversations, I sensed that I was not only a guest but also a source of comfort for Bill in his grieving process.

Between our jobs on the farm, we went fishing. The sandy coast there is famous for flatfish and shellfish and we often took our small boat out and went to catch our meals. I don't think you can beat the taste of freshly caught fish.

On some days, I took Troy for long walks along the rugged coast, and to my surprise, Bill asked, "Would you mind if I tagged along, I must say I've never really taken time to do any sightseeing."

It seemed as if he was rediscovering his own land through fresh eyes. He would pause and gaze at the scenery. "Well I never knew that was there," he'd say pointing to some feature in the landscape.

In many ways we were kindred spirits, we both were looking to find inner peace and these walks certainly helped with that.

Our time together during that winter was a period of healing and rediscovery for both of us. As we worked the land, went fishing and roamed the fields with Troy, the bonds of friendship and the magic of the landscape transformed our lives in ways we had never anticipated.

I spent Christmas with him. We ate a duck from his yard and huge potatoes from his field. In front of a roaring fire, we listened to a carol service on his brand-new radio and drank a little more beer than we should have. There was no king's speech back then just some pompous chap from the BBC wishing us all a Merry Christmas."

Walter paused as he thought back to his old friend.

"There was a really heavy snowfall that year and although Bill's sheep were hardy enough, we spent hours digging them out of snow drifts and taking them nearer the farm. We'd been extra busy and I was frozen to the bone by the time we got into the shelter of the barn. It was obvious that Bill wanted to ask me something. He was also feeling the cold, he wore a couple of sacks around his shoulders on top of his heavy coat. He leant on his crop and asked "Can you stay a few weeks more and help bring the sheep in for lambing? This is the coldest winter I can remember for some while."

"Yes, of course, I'll stay and help if you like," I offered.

"We've got to set up some pens in the big shed for the expectant ewes," he said, a smile replacing his usual weary expression.

I stayed on at the farm, for that spring's lambing season, and what a remarkable period it turned out to be.

Each day was an adventure, and the farm was a bustling hub of life and anticipation. While most of the ewes were capable of managing the births on their own, there were occasions when we had to intervene, and those moments were nothing short of exhilarating.

The chilly nights often gave way to crisp, early mornings filled with the hopeful bleating of expectant mothers. Armed with our lanterns, we'd make our way to the lambing shed, where the atmosphere buzzed with an air of expectancy. The straw beneath our feet whispered with anticipation and each ewe carried the promise of new beginnings. Our breath hung in misty clouds around our faces and our cheeks shone bright red as we worked.

I can still vividly recall the sensation of helping my first new life onto the planet. The sheer joy and sense of accomplishment that coursed through me when the lamb was born safely was indescribable. I had knelt in the straw to assist with the birth, and when the lamb emerged, wet, fragile, and bewildered, I just sat back on my heels, awestruck. 'Good Lord, will you look at that,' I muttered.

It was as if I had been granted a front-row seat to the miracle of birth, a privilege that left an indelible mark on my heart.

"That feeling never grows cold," Bill said a huge smile across his face. "I've helped birth hundreds of lambs and calves and it's always the same. Folk say farmers are tough old sods but that sight as new life appears, it brings a tear to your eye."

I helped the mother clean it up using fresh straw, and, of course, she licked her new baby clean. Within minutes, the lamb was up, and the bond with her mother strengthened with each nuzzle and lick. When it finally realised that there was a meal on offer, it latched onto the ewe, its little tail wagging appreciatively.

Our days were filled with assisting ewes in labour to ensure the newborns received the care and warmth they needed. We'd watch as the cutest of lambs took their first tentative steps, their small, wobbly legs gradually gaining strength. It was a daily spectacle of resilience, a triumphant reminder of life's persistence in the face of adversity."

As the weeks passed and the lambing season reached its peak, the farm was transformed into a joyful chorus of bleats and laughter. Bill and I worked in harmony. We'd always have something to tell each other.

And through it all, Troy, my steadfast companion, became an honorary member of the farm. It seemed as though he got great pleasure listening to the lambs shouting for their mothers. He'd watch over the lambs, his presence a calming influence on both the animals and us. The farm had become our shared sanctuary, a place where new life bloomed in abundance, and the seasons turned with a sense of wonder.

The spring's lambing season was a chapter of life filled with twists and turns, unexpected joys, and a deep connection to the rhythm of the land. It was an unforgettable journey, one that left me with a profound appreciation for the beauty of nature and the boundless capacity of the human heart to find joy in the simplest of moments."

Joe switched off his tape and smiled happily at Walter. "It sounds as though you were enjoying life."

"Yes, the lifestyle was addictive but my itchy feet began nagging at me. Anyway, for the next few months, I felt that I was needed by Bill and I owed him a great deal for the joy we had shared during the lambing."

Walter suddenly continued and Joe was caught off guard and had to hurriedly switch his tape back on.

"One day, the inevitable happened. I found myself standing at the farm gate, gazing wistfully along the winding road that stretched out into the countryside. The sense of wanderlust had been building within me for some time. It was then that I felt a familiar presence beside me… a comforting, gentle weight against my side. It was my old faithful friend, Troy.

Troy, with his majestic presence and soulful eyes, stood with me. As we both stared out into the vast landscape, he leaned in and gave me a gentle nudge with his massive shoulder. I responded with a fond slap on his neck, a gesture that we had shared countless times over the years. In return, Troy placed his head on my shoulder, as if to say, "Come on, my friend, it's time we hit the road again."

I had prepared for this moment meticulously. The Vardo, our faithful travelling companion, had been carefully inspected. All the wheels had been removed and the axles greased, ensuring a smooth journey ahead. The farrier had paid a visit, and he had tenderly reshaped Troy's hooves and fitted him with new shoes for the road that lay ahead. They were cleverly designed so that I could knock studs into them if I needed more grip, a bit like football boots really.

I turned to my dear friend, and with a sense of gratitude, I shared, "I'm afraid I think that it's time to move on. Bill, you've been a gracious host during my time here and I'm very grateful to you for sharing your world with me."

Without a word, he reached out and placed a hand on my shoulder, a silent reassurance that spoke volumes about the time we had spent together.

In that brief touch, I felt the weight of his unspoken appreciation. With a nod, he said, 'You'll always have a place here, should your journey bring you back this way.'"

With Troy by my side and the Vardo prepared, I felt the familiar thrill of adventure coursing through my veins. The open road beckoned, promising new landscapes, encounters, and the freedom that only a nomadic life could provide. It was time to continue our journey, and with a final farewell to Bill and the farm and the clip-clop of Troy's feet I set out once more, guided by the ever-enticing horizon."

Joe studied his friend a moment, "Were you sad to leave? You and Bill had become friends and shared your life stories."

"Yes and no, I wasn't ready to settle down, and yet, as you say we were good friends." Walter thought about the situation for a moment.

Joe clicked off his tape, "Maybe, that's a good place to leave it for now."

Yes, I think you're right," Walter replied thoughtfully. "Will you have time to call tomorrow?"

Joe took his diary from his jacket pocket and flicked through its pages.

"Yes, I think we can make an early start. Is there anything I can bring for lunch?"

"You mean dinner, we don't do lunch around here, tea times what you call dinner," Walter laughed.

Joe left and soon after Walter settled back down with his book but his mind was on the next part of his walk.

Chapter Twenty-Three
Scotland.

   I continued heading northward to the picturesque landscapes of Scotland. My life had taken on the nomadic rhythms of a tinker, just like the ones I used to meet in the marketplaces when I travelled the canals. I took on various odd jobs wherever the opportunity arose. Along the way, I picked up a few practical skills, including the use of a hand-operated grinding stone. I became quite handy at sharpening knives and garden shears for the folks I met on my travels, I even had a sign on the back of the Vardo advertising my services.

   I had a knack for fixing what seemed beyond repair, just like Owd Jos used to say, "There's nowt that can't be fixed with a bit of elbow grease."

   I salvaged lawnmowers, breathed new life into old bicycles, and set right a few garden gates that had seen better days. It brought me satisfaction, but the rewards weren't always in the form of cash, mind you. Sometimes, it'd be a simple meal or one time, I repaired a man's ladders that he used for apple picking, and he thanked me with a bag of his apple harvest.

   But the most peculiar payment that sticks out was after I'd fixed a woman's gate, which had fallen off its hinges. She welcomed me into her cosy home and offered a good, strong cup of tea, served in the finest china, and laid out on a beautifully hand-crafted cloth. The room had a calm, soothing ambience, and there was a faint trace of lavender in the air. I was fascinated when she set up a card table and proceeded to give me a Tarot Card reading. I was fascinated by it all and she was remarkably accurate about my past, although I reckon she was just good at reading people.

   Life was simple and straightforward in those days, and I knew I had my bank account to fall back on if needed. To the best of my recollection, I don't think that I ever needed to withdraw a single penny during that time.

   It was during these travels that I stumbled upon an interesting opportunity. I was enjoying some local hospitality, a beer, and a steaming bowl of broth when I heard about a job opening on a sprawling estate, nestled in the heart of the Scottish Lowlands. They were in dire need of assistance in moving timber, but the rugged terrain made it impossible to bring in any form of machinery.

   The challenge intrigued me, and the prospect of working amidst the untamed beauty of the Scottish wilderness was a bit of a lure. Little did I know that this decision would not only change the course of my journey but also lead to a chapter in my life filled with unique adventures and unexpected encounters."

Walter stopped a moment to clear his mind. The pause in their conversation allowed Joe to absorb the unexpected twist in Walter's story. Walter acknowledged the need for more coffee, knowing that the next part of his story would be quite unbelievable and entirely unexpected.

"I think we need a coffee, Joe."

"Yes, I think so too. I'll only be a jiffy."

Off he went and boiled the kettle. On his return, they both sipped their coffee, Walter was ready to continue his narrative:

"The next stage of my journey was truly extraordinary. You see, the estate manager in Scotland, the very man I was to work for, turned out to be none other than my old Captain from the past. Initially, he didn't remember me, of course, it had been years and my appearance had surely changed. However, as I recounted some of my memories and showed him my medal, he finally remembered who I was.

Our reunion was not one filled with old friendship but rather a mutual acknowledgement that our paths had once crossed, albeit under very different circumstances.

We were given the task of hauling timber from the forest onto the well-trodden paths across the estate. Troy and I handled the challenging parts, such as climbing hillsides and navigating through dense trees. After that, another team would collect the timber we left behind. It was mostly just Troy and me, working day in and day out amidst stunning landscapes. However, it wasn't without its risks. Some of the hills were too steep for Troy, and the ground was treacherous; our feet would get stuck in soggy patches, and broken branches often snagged at our legs.

Yet, occasionally, the bright autumn sun would illuminate the forest's golden-bronze bracken, casting a spell of enchantment around the trees. On certain hill slopes, there were inviting patches of lush green grass where we'd take a break. While Troy contentedly grazed, I lay down and listened to the forest's melodies. I'd hear a golden eagle's call somewhere in the distance or a stag's bellow in the morning mist. The wind created a unique symphony as it weaved through the tall pine trees.

Gazing at the drifting clouds above would remind me of my carefree childhood days spent with Jack, searching for dragons and monsters amongst the clouds. I recalled our trek over the moors from Marsden and the captivating, spirited Mary Hendrick whom we assisted in Manchester. Thankfully, thoughts of the trenches were few. The beauty and solace of nature acted as a balm for my troubled soul.

It was autumn, two years since my last stint on Bill's farm and I realised that I had come a long way mentally since then. I found companionship amongst the lads working as lumberjacks in those remote woods. Some of whom had also just returned from the trenches. We were kindred spirits and I could see in their eyes what that brief life had done to them.

Often the clouds would cover the hilltops and there would be a slow rumble of thunder echoing down the glens and I knew that just like me those rumbles took them back to the stinking hell we had left. Then a constant rumble of gunfire was our daily bread and fear was smeared across it. The horses were stabled overnight in crude briers in sheltered glens safe and warm under their blankets. We were never short of firewood and we'd gather around a roaring campfire, swap stories, and cook sausages on wooden sticks. Our laughter and tales of adventure filled the nights, making us feel alive with possibilities. Later and usually after a beer or maybe a local whiskey or two we'd fall asleep under the vast, starlit skies.

Every day, they'd give me directions to the timber that needed moving but really all I had to do was follow the sound of axes and saws felling the timber. The work was more rewarding than I could have imagined, both in terms of friendship and finances." A sudden thought seemed to jolt Walter's memory. "One time, it was Troy and me to the rescue. One of the lumberjacks had fallen over a steep cliff, he had managed to grab a branch sticking out from a fallen tree but he was precariously placed with a drop of maybe sixty feet below him. I peered over the edge and had a clear view of the lad. I backed Troy towards the edge and lowered our towing rope down to him. A few of the other lads came to help. The stranded lad tied the rope around his middle and slowly Troy managed to haul him back to safety. We all had a few extra beers that night. Before I left that lad gave me a wonderful tartan plaid," Walter points to where Joe is sitting, "You're sitting on it now." Walter paused briefly and stared into the distance. "But then, one day, Troy stumbled, the logs we were hauling kept moving and almost pulled Troy over. I couldn't ignore the signs of his ageing. He wasn't hurt, but he told me in his own way that he'd had enough. And so, with a heavy heart, I made the difficult choice to hand in my notice. It was time to prioritise Troy's well-being over everything else. Together, with a very fat wallet, we embarked on a steady journey back to Yorkshire. I thought about calling to see my friend Bill on his farm but the weather was closing in for winter and I was aiming for home."

Joe couldn't help but smile, his eyes reflecting the warmth and admiration he felt for Walter. "My words, Walter," he said with a contented sigh, "You are becoming a very skilled storyteller. I find myself completely absorbed in your tale instead of merely being your scribe."

Walter's face, broke into a modest grin. "Well, Joe," he replied in his measured, plainspoken way, "It's not every day that I get to share these memories with someone who truly listens and cares. Your presence, and your words, breathe life into my stories. But after all the books and the stories I've enjoyed, told by master writers, well then it's not surprising that I can put a tale together"

In that shared moment, seated comfortably, Joe and Walter's roles transcended the mere recorder and storyteller. They had become partners in the art of storytelling, forging a connection that went beyond words. It was a testament to the power of their friendship and the magic of stories that bound them together.

"Please continue, Walter."

"So, there I was," Walter said, his voice tinged with a mix of nostalgia and melancholy, "Back in Huddersfield, with the realization that my days of travel were behind me. It was a bittersweet homecoming, I retired Troy to a sanctuary for old workhorses, a decision that weighed heavily on my heart but I knew he'd be well looked after and he could live out his days in peace."

He paused for a moment as if lost in the memories of that parting with Troy, before he continued, "Leaving Troy behind was one of the hardest things I've ever done. He had been my constant companion, my confidant, and my friend through thick and thin. But I knew it was time for him to enjoy his well-earned rest."

Walter's voice grew softer as he spoke of Troy, "I visited Troy often at the sanctuary, and even though he was in a place of comfort, I couldn't help but feel a pang of sadness each time I left him.

I took lodgings near the centre of town and sold the Vardo to a family of travellers who wanted to hit the road in traditional style."

He shifted his focus to the house across the road, his childhood home, "And then, I stumbled upon this house," he said. "It was advertised in the evening news and well within my price range. I felt like fate had brought me back to where I began, a chance to reconnect with my roots and the memories of my youth."

Walter's gaze drifted out of the window, his thoughts returning to those quiet streets. He concluded with a wistful smile, "It's a reminder that no matter where life takes you, there's always a place to call home, a place where memories linger and maybe new adventures await."

Walter's story continued, his voice a mix of vulnerability and hope, as he sought to navigate the uncertain road that lay ahead, finding a new sense of purpose without his cherished companion.

"I missed Troy's company and I decided to start frequenting horse shows and sales, not with the intention of buying but more out of interest. It was at one such sale that I met Alice."

Joe smiled, "At last, I've been waiting for this bit." He declared rubbing his hands with glee.

Chapter Twenty-Four
Alice

"We met at a horse fair and auction, I was not there to buy, just to look but she was there to find a new pony. We hit it off straight away. She was a bonny lass, clever too, she'd had a grammar school education."

Joe notices that Walter's mood has lifted as soon as he starts to talk about her.

Walter leaned back in his chair, lost in memories of a time long past. "We were from different ends of the pond," he continued, his voice tinged with nostalgia. "Her father was a solicitor, well-to-do in every sense, and her mum, she ran the Girl Guides and baked scores of cakes and scones for various fundraisers, always so proper and prim." He paused, his gaze distant as he recalled those days.

"I had just bought this house, one hundred and sixty pounds it cost." Walter shook his head, a wistful smile on his face. "I can't believe it, one down the road sold for forty thousand a week or so ago; that was some investment."

Joe interjected eagerly, "You were talking about Alice."

Walter snapped back to his memories, a fond twinkle in his eye.

"Oh aye, Alice," he said with a warm grin. "I'd seen her a few times at various shows but never dared approach her, I suppose I didn't think she'd be interested in a chap like me. Then, out of the blue, I got a chance to talk to her. I was leaning against the gate and when she'd finished in the showring I opened it for her. She slipped out of the saddle and thanked me.

Alice was a vision in the saddle, she had an air of elegance that drew me in like a moth to a flame. Her eyes sparkled with an alluring curiosity as she gazed at me, and a mischievous smile played on her lips. Her presence was like a magnet, pulling me closer.

"I've seen you at a few shows," she said, her voice as melodious as a songbird. "Do you know anything about horses?"

I was surprised that she'd even noticed me. "Not much, maybe a little bit," I replied humbly, my heart pounding like a drum.

"I think you are being modest," she remarked her words a gentle caress on my soul. Our eyes remained locked, and I felt my mouth go as dry as the straw in the field.

"Will you wait for me?" Alice's request was a symphony of hope and anticipation, and my chest tightened with an overwhelming surge of emotions. I wanted to say, "I'll wait forever if you wish," but the words caught in my throat, so I simply nodded, my voice failing me.

As Alice led her horse away, I watched her with a mixture of awe and longing. I wished I'd worn a better jacket as if that would have made any difference. The minutes felt like hours as I waited, my thoughts consumed by the enchanting woman who had just walked into my life.

When I saw her again… time seemed to stand still. Alice was a vision of loveliness as if she had stepped out of a Hollywood set. She wore a perfect white dress, reminiscent of the Art Deco style that film stars of that time were famous for wearing. Pink roses adorned her attire, and a delicate lace trim around the hem matched her gloves. I gasped for breath as if I'd been punched in the chest. It was love at first sight, or perhaps the moment when my heart truly awakened from its slumber."

Walter's tale continued with a wistful smile, his memories vivid and his heart still warmed by the recollection.

"I helped her select a new pony, a skewbald thing with lovely markings. A gipsy lad was selling it, and Alice was going to pay the asking price, but I haggled with him and saved her five pounds. In 1922, that was a sizable amount, you know."

Joe couldn't help but interject, "You old romantic," he said, his voice filled with admiration.

Walter chuckled and continued. "Well, what can I say? Love makes a man do strange things. That pony, Beauty, became part of our story, and I like to think it was my first gift to the woman who would become my life partner. I had an instant daydream of us riding through the meadows, our laughter carried by the wind, and I knew then that my heart had come back to life."

He leaned forward, his voice growing softer as he continued. "Alice was quite taken by my spirit and resourcefulness that day. We laughed and I mustered the courage to ask her if she'd like to walk around the fair with me. I felt so shy and awkward.

In those days, the fairground rides were steam-driven marvels, brightly coloured horses chased each other to the sounds of steam-driven pipe organs belting out popular songs. Traction engines filled the air with smoke and the sound of spinning flywheels. There was the aroma of food cooking all mixed with the smell of horses and steam engines. At one end of the field, a brass band in bright purple uniforms played lively tunes. I bought her a toffee apple, and we went on a couple of roundabout rides. Folks were singing along, and I reckon they were just glad to forget their problems for a few moments."

His eyes twinkled with nostalgia as he continued, "I noticed that every man we passed turned to take a second glance at Alice. I tried to win her a cuddly toy at the coconut shy, but those coconuts seemed to be glued down. However, I had better luck with air rifle shooting, after all, I was a professional at shooting. I managed to win her a large teddy bear… it's still perched on top of the wardrobe upstairs."

A fleeting smile graced Walter's lips, but it was accompanied by a trace of bashfulness. He wiped a solitary tear from the corner of his eye and carried on, "When it was time for us to part, she asked me 'Will you want to see me again by any chance? I'm riding in the Gymkhana in Bingley next week.'

I was at a loss for words, I couldn't believe that she actually wanted to see me again. I mumbled a response, "That would be very nice… I'll make sure that I'm there."

Walter's memories continued to flow, and he paused, his thoughts turning inward as he remembered those early days of their courtship.

"Sounds like you were well smitten," Joe jibed, a mischievous glint in his eye.

Walter grinned and replied, "Aye, Joe, love at first sight, it was for both of us, I reckon."

"And did you turn up at the next gymkhana?" Joe probed, eager to hear more.

Walter's voice brightened at the thought of it. "You can bet your last penny I did. It took me several changes of tram but I eventually reached Bingley," he said with glee, his excitement and anticipation from all those years ago still apparent in his eyes.

Walter continued his story with a nostalgic smile, he was almost overpowered by the intensity of his memories.

"We'd met up a couple of times, but only at horse shows, and slowly we got to know each other over cups of tea. One time, we'd been walking around the fair for a while and she linked arms with me. It took my breath away. I didn't dare say anything; I just walked on as if it was the most natural thing in the world.

"Since I'd met her I'd been inspired to go into town and buy some smarter jackets and one of those Barbour coats, it was blooming expensive but I thought she was worth it. I think it was the first time in my life I'd been a little bit extravagant and it felt good. It looked stylish, with a neat tartan collar and I looked every bit the country gent. Alice checked me over, and her expression told me at once that she agreed.

'Come on, Walter,' she said, her voice filled with warmth. 'I want you to meet my parents.'"

As Walter recounted these moments, it was clear that the passage of time hadn't dimmed the vividness of these precious memories. However, his eyes clouded with sadness as he delved deeper into the story.

"But you see, Joe, those were different times," he began, his voice tinged with nostalgia and resignation. "Her parents didn't think I was the right match for their daughter. There were a lot of snobs about and class distinction was still widespread. White-collar workers had a certain arrogance about them, hardly wanting to associate with the working class. Still do, in some places," he sighed, wistfully.

From the moment we met, it was clear they were unimpressed by me. Their expectations for their daughter were sky-high as if she deserved nothing less than a lawyer or a business mogul. I watched as they clung to their notions of propriety and control, even though Alice was nearly 20 years old.

One day we met in a café about a mile from her home and she broke the news to me that her parents had forbidden her to see me again. I was dismayed, my heart heavy with disbelief. After all, I had faced hell to protect their cherished way of life. Anger and frustration welled up inside me, but Alice, ever the optimist, suggested we meet in secret. It seemed deceitful, and it took me back to my time with Florence but the allure of being with her overcame any reservations.

With no permanent job to tie me down, my days were free, allowing us to sneak moments together. We'd steal away for clandestine meals or rides into the countryside, the thrill of our hidden romance adding a layer of excitement to our days. The challenges were particularly pronounced at horse shows and fairs, where her parents always watched her ride.

It was like a scene from a spy movie. At the fairs, we'd duck behind marquees, and I'd watch her ride from the safety of the crowd, hidden in plain sight. It was unconventional, yet strangely, it was exhilarating. Our love grew under the cloak of secrecy, forging a unique bond between us. If anything, it made us closer, I think that it is something about the human spirit that if someone says you can't do something, well then, you want to do it even more."

Joe chipped in, "Yes like when you're on a diet and crave fish and chips."

They both laughed and for a moment the pain of Walter's strained relationship with Alice was forgotten.

"For truly private moments, she would venture here to our secluded hideaway, far from her parents' prying eyes. We'd spend hours in the park, or on warm summer evenings, we'd listen to the brass bands playing while enjoying a quiet picnic. These moments were our sanctuary, where love and determination triumphed over the rigid boundaries of class and the disapproval of her family. Fortunately, she had lots of school friends who were willing to provide her with an alibi. This rather odd, almost bizarre relationship lasted for about three years, I know that there were three Christmases when we had to meet secretly and the gifts I bought for her had to stay here so that her parents didn't see them. We had so much in common and shared the same views on endless subjects.

I did manage to find work on the canals again, firstly loading cargo on one of the wharves and then on a barge. By chance, I met up with Owd Jos who had a barge again, he and Dolly were still plying their trade along the waterways. They were delighted to see me and employed me in an instant. Their new barge had a Lister diesel engine, with a very distinctive knock as it pushed us through the water. It did not have a soul like Troy's but it was fun to tinker with and I wondered about buying a garage or workshop and making that my profession. Alice spent a weekend on the boat; she told her parents she was staying with an old school friend. I know it was a lie, but we were in love and any moment apart was a waste of time.

At least we had lots to talk about," he mused, his eyes wandering to the photograph on the mantelshelf.

"And so, do we," Joe replied, his voice warm, "But let's take a break."

Walter's face lit up, a fond and wistful glint in his eye. "Another coffee, I suppose," he said, as the memories of Alice filled the room. The very mention of her name brought a bittersweet smile to his face.

As they took a pause from their conversation, Walter's thoughts drifted back to the days when Alice was part of his life. They had been through so much together, and the mere mention of her name was enough to transport him back to those times of joy and innocence.

Walter thought about the secret meetings in the park, the stolen moments behind the marquees at fairs, and the shared picnics while listening to the distant brass bands. Those were the moments when their love had blossomed, strong and resilient in the face of objections.

With their cups of coffee in hand, Joe and Walter sat in companionable silence, their friendship only a few months old, but already enriched by the memories they had begun to share.

Walter's curiosity about Debbie's new school broke the silence, his genuine interest evident in the furrowed lines on his forehead.

"How's she doing at the new school?" he asked.

Joe looked up from his coffee, bringing his mind back to the present, his eyes reflecting a mix of fondness and concern. "Good," he began, his voice tinged with fatherly pride. "She seems to be pretty settled... she won't start full-time until after Christmas. She chats about her new friends and her new teachers when she's at home and she's told Grandma and Grandad the whole story. The emphasis is always on 'the new.' She seems happy, and that's all that matters."

Walter's eyes wandered to a large potted plant on the window sill. He gestured toward it, drawing Joe's attention.

"You see that plant? It's called a Parlour Palm." Walter began, a hint of nostalgia in his voice.

Joe looked quite confused with this new direction of their conversation.

Walter continued, "When I bought it, it was quite tiny in a little pot, just a couple of green sticks with a few fronds sticking out.... then, after a while, I needed to re-pot it because the roots were showing, its fronds reached further out into the room and formed the plant you see now. Over the years I've had to keep finding a bigger pot for it." Walter's eyes seemed to hold the weight of life's lessons learned through the years. "Life's like that, Joe," he continued, "We outgrow our own little pots, we expand our roots, and throw our arms out wider and wider until we reach our full potential. Debbie will have to do the same, keep changing pots until one day she'll find a pot the right size."

Joe chuckled at Walter's wisdom, his eyes crinkling at the corners. "That's a nice analogy," he said, appreciating Walter's perspective. "Perhaps you missed your calling; you should have been some kind of Guru."

Walter grinned, his new friendship with Joe enriching his life in unexpected ways. "Well," he said, "I've certainly learned a thing or two about life's pot changes and growth from the experiences I've had. Sometimes, the best wisdom about life comes from living it."

Walter smiled the creases beside his eyes deepening as he remembered an important night in his relationship with Alice.

"I'd been looking forward for weeks to a special plot night celebration organised by the local Round Table. I'd managed to secure tickets to their fireworks display… they were raising money for a local charity helping war orphans find homes and comfort. I couldn't wait to surprise Alice.

As the sun dipped below the horizon, Alice arrived here, she'd told her parents that she was going out with some friends to a plot night celebration. I greeted her with a bouquet of her favourite flowers and a wide smile on my face. 'Alice, I have a surprise for you,' I said, handing her the bouquet.

Alice's eyes lit up with delight as she took the flowers. 'Oh Walter, you always know how to make me feel special,' she said, giving me a warm hug.

Wearing warm coats and hand in hand, we made our way to the event, the cold evening air buzzing with anticipation. The fireworks display was known to be one of the best in town, and I couldn't wait to share this experience with Alice.

We arrived at the event, and the night was alive with energy. The smell of toffee apples, roasting chestnuts, and of course, the comforting aroma of pie and peas wafted through the air as we joined the crowd. Children laughed and ran around with sparklers, their excitement infectious, and the atmosphere was one of joy and togetherness. The local brass band was playing old favourites, their tunes floating on the chilly night breeze, adding to the festive ambience. The music provided a heartwarming soundtrack to our evening, underscoring the sense of community and tradition.

I had reserved a prime spot near the lake where the fireworks would be reflected in the water, and as we settled in, the sky began to darken. The first fireworks burst into a shower of colours, and for a moment, my memories of the trenches rushed back. It was an uncomfortable feeling, but Alice clung to my arm, her presence a reassuring anchor amidst the dazzling display above.

As the fireworks continued to paint the night sky with vivid hues, we shared our laughter and stories, finding warmth in our closeness. The bursts of light seemed to echo our shared joy and excitement. We held each other close, our hearts warmed not only by the brilliance of the fireworks but by the presence of one another.

The crowd's attention shifted as they lit the bonfire, and people drew nearer to chase away the chills of the night. Someone had artfully created a straw-filled Guy to sit on the top. Some joker had dressed the Guy to look like the Kaiser showing that no one had forgotten those dreadful years. The bonfire crackled, casting its warm, flickering light on the faces of the gathered crowd, creating a sense of unity and cosiness.

The night was alive with a symphony of colours, a sky ablaze with fireworks that mirrored the burst of emotions within me. Then, with a heartbeat so loud that I thought I'd drown out the fireworks and brass band I found the courage to drop a bombshell of my own.

I turned and stood in front of her, our eyes locked and I wondered what thoughts lay behind those perfect pools of love. I don't know how I kept calm but without any hesitation, I said, 'This night, with all its splendour, pales in comparison to the light you bring into my life.

She gave me a curious stare, 'What is it Walter?' I think that for some reason she anticipated something awful.

'Will you marry me?' I blurted out kneeling before her, offering a small red box.

'Walter,' She put her hand to her mouth, speechless, but with trembling hands, she took the box and prised open the lid.

Her eyes filled with tears and her lips quivered. "Oh, my, Walter, what can I say?"

With a voice filled with emotion, I said, "Say yes, of course."

There was a pause a moment of horror for me, was she going to refuse my offer?

"Yes," she whispered, her voice barely audible amid the roar of the fireworks. 'Yes, Walter I'd be honoured to marry you.'

With tender delight, illuminated by the fireworks, she placed the ring on her finger its sparkle a perfect echo of the joy in her eyes.

At that moment, as the fireworks painted the sky, time stood still for us both. Our unspoken connection spoke volumes, echoing the trials we'd conquered and the promise of an unwritten future.

As the grand finale approached and the sky erupted into a vibrant display, Alice and I stood together, lost in the magic of the night. The brilliance of the fireworks dimmed against the warmth of our embrace and the profound memory we had just created."

Walter's reminiscences brought back vivid memories of that enchanting night, "Nowadays, they'd say that there was an elephant in the room and we knew that this joy was tinged with the knowledge of the unresolved situation between us and her parents." He sat in silence, staring at his hands, his thoughts transporting him back to that pivotal moment.

"I knew there was something on her mind as I walked her to the tram stop. She took off my ring and placed it back in the box."

"Forgive me, Walter," she said, her voice trembling with a mixture of love and hesitation, "I do want to marry you, but I must find the right time to tell my parents."

My heart raced, and for a moment, the desire to be with her and start our life together overpowered me. "We could just elope," I suggested, my words fuelled by love and impatience. "I own my house, and I have a little money in the bank."

But Alice's eyes pleaded with me to understand the predicament she was in. "Please, Walter," she implored, her gaze filled with a mix of longing and worry, "Give me time."

The tram arrived, interrupting our conversation, and I waved her off with a heavy heart, the box still clutched in my hand. It was a cold night, but the chill in the air seemed to have seeped deeper into my bones. Our love was undeniable, but the obstacles we faced were equally apparent, casting a shadow over our otherwise bright future.

With a heavy heart, I watched her tram disappear into the night. The uncertainty of our future gnawed at me, the love we shared now intermingled with a sense of impending challenge. How would the story of our love unfold in the face of tradition and the high expectations of her family?

"Phew," Joe said, his voice tinged with empathy as he leaned forward, his hand finding its place on Walter's arm. His touch was a silent reassurance to let his friend know that he wasn't alone in this emotional journey. "That's a tough pill to swallow; I can't imagine how you felt."

"I can't find the words to express the profound mixture of love, longing, and anxiety that had defined those moments. Even now, there's a lump in my throat." Walter looked sad but resolute.

"We still saw each other whenever we could," Walter continued, his voice bearing the weight of our unspoken challenges, "But still, Alice could not find the courage to tell her parents. I knew she didn't want to hurt them, and it was her sense of loyalty, not cowardice, that was dictating the event."

Our clandestine love story became a medley of emotions, woven with threads of passion, devotion, and the complexities of family loyalties.

Nevertheless, we shared some remarkable evenings. Alice had a knack for talking me into ventures that I wouldn't normally entertain. So, when she proposed an evening at the theatre in Bradford to watch an opera, I hid my apprehension and agreed, just to see her joy.

'Oh please, Walter. I love Puccini's music. The theatre in Bradford is so beautiful.'

'Yes, of course, I've never been to an opera," I confessed.

'Just one tiny thing,' she gave me a coy smile and I was immediately suspicious.

'What might this, one tiny thing be, Alice?'

'You'll need to wear a black tie and dinner jacket.' Her smile was convincing. 'People tend to dress up for the opera.'

"Throwing caution to the wind, I dug deep into my pocket and secured us a private box beside the stage. Little did I know, that it was just the beginning of the expenses for this outing. I ventured into Huddersfield, sought out a tailor, and had a jacket tailored specifically for the occasion… that was a first for me too. The tailor a very serious character, bustled around me, pins held deftly between his lips as he marked the fabric with chalk. He also took measurements for a pair of trousers. 'Return next week for a fitting,' he instructed.

Following his guidance, I returned for the fitting and found myself lured into purchasing not only two dress shirts but also a waistcoat. As I stood before the tailor's full-length mirror on the day of my final fitting, I felt special. Alice had joined me for this ultimate fitting, observing from the sidelines. As I emerged from the dressing room, her sheer excitement radiated through a grin that spanned the width of her face. Her eyes sparkled with a joy that she couldn't contain, and the warmth of her happiness engulfed the room. It was a smile so vast, so genuine, that it revealed her exhilaration without a single word. The mirror reflected her enthusiasm as much as it did my transformed appearance.

As the tailor's assistant wrapped the suit for me, Alice linked arms with me, she smiled up at me and without taking her gaze from my eyes, she announced to the whole shop, 'Don't you agree… I have the most handsome man in Yorkshire if not the country as a fiancé.' The assistant smiled and even the tailor nodded in agreement.

I just hoped that I would like the opera because the whole thing had cost me almost three weeks' wage.

On the night, we dressed in our best attire… Alice in an exquisite mauve dress adorned with a silk cravat, reminiscent of the Hollywood icons of that era. I wasn't as glamorous, although I did sport my new dinner jacket and for the first time, I wore a dickie bow, you know, a bowtie. I felt a bit self-conscious as we left the house, I was definitely in uncharted waters. We hired a cab and I'm sure all the neighbours were squinting through their curtains to watch us leave.

Alice told her parents that she was to attend a ball with a few well-to-do friends of hers and her mother had gladly bought her a new outfit for the occasion.

As we stepped out of the cab into the rainy streets of Bradford that evening, the brilliant lights of the theatre created a mesmerizing spectacle, casting shimmering reflections all around the grand building. Each raindrop seemed to catch the glow, illuminating the surroundings in a dance of light and water. Upon entering the foyer, there was an excited hum in the air. The audience bustled around, their excitement tangible, as they eagerly awaited the moment to take their seats. Conversations buzzed with enthusiasm, laughter, and snippets of discussions about the night's performance, creating an electric atmosphere that heightened the anticipation for the upcoming spectacle.

We proudly took our rather expensive seats and waited. When the house lights dimmed and the first bars of the prelude filled the theatre I was as excited as Alice. During the performance, my attention wasn't solely fixed on the stage. Rather, I found myself enchanted by Alice's reactions, I was utterly absorbed by her expressions as she became engrossed in the unfolding tale. Her eyes shimmered with delight, thoroughly engaged in the story, and her enthusiasm was contagious. In those moments, it felt as though the world around us dissolved, leaving only Alice, the performers, and the enthralling melodies."

The interlude between acts came, and the house lights illuminated the grandeur of the auditorium. As I turned to say something to Alice, my gaze landed on a sight that sent a chill down my spine. Her parents, the very people who had forbidden our meetings, were seated directly below us in the stalls.

The realisation struck us like a bolt of lightning, and a mixture of shock and fear crossed Alice's face. I knew we couldn't stay there any longer, not with her parents so close. We exchanged a quick, panicked glance, and without saying a word, we slipped out of our private space and into the chill of the theatre steps.

As the final act began, Alice and I clutched each other's hands and made for the exit. It was a frantic escape down a flight of stone steps. Our hearts raced, and our breaths quickened as we ran for the door. The orchestra was hitting a dramatic height that seemed to fit our predicament. The music continued behind us, but our focus was entirely on avoiding her parents.

We burst from the theatre and into the cool night air, relieved to be free from the potential confrontation. Our covert escape from the theatre had gone off without a hitch, and as we strolled away hand in hand, Alice couldn't contain her laughter. 'That was a close one,' she chuckled, and soon, her infectious laughter had me joining in.

We slipped into a nearby hotel restaurant to share a satisfying meal. In our fine clothes, we certainly looked to fit in amidst the finery of the restaurant. We shared a small secluded table for two where the light from the candle between us sparkled in her eyes and at that moment I knew the real meaning of being in love.

As she delicately wiped her mouth, she inquired, 'So, what did you honestly think of the opera?'

'It turned out to be more thrilling than I ever anticipated,' I replied with a smirk.

'You know what I meant,' she retorted, slightly perturbed.

Our conversation was interrupted by the waiter, presenting dessert options. I chose the traditional sticky pudding which I think tasted better for the surroundings and my three-piece suit.

'Well?' she prodded.

'Yes, I did enjoy it. We could give it another go sometime. But I must confess, you in that dress, is the most unforgettable part of this wonderful evening.'

Her hand reached out to touch mine. 'Don't ever grow up or change… Walter Middlebrough I love you.'"

It was another adventure to add to our collection."

Joe reached out and stopped the tape, a playful glint in his eye. "Sorry, Walter," he said with a grin, "but duty calls. I must make tracks for home before my wife thinks I've got a fancy woman."

Walter chuckled, appreciating Joe's witty remark. "Of course not, Joe."

With Joe's theatrical exit still fresh in his mind, Walter couldn't help but smile at his friend's dramatic flair. He knew that their next encounter would be just as interesting. Somehow, he appreciated the space to enjoy his memories of that very special night.

When Joe hurried away, Walter's room seemed to be rather empty, he turned his attention to the rows of books neatly lined up on the shelves. They summoned to him like old friends waiting to be revisited. Walter moved along each shelf, straightening the volumes as if he were a sergeant inspecting his troops on parade. Occasionally, he'd stand back to survey his handiwork, ensuring that every book stood at attention.

Once satisfied with the meticulous arrangement of his beloved collection, he reached for one of his perennial favourites, gently easing it from its place on the shelf. 'Come on, Heathcliff, let's spend some time together,' he murmured to the book, as though it held the essence of a cherished confidant. With the precious Brontë classic nestled in his palms, he settled into an inviting, well-worn chair, embracing the comfort it offered.

As he delved into the pages, he felt the familiar embrace of the Yorkshire Dales enveloping him, each word a pathway to the enigmatic world within. The mysteries and passions woven within the novel beckoned him, offering an escape into a realm where the moors whispered secrets and the characters' emotions danced across the pages, inviting him to lose himself within their timeless tale.

Chapter Twenty-Five
Doubts Set In.

Joe returned home after his heart-warming conversation with Walter, his face showed signs of weariness. Julie, who had been waiting by the door for him, glanced at him and remarked, "You look tired love. How was your day?"

Joe sank into an armchair, his eyes filled with a mixture of exhaustion and satisfaction. He began to recount some of Walter's love story to Julie. He described the emotions and trials that Walter and Alice had gone through, painting a vivid picture of their journey. Julie listened and could only sympathise with the young couple's plight.

As the evening progressed, Joe suggested. "Come on get your glad rags on, we'll go to the Red Lion for a meal."

"I know what you are up to, it's quiz night," Julie replied with a knowing shake of her head.

As they entered the pub, Joe took a deep breath of the familiar welcoming aroma of freshly pulled beer that greeted them. They had arrived just in time for the start of the pub's quiz night, and the atmosphere buzzed with the energy of friendly competition. Joe and Julie joined in, Joe made the occasional fist-pump as he made the right answer.

After the quiz, over plates of hearty pub fare and pints of ale, they savoured the flavours and cheerful ambience. Laughter and conversation flowed effortlessly, as a few friends joined them.

When they eventually left the pub, the night had taken a romantic turn. Gentle raindrops began to fall, creating a soft melody on the streets. Instead of rushing to take cover, Joe and Julie exchanged a knowing look and shared a spontaneous decision to walk home in the rain.

The cool droplets soaked through their clothes, clinging to their skin. Yet, the experience felt liberating, a testament to their love's ability to find joy even in the unexpected. They held hands, their laughter ringing through the quiet streets as they twirled and danced, their faces illuminated by the glow of streetlights.

The raindrops sparkled like a thousand tiny diamonds, and as they reached their doorstep, Joe and Julie exchanged a profound, passionate kiss. It was a moment of connection, of sharing life's simple pleasures, and of embracing the love that bound them together. In the gentle embrace of the night, they found a deeper understanding of each other and an unspoken promise to cherish every moment they had together. Just after the lights were turned off Joe whispered, "Can you arrange for Debbie to stay at your mother's again sometime?"

Joe arrived back at Walter's, a contented smile on his face still buzzing after the fun of the night before.
"You look well today," Walter commented pleased to see his friend looking so refreshed.

Joe smiled with a mischievous wink he said, "We had a great night out, first time in ages that we've managed a night in the pub on quiz night. We used to be regulars… our old teammates were pleased to see us."

As he settled into the familiar chair, he delved into a bag beside him and retrieved a couple of paper bags. "Julie sends her regards," he said with a grin, producing a couple of pasties. "She thought we might enjoy these while we continue with your story. She's good at thinking of the little things."

Munching on their pasties, they delved back into the complications of Walter's love story, the tale that had captured Joe's heart and had now he yearned for more.

"Oh, let me stop a minute Joe, we must have the brown sauce," Walter said and made a rather slow dash into the kitchen. He returned holding the sauce bottle above his head.

"So, Walter you explained about your rather unorthodox courtship but how did you finally get together?" Joe probed for more details.

Walter's gaze turned distant, lost in the painful recollection.

"I read a few chapters of Wuthering Heights last night," Walter said thoughtfully, "The winter of twenty-nine I did a lot of reading. I'd not seen Alice for over a month, which was strange. I was worried. Of course, calling to see if she was alright was out of the question. I suppose I was feeling a little bit insecure… I was having all sorts of doubts. I didn't want to believe that she had changed her mind about me." His voice trembled and his eyes welled up with tears. "Well, one day, just before Christmas, she turned up here. When I opened the door to her knock I couldn't believe it… she looked soaked and she was shivering. I pulled her in as quickly as I could. It was hailing and snowing, and the weather was so bad that the trams had stopped running. She had to walk for over a mile in near-blizzard conditions, and she was heartbroken. It took me ages to sort out what was going on."

Joe listened intently, but could not suppress a question, "What happened?" he asked, his voice hushed.

Walter continued, his words heavy with pain. "Eventually, she managed to tell me what had happened. 'I'm sorry… not to have called or anything,' her voice trembled with pain. 'My family's world has come apart… Father has committed suicide and mother has gone insane.' Her words cascaded out in a painful torrent.

I reeled in shock, unable to believe it. Her father was so well known in the community, what you might call a pillar of society.

Alice poured her heart out to me. 'He's let us all down.' Tears streamed down her face.

I wrapped her in a blanket and left her in front of the fire while I made her a hot drink. For some time, she sobbed with her head in her hands, seemingly ashamed of what had happened."

Walter fixed Joe with a stern gaze. "Let me remind you about that period of history. The bubble of the Roaring Twenties was just about to burst, and the shock waves of 'The Great Recession' were on the horizon. There were strikes, rampant unemployment, and families struggling to make ends meet. Not much in the way of social care back then and families were virtually dying from starvation.

Anyway, when she finally managed to get it out, it seemed that her father had been a secret drinker and gambler, a man tortured by his own demons. His investments had crumbled with the recession, and it was out of despair and shame that he took his own life. He had lost everything… their savings, their home, their future. Alice was in a dreadful state, she sat numbed to the core by the situation.

Later, there was a dreadful scandal, and the newspapers ran all kinds of hurtful headlines about her father and the family in general."

Joe, his heart heavy with empathy, could barely find words. "Oh, my Walter," he whispered, "What a devastating tragedy."

Walter nodded, his gaze fixed on the photo on the mantle as he recounted the challenging ordeal.

"It was a tough time for her," he sighed softly. "Losing her father was just the beginning. With their finances in turmoil, she had to part with her beloved ponies... and that shattered her. Soon after, her mother faced a mental breakdown, landing her in Menston Mental Hospital. To make matters worse, heartless bailiffs evicted Alice, leaving her with nowhere to turn. That's when she found refuge here."

Walter paused, his voice now laced with profound sorrow.

"I was honoured that she had come to me for comfort," Walter continued, his voice softer now, tinted with the warmth of fond memories.

"That Christmas after the loss of Alice's parents we grew even closer, finding comfort in each other's presence, but the festive season was tinged with the heavy shadow of Alice's loss.

We exchanged gifts, and as we unwrapped them, our smiles were genuine, yet there was an unspoken weight in our hearts. The decorations seemed to shine a little less brightly that year.

One evening, as we sat together by the fireplace, the crackling flames casting flickering shadows on the walls, Alice turned to me. Her eyes held both grief and hope, a reflection of the mixed emotions that had defined this season.

"Walter, I miss them so much... but I'm so glad we have each other," she confided, her voice quivering with emotion.

I reached out and gently took her hand, trying to comfort her. "I know," I said quietly, there were no other words that could help.

We sat in silence, the warmth of the fire enveloping us, as we faced the stark reality of her loss. My love for her grew even stronger at that moment, and I decided that I needed to express my love.

'Alice,' I began, 'I love you with all my heart, and I can't bear to see you suffer like this. I want to be there for you, to make you smile, and to create new memories.'

Alice looked at me with a mixture of surprise and curiosity. 'What are you saying?'

I took a deep breath, my determination unwavering but my silly sense of humour took over, 'Can you make Yorkshire puddings?' I asked.

She looked confused and I know it was a silly thing to say but I just wanted to lighten the mood.

She smiled curiously at me, 'Yes, of course, I can, what Yorkshire Lass can't?'

'Okay, well I'm saying that I still want to marry you. So, will you marry me?'

I handed over the little red box again. Tears welled up in Alice's eyes, but they were no longer solely tears of sorrow. They were tears of gratitude and the promise of a brighter future. She slipped the ring on and held it up to the light to admire.

'Walter,' she whispered, her voice filled with love, 'Yes, with all my heart I want to marry you, too.'

And so, against the poignant backdrop of the Christmas season, Alice and I made a promise of love and commitment that echoed through the wintry air. As the season's magic surrounded us, my mind buzzed with a flurry of questions and doubts; it marked a significant step for both of us.

In the days that followed, we embarked on the joyous journey of selecting new furniture. The pieces I had back then were basic, and the act of choosing and arranging brought a touch of brightness to our lives, lessening the weight in Alice's heart. I couldn't bear the thought of leaving her alone, fully aware of her vulnerability. Consequently, I made the decision to leave my job, opting to prioritize our time together over professional pursuits.

The metamorphosis of our living space was a joint venture. Despite the modern amenities at our disposal, remnants of the past lingered in the form of unused gas mantles on the walls, a testament to a time before electricity had been available.

Undeterred by the traces of the past, we undertook the task room by room, immersing ourselves in the process of redecoration. Each space became a canvas upon which we painted the hues of warmth and the essence of a new beginning. The installation of electricity was a major upheaval as the company we hired was forced to dig through the wall plaster and lift floorboards to install the cables. We decided that while we had all the dirt and upset of the electricians we would also have new plumbing installed. The walls, once adorned with gas mantles, now bore witness to the transformation we were bringing about.

Venturing upstairs, we introduced a modern luxury that spoke of progress... a new bathroom. In our neighbourhood, I believe our addition marked us as pioneers and I'm pretty sure that we were among the first to enjoy the convenience of an inside toilet. As the fixtures and tiles found their places, we enjoyed days of tramping around the shops and markets looking for bargains.

As the scent of fresh paint and the echoes of laughter filled our home, the sad pains of the past began to recede and we set the date for our wedding.

We got married the next February, and as fate would have it, it snowed all day, blanketing the world in a pristine layer of white. It felt like a poetic reflection of our new beginning, a fresh canvas for us to start our life together.

Owd Jos, my trusted friend and confidant, stood by Alice's side, proudly giving her away. His eyes held the wisdom of years and the warmth of a friendship that had been tested and strengthened. It was a symbolic passing of the torch, and I felt a profound gratitude for his support.

Dolly, always the lively and spirited one, stepped into the role of maid of honour with an infectious enthusiasm. Her vibrant energy added a touch of charm and joy to the occasion and her enthusiasm carried us forward.

The small village church, with its weathered stones and rich history, bore witness to our union. The scent of ageing wood and the soft strains of the organist's music filled the air as we exchanged our vows. It was a simple and heartfelt ceremony, we exchanged our vows and relished the thought of our new life together.

The vicar, a gentle chap with a kind smile, blessed our union, and the church's caretaker, who had dedicated her life to tending to the blossoms and greenery in the sacred space, joined in our joy and acted as witness.

After the ceremony, we all retreated to the warmth and cosiness of the local pub. The rustic atmosphere, with its polished wooden beams and a crackling fireplace, became the backdrop for our celebration. We shared stories, laughter, and a hearty meal, the clinking of glasses a joyful chorus to our love.

I joked with Jos, "You know the father of the bride or the one giving her away has to pay for the meal."

He had by that time sunk several drinks. "Don't you worry my boy, I've already taken care of the bill." He looked at the barman. "Isn't that so," he called out proudly. The barman returned a solemn nod of agreement.

"I was only kidding," I said.

Dolly threw her arm around me. "Don't worry lad… it'll do him good to have to open his purse for once. It's a wonder that he remembers how to do it." She gave a huge hearty laugh and crushed me to her bosom.

We stepped out on our journey as husband and wife in the company of a select few who held special places in our hearts. The simplicity and intimacy of the occasion made it even more profound, a reminder that love, when genuine, is the most beautiful and enduring treasure of all."

Joe could picture the scene, as a simple and intimate wedding amid a snow-covered landscape. He leaned in, "It sounds like a wonderful wedding, especially after the rather stormy courtship."

Walter's eyes seemed to sparkle with a blend of joy and melancholy as he reminisced.

"We had a simple honeymoon in Saltaire, taking the tram from Bradford to an inn there. Despite the month and the weather, we walked up on Shipley Glen every day, but our laughter was muted by the pain that still clung to our hearts. Alice would still have weepy days, and I tried my best to comfort her."

But as Walter recounted these moments, the weight of the past resurfaced, and he had to pause once more. His eyes welled with tears, the emotions of the past still very much alive within him. Joe, deeply touched by Walter's story, continued to listen and record every word, respecting the depth of love and loss that had marked this chapter of Walter's life.

Chapter Twenty-Six
Fateful Day.

"How were you employed at that time?" Joe asked, careful to tread lightly as he explored this deeply emotional part of Walter's story.

Walter, his voice quivering with the pain of the past, replied, "Once we were settled and I was certain I could leave Alice I went back to doing odd jobs; there was no steady work to be found. But Owd Jos knew plenty of people and kept me going. To my surprise, Alice, on the other hand, found the perfect job as a stable hand.

Her bosses, upon learning about her many medals from Gymkhanas and shows, promoted her and allowed her to teach riding to their well-to-do clients. They even entered her into shows. It was perfect for her, and I'd go along and help her muck out the stables. It reminded me of Troy, which was a sentimental memory.

We settled into a comforting routine but one day as Alice arrived home from work she looked to have a secret to tell.

"Walter," she said sheepishly, "I called at the clinic."

"Why?" I was concerned about her health. "Are you ill?"

"I think you had better sit down." She took my arm and guided me into my chair. I feared for the worse but her eyes were telling me otherwise.

"We're going to have a baby!" she exclaimed.

I couldn't contain my excitement; this was a new adventure we were about to embark on together. "Oh, my words!" I exclaimed. I wasn't sure what to say. "We must tell Dolly and Jos, they'll be delighted."

I remember tenderly placing my hand on her tummy as though I could already communicate with the miracle that was happening inside.

For the next few weeks, we busied ourselves with all the usual preparations, transforming the spare room into a cosy nursery and making grand plans for the future.

But, as it often goes, fate had a different script in mind for us. When Alice was around four months pregnant, her bosses insisted she participate in a prestigious gymkhana run on one of the North Yorkshire country house estates. It was a three-day event, and it meant we would be living closely with the horses, spending our nights in a barn which rekindled lots of memories.

Walter paused, a smile gracing his lips as he reminisced about those days. "It turned out to be quite an adventure, and initially we enjoyed every moment of it.

The dressage event had gone really well, and Alice had looked stunning in her impeccable hunting attire, with shiny boots that seemed to mirror her radiant smile. The arena was alive with the rhythmic hoofbeats and the elegant dance of horse and rider. Alice's performance was nothing short of captivating, and the judges had taken note, awarding her the praise she rightly deserved.

Yet, as the second day of the gymkhana loomed, an intense tension began to weave its way into my heart. This was the day of the cross country, a thrilling but treacherous challenge that made my heart race with apprehension. The jumps were no mere showpieces; they were colossal, daunting obstacles carved from solid tree trunks. There were dips with water splashes and climbs that would test both horse and rider and could send even the most skilled riders tumbling to the ground.

I couldn't shake the unease that clung to me like a shadow. The dangers were real, and I feared for Alice's safety as she prepared to face these formidable hurdles. Her unwavering confidence was admirable, but I couldn't help but worry.

As the event unfolded, I watched anxiously, my heart leaping with every jump she and her horse cleared. The crowd held their collective breath, the suspense in the air almost suffocating. Yet, Alice's determination and her bond with her horse carried them through. She navigated the course with grace and fearlessness, her sheer skill evident in every jump they conquered. Just once when she reached a castellated stone wall did her mount look uncertain but somehow it fed off her confidence and bravely leapt over that unyielding obstacle.

By the end of the day, Alice, with her face and clothes splattered with mud had secured second place, an incredible accomplishment that left me both relieved and immensely proud. The exhilaration of her victory mixed with the lingering worry that had plagued me earlier.

We celebrated her achievement with her bosses, who treated us to a sumptuous meal at a local hotel. Laughter and joy filled the evening, temporarily masking the underlying tension that the final day of the event held. Everything seemed to be falling into place, but the uncertainty of the upcoming day lingered in the shadows, an unspoken reminder that she would have to take risks and push herself and her horse to the very limits to win.

The show jumping day arrived, and the showground was bustling with activity. The atmosphere was electric, charged with excitement and anticipation. Families bustled about, and children's laughter filled the air as they clutched candyfloss and balloons. Stalls and food vendors lined the perimeter, their savoury and sweet aromas mingling with the scent of hay and horses.

Competitors, dressed in their finest riding attire, were busy preparing their horses. They meticulously groomed the animals, and nervously polished their tack. The elegant thoroughbreds and sturdy ponies pranced and neighed, sensing the tension that surrounded them. There was a slight mist that morning and their breath was visible in the crisp morning air.

Spectators began to gather around the jumping arena, lining the fences with eager expressions. Friends and families cheered for their loved ones, waving flags and banners. The judges in their bespoke jackets adorned with official rosettes conferred and reviewed the course, ensuring it presented a fair challenge for the riders.

Over by the entrance, the event organizers huddled together, ensuring every detail was in place. The public address system crackled to life, announcing the commencement of the first event. The show jumping day was off to a good start with the pony classes going first over less challenging jumps than faced their seniors. It promised to be a day of thrilling competition, there would be winners and losers but everyone would be thrilled by the experience.

In the paddock, I helped Alice into her saddle and gave her a good luck kiss. She smiled down at me from the saddle and tapped my shoulder with her crop. "Wish me luck," she said. I knew that her mind was on her parents and how proud they would have been of her achievements. I kissed my fingers and touched her boot as she set off, "Good luck," I whispered to her. I was aware that luck had nothing to do with the outcome, the bravest and most determined would take the day. I was confident she would win.

The early rounds went well and Alice performed spectacularly. She was in third place, which earned her a place in the final round, which was a nail-biting race against the clock. Points were close for the top five riders and so, if her time was good she could win the competition. I watched with a mix of pride and fear as the bell signalled the start of her final run. Her mount began a paced canter around the ring before lining up for the first jump. As she leapt over poles, gates and fences made of shrubs she was doing exceptionally well, her timing outpacing that of her competitors. Hope surged within me as I dared to imagine her victorious ride.

She was pushing hard, clipping corners trying to save strides and time and then, in an instant, the world shifted into slow motion. As Alice and her horse approached a tight corner, disaster struck. My heart pounded and I watched in horror. The horse's front foot caught on the decorative hedge beside the jump, it tripped and then both horse and rider somersaulted through the jump. The brightly painted woodwork splintered and flew into the air, I remember watching it spin. They landed in a jumble of limbs. I feared that her mount had landed on top of her.

My immediate instinct was to act. I leapt over the barrier and raced toward Alice, my heart pounding with anxiety. By the time I reached her, a crowd had gathered, and two medics in white coats carrying a stretcher were already on their way.

I reeled as panic welled up within me, and I felt a wave of nausea wash over me. The sight of the rushing medics instantly took me back to the war, to the chaotic scenes of bombs and destruction. I had to take a deep breath, my mind seemed to be in a fog and my heart was pounding like a traction engine.

My foremost concern was for Alice, and my relief was obvious when the medics sat her up and assured us that she was all right, albeit slightly winded. However, her complexion was ghostly pale, maybe it was the shock but I couldn't help but feel a lingering unease. The medics insisted on carrying her to their post for a thorough check-up, a wise precaution, given the circumstances. As they carefully attended to her, my mind was a whirlwind of emotions, from the fear of the accident to the haunting memories it had unexpectedly stirred.

However, the reassurance that came with the medics' presence was short-lived. Suddenly, without warning, Alice was violently sick, her agonized screams cutting through the air. She clutched her stomach, rolling listlessly onto her side, her face contorted in pain.

In that horrifying moment, the doctor pushed me out of the tent, his words an attempt to console my growing dread. "Don't worry," he said, but his voice carried a solemn weight that told me otherwise.

I stood just beyond the tent's entrance, feeling numb, my stomach churning with anxiety. Fear gripped me like a vice, and I instinctively knew that something was terribly wrong.

My mind raced, and my heart pounded in my chest as I braced myself for whatever news would come next. As I stood just outside the tent, fear and helplessness washed over me like a relentless tide. I felt an unexpected, desperate urge to reach out to a higher power. It was a yearning that had long been dormant, buried beneath the weight of the harrowing experiences I had witnessed during the war. In those dark moments, my faith in God was lost as were so many boys' lives. I questioned the existence of any benevolent force in the universe, I reasoned that, if I were to ask for help and an enemy soldier praying to the same God asked for help which of us would he choose?"

Walter's voice echoed the excitement and anguish of that moment and Joe reached over to try to calm him.

Walter continued, "Yet, now, faced with the stark reality of Alice's suffering, my scepticism crumbled. In the depths of my soul, a fervent prayer welled up, a plea for divine intervention, a hope against hope that God any God would hear my plea and guide Alice through this tragedy unscathed.

With every fibre of my being, I sent out that silent prayer into the universe, a desperate call for mercy, for a miracle to spare the woman I loved from further anguish. The darkness around me seemed to close in, but I clung to that fragile thread of hope, willing it to lead us toward the light, toward a future where Alice would emerge from this ordeal intact."

Walter who had moved to the edge of his chair blew a sigh of relief and sat back.

"Sorry Joe, I got a bit carried away there,"

Joe, thoughtful as ever gave Walter a reassuring smile. "I can understand."

Walter closed his eyes and continued.

"Time felt suspended, the world held its breath, and I waited in agonising uncertainty for any sign, any glimmer of reassurance that my plea had been heard. The stable managers fussed about but I had the sense that they were more interested in making sure that any blame for the accident was not theirs.

As I anxiously waited outside the tent, my heart heavy with both fear and hope, I saw the doctor emerge from the tent. His face, once stoic and professional, now bore an expression of disappointment and genuine sorrow. Dread settled like a leaden weight in the pit of my stomach.

Without hesitation, I rushed over to him, my heart pounding in my chest, my voice trembling as I implored him for news. His eyes, filled with compassion and a profound understanding of the emotions raging within me, met mine.

"I'm sorry, son," he said gently, his words delivering a cruel verdict that sent my world into a tailspin. My heart felt as though it were in the grip of some monstrous force. "Your wife will survive," he continued, offering a glimmer of relief, "but I'm afraid she has miscarried."

The conflicting emotions that surged within me were overwhelming. It was as if elation and devastation waged a fierce battle for dominance within my soul. Relief flooded my senses, knowing that Alice would be alright, that she had survived the ordeal. Yet, there was profound sadness and grief over the loss of our child, it seemed a cruel blow.

In that moment, I stood at the crossroads of joy and sorrow, my emotions in turmoil, torn between the relief of Alice's survival and the deep anguish of our shared loss. It was a bittersweet moment that would forever mark our lives, a reminder of the fragility and resilience of the human spirit in the face of adversity."

"Wow," Joe murmured, his voice tinged with empathy as he absorbed Walter's harrowing recollection. "Oh dear, Walter, I am so sorry. I can't even begin to imagine what you went through at that time."

Joe shifted closer to his old friend, their connection deepening in that moment of shared understanding. He gently placed his hand on Walter's, a silent gesture of support and friendship.

"That's enough for today," Joe continued softly. "You must be exhausted, and I have to admit, I'm quite shattered myself."

Walter, his eyes reflecting gratitude and a host of unspoken emotions, managed a simple yet heartfelt "Thank you."

There were so many thoughts and feelings bottled up inside him, memories and stories waiting to be shared, but for now, the weight of the past had left them both drained.

With a sense of companionship that could not easily be put into words, they rose from their seats, ready to part ways for the day.

Joe leant against the door as he was leaving, "Don't forget it's the weekend, I'll not be here for a couple of days."

Walter was disappointed that it would mean days on his own with his friend missing.

"Oh yes, I'd remembered. I've plenty of jobs to keep me busy, plus there's plenty of football on this weekend. "I might ask Mr and Mrs Singh for a meal, she makes the most incredible curries."

Joe smiled he had only admiration for Walter's stoic resolve.

Walter felt quite depressed after Joe left, the burden of his memories had taken a toll and now he felt alone and isolated. He decided to prepare a simple meal, he opened and heated a tin of soup. With his humble dinner ready, he settled in front of the television, the glow from the screen providing a small source of comfort.

As he sipped his soup and watched the evening news, Walter's mood began to brighten, albeit slowly. Memories of the fun outings he had shared with Alice floated back into his consciousness. He recalled the laughter, the shared adventures, and the simple joy of walking hand in hand in the park. The warmth of those memories provided a glimmer of comfort in his otherwise quiet evening.

Determined to share these recollections with Joe the next time they met, Walter took another sip of his soup and felt a sense of anticipation for their future conversations.

A thought suddenly struck him, like a beam of sunlight breaking through dark clouds, and it brought a grin to his lips. Walter rose from his seat and walked over to the sideboard cupboard, its wooden surface bearing the marks of years of use.

He opened the middle drawer of three and gently pulled out a dog-eared cardboard shoebox, the shoes that were in the box were worn out years ago. But the box had endured, its contents a treasure trove of photographs capturing the precious snippets of their past.

Walter felt quite excited as he carefully opened the box, he wondered if it was time for a new box this one was definitely past its best. The large elastic band that held it together had slowly cut its way through the box lid and when he removed it, the lid almost fell in two. Once opened the box had a slightly musty smell proving just how long it had been since he delved into it.

He began to flip through the photographs one by one. Each image held its own story and it was a fragment of their shared past. He marvelled at the smiles, the laughter, and the love that radiated from those captured moments. He chuckled at pictures of himself as a younger man. Occasionally, he would stop at one and remember its details even the conversations from that scene.

There was one picture in particular that made him smile; it was of Alice snuggled up to him, he had his arm around her shoulders and they were both smiling at the camera. He remembered that day, he asked someone to take the picture while Alice and he posed. Walter remembered so much background to that photograph. It was taken in a park in Scarborough, during a wonderful week's holiday. The weather had been kind and most days they had enjoyed time sitting in a deck chair on the beach. Alice had drawn a huge love heart in the sand and they had watched as the tide had eventually carried it away. The evenings were filled with visits to the theatre or the simple pleasure of walking on the promenade or on the beach under the stars... he took a deep breath and he could almost smell the sea, feel the cool breeze, and hear the constant calling of the gulls. Except one morning when the famous sea fret had descended on them. They did not let it dull their spirits despite it feeling a little chilly in fact he remembered Alice saying, 'I fancy an ice cream, come on it'll be fun.' The memory of them buying an ice cream from across the road to the beach and sitting and eating it in the fog. There was another photo taken on the beach. They'd made friends with a family from Leeds and he remembered spending hours building sandcastles with their two children. Alice had watched him and he saw a far-off look in her eyes and he knew she was wishing that the children were theirs.

In those photographs, he found memories, some that he had not thought about for years. He found a rare one of Alice on horseback, he remembered how beautiful she was and thought himself lucky to have been able to share so many years with her.

Among the photographs, there were moments of happiness, times when they could put aside the pain of their past, if only for a while, and simply revel in the joy of being together. Their shared grief over the loss of their baby had never truly faded, but these snapshots of brighter days provided a respite from the guilt that had haunted them.

He took a deep, satisfied breath enjoying the sudden calm that settled in his breast. Happy and comforted by the visual journey through their shared history, Walter gently replaced the lid on the shoebox, securing it with a few well-worn rubber bands. He then returned it to its place in the cupboard, where it would rest, a silent witness to their love story, waiting to be revisited whenever he needed a reminder of the happiness they had shared.

The television continued to play in the background, and Walter watched part of a program on farming, the familiar scenes of rural life lulling him into a state of drowsiness. Eventually, he nodded off, finding rest in the embrace of his dreams as he prepared to face whatever the next chapter of his life would bring.

Chapter Twenty-Seven
I've Found Elsie.

As Joe drove home, he felt exhausted. Today's emotional journey with Walter had left him feeling mentally drained, his mind was swirling with the vivid and painful memories from Walter's past. He found himself overwhelmed and pulled his car over into a layby to escape the mad teatime traffic that rushed past him in a blur. He sat for a moment to compose himself watching the taillights and nameless traffic and wondering about the lives of the drivers. It took a few moments but eventually, he restarted the engine and headed home, a heavy cloud of emotions trailing behind him.

Julie pulled into their driveway just as he arrived, and offered a warm wave. Joe tried his best to muster a smile in response, though it didn't come easily.

Meeting on the front step, they exchanged a brief yet comforting kiss. The warmth of Julie's lips against his own provided a soothing balm for his weary soul. Sensing that something was amiss, Julie asked him with genuine concern, "Are you okay?"

Joe's response was heavy with the burden of the past hours.

"Yes and no. At last, I've met Alice in Walter's story," he began, his voice tinged with melancholy. "But the joy didn't last long and the story so far is quite tragic. Well, I was really excited when he opened up about Alice. She was incredibly special to him. It was an unconventional love story, really. They met secretly at first, and their relationship blossomed amidst challenges and her parents' disapproval. They even got engaged during a stunning firework display by the river one night." Joe paused his emotions flaring up, his cheeks reddened and for a moment he was speechless. "They were married under difficult conditions and just when they thought they were on the level, Alice miscarried." Joe stopped abruptly.

Julie could see that he was upset. she reached out to him and held his hand and then offered him a glimmer of hope.

"Oh dear, I've got something that might cheer you up a little." She gave him a cheeky wink.

They made their way indoors and the routine of making coffee provided a comforting distraction. Joe switched on the kettle while Julie prepared the coffee granules.

"So, go on then," Joe said, taking a sip of his coffee, "Cheer me up."

Julie paused for a moment, savouring the anticipation.

"I called in at the newspaper office this afternoon and did a little more research," she said.

"How was Danny? I bet he was glad of some company."

"Do you want my news or not?" Julie sounded irritated.

"Go on then tell me?" Joe asked impatiently, "What have you found?"

"Not what, but who… Elsie," Julie said triumphantly, "And can you believe it… she lives just on the other side of Huddersfield only about three miles from Walter. I have her address. Why don't we call and see her but keep it a surprise for Walter?"

"Oh, my goodness, I can hardly believe it." Joe looked amazed, "Do you have her phone number, my words, she was Walter's elder sister so how old will she be?"

Joe and Julie spent most of the evening discussing what they could do. The prospect of connecting with 'Elsie,' Walter's elder sister, filled them both with a sense of excitement and wonder. They mulled over the details, wondering how she would react to their surprise visit and what stories she might hold about Walter's past.

As Julie sat snuggled up to Joe, her fingers were gently tracing the edge of the letter from Debbie's school. Her eyes were bright with anticipation as she turned toward Joe, who was staring into space still thinking about Elsie and what she would feel about meeting her long-lost kin.

"Joe," she began, her voice filled with a mixture of excitement and pride, "I received a glowing report from the school about Debbie."

Joe came back to reality, a warm smile spreading across his face. His eyes met Julie's, and there was a softness in his gaze.

"That's wonderful news, I'm sorry love, I'm a bit distracted. Debbie's wellbeing is the most important thing," he replied, his tone laced with genuine happiness. "I think she's been much calmer since she started there, don't you?"

Julie nodded enthusiastically, her hope shining through her eyes. "Definitely," she affirmed, her voice tinged with pride. "Oh yes, it's early days but the omens are good. And she's even made a special friend."

A sense of warmth and contentment filled the room as they discussed Debbie's progress. Joe, feeling the significance of the moment, suggested, "Maybe we could let her bring her new friends over sometime, you know, for tea or something?"

Julie's face lit up at the idea, her enthusiasm contagious. "Yes," she agreed, "I'm sure she'd love that."

They sat together listening to the late news on the television, as the weather report finished Julie said. "I think we should pay Elsie a surprise visit but how do we know it's the right woman?"

Joe thought about it carefully before responding, "Well, there's only one way to find out. We don't have a phone number, so I suggest we go look."

"Debbie is going to stay with Mum tomorrow… Mum wants to take her shopping in the morning."

"Okay, well we'll drop her off and go investigate this woman," Joe announced.

With their determination in place, Joe and Julie embarked on a journey into the depths of suburbia. They stopped briefly to drop Debbie off and then the drive took them along winding roads until they reached a new housing estate with large detached houses. They looked for the address they thought to be Elsie's.

Julie counted off the house numbers as Joe slowly drove along. She suddenly announced, "Number thirty-three... here we are. It looks very nice."

It was nestled within a row of detached houses, tracing the gentle curve of the road that snaked through the estate, each residence boasted meticulously tended front gardens and spacious driveways leading to sizable garages. Pulling up to the curb, they parked their car and lapsed into a momentary silence, fixated on the house looming ahead. An air of anticipation mingled with uncertainty hung between them.

Julie's voice broke the stillness, tinged with a hint of caution. "Do you think we should? I'm not sure..."

Joe glanced at her, sharing her unease. "It's a big decision, I know. But maybe it's worth a shot?"

"Dare we do this?" Julie eventually voiced, her question hanging in the air, laden with the weight of their uncertainties.

"Well, we are here now… let's do it." Joe was desperate to fill in a few more gaps in Walter's story.

The path to the front door seemed to stretch before them, and they were both acutely aware that this visit could hold significant meaning, not just for Walter but for their own journey of discovery as well. With a shared glance of determination, they finally mustered the courage to tread the path to the front door, ready to uncover the mysteries and stories that lay behind it. They pressed the bell and heard its musical chime from somewhere inside.

The lady who answered the door turned out to be quite a surprise. Joe and Julie had both envisaged a frail old lady, but they were way off target. Elsie had a youthful glow about her. She wore stylish slacks that gracefully draped over her slender frame, and her hair, freshly dyed and neatly swept back into a ponytail, added a touch of contemporary flair.

She opened the door and asked, "Can I help you?" her smile was welcoming.

Julie took the lead, her excitement palpable. "Are you, or were you Elsie Middlebrough?"

Elsie appeared genuinely surprised as she replied, "Why yes." She was suspicious and wondered about the purpose of this unexpected visit. "Are you from the Jehovah's Witnesses? I had two of your brethren here last week," she said.

A warm smile cracked Julie's face as she clarified the situation, "No, not at all. We have some news, it's about your brother... Walter."

Elsie's expression shifted from surprise to shock, clearly, she was not expecting this revelation. Her hand shot to cover her mouth

"Oh my, goodness gracious," she whispered through her fingers, her voice filled with a mixture of astonishment and emotion. It was as if a long-closed book had suddenly been opened, and a rush of memories flooded back into her consciousness.

Elsie's eyes sparkled with anticipation as she leaned forward, her voice bubbling with excitement, eager to uncover more about their news.

"So, how do you know our Walter? Who are you?"

Joe smiled, he was pleased to see how eager she was for news of her brother.

"I'm his social worker." Joe held out his name tag as proof of his identity. "but I'm writing an article for the local paper about him... well, it started off that I was interested in his war stories, but it has developed way past that."

Elsie nodded, her interest aroused. "Well, you had better come in. So, how is he?" she inquired.

"He's doing well," Joe assured her. "He's very independent, and we try to keep a close eye on him. I take him on walks occasionally."

Julie couldn't help but interject with a smile, "And for the occasional curry."

Joe chuckled, "Yes, that's right," he admitted. "He's quite the fan of curries."

Elsie's eyes seemed to light up at the thought of seeing her brother again. "I'd love to see him again," she said warmly. "It must have been at the end of World War One since I last saw him. Where does he live?"

Joe's response was filled with a sense of serendipity as he revealed, "Would you believe, he has a house almost opposite to where you all grew up as children together."

Elsie's surprise was evident as she exclaimed, "No... I've been down there lots of times over the years."

The idea that her brother had lived so close all this time seemed to fill her with a mixture of nostalgia and excitement. "I can't believe it." Her tears ran uncontrollably across her cheeks.

Julie couldn't help but compliment Elsie, saying, "What about you, Elsie? You look very fit and well."

Elsie beamed with pride, her lively spirit shining through as she replied, "I am indeed. I run a keep-fit class for us old folk down at the centre. I love it, and it keeps me on my toes too."

Joe chimed in, offering his own compliment, "Well, you look well on it."

Julie, ever the conversation starter, brought up Elsie's history, saying, "I understand from Walter that you were still a nurse when you last saw him."

Elsie nodded, her eyes filled with memories that spanned many years.

"Yes, oh, let me think. We met a couple of times in a field hospital somewhere in Belgium, and then when he returned to Blighty... I saw him then. Sorry, it's quite a shock my memory has all gone a bit fuzzy." She paused a moment and then as her instincts took over she offered them a seat.

As their conversation continued to flow, Julie's curiosity got the better of her, and she asked, "We're hoping that you can fill in a few blanks for us about his early years and your family. For instance, what did you think when your dad put him to work on that barge? Were you surprised?"

Elsie smiled at them both, appreciating their interest, and replied, "I think that this calls for a large brew of tea. Will you share one with me?"

While Elsie busied herself making tea, Joe took the opportunity to look around the room. The cosy living room exuded warmth and comfort. The mantelshelf, adorned with several generations of cherished family photographs, told the story of a life well-lived. Each frame held memories preserved in time's embrace, capturing weddings, birthdays, and adventures through the years. Among the photographs, he noticed an older man who he assumed was her husband, along with four young boys.

Elsie rolled in a gleaming bronze-coloured tea trolley, its wheels gliding silently across the Axminster-covered floor. The scent of freshly steeped tea leaves wafted through the air, promising a comforting brew to come.

As she poured the tea and offered around the cups, a warm smile graced her lips. "Help yourselves to biscuits," she encouraged, her tone inviting. Then, with a gentle smile, she added, "Would you like to hear my story too?" she made a self-conscious gesture and adjusted her hair with a delicate sweep of her hand.

Joe and Julie exchanged an eager glance, their anticipation evident. "Oh, that would be incredible," Joe exclaimed, his enthusiasm palpable. "A complete family saga. My newspaper boss would absolutely love that."

Elsie settled into her chair, the years gracefully fading away as she crossed her legs with the agility of a much younger person. She furrowed her brow, contemplating the weight of the past that had been stirred by Joe and Julie's questions. A deep breath signalled her readiness to share a part of her family's history that was both painful and poignant.

"Oh, yes," she began, her voice carrying a mixture of sadness and nostalgia. "You asked about our father's decision to leave Walter to work on the boat." Her eyes momentarily glistened with unshed tears as she delved into the memories. "There was no doubt that Dad was heartbroken when he returned, he had so much to deal with at that time; Mum had passed away and he really didn't know how to deal with it. In those days, there were no social services or counselling to help him cope with his grief. Some turned to the church while others turned to the bottle."

Elsie paused, her gaze distant as she recalled those trying times. "Walter was the youngest and the only one not bringing in any wage. The rest of us kids were still part-time in school, the rest of our time was in the weaving sheds but we barely earned enough to make ends meet. Tilly, the brightest among us, was particularly affected by Mum's death. Grandma died too and we were in a pickle." She grimaced slightly and continued, "Dad had no choice but to pull her out of school to help look after us. She resented it deeply, and unfortunately, she took her frustrations out on Walter, the youngest of us."

Tears welled up in Elsie's eyes as she continued, her voice trembling with emotion. "Tilly said some truly awful things to him, and at times, she was terribly cruel. But you know, Walter never got cross back with her. It was not his way even though I know he was hurt by it. It was a difficult period for all of us, it was marked by loss, responsibility, and the strain of us trying to get back on our feet."

Elsie leaned forward, her eyes sparkling with anticipation, her enthusiasm infectious. "I wonder when we might meet Walter," she pondered, a gentle smile touching her lips. "Does he know you've found me?"

"No, not yet," Joe replied with a serious expression. "We needed to make sure that you were the right person first, and that you wanted to be reunited."

Elsie nodded a nostalgic glimmer in her eye. "He was always a good kid with a heart of gold, even back then," she reminisced. "I recall how devastated he was when Mum passed away. Dad took him to work on the boat, not out of malice, but to ease Tilly's burden and perhaps because it meant one less mouth to feed. The next time I saw Walter was after Dad and Joyce had also passed. He seemed to be thriving on his new life on the barge, brimming with stories about his newfound family."

She chuckled, her laughter ringing with genuine affection. "He had quite a fan club, too," she added playfully. "All my friends fancied him. I think it was his kindness and gentle soul that made him even more attractive. Oh, yes," she said with a grin, "I remember the giggles and secrets the nurses in the field hospitals shared about him. Walter was always such a gentleman, never letting it go to his head."

As they shared these moments of mixed emotions, the anticipation of meeting Walter hung in the air like a promise of rekindled connections and the chance to revisit a time when life was simpler, even amid its challenges.

Elsie noticed that Julie's gaze was drawn like a magnet to the captivating photo display, which unravelled the rich tapestry of her family's history. Time had cast a gentle fading spell on the old photographs, yet they clung fiercely to their stories, each one a portal into a different era. The pictures seemed to whisper to Julie, beckoning her to step into their world. Elsie couldn't resist the opportunity to peel back the layers of her family's past, understanding that these images held tales of bravery, sacrifice, and enduring love.

A proud smile graced Elsie's face as she gestured towards her cherished collection of photographs. "These pictures… you see, they're my family… my beloved darlings. They've all left indelible marks on the pages of history."

Julie's eyes sparkled with genuine intrigue. "Elsie, I'd love to hear about them."

Elsie's voice carried the burden of years gone by, it was filled with nostalgia.

"Let's take a stroll down memory lane, shall we? We'll begin with Arthur, my dear husband." She pointed to a distinguished man captured in his army doctor's uniform. "Arthur was a doctor, as you can see. He served in both wars, tending to the wounded. That's where we met, just behind the trenches in a bombed-out hospital in Belgium. It was also where I reconnected with Walter. Arthur won me over right away. He was very handsome and his compassionate nature made him a favourite among his patients."

Julie interjected, "Being a doctor during the war must have been incredibly challenging."

Elsie nodded in agreement. "Indeed, it was. Arthur bore witness to the raw horrors of war up close but he never faltered in his duty."

Her gaze shifted to another photograph, this one featuring a young man in a dashing RAF pilot's uniform. "And this young man here is, Arthur Jr."

Elsie's smile wavered, and a touch of sadness brushed her voice. "Yes, we were very proud of him. He aspired to be a doctor, following in his father's footsteps, but the Second World War intervened. He joined the RAF as a pilot and fought valiantly. Unfortunately, my dear, while on a mission over Germany, he was shot down. For a long while we hoped that he had been taken prisoner but he didn't make it back home."

Julie whispered her condolences, "I'm so sorry, Elsie."

Elsie's response held warmth. "Thank you, Julie."

She then directed Julie's attention to another photograph, portraying another young man in a similar uniform to his brother's.

"That's my next oldest, Mark. Another courageous pilot, another heartbreaking loss to the war." Elsie's emotions showed and her voice trembled slightly.

Julie commented thoughtfully, "Your family has made tremendous sacrifices for our country."

Elsie acknowledged with pride, "Yes, they have, dear. And then there's Jack, he's named after his uncle my brother of course." She indicated a photo of a cheerful man clad in a butcher's apron. "He served in the army, returned home, and started his own family and business. He's quite a character, just like his namesake was."

Julie's curiosity persisted, "And what about the one in the navy uniform?"

Elsie beamed with maternal pride. "Ah, Walter, named after my baby brother; of course. He became a solicitor and served in the Royal Navy. Just look at that picture, Julie." She points to a family portrait where Walter stands tall, surrounded by his four children. "He had quite the brood, didn't he?"

"Your family's legacy is remarkable, Elsie."

"Yes, dear. They were all brave in their own ways. These photos, they're more than just images; they're a testament to the strength and love that held us together, even in the darkest of times."

As Elsie shared her family's history with Julie, the room seemed to transform into a time capsule, where the past came alive through stories, laughter, and even tears. The old photographs bridged the gap between generations, and Julie felt a profound connection to this family's enduring spirit.

Elsie squared up to Joe, "So, when can I see him," she asked bluntly.

Joe smiled and grimaced all at one time. "I think we should have a party somewhere, maybe at a restaurant…"

Julie jumped in, "What about the curry house? Do you like curry, Elsie?" there was intrigue and excitement in her voice.

"Yes, I've been known to munch the odd poppadum."

"Sounds like a plan! I won't spill the beans to Walter, and we'll throw a surprise party," Joe proposed eagerly.

Elsie glanced at the clock on the wall, her eyes widening in surprise. "Oh, goodness me," she exclaimed, "I've got an appointment to get my hair done in town. I'm afraid I'll have to ask you to leave, in the nicest possible way." With a graceful movement, she rose from her chair.

Joe, ever the gentleman, smiled warmly in response. "Of course, Elsie."

Elsie, with a playful glint in her eye, inquired, "Can you come back tomorrow?"

Joe's delight was evident as he replied, "Why yes, I'd be delighted to."

"Walter, my other Walter that is, and a couple of his sons will be visiting for Sunday lunch," Elsie continued, her tone filled with fondness. "He comes one week, and Jack and his family the next." Her laughter bubbled up, and she tilted her head back. "I can't handle them all at once these days," she confessed, "but I'd love for you to meet them." Pride coloured her words.

Joe and Julie bid a warm farewell to Elsie's cosy home, leaving Elsie feeling amazed and very happy.

They made their way to Grandma's house, where the anticipation of their arrival had Debbie practically bouncing with excitement. Her eyes sparkled as she embraced her parents, her small hand slipping trustingly into theirs.

Together, they embarked on a leisurely walk towards the nearby park. The air was alive with the symphony of children's laughter and the distant serenade of birdsong. Debbie's boundless enthusiasm permeated the atmosphere, a tangible reminder of youthful wonder.

"Mum," Debbie burst out, her voice brimming with both eagerness and innocence. "I want to grow up soon, like you and Dad."

Joe and Julie exchanged affectionate smiles, their hearts warmed by their daughter's curiosity. Joe leaned down, his eyes twinkling as he explained, "Well, sweetie, being an adult does come with more freedom, but it also brings more responsibilities."

Curiosity gleamed in Debbie's eyes as she asked, "What kind of responsibilities, Dad?"

Julie chimed in, her voice gentle and reassuring. "Responsibilities like going to work, paying bills, and taking care of your own family someday."

"But that sounds boring," Debbie exclaimed, her youthful exuberance undiminished. "I want to have fun all day long."

Joe and Julie shared a knowing laugh, the kind that only parents could understand. Joe continued, "Debbie, there are plenty of fun things that adults get to do, but they also work hard to be able to do those things."

"The secret is, to find a job that is fun to do," Julie added.

Undeterred, Debbie declared, "I don't care; I still want to grow up soon."

Joe and Julie exchanged an amused glance. They knew that as Debbie grew older, her perspective would evolve. They found a bench and settled on it, watching their daughter play on the swings with a mixture of pride and nostalgia.

"The school is really helping her," Joe remarked, his gaze never leaving Debbie's playful antics. "I've never seen her so chatty."

Julie nodded in agreement. "Yes, I'm hoping that when she's there full time there will be more changes. She's growing up so fast," she mused.

"It feels like just yesterday she was a little baby," Joe said, a touch of sentimentality in his voice.

Julie smiled, her eyes reflecting a mixture of emotions. "She's still our little girl," she said. "But soon she'll become a young woman. It's both exciting and a bit scary."

Joe nodded, his voice filled with pride. "I'm really proud of her," he admitted. "She's smart and independent. I know that despite her problems, she's going to achieve great things in life."

Julie's agreement was heartfelt. "I feel the same way," she said.

They continued to watch Debbie play, allowing themselves a moment to appreciate the unique journey of parenthood. As they headed home, Debbie's chatter about growing up continued. Joe and Julie couldn't help but laugh, recognizing that their daughter's dreams and aspirations were a sign of her growing maturity.

Once home, Debbie headed straight to her room to watch television. Joe and Julie settled onto the couch, reflecting on the day and their daughter's journey ahead.

"I think she's ready for more responsibility," Julie suggested.

Joe nodded in agreement. "Perhaps we should start giving her more jobs around the house," he suggested, a sense of anticipation for the future lingering in the air.

The following morning was a crisp Sunday morning, Joe awoke with a sense of eager anticipation. Today held the promise of a long-awaited meeting with Walter Jr. and Elsie. He quickly went about his morning routine, shaving and showering, eager to begin the day's events.

Debbie's newfound sense of independence had her up and dressed before Julie could assist her, however, they decided that she should change from football boots to more practical footwear.

During breakfast, Joe couldn't contain his excitement. "I'm really looking forward to meeting Elsie and her sons," he announced with a smile.

Just before noon, they embarked on a journey across town, navigating the bustling streets filled with weekend shoppers. There had been a road accident at a nearby junction and they were diverted along a different route. Their car weaved through the traffic until they arrived at Elsie's home.

Elsie greeted them at the door, her eyes were bright with anticipation, and she welcomed them warmly as they stepped out of the car.

"Come in, come in," she beckoned with genuine enthusiasm. "Walter's already here... I've told him all about you and your quest to reunite our family."

As they entered, Walter stood by the photo collection smiling at the picture of his Dad. He greeted them, "Hi there, Mum's told me all about you."

Inside, as they settled into the cosy living room, conversations flowed naturally. Walter Jr. shared stories of his own family and the challenges life had thrown at him, his voice tinged with a mix of nostalgia and resilience.

Joe leaned forward, his eyes filled with genuine curiosity. "Walter, tell us about your father, about the man he was."

Walter Jr. nodded, a reminiscent smile gracing his lips. "Dad, was a brilliant doctor," he began, his voice tinged with both fondness and sorrow. "I was only a young teenager when he went away to war. Mum, God bless her soul, assured us he'd be back soon." He shook his head, "Unfortunately, fate had other plans for him and my brothers. Somewhere in North Africa, working in a field hospital with the Eighth Army, he met his end."

Elsie's voice joined in, her tone carrying the burden of shared grief. "I couldn't believe it. After everything we'd gone through in the First World War, it just didn't seem fair. I lost my two sons in the same month, both of them shot down over Germany. If it hadn't been for Walter and Jack, I don't know how I would have survived. Of course, I worried about their safety and every day I lived in fear of another telegram dropping on the mat."

Silence settled over the room, heavy with the weight of their collective losses. Yet, in that shared grief, there was also a profound sense of resilience and the enduring bonds of family that had carried them through the darkest of times.

As they continued to share stories and reminisce, the room once again filled with laughter and warmth, proof of their inner strength and the enduring power of family ties.

Walter Jr. recounted tales of his own family, and Debbie listened with wide-eyed wonder.

The afternoon continued with a traditional Yorkshire meal, a hearty spread of roast beef and Yorkshire puddings.

"Oh, my words Elsie, you're a wonderful cook I can never get my Yorkshires to rise like that," Julie commented as she helped Elsie with the washing up.

Time seemed to slip away as they shared stories and exchanged laughter. The room resonated with the echoes of family tales, weaving a tapestry of shared memories and hopes for the future.

"So, when can we meet up with Uncle Walter?" Walter Jr. asked, his eyes shining with anticipation.

Joe smiled, his heart warmed by the prospect of reuniting the family. "We had talked about a party for all of you... I mentioned the article I'm planning to write. What if we ask the local newspaper to send a photographer?" Joe suggested, his excitement evident.

"Oh, no, Joe," Julie intervened, concern in her voice. "They'll want it to be private, surely."

Walter suddenly interrupted, his eyes twinkling with an idea. "We could hire a photographer; we'll certainly want some photos to capture this special day. Do you have a venue in mind?"

Elsie thrilled by the idea chipped in, "We certainly do… the curry house on Market Street, Joe and Walter visit it at times."

Walter looked surprised, "Sounds good to me."

Joe was feeling excited as the intrigue of the party filled him with joy. "You'll get a surprise… Walter speaks Urdu like a native, he had the staff there in stitches. I've no idea what he was telling them."

"Does Jack know yet?" Walter asked his mother.

"No, it's all been a bit of a shock. I've not had time yet."

"I'll call around and see him." He turned to Joe and Julie. "If you can arrange this party… Jack and I will pay for it."

They all paused, pondering the suggestion. Julie was the first to offer a solution.

"It's Christmas in two weeks," she suggested, "why don't we arrange something for New Year's Eve? What a way to start the New Year."

Elsie clapped her hands in glee, "I love it, I can't wait."

There was a general consensus on that idea, and so it was agreed. The room buzzed with excitement as plans for the family gathering took shape. It was a moment of shared anticipation for the joyful reunion that lay ahead.

"Could we contact anyone else?" Julie asked, her curiosity piqued.

Elsie looked sad and shivered a little. "No, I'm afraid not. I know Tilly passed away some years ago. She married a farmer from up Skipton way, but I don't think she was very happy." She paused to think. "Claire, I saw her just before the Second World War. In fact, it was outside our old house. By chance, we'd both gone on a nostalgic journey. She'd moved to London, and from what she told me of her new life, I was convinced she'd fallen in with a bad crowd. I'm certain her husband was a bit of a gangster in the East End. I heard nothing from her after the blitz." Elsie looked sad, the reality was something she did not like to face.

The room fell into a moment of reflection, each person lost in their own thoughts about family members who had drifted away or faced difficult circumstances. The forthcoming gathering seemed all the more precious in light of these unspoken stories and the bonds that had endured through time.

Chapter Twenty-Eight
A Stroke of Luck.

Joe pulled up outside Walter's house, the rain pounded the windshield relentlessly, so hard that the wipers could hardly cope. He couldn't wait to share his news about Elsie and her family with Walter, but he had promised the family to save it for the secret party. He paused for a moment, hoping the rain would relent, but the deluge showed no signs of abating. With resolve, he dashed out of the car, crossed the pavement, and lightly tapped on Walter's door before entering without waiting for an invitation.

Walter was taken aback, his surprise evident in his expression. "By gum, Joe, you're in a hurry this morning," he remarked with a warm smile, clearly pleased to see his friend.

Joe, soaked from the rain, grinned apologetically. "Sorry about that, Walter. It's absolutely pouring out there. How are you this morning? I hope you managed alright without me these last couple of days."

Walter reassured him, "Oh, yes, of course. I watched the football on Saturday afternoon, and then I watched it again in the highlights later on. It was a good match."

Joe, ever thoughtful, produced a paper bag. "I brought you a couple of pasties again. I had thought we might go out for a walk this morning, but considering the weather, I think we're better off staying at home."

Walter nodded in agreement, his eyes reflecting a sense of contemplation. "Yes, I think you're right, Joe. Hang your coat up on the airer to dry. Shall we do some recording?"

Walter had been reflecting on his life story, and he realized that sharing it was quite therapeutic and was helping him come to terms with the loss of Alice.

The rain outside continued its relentless downpour, creating a soothing backdrop for the cosy scene within Walter's home. As they prepared for another recording session, Joe and Walter followed a familiar routine, they found their comfortable spot in the living room. Walter, ever the gracious host, had prepared a pot of coffee, and the room was filled with the comforting aroma of the fresh brew.

Joe meticulously checked his recording equipment, ensuring the microphone was in its proper place and that every wire was connected securely. A notebook lay open on his lap, ready for jotting down important details and notes from their conversation.

Before diving into the new tales, Joe took a moment to review their previous recordings. It was a way for Walter to reflect on the journey they had embarked upon, to see how far his life story had come since that first rainy day.

Walter, his eyes filled with memories, handed Joe a cup of coffee, and they exchanged a nod of readiness. Joe began with open-ended questions, inviting Walter to share more about his past, his experiences, and the emotions woven into his life's tapestry.

"We left off on rather a sad note, where you lost your child," Joe said, a hint of sadness shimmering in his eyes. "How did you pick yourself up after such an event?"

Walter's gaze turned introspective, and he paused for a moment, collecting his thoughts.

"I'm not reight sure, lad. It was a long and painful process, and to be truthful, I don't think either of us ever truly got over it. But I believe it was our mutual love that helped us find some semblance of healing."

Joe smiled, admiring the courage he saw in Walter's eyes. "So, what about work?" Joe enquired.

Walter's eyes brightened as he continued, "Well, obviously, Alice had to leave her job at the stables. There was no compensation in those days, no support for her mental state either. Unless you were wealthy, it seemed like no one really cared. So, I suggested a change of scenery, a holiday of sorts. Alice had always fancied a holiday in Scotland, I'd told her about my adventures there with Troy. I had some very fond memories of when I worked there."

Walter's mind drifted back to that time, his voice carrying the heavy load of his memories.

"It was a memorable holiday. We made our way north, staying overnight in Carlisle. The next morning, we took a train to Castle Douglas and then we took a horse-drawn cab to reach our final destination. Which was a little inn, well known to travellers, I'd stayed there once before when I was on the road with Troy. Let me paint the scene for you. "Walter smiled obviously the place had a special meaning for him.

"Nestled on the coast, our quaint Scottish inn exuded charm and history. As we stepped inside, there was a cosy ambience created by low wooden beams that crisscrossed the ceiling, evoking a sense of warmth and romance, we were made very welcome right from the start and I sensed it was going to be a worthwhile venture. We booked our stay for six nights. Our room had a wonderful view out over the scenic landscape around the Solway Firth."

Joe was drawn in; his mouth was almost watering at the thought of the place.

Walter continued, "The main highlight and comfort in the inn was a roaring log fire, that cast an amber glow across the room. Its smoky aroma mingled with the earthy scent that is common in old public houses."

"Wow, Walter you've sold me this place already."

Walter chortled and continued.

"I'm just getting into my full flow now… on the walls were majestic antlers of proud Scottish stags, their presence sort of authenticated the scene. So, picture this Joe, at the heart of the inn stands the bar, a grand structure crafted from polished wood and etched glass that reflected the light on its smooth surfaces. Bottles of various fine Scotch whisky lined the shelves behind the bar, their amber nectar a joy to behold. The barman, with a friendly smile, expertly pours drams of these fine local spirits for the inn's patrons."

"Blimey Walter what time's the train there… it sounds like heaven. What was the landlord like?"

Walter smiles pleased that he has amused Joe. "He was a fine character with a hearty laugh and a twinkle in his eye, he welcomed us like long-lost family. He bowled Alice over with his traditional attire; he wore a tweed jacket and tartan tie, his rugged, weathered face told tales of years spent in the Scottish wilderness, and his stories of local lore and legends kept the patrons entertained late into the night. With a warm, thick brogue, he offered recommendations for the finest whiskies and hearty Scottish dishes, ensuring that every guest felt at home in this charming retreat.

That evening, quite coincidentally, my old Captain and his wife were also dining there. After our meals, we found ourselves in the lounge together."

There was a short pause as Walter sipped his cold coffee and then he continued, "It's good to see you again." The captain said, "Don't think me presumptuous, but if you are interested, I have a job that I believe would suit your skills perfectly.' I gave him a curious look. 'Not lugging timber this time, but something I think will be just up your street; the annual cull of our red deer is happening next week. I know with your shooting skills it's something you'd excel at. Perhaps if we offer you and your charming lady wife accommodation at the Hall, you might consider helping us with this task.'"

Walter's face lit up with excitement as he recalled the offer. "I was utterly gobsmacked. It was a fantastic opportunity to earn some extra money, and extend our holiday."

Walter leaned forward, his eyes reflecting the vivid memory playing out in his mind.

"The next day," Walter reminisced, a soft nostalgia lingering in his voice, "The Captain's arrival was as commanding as ever, astride a magnificent chestnut steed that exuded a sense of regal bearing. His gillies, clad in rugged Highland attire, stood by his side, a stark contrast to the Captain's polished image.

"'Have you given my proposal any thought?' the Captain inquired, his tone measured yet expectant.

"Yes, sir. I'd be honoured to return to your service," I replied with genuine enthusiasm, feeling a mix of anticipation and readiness for the opportunity. "When do you require me to start?"

"The Captain, characteristically concise, simply nodded a glint of approval in his steely gaze. 'Good man,' he acknowledged before urging his mount forward. As he began to ride away, his commanding voice carried back to me, 'I shall send a gig for you at the end of the week,' his words resonating across the tranquil countryside as he disappeared into the horizon."

Walter's voice carried the importance of that moment, it was the beginning of a new chapter in his life, one filled with the promise of adventure and the unknown. As Walter recounted this turning point in his life, Joe couldn't help but admire someone who could make a decision without tripping over all the possible obstacles.

"Did you not discuss your pay with the captain?" Joe asked.

"Didn't need to, don't forget I'd worked for him before and I knew the wage would be acceptable."

"We cherished the next six days, finding solace and serenity in the heart of Scotland's rugged landscapes. Most mornings, we set out on leisurely walks, our footsteps echoing through the hills, or we would sit by the shores of the Firth and watch the countless birds that pecked at the sands and swirled in the air. It was a time of quiet reflection, a respite from the tumultuous storm that had shaken our lives. It was as you might say just what the doctor ordered."

Walter smiled and stared into his empty mug, as he said, "Time for a cuppa, I think."

They paused their storytelling, and Joe rose to his feet to put on the kettle. The comforting sound of boiling water soon filled the air, mingling with that familiar aroma of freshly brewed coffee. As Joe worked, Walter took the opportunity to open his shoebox.

"I've got some photos from that break," Walter's voice carried the weight of nostalgia and excitement. "The Leica I bought then was my first-ever camera. Handheld cameras were a rarity back in those days, but a new shop had just opened in town, offering cameras, film, and developing services."

With tender reverence, Walter sifted through the box, each photograph a silent storyteller encapsulating moments frozen in time. Carefully selecting a few from the pile, he laid them out on the table. Grainy black and white images emerged, revealing landscapes painted in serenity, where heather-dressed hills sprawled against the sky. Yet, it was the portraits, faces etched with laughter, determination, and quiet love, that stole the breath away.

In the midst of the aromatic coffee and the quiet bubbling of the kettle, Walter and Joe found themselves transported once more to that distant past.

The images, artefacts of a bygone adventure, now breathed life into the room, infusing it with the vibrant hues of their shared journey.

"That's Alice, the landscape was truly grand… but compared to her it was very dull." He laughed.

"She was very lovely," Joe admitted, "She looks like a film star the way she poses for you."

Walter chuckled as he pointed to a particular photograph, a moment captured and preserved. In the image, he was dressed in a kilt and a tweed jacket, an expression of mischief dancing in his eyes. He began to narrate the story behind the photo, his voice tinged with fondness and nostalgia.

"You see," he began, "The landlord of the inn and I decided to play a little joke on Alice. We concocted a tale about going on a 'Haggis Hunt,' one of those mythical creatures from Scottish folklore. Of course, she didn't quite buy into our boyish prank, but she humoured us, deciding to join in the joke." Walter continued a hint of amusement in his tone. "The landlord generously lent me the kilt for the photograph and gave Alice a shawl to wear. He told us it was a magical shawl, one that the Haggis couldn't resist; 'they'll flock to you,' he claimed. He even provided us with a detailed map and directions, promising that they would lead us straight to the haggis in their 'natural habitat.'"

Walter's eyes seemed to sparkle with the memory of that day. "So, off we went on our little adventure, me striding out in the kilt and armed with our map to guide us. The directions led us into a magical glen, a place of breathtaking beauty. Steep rocks framed our path, their surfaces were adorned with a lush, green moss that seemed to drip with water so pure you could drink it. It gave the whole place an otherworldly, almost ethereal quality. Alice said it was how she imagined a Fairy Dell to be."

Walter's voice grew more animated as he described their journey. "As we climbed higher through that glen, our spirits soared beside us. It felt like a spiritual pilgrimage, a rediscovery of hope in the heart of the Scottish wilderness. You see, I had lost my faith amid the blood-soaked fields of Belgium, but that day, in that glen, I found something special once more."

A warm smile graced Walter's face as he concluded, "When we finally emerged from that enchanted glen, it was as if we had been reborn with a newfound hope, ready to embrace the world once more."

"The heather was in full bloom, cascading like a royal carpet across the undulating hillsides, as far as the eye could see. Its vivid purplish hue adorned the typically green slopes, transforming the landscape into an artist's vision. Nature seemed to be orchestrating a symphony of hues, painting a picturesque scene of healing and renewal across the hills.

"I remember that moment vividly," Walter reminisced with a soft sigh. "The air, thick with the earthy fragrance of the heather, was rejuvenating. Each breath I drew felt like a gulp of tranquillity, as though the very essence of nature's serenity had seeped into the air. It was a remarkable sensation, standing amidst such natural splendour."

Walter paused, his gaze distant as he delved into the depths of his memory.

"But it wasn't just the scenery. I saw a change come over Alice during those days. Though I knew she still carried the pain deep within her, I believe she found a measure of peace in the embrace of nature. It was as if she started to accept the world for what it is. That night, back in the inn, there was only one food we could try for supper, and, yes, you've guessed it, Haggis, neeps, and tatties, all accompanied by a very generous tot of whiskey. Everyone in the inn that evening joined in the fun, and before long, it turned into a lively party, with the barman playing his bagpipes. I saw Alice truly enjoy herself and laugh for the first time in a long while."

"As arranged, at the end of our stay at the inn, the Captain sent a horse and buggy to convey us to the Hall. I thought it was a generous gesture by him. The Hall itself, well, it was nothing short of a masterpiece… a Gothic marvel that seemed to embody the very essence of power in that ancient, imposing landscape."

They provided us with a comfortable cottage, and as we entered, the sight of it brought a radiant smile to Alice's face. We'd a cosy living room, complete with a log fire that crackled with warmth. A stag's head above it on the chimney breast kept its beady eyes on our every move. I can still hear the excitement in her voice, she was so delighted, as she turned to me and said, 'You go off shooting, my love. I shall find my bliss in the pages of a good book amidst this stunning backdrop.' With a theatrical flair, she flung herself onto a colossal couch, her exclamation of 'Perfect!' echoing through the room. We shared a hearty laugh, the promise of adventure dancing in our eyes.

The following day, two of the Captain's gillies arrived at our doorstep. They were armed with all the necessary hunting gear and there was a sense of old friends because I had met them before when Troy and I helped with the logging. They presented me with a camouflaged jacket and trousers, and as I donned them, I felt proud, it was like putting on my old uniform and I felt the part.

We set off, heading up the glen, the lads had a hip flask or two which we shared as we climbed. It didn't take long before we spotted a gathering of stags. They were truly majestic, their antlers sprawling like crowns of the wilderness. I couldn't help but feel a pang of sorrow at the thought of taking their lives, but then one of the gillies pointed out a particular stag, noticeably weaker than the others and clearly ailing.

Making sure we were downwind of our quarries, I lay down in the soft heather and took aim. At that moment, as I stared down the rifle's sights, indecision gripped me. Memories of the past came rushing back, vivid, and haunting. The rumble of distant gunfire and the anguished cries of the wounded and the dying replayed in my mind. The gillies must have sensed something amiss but they couldn't possibly fathom the ghosts that lingered within me. I took a deep breath, steadying myself, and then I fired. The shot was, even if I say it myself, impeccably precise, the animal fell swiftly. It was a clean kill, one that didn't send the other deer into a frenzy of fear.

And so, this pattern continued for the next ten days. I hunted and took down fifty-two deer, their noble spirits returning to the earth, and I even shot a few rabbits to provide sustenance for the gillies and myself. It was a blend of exhilaration and melancholy, a unique interplay of emotions that defined those days in the heart of Scotland's wilderness.

The Captain expressed his genuine delight with my work, commending my skill in aiding the cull of the creatures. He assured me that he would summon me as soon as the need arose for further culling. And as if the sense of accomplishment weren't enough, I was handsomely rewarded for my efforts. It was a generous payment, a recognition of the vital role I had played in maintaining the balance of the local wildlife.

But that wasn't all. As a further bonus, we were allowed to retain the cottage for an additional two weeks. It was an unexpected gift, an extension of our break amidst the serene Scottish landscapes. Those extra weeks provided us with the precious opportunity to further immerse ourselves in the beauty of the natural world almost as if nature herself had chosen to embrace us with open arms."

"It truly was a great adventure and a fortunate turn of events," Joe remarked. "You seemed to have landed squarely on your feet."

"Indeed, Joe, but the story doesn't end there. More opportunities came our way.' Walter's voice carried a sense of wonder as he continued. "As word of my skills as a sharpshooter spread, two more lairds from neighbouring estates sent me offers of work. So, it transpired that we were away from our Yorkshire home for almost six months. At one of the farms, something remarkable happened. Alice, my dear Alice, found the courage to get back in the saddle once again. I remember the worry etched on her face the first time she mounted the horse, but her love for riding, her indomitable spirit, soon triumphed over her apprehension. While I was away, walking through the glens, rifle in hand, she was riding across the countryside, the wind in her hair, and the Scottish landscape unfolding around her."

Walter's eyes twinkled with the memory, the joy of that time evident in his expression. "But, as with all good things, our time away had to end. We reluctantly returned here but we were glad to be home. Yet, even as winter's icy grip tightened around us, our spirits remained buoyant. We were filled with a euphoria that warmed our hearts, a residue of the adventures we had, and a very nice sum to deposit in the bank… enough to carry us through the winter."

Walter's words carried a profound sense of nostalgia, an echo of the happiness they had found in the midst of adversity, and the enduring spirit that had carried them through those transformative months.

At the end of their session, as the rain outside continued its rhythmic drumming, Joe and Walter reflected on their conversation. They discussed what they had covered, revisited the topics they planned to explore next and set their goals for the continuing voyage into Walter's life story.

"Oh, I nearly forgot," Joe said, "We were hoping you'd like to share Christmas with us at our house?"

Walter looked stunned, his eyes filled with tears, and his throat seemed too tight to speak at first. "What can I say? That is so generous… but I'd hate to be a burden."

"Don't be silly," Joe said, taking hold of Walter's hand. "We can't bear the thought of you being on your own for Christmas. We'd be honoured if you'd come."

Chapter Twenty-Nine
This is Jack.

Julie's heart danced with excitement as Joe's footsteps echoed through the hallway. She turned from the window, where she'd been eagerly waiting, her eyes alive with anticipation.

"Guess what?" Julie began, her voice brimming with excitement, her eyes sparkling like stars on a clear night.

Joe entered the room, his curiosity piqued. He pulled her into a warm embrace, his eagerness matching hers. "Don't keep me in suspense," he urged, a playful grin on his face. "What's the news?"

Julie couldn't contain her enthusiasm. "Elsie rang me earlier," she exclaimed. "She mentioned that her other son, Jack, is coming to visit tonight, and she asked if we would like to meet him." She ended her revelation with a tender kiss on the tip of Joe's nose.

A flicker of anticipation danced in Joe's eyes. "And you said yes, I assume?"

"Of course," Julie replied, a playful lilt in her voice. "What else would I say?"

Joe chuckled in agreement. "Fair point. What time is this happening?"

Julie paused, her mind racing. "Elsie said around seven. Mum's coming over to babysit."

The seconds seemed to stretch as they waited for Julie's Mum to arrive. Joe's heart raced with the prospect of meeting Jack, while Julie fidgeted with a mix of joy and nervousness, the anticipation making her unable to sit still.

Their conversation was punctuated by the sound of the doorbell. Julie's mum had arrived. As Joe and Julie made their way to the door, their smiles mirrored their shared excitement for the evening that lay ahead.

"We won't be long Mum," Julie said. "Debbie's already in bed but I think she's waiting for you to go read her a story.

As they drove to Elsie's house, Joe and Julie engaged in a conversation about their plans for Walter's visit at Christmas.

Julie said smiling, "I wonder if he has any preferences for his Christmas dinner? It's such a wonderful idea."

Joe nodded, he was trying to concentrate on the road, the conditions were dreadful, ice, fog, and dazzling lights of other motorists.

"He's not said, I doubt if he'll be very fussy about what we have. I think the company will make him happy enough. It's a great way to make his Christmas special," He paused to check for traffic as he turned off the main road. "Especially after all he's been through. And I think it'll be lovely for him to spend the day with people who care about him."

Julie: "Absolutely, and I've been thinking about what we could do to make it even more memorable for him."

Joe parked the car and answered, "Well, Walter mentioned he enjoyed a traditional Yorkshire meal. Let's go all out with roast turkey, stuffing, and all the works. I'll bet he'll love it."

"And we can decorate the house with lots of Christmas lights and ornaments. You know, give it that festive feel."

Joe looked thoughtful, "Well, Debbie will love that too, I can almost see her face lighting up when she sees all the decorations. And we'll have to put up a Christmas tree, of course."

Julie looked happy. "Of course! And let's make sure we have some carol singers for a little Christmas music. It'll be a day to remember."

"You know, Julie, I think Walter will really appreciate it. He's been through a lot, and this will be a way to show him how much we care."

Julie: "Exactly, Joe. It's not just about the decorations and the food; it's about showing him the warmth of a family that cares about him. It'll be a Christmas he won't forget."

Their conversation was filled with excitement and a shared determination to make Walter's Christmas special, and as they arrived at Elsie's house, their hearts were filled with the spirit of the season and the joy of giving.

"Do you happen to know what date is Walter's birthday?" Julie inquired, her mind already formulating a plan.

Joe pondered for a moment. "Well, he mentioned to me that he had no idea about his real birthday. Maybe Elsie will have some information about it. On his paperwork in the office, it mentioned July twelfth."

Elsie welcomed them at the door. Her face wrinkled into a huge smile, her eyes sparkling with excitement.

"Come in, hurry up or you'll catch your death out there tonight. I'm so glad you could come," she said. "Jack's in the living room. Let me introduce you."

The living room felt cosy and warm as they entered. A heavy-built man of about fifty sat, dressed in denim jeans and a tee shirt printed with the image of a guitar across his chest. Elsie gestured towards him, introducing, "Jack, these are the lovely people I was telling you about, Joe and Julie."

Jack's warm greeting and strong handshake left a positive impression. The firmness of the handshake and the strength of that hand revealed much about Jack's life. Joe couldn't help but notice the calloused hand, a testament to a life of hard work and dedication to his craft. It spoke of a man unafraid of hard toil.

Elsie fussed about taking Joe and Julie's coats.

"Jack, these two kind souls are friends with your Uncle Walter… of course, you've never met him. They are helping him with something special. Now, I know you once delved into the family history, and I wondered if you might know his actual birthday?"

Jack sounded surprised, "My uncle Walter? Do you mean your brother Walter?" His brows furrowed in thought. "Well, that's fantastic… Mum's often mentioned him and Uncle Jack." He looked thoughtful, "There might be some old records or family documents that have that information. I'll see what I can find."

"Tea, everyone?" Elsie asked, her voice tinged with warmth as she disappeared into the sanctuary of her kitchen.

As the kettle hissed and cups clinked, Jack settled into a chair, his eyes flickering with curiosity. "So, what's all this about?"

Joe sighed, a mix of apprehension and fondness in his tone. "I'm Walter's social carer, but when I first brought up the idea of him going into a care home, it didn't go down very well. Somehow, we started talking about the past. I've always dreamt of being a journalist, so I thought of writing an article about him. But it's become much more. In the short time I've known him, he's filled a void for me that I never realized I had… a father figure."

"Sounds like your meeting was good for you both," Jack said.

Joe nodded, his eyes shimmering with unspoken stories. "I wanted to help Walter reconnect with his family. The catch was that we were not sure if any of his siblings were still around."

The room fell into a contemplative silence, the weight of uncertainty hanging in the air like a dense fog. Elsie reappeared with her tea trolley, and a playful banter ensued.

"Oh, mother, are you still pushing that old thing about."

"Don't you be cheeky… there are miles left in this trolley," Elsie retorted with a twinkle in her eye.

Joe relished the lively exchange between them. "Do you know about the New Year's Eve party we're planning?" he asked Jack.

Jack grinned, "Well, only what Mum's told me since I arrived here tonight, and that I'm footing the bill." His willingness to participate was clear.

As Joe outlined the party plans, Jack's enthusiasm was infectious.

"Sounds like a blast. I've got just the guy for the photos." He was genuinely excited about contributing.

Joe reached into his pocket and handed Jack a folded paper. "Here's something we found about your namesake, your Uncle Jack served in the Royal Navy."

Jack paused to read the press release. He turned to Elsie, "Crickey, this is amazing. Did you know about this?"

Elsie replied, "No, when this news was in the paper, I was still serving in France. I was amazed too when Joe showed it to me."

Jack couldn't hide his amazement. "Wow, I can't believe it. Thank you, Joe, that's fantastic."

Joe chuckled, "Well if you like that story, you just wait until you hear your Uncle Walter's stories."

The room was filled with anticipation and shared stories, creating an atmosphere of excitement and warmth as they delved into their family's history.

As the evening unfolded, Elsie shared cherished memories of Walter from their childhood.

"He was always up to something, he drove our parents up the wall at times. We never knew where he was, he was always off somewhere. I'm not surprised he enjoyed walking along the canals." Elsie spoke with a tear meandering over her aged cheek.

"He told me he was always in trouble at school, and with Tilly," Joe probed for further background.

Elsie shared more about Walter's earlier years, and Joe listened intently, eager to uncover more details for his story.

Elsie continued, "When he was at school, it felt like he was getting the cane all the time. It seemed like he'd do anything to avoid it, including bunking off. There was this one time when he'd been missing for two days and the police brought him back from Littleborough, on the other side of the Pennines. He told them he had just gone for a walk, got lost, and had to ask them for help. He was only about eight at the time. I suspect he might have handed himself in because he couldn't face climbing back over the mountains." She shook her head in dismay. "Mum nearly had a heart attack when the Black Mariah pulled up outside the house. Of course, all the neighbours were out being nosy, as they always are."

Joe absorbed these stories, which helped paint a more vivid picture of Walter's adventurous youth. It was clear that his early years were filled with both misadventures and unexpected encounters, making his journey through life even more intriguing.

"I still take him down to the towpath on fine days, he loves to reminisce about his years on the canals. Unfortunately, he needs the use of a wheelchair these days to get out and about."

They shared a delightful trip down memory lane, and Joe and Julie couldn't help but smile as they listened to stories about the man they had grown to admire so much.

"Unfortunately, there are no photographs of him, dad didn't own a camera," Elsie said her voice edged with regret.

As the evening ended, Elsie promised to dig through old family records to find any information about Walter's birthday.

Touched by the gathering, Elsie expressed her gratitude for their interest in her brother's life story. It was a night filled with hope and the promise of uncovering more about Walter's past, all thanks to the newfound connection with his family.

Chapter Thirty
The Secret

Joe wasn't very good at keeping a secret and so, the next day when he met Walter, he had to be on his guard. Otherwise, his excitement at the thought of bringing Walter's family together would make him spill the beans.

Almost as soon as he entered Walter's kitchen he smiled and asked Walter, "What would you like to do today?"

Walter considered for a moment before replying, "If it's not too cold, what about a walk to the park? We can wrap up well. They've forecast snow for the weekend; maybe we'll have a white Christmas." He looked happy as he said. "Thank you for your invitation. I've not shared Christmas with anyone for the last ten years since Alice died."

Joe nodded, touched by Walter's openness. "A walk to the park sounds like a lovely idea, and it will be an honour to share Christmas with you, I'm sure it will be a special day."

As they set off for the park, there was a flurry of snowflakes and a chilly wind that made them both shiver.

"Blimey Joe, do you think we need snow chains for my wheels?" They both laughed heartily at the suggestion.

Joe adjusted the blanket across Walter's knees making sure that it was well tucked in.

The prospect of a snowy Christmas filled Joe with cheer, and he couldn't help but smile. "A walk in the park, a chance of snow, and good company? It sounds like the perfect day."

As they made their way down to the towpath, their banter floated on the chilly air. Walter, wrapped in layers of warm clothing, hummed a little tune, his spirit undeterred by the cold.

"Come on, Joe, put your back into it, it's too cold to hang about," Walter teased, his eyes sparkling with mischief.

"You're a hard slave master, Mr Middlebrough," Joe quipped back, pushing the wheelchair a little faster. His breath was visible in the cold air. Their laughter mingled with the crisp winter breeze, creating a lively atmosphere.

They stopped by the canal to watch the ducks. Parts of the water were frozen over and the ducks were comically waddling across the ice to find places to swim.

Walter pulled his scarf around his chin, shivering slightly. "I'm not sure that this was such a good idea, Joe," he admitted, his voice muffled by the scarf.

"We'll have a quick spin around the park," Joe said, his tone confident and cheerful. "I believe they've got the Christmas tree up and decorated somewhere near the old bandstand."

As they strolled, they couldn't resist the urge to burst into Christmas songs, their voices harmonizing in the crisp winter air.

"I do enjoy Christmas," Joe confided a hint of nostalgia in his voice. "After my Mum and Dad left me with my Aunt, she always made sure that I had a really special time. I remember lots of warm, cosy moments."

The memories of past Christmases brought a sense of warmth to the chilly day, and the anticipation of the grandly decorated Christmas tree ahead filled them both with excitement. Amidst the wintry atmosphere, a few people gathered around the majestic tree, standing tall, at least twelve feet high, adorned with shimmering tinsel, flashing lights and an array of vibrant decorations.

"Goodness, what a spectacle! The council seems to have pulled out all the stops this year. Probably explains why my rates are sky-high," Joe quipped in his typical dry humour.

"Ah, but look at those little ones over there," Walter countered, his smile infectious. "Their faces are full of joy, it's like witnessing magic. Sometimes, it's the little moments that make it all worthwhile."

They stopped for a moment, watching the lights that twinkled and flashed, sometimes randomly, other times in delightful patterns.

Walter nodded appreciatively, "I must say, Joe, there is something to be said for modern electrics; we could never do that with real candles."

Joe laughed secretly at Walter's comment and then continued their walk.

Despite the cold, the camaraderie between Joe and Walter created a heart-warming atmosphere, reminding them that the holiday season was not just about the weather but the warmth of shared moments and cherished memories.

Indoors, Joe cranked up the heating. "I'll tell you what, Walter, it's shaping up to be a proper cold winter."

"I've got a batch of sandwiches prepared, Joe. Could you fetch them?"

As Joe began setting out their simple meal on the table, a faint knock came at the door. Joe was taken by surprise when he opened it.

"Julie! What a pleasant surprise," Joe's voice exuded a blend of delight and mild concern. "Is everything all right? Come in, Walter's in the sitting room." he enquired.

Julie stepped into the room, her presence bringing an unexpected joy. Walter, a mixture of confusion and pleasure on his face, stood up to greet her.

"Hello, Mr Middlebrough, Joe's told me so much about you that I feel I already know you."

"Please call me Walter," he said simply. "May I call you by your first name?" Walter asked, displaying his old-fashioned chivalry. "The house is a bit of a mess, and we were just planning to share some sandwiches. Will you do us the honour of joining us?"

Julie smiled warmly. "If there's enough for one more, I'd be delighted. Joe's spoken of your generosity. But, I come bearing gifts. I've heard about your liking for pasties, so I've brought some with me."

Walter responded with a twinkle in his eye, "He's mentioned you as well, but he's never let on what a bonny lass you are."

Julie chuckled, her laughter filling the room. "And he certainly hasn't revealed your talent for flattery."

When they finished their lunch, Walter went to his secret stash of biscuits.

"Scottish shortbread biscuits," he said with a smile, holding out the box. It featured pictures of the Scottish glens with tartan patterns. "Mrs Singh especially gets these for me because she knows I love them."

Walter handed the box to Julie, saying, "Why don't you have the first pick? It's a fresh box."

He then turned to Joe and said, "I have a small errand to run, just down to see Mrs Singh."

Julie offered, "Can I go for you?"

Walter politely declined, replying, "No, that's a kind offer but not really. It's something I must do myself."

"Well, let's go now. The snow has stopped for the moment," Joe observed, looking out the window. "You'll need your coat and scarf again."

The pavement was covered in a layer of wet slush and ice, as cars passed them they constantly had to duck away from the spray off their tyres. Balancing became an intricate dance; Joe found himself relying on the wheelchair for stability."

Inside the shop, Mr Singh warmly greeted them, saying, "Mr Walter, it's a pleasure to see you out and about in this lovely Yorkshire weather."

Walter asked, "May I speak with Mrs Singh?"

Dressed in a turquoise sari and a headscarf, Mrs Singh appeared from behind a beaded curtain, having overheard her name, she recognised Walter's voice. They greeted each other and spoke in Urdu, Joe observed their exchange, noting Walter's questions and her responses through smiles and various hand gestures and nods.

Walter turned to Joe and with a rub of his hands said, "All sorted, let's get off home."

Curious, Joe couldn't help but ask, "What was that all about?"

Walter dismissed it with a wave of his hand, "Nothing for you to worry about."

As she waited, Julie took it upon herself to tidy up. She gracefully moved around the kitchen, lathering the dishes with soap, and rinsing them under the warm stream of water. The hum of the vacuum cleaner filled the living room as she meticulously glided it across the carpet, erasing the faint traces of dust and bringing a fresh vitality to the space.

Her eyes wandered toward the bookshelf, a treasure trove of knowledge and stories. A soft smile played on her lips as curiosity tugged at her. With a gentle touch, she slid a couple of volumes from their places, careful not to disrupt their order. The weight of the books felt reassuring in her hands as she leafed through the pages, briefly immersing herself in their worlds before delicately returning them to their spots.

With her tasks complete, Julie sank into a cushioned chair, relishing the serene atmosphere. The room exuded tranquillity, an embrace of warmth and familiarity. She let herself melt into the quietude, absorbing the cosiness of the surroundings. Each corner held a story, each object a piece of Walter's history. It was more than a room; it was a sanctuary of memories and comfort.

As Walter and Joe trudged back from their snowy adventure to Mrs Singh's shop, a mischievous grin crept across Walter's face. He turned to Joe and said, "You know, Joe, I've just realised something."

Joe raised an eyebrow, intrigued. "What's that, Walter?"

Walter chuckled, "I think you need to invest in some snow chains for your feet. It looked like you were auditioning for a part in a slapstick comedy, the way you were slipping and sliding on that slush."

Joe couldn't help but laugh, "Well, it was quite a performance, I must say."

They continued their walk, now sharing light-hearted banter about the snowy escapade. As they approached their destination Joe couldn't resist poking fun at himself. "Let's hope Mrs Singh didn't think I was trying out for the Yorkshire Winter Olympics team."

Walter grinned, "Oh, I'm sure she was thoroughly entertained by the sight of you."

Their playful banter continued all the way back home, making the snowy journey not just an errand but a memorable and humorous adventure.

As soon as Walter entered he knew that Julie had been busy while they were away. "What have you been up to?" Walter asked Julie.

Julie replied, "Just thought I could help. I don't mind."

"It's kind of you to help, but your husband is trying to get me into a home and I don't want to give him any excuses."

Julie whispered in confidence to Walter, "I think he's given up any such notion, we'll make sure you are looked after here."

Joe, keen to hear more of Walter's tales, suggested, "So, Walter, we've got a couple of hours. How about continuing with your saga?"

Julie chimed in enthusiastically, "Oh yes, please! I'd love to hear them in your voice instead of just the tape recordings."

Walter settled into his chair, taking a moment to let his memories resurface.

"I'm not used to an audience," Walter said almost embarrassed. "I think we'd got to the thirties and with us going to work in Scotland. Well, right up to the start of the Second World War, life just bumbled along in a delightful rhythm. Our annual Scottish holidays, financed by the proceeds from the various culls, became the highlight of our year. For a few precious months, we'd immerse ourselves in the breathtaking landscapes, where I'd be out shooting on different estates, and Alice would gracefully traverse the glens on horseback. It was during these moments that she radiated with vitality, a vision of health and happiness.

Our stays were never just about work; they were a celebration of our life. Invitations to dinners and parties flowed generously, and we revelled in the friendship of those Highland gatherings. We forged enduring friendships, creating a network of kindred spirits in the north. The anchor of these experiences was the familiar embrace of the same hotel, the one we had first visited. Our room there was almost as familiar as home.

"The landlord and his family became more than hosts; they evolved into cherished friends. Our connection grew so deep that we stood as godparents to their second son. The bonds we formed in those Scottish retreats were not just temporary; they became threads woven into the very fabric of our lives.

"As the world teetered on the brink of another war, these memories stood as beacons of a time when life, though not without its challenges, unfolded in a harmonious melody. Little did we know that the symphony of our existence would soon be disrupted by global conflict."

Walter paused, reflecting on the past. "But war was looming again. I didn't wait. I was too old to be conscripted, so I joined the Home Guard as soon as Anthony Eden asked for volunteers. What a ragtag army we were! Brush handles for rifles, tennis balls as grenades, and one set of binoculars between us. I showed them my stripes from the last farce and immediately got promoted from private to sergeant. We were nicknamed 'Dad's Army,' and to some, we were a bit of a joke. But we were all this country had after Dunkirk." Walter's eyes sparkled with the memories of those challenging times as he continued with his tale.

"We had several experts turn up at the meeting hall. They were usually chaps who were specialists in some form of defence. They showed us how to use canals and rivers as obstacles and how to use the lock gates and elevated areas to site machine guns. And then there were the sticky bombs and Molotov Cocktails for destroying tanks.

We eventually had explosives experts showing us how to make bombs, but there was a problem, we didn't get any explosives issued. Alice, never one to shy away from action, eagerly joined the WVS (Women's Voluntary Service). Her fiery determination crackled in her eyes as she sought to contribute more actively to the war effort. Despite her fervent desire for a rifle, she found herself handed a tea trolley, a customary role for women at that time. Undeterred by the unexpected assignment, she dived headfirst into the task, determined to make a difference.

Refusing to let conventions limit her ambitions, Alice sought opportunities to step beyond the expected. She delved into driving for the army, embracing each challenge with an unwavering resolve. Fuelling her passion for learning, she enrolled in a car mechanics course, the grease and grit of the workshop becoming as familiar to her as her own reflection in the mirror. With dedication and perseverance, she earned herself a license to drive bulk loads in wagons, akin to today's HGV license.

Despite her proficiency behind the wheel and her undeniable skill in navigating the intricate mechanics of vehicles, I don't think the oil-smeared face and brown overalls were her best look. Her commitment and competence spoke volumes, far outweighing any fashion concerns.

Around 1942, I received an unexpected visit from my old Captain, accompanied by two imposing MPs. I thought he'd come to ask me to go to Scotland for a cull but I was wrong." Walter paused he gave Julie a smile as he retraced his memories. "The Captain, who was visibly frail and under pressure, delivered the weighty message. "Walter," he began, sitting where Joe sits now, his voice was thin and frail but held onto its sounds of the glens, "I'm afraid your country needs you again."

In a moment of poor taste, I quipped, 'What do you need, are you looking for someone to shoot Hitler?' The Captain brushed aside the jest and continued soberly, 'I need you to come with us. A couple of weeks, that's all, I promise.'

Shaken and afraid, I enquired, "Why, what is it?" The Captain remained tight-lipped, revealing only the urgency of the situation. Alice and I exchanged glances, I could see the concern on her face. She gave me a weak smile and said, "Of course you must go, Walter, I'll be alright."

Torn between duty and my concern for Alice, I reluctantly agreed." Walter drained his mug, it was more of a plea for another coffee than anything else.

It was the first time since our wedding that we were separated, but duty called, and I was trained to respond. I felt a strange mix of flattery and fear, not knowing what I was needed for. Alice helped me pack my old kit bag and that night, I rode a train, unaware of its destination. I must have nodded off because I was abruptly awakened by the guard.

'This is your stop sergeant.' His voice was friendly but weary.

I took a deep breath as I stood on that anonymous station and knew straight away that I was back in Scotland. There was a faint essence of spruce mixed with the earthier smell of heather that I knew so well. I didn't have to wait long, I heard the sound of a wagon engine and then a young squaddie charged onto the platform.

"Sorry I'm a bit late, sir, is it Mr Middlebrough?" He carried my kitbag and then chucked it into the back of his wagon. We drove through a dense mist that seemed to be rolling down through the forest and onto the road. As soon as I arrived at a huge old house buried deep in a forest, I was directed into what was the old kitchen which was serving as the mess.

A young officer greeted me after my meal. 'May I call you Walter?' he asked. I warily nodded that it was all right for him to do so. "The thing is… Walter, come sit down and I'll explain while we eat. I'm blooming starving.' We sat across an old wooden table. 'I'm part of a group sending operatives overseas, usually behind enemy lines. We parachute them in and hope that they will meet up with local resistance groups.' There was a pause as the officer, I never knew his name continued.

'We are losing too many due to their inability to look after themselves until they meet up with friends. In a nutshell, Walter, I'd like you to help our team here to come up with a strategy of how to live off the land and to survive that we can teach to our young operatives."

'Are you sure I'm the right man?' I wasn't sure they'd got the right man.

'You come with glowing credits to your name. Yes, we are sure that you are the man we need.'

The next morning after a breakfast that could have sunk a barge, I was shown to what must have been the old parlour. The walls were decorated with paintings of past lairds and misty waterfalls. Three young chaps were waiting. For the next ten days, we discussed survival. They were eager and willing to accept my experience as a guide. We had quite a few walks in the forest and I tried to show them how they could make a temporary shelter, which plants and berries to eat and which to leave well alone. My experience in France and Belgium was invaluable because I knew what might be available to them. They were nice lads and our walks were very pleasant, I was just sad that Alice was at home on her own. I knew that she would keep herself busy with her driving.

We put together a small survival kit that contained the very basics that someone would need which included; fishing hooks, a compass, a sharp knife, and a sewing kit. It all had to fit into a small traveller's suitcase but mostly it hadn't to look like a survival kit."

Walter fell into a reflective silence as the room was bathed in the peculiar glow of the gloomy winter light.

"Did they pay you for this work?" Joe probed, eager for more details.

Walter's face lit up with a reminiscent gleam. "They certainly did. I reckon I got more than the Prime Minister for those weeks. Alice, always practical, suggested we put it in our holiday fund for after the war."

Julie rose to switch on the lights, adding, "But you had no idea how long the war would last."

"That's one of the worst parts of it, the uncertainty. At least back then, no one was making promises about it being over by Christmas like they did in the past," Walter shared, the weight of the unknown evident in his words.

"I think we'll brew you some coffee, Walter, and I'll whip up a little something to eat before we head home to pick up Debbie from Mum's," Julie proposed.

"Thank you," Walter expressed his gratitude. "It's been really nice having your company."

Julie chimed in, "The next time we meet, it'll be Christmas day. Joe will swing by to pick you up around eleven. How does that sound to you?"

Walter's smile widened, and he replied, "Sounds like a dream to me." The satisfaction in his expression painted a picture of anticipation for the upcoming festive day.

Chapter Thirty-One.
Merry Christmas.

Christmas Day dawned, but the world was still cloaked in pre-dawn darkness when Walter stirred from his slumber. He felt the chill seep into his bones as he padded into the kitchen to put on the kettle.

'Right, I need to get upstairs and get my best clothes'. Each step creaked in symphony with his elderly joints as he ascended the stairs, a sign that they were both ageing. Yet, his heart danced with anticipation, undeterred by the physical reminders of his age.

A melody escaped his lips, "Jingle Bells" hummed softly, a cheerful tune cutting through the quiet of the early morning. With each note, the festive spirit swirled around him, enveloping him in warmth.

Reaching the top of the stairs, he paused, drawn to the window. Peering through the glass, he beheld a wintry scene bathed in darkness. The night had bestowed a generous gift of snow, a pristine blanket veiling the world in hushed tranquillity. Yet, even in the dimness, the twinkling lights of dawn hinted at the promise of a new day.

He took new clothes from his cupboard and his suit from his wardrobe. After washing and shaving he dabbed sandalwood aftershave around his chin and then dressed paying meticulous attention to how he looked. Standing before his reflection for a moment and whispered to the bear above him on top of the wardrobe. "Oh, Alice how you would have loved today."

Joe arrived with a green elf hat pulled down to cover his ears.

"Merry Christmas, Walter. Are you ready?" A rush of cold air suddenly flooded the kitchen as he entered. He rubbed his hands together in glee anticipating that they were all set for a great day.

Walter appeared dressed in a three-piece suit complete with a gold watch chain and a tartan bow tie.

"Hey, Walter you look like the Lord Mayor with your gold chain. You look great."

"Here Joe that's for your family." He pointed at a large cardboard box covered in festive paper and decorated with several large bows.

"Wow, Walter what's all this about and how have you managed to do this shopping." Joe gave him a suspicious look.

"Mrs Singh helped me. Do you remember the chat I had with her, we spoke in Urdu, we were not being rude but I needed to keep a secret?"

"Oh. So that's what that was all about, I did wonder," Joe confessed.

"I admit that she did the wrapping and even selected a few of the gifts," Walter added with a broad grin.

Walter placed another box on top. "Mince pies," he declared and then took another parcel from the fridge, "White Stilton, Mrs Singh brought that as a treat for me."

The festive spirit filled the room as Joe picked up the beautifully wrapped gifts and the delightful mince pies and Stilton. Walter's efforts to make Christmas special warmed Joe's heart.

"Walter, you've really outdone yourself! This is incredible," Joe exclaimed, his eyes widening with appreciation.

Walter chuckled, "Well, I thought I should contribute something to the festivities. Now, let's load these into the car. We don't want to keep your family waiting and I'm rather excited myself." Walter went and retrieved another parcel. "This is special, I need us to make a call on the way to your house will that be alright Joe?"

Joe looked rather puzzled but he did not question the request.

As the gifts were carefully placed in the car, Walter couldn't help but ponder the transformation of his anticipated solitary Christmas morning into a day filled with unexpected joy.

"Are you all right, my friend?" Joe asked.

Leaning against the car boot, Walter sighed. "I can't believe how fortunate I am to have company today. Just a little over a month ago, before we crossed paths, I stood at the cenotaph feeling terribly alone. Most of the veterans I had grown accustomed to meeting there on Remembrance Day have passed away. One of the last, a man I vaguely knew as George, I have no idea about his surname, passed away earlier this year. His son was there in his stead, and we briefly spoke. That's when he shared the sad news of his father's passing."

Joe placed a comforting hand on Walter's shoulder. "The funny thing about Christmas is that, although it's a time of celebration, it also stirs up so many memories from the past."

"That's very true... but today is a day of good cheer, a day to celebrate life and good friends." Walter took a deep breath, a beaming smile rearranging the wrinkles of his weathered skin.

As the wheels rolled toward Joe's house on this festive Christmas Day, Walter's face radiated an infectious joy, heightened by the snowy wonderland enveloping them. The serene landscape, blanketed in pristine snow, lent an enchanting aura to their journey.

Glancing out of the car window, Walter's gaze lingered on the many houses that were brightly lit. He tried to imagine the scenes within as families fought their way through brightly coloured wrapping paper. The air would be filled with the smell of roasting meats and chopped vegetables sitting patiently on the hob waiting for a hearty feast.

"Down here, Joe," Walter suddenly alerted Joe. "Just turn at this corner, down this street. Please, just stop," Walter suddenly directed.

Puzzled but trusting Walter's guidance, Joe pulled over near a patch of wasteland, confused by their unexpected stop.

"I've come to visit an old friend of mine. We've been mates for years. Will you give him the other parcel, Joe, please?" Walter requested. "I can't make it… my old legs you know."

Stepping out onto the snow-laden ground, Joe noticed a makeshift shelter, built from wooden pallets, and shrouded in blue plastic. Nestled within it sat an elderly man, bundled in tattered garments and a blanket. It struck Joe that Walter was determined to make this Christmas special for his friend, despite the circumstances. Approaching the elderly man, Joe extended the parcel.

"Your friend Walter sent this for you. And I'd like to wish you a Merry Christmas too," Joe spoke warmly.

Grubby hands with fingerless gloves gratefully accepted the parcel, and the old man's eyes twinkled with gratitude. "Please pass my thanks to Walter. He's allus been a good mate," the man expressed softly.

As Joe returned to the car, a solitary tear traced its path down his cheek. In this moment, witnessing Walter's selfless act of kindness, Joe discovered a new dimension of his friend a profound generosity and a heart brimming with compassion.

Walter was absorbed by the scenery and didn't seem to notice that Joe was subdued on the way home. Upon arrival, Joe's family welcomed Walter with open arms. The warmth of the home and the inviting aroma of Christmas dinner created a comforting atmosphere.

"Welcome, Walter!" Julie exclaimed, she wore a Christmas jumper complete with flashing reindeer. We're so glad you could join us," Julie greeted him with a warm hug, her eyes sparkling with excitement.

She tweaked his bowtie saying, "My words Walter, you look pretty special."

The beautifully decorated Christmas tree in the corner and the soft glow of fairy lights illuminated the room added further magic to that moment.

"Like all good visitors at Christmas, I come bearing gifts," Walter announced, his eyes sparkling with genuine pleasure. "Thank you for inviting me. These are for you and your lovely family. I hope you like them."

Walter's smile widened as he watched Joe present his gift box to the family. He could sense the warmth of the moment, appreciating the simple joy of sharing during the festive season.

Julie's daughter, Debbie, approached Walter with a curious smile. The room held a brief pause, as Julie, somewhat nervous, observed the interaction. Debbie, however, surprised everyone by staring into Walter's eyes for a moment. In that instant, a basic instinct seemed to guide her, assuring her that this stranger could be trusted.

The tension melted away, replaced by a sense of connection.

"Did you bring me anything, Walter?" Debbie inquired.

Walter chuckled, handing her a small soft package. "A little something to make your Christmas brighter, Debbie. I hope you enjoy it."

Carefully taking the parcel, Debbie sat down at Walter's feet and ripped it open, revealing a colourful tiger.

"It will bring you good luck... do you like it?" Walter asked.

She held it close, cuddling it like a baby. "Oh yes, I've never had a tiger before." Her fingers traced its stripes, and then she looked into its mouth. "Oh, it has very big teeth."

"Tigers need big teeth, but they will not hurt you."

The dining table was adorned with fine china and crystal glasses, creating a warm and inviting atmosphere. The family gathered around the table, sharing laughter and stories as they enjoyed the delicious feast.

"This turkey is absolutely delicious, Julie!" Walter exclaimed between bites. "You're quite the cook."

Julie blushed, appreciating the compliment. "Thank you, Walter. It's an old family recipe. I'm glad you like it, it cooked overnight." She wore a bright yellow crown from the cracker she had pulled with Walter.

They moved to the living room, where Debbie pulled her small chair up beside Walter.

"What did you do at Christmas before you came here?" she asked curiously.

The warmth of the fire flickered in Walter's eyes as he shared his Christmas traditions with Debbie.

"Oh well, we did all kinds of things. Alice, that was my wife," he reminisced with a gentle smile. "We used to like to go to chapel and sing carols. A group of us used to set off at about ten o'clock on Christmas Eve and go around other people's houses, singing at their door."

Debbie looked aghast, "What did they do?"

"Sometimes they would offer us mince pies and donate to whatever charity we were helping that year. Early in the morning, maybe two o'clock, we'd all gather at someone's house and eat mince pies and drink hot tea to chase away the cold."

"I think I'd like to sing carols and get paid with mince pies, I'm not sure about being out in the cold though." She shivered.

Everyone laughed at her remarks.

Walter continued. "To make the room smell festive, we used to stick cloves into an orange and hang them from the tree." Walter could almost smell that distinctive Christmas aroma. "It was a time filled with warmth and laughter. We didn't have any children, so sometimes we'd go stay with some friends in Scotland." Walter paused, those memories of cosy warm holidays with their Scottish friends were special.

Debbie's eyes lit up with curiosity. "That sounds wonderful. I wish we had such traditions here."

Walter continued his journey down memory lane. "One Christmas, we had a change from our usual routine and headed for the West Coast, spending a fortnight in Blackpool."

Joe chimed in, "That must have been fun."

Walter chuckled, "Not really, it was freezing. Even the sea was frozen on the beach. We changed hotels after a couple of days and fortunately found one that had a bit of heating on."

Julie suggested they gather by the fire to open presents, Walter felt a sense of joy and fulfilment. He clutched the precious presents Julie and Debbie had given him.

After the Queen's speech had finished, Julie's parents arrived with even more gifts and goodwill. The day unfolded into a celebration of companionship and love. Christmas, once a lonely day for Walter, had transformed into a day filled with laughter and shared moments, creating new memories that intertwined with the tapestry of his life.

They put Debbie to bed as Walter left and that night she fell asleep clutching her new soft cuddly friend, the tiger and dreamt of singing for mince pies in the snow.

Later that evening, Joe saw Walter safely back into his home. He made a coffee and laid out a few mince pies for his friend. There was an embarrassing pause which was finally brought to an end when they embraced. They both realised that they had found part of what was missing from their lives.

"Thank you for a wonderful day, son," Walter said with a brief sniffle.

"The pleasure is mine, I can't explain how wonderful it was to share this day with you," Joe's voice trembled as the emotion welled up inside. "I'll call and see you tomorrow."

"Nay lad, have a day off, that lovely missus and your daughter would rather you be with them. There's allus plenty of stuff on tele, and Match of the Day will be busy, it always is Boxing Day. I've plenty of grub, Julie gave me a parcel of cold roasts. I think I could do with a rest too."

"Well, if you are sure. I hope we didn't wear you out today?"

"No, it was perfect… honest, just perfect."

Chapter Thirty-Two
Boxing Day.

As Boxing Day unfolded, Walter's cosy home was filled with the delightful aroma of spices after Mr and Mrs Singh arrived, bearing the gift of a delicious homemade curry for lunch. The lively chatter and warmth of their presence added another layer to the festive atmosphere.

As the delightful aroma of curry wafted through Walter's home, the Singhs settled around the table, bringing with them not just a culinary treat but also an air of warmth and camaraderie.

Mrs Singh, with a twinkle in her eye, said, "Walter, my friend, we couldn't let you miss out on our homemade curry. It's a small token of our appreciation for your friendship."

Walter chuckled, "I'm honoured to be on the receiving end of such a delicious gift. I must admit, my culinary skills are nowhere near as refined as yours."

Mr Singh, with a playful grin, added, "Well, we can't have you surviving on mince pies alone, can we? Variety is the spice of life, as they say!"

The room erupted in laughter, and the conversation flowed seamlessly. Walter, always the storyteller, shared anecdotes from his Christmas day, highlighting the joy he experienced with Joe, Julie, and Debbie.

"Thank you, Mrs Singh, your choice of gifts for my friends was just right... and they were well received especially the tiger. Debbie took to it straight away."

"A cousin of mine from Bangalore makes them and other soft toys. She is very skilled; the money goes to a children's fund."

"So, Mr Walter you have found a new family. We are very happy for you," Mr Singh said.

"Yes, I have been a bit lonely since Alice passed away."

"It must be ten years now," Mrs Singh added.

The exchange of stories, the blending of cultures, and the shared appreciation for good food created a beautiful tableau of unity and friendship

Mrs Singh, ever thoughtful, reached into a bag she had brought with her. "Walter, we thought you might enjoy this," she said as she handed him a beautifully wrapped parcel.

As Walter unwrapped the beautifully adorned parcel from the Singhs, a spark of curiosity gleamed in his eyes. The anticipation hung in the air, and with each careful unveiling, the layers of wrapping revealed a collection of traditional Indian spices. The vibrant colours and aromatic scents filled the room, awakening his senses.

"Oh, you shouldn't have!" Walter declared his lower lip quivering with joy.

"Well, you have been a loyal and good customer over the twenty or so years we've been here and I feel that we are also friends. Some around here were not so welcoming as you were."

Walter's face lit up with a radiant joy that transcended a mere exchange of gifts. It was a moment of genuine delight; a reflection of the unexpected pleasures life had recently unveiled for him. The spices, a tangible representation of the Singh's' thoughtful gesture, held the promise of new culinary adventures.

Walter's face lit up with appreciation. "This is fantastic! I'll have to learn a thing or two from you about using these. I might even attempt my own curry someday."

Mr Singh chuckled, "The secret is in the blend, my friend. We'll have to organize a cooking session one day."

In receiving this simple yet profound gift, Walter felt a profound sense of acceptance and belonging. The spices, a treasure trove of flavours and aromas, became a bridge between his friend's culture and his world.

The afternoon unfolded with shared laughter, stories, and the joy of newfound friendship. The simplicity of the gathering, marked by the exchange of cultural delights and thoughtful gifts, created lasting memories for everyone present.

The Boxing Day celebration at Joe's home was filled with the warm glow of friendship and family. Debbie, Julie, and Joe gathered around the dinner table, joined by Julie's parents. The air buzzed with the joy of the season, and the aroma of a hearty meal lingered in the cosy atmosphere.

Debbie, still enchanted by the tiger gift from Walter, clutched it close, her eyes sparkling with delight. Julie's parents exchanged amused glances at Debbie's newfound furry companion.

Joe, with a playful grin, teased, "Looks like Walter's gift has won the coveted position of favourite, eh, Debbie?"

Debbie nodded enthusiastically, her words filled with childlike excitement, "It's the bestest tiger ever! I'm going to call him Mr Stripes."

Julie's parents chuckled, and her dad, raising an eyebrow, remarked, "Mr Stripes, eh? Sounds like quite the distinguished tiger."

Debbie giggled, "Oh, he is!" as she lifted the tiger to illustrate her point.

Julie leaned over and ruffled Debbie's hair, "Well, Mr Stripes is welcome to join us for dinner. I'm sure he's got some stories to share."

That afternoon they watched the cartoon film Jungle Book, Debbie was appalled that the tiger was the villain of the story. "Mr Stripes is not a mean tiger like that one… in fact, he'd bite the tail of that bad one if he could."

The dinner conversation flowed seamlessly, filled with anecdotes, laughter, and the clinking of cutlery against plates. Julie's roast dinner, a tradition in itself, earned praise from the table.

Once the meal concluded, they settled into the living room, the warmth of the fire casting a soft glow. Julie's parents shared tales of their own Christmases, creating a tapestry of memories that blended seamlessly with the spirit of the day.

As they enjoyed the calm after the festive storm, Joe glanced at Julie, a silent acknowledgement of the joy that filled their home. Walter's presence lingered in the shared stories, the laughter, and the simple, heartfelt moments that had woven the threads of their unconventional but deeply cherished Christmas celebration.

The next day, Joe, Julie, and Debbie made their way to Walter's house, carrying a parcel of leftover food from their Boxing Day feast. The crisp winter morning air carried a festive cheer as they entered.

"How are you this morning, Walter?" Joe greeted, noting the kettle's familiar hum.

"I'm doing well, thank you," Walter replied warmly.

Excitedly, Debbie rushed towards Walter and jumped onto his knee.

"Do be careful, Debbie. You don't want to hurt Walter," Julie cautioned.

"Oh, I didn't hurt you, did I, Granddad Walter?" Debbie asked innocently.

Debbie's innocence melted any initial surprise Walter felt at being addressed as 'Granddad.'

Walter grinned, feeling a sudden kinship with Joe and his family. "Not at all, my dear."

Julie proposed sharing the leftovers. "I thought we could have lunch together. It'd be a shame for this food to go to waste. I've left some in your fridge for you."

Around the table, laughter and stories intertwined, filling the room with warmth. Debbie, unable to contain her excitement, burst out:

"Granddad Walter, guess what we named the tiger?"

Walter, intrigued, leaned forward. "Do tell me, what's the tiger's name?"

"Mr Stripes!" Debbie announced proudly, setting off a round of laughter.

Walter chuckled, "Mr Stripes, a splendid name indeed."

Julie explained the tiger reference, relating it to 'The Jungle Book.'

"That's a favourite of mine," Walter acknowledged with a smile. "There's more to 'The Jungle Book' than just Mowgli's story. I have the books somewhere on my shelf."

"Could you read them to me sometime?" Debbie asked, her eyes gleaming with anticipation.

"How did you manage yesterday, Walter?" Joe asked.

"The Singh family, you know from the post office and grocers down the road, brought the most fantastic curry for me. It was a treat!"

He showed them the gift of spices they had also given him.

As they were about to leave, Joe, with a sly grin, suggested, "Walter, how about joining us for New Year's Eve? We're planning something special."

Walter, intrigued, agreed, "Sounds like a plan. I could use some company on New Year's Eve."

Joe and then Julie embraced Walter on their way out. Debbie, held in her father's arms reached out and kissed Walter, a rare gift only usually reserved for parents and grandparents.

"My words, you are honoured," Joe said, "I'll pick you up about six-thirty on New Year's Eve, is that all right for you." Joe gave Walter's shoulder a friendly pat.

"I can't wait, what shall I wear?" the excitement was obvious as he spoke.

Julie bobbed her head back in through the doorway, "Put your nice suit on," Julie added with a radiant smile.

The day before the party, Walter sat contentedly at the kitchen table, relishing the last remnants of turkey in a sandwich. He basked in the satisfaction of the past few days, dressed in the pyjamas gifted by Julie for Christmas, adorned with Tartan patterns that showed she paid attention to his stories. As he savoured his meal, he reflected on the significant changes in his life, particularly since Joe had become his carer. Ever since Alice's passing, he had lost interest not only in Christmas but in life itself. However, the unexpected encounter with Joe transformed his world entirely.

Finishing his meal, he cleared away the dishes and glanced out of the kitchen window. The snow had nearly vanished, leaving only faint traces along the edges of his yard. "I must tidy up the yard once it warms up," he mused aloud to himself.

Earlier that morning, Joe had stopped by for a brief visit, ensuring Walter was doing alright.

"It's still too cold for a walk around the park," Joe remarked as he stocked Walter's fridge with food.

Grinning, Joe added, "I must confess, I'm getting tired of turkey. I reckon most folks have used up their bird in curries and omelettes. Apologies, I can't stay long today; I'm off to Julie's parents for a meal. Debbie is still tightly hugging Mr Stripes."

With a nod, Walter bid farewell to Joe, grateful for the care and company that had unexpectedly brightened his life.

"In the warmth of his snug living room, Walter meticulously adjusted the handful of Christmas cards that had arrived, particularly cherishing the familiar ones from his Scottish friends. The familiar handwriting and heartfelt messages triggered a surge of nostalgia, reminding him of the lasting bonds that transcended the passage of time. Fifteen years had slipped by since their last meeting, yet the enduring remembrance in the form of these cards evoked a sense of deep gratitude and a pang of longing for the companionship he had once cherished.

As he arranged the cards on the mantelpiece, Walter's thoughts meandered into the realm of possibility. Joe's unexpected presence in his life had ignited a spark, reigniting a dormant desire for connection. The notion of rekindling those old friendships surfaced... a prospect that, until now, felt distant and improbable. Yet, spurred by Joe's friendship and the anticipation of the upcoming party, Walter allowed himself a glimmer of hope. The idea of visiting his friends when the weather relented seemed less daunting, more inviting, and, dare he admit, somewhat exhilarating.

Gently setting aside the partially read copy of Ivanhoe, its weighty prose feeling momentarily burdensome, Walter reached for Kipling's Jungle Book. The familiar tale, etched with memories of childhood enchantment, beckoned him into its world, offering solace and familiarity amidst the flurry of thoughts about the impending party. He was determined that he should read passages of it to Debbie and of course Mr Stripes.

Despite the lingering anticipation of tomorrow's gathering, Walter relished this small indulgence, finding comfort in the pages that momentarily transported him away from the hustle and bustle, into a realm of the tiger where cherished memories and wistful dreams languished in the heat of the jungle.

Chapter Thirty-Three.
The Reunion.

Despite the poor weather conditions, sleet had been pounding the streets for several hours, Joe arrived punctually on Walter's doorstep, his enthusiasm for the surprise party was evident in his eager call. "Come on Walter, are you ready?"

Dressed neatly, Walter, although outwardly prepared, emitted an air of reluctance that Joe immediately noticed. "Is everything alright, Walter? You seem a bit different today. You're not feeling under the weather, are you?" Concern laced Joe's voice.

Struggling to contain a surge of conflicting emotions, Walter steadied himself before speaking. "I'm sorry, Joe. I can't help but feel that I'm imposing on you and your wonderful family. You've all been incredibly kind to me and I never intended to be a bother. It's one reason why I've been so hesitant about accepting your help."

Joe closed the distance between them, enveloping Walter in a heartfelt embrace. "You're not a brother, Walter. Not in the slightest. You've added warmth and light to our lives. We're thrilled to have you as part of our family, not just today but always. Come on, let's get your coat on; the party's waiting."

Walter's eyes reflected a mix of gratitude and insecurity. "Thank you, Joe. But sometimes, I can't shake this feeling that I'm intruding."

Joe's reassuring grip on Walter's shoulder conveyed unwavering support. "You're not intruding, my friend. You're a cherished part of this celebration. Trust me, your presence brings us all joy. Now, together, let's head to the party and make some memories."

Walter and Joe made their way quickly toward the waiting car, an indescribable warmth enveloped Walter's heart. Joe's reassuring words and the prospect of joining in the festivities with newfound friends ignited a spark of anticipation within him. The drive to the party was quiet, Walter's memories of other New Year's Eves haunted him. The snowy streets outside seemed to fade away, eclipsed by the ghosts of the past.

The sight of the curry house as they arrived prompted Walter to quip, "Curry for a celebration, Joe? Now, that's my kind of festivity!"

Joe offered a steadying hand as they traversed the pavement. "Take it slow, Walter. The path can be a bit slippery."

Stepping into the curry house, Walter was greeted by a chorus of applause. The air crackled with palpable excitement as arms opened wide to embrace him, and the restaurant staff, dressed in their traditional outfits, formed an unexpected guard of honour for him. Overwhelmed by the warmth of the reception, Walter found himself struggling to absorb the enormity of the moment. His gaze swept the room, and there, amidst the gathering, were the Singhs, his dear friends whose presence added to the overwhelming emotions surging within him. The tears pooling in Walter's eyes mirrored the explosion of emotions swirling inside him, like a radiant firework display. The sheer weight of this unexpected celebration seemed to render him momentarily speechless.

"What's happening, Joe?" Walter's voice trembled with a blend of emotions, bewilderment, joy, and a touch of curiosity, as he tried to make sense of the unexpected spectacle.

Joe's smile held an underlying warmth as he explained, "Do you remember the TV programme, 'This Is Your Life'? Well, tonight, Walter, it's your turn. We want to honour your life, surrounded by the very special people who share this evening with you."

Walter found himself manoeuvred to the heart of the room and seated at a small table, enveloped by an atmosphere brimming with anticipation and camaraderie. One of the waiters brought him a plate of freshly cooked popadums.

"Are you comfortable?" Julie's gentle inquiry broke through the moment, her eyes reflecting a depth of care and affection for Walter. "Please enjoy these, Mr Walter," the boy said with a bow of respect.

Debbie, in her exuberance, clambered onto Walter's knee, clutching Mr Stripes tightly. The air in the curry house filled with an unexpected yet heart-warming sound, one that echoed the spirit of the Glens of Scotland.

Suddenly, a familiar figure emerged from the staffroom, dressed in magnificent Scottish regalia, a dear old friend from Walter's days at the hotel in Scotland. The room burst into applause as the enchanting melody of bagpipes filled the air, encircling Walter in a joyous, uplifting rhythm.

Clapping along with sheer glee, Walter couldn't contain his infectious enthusiasm. His hands extended outward in appreciation and delight, encapsulating the spirit of this unexpected celebration in his own unique way.

"You might have thought that was a surprise," Joe declared with a grin, "but hold on to your sporran, Walter."

There was a line of chairs facing Walter and one by one they filled with characters that Walter didn't quite recognise although there was something about them that seemed familiar. The last lady was crying soulfully and just as she was about to take her place she hesitated and then rushed over to Walter and embraced him. There was something so familiar about that touch that Walter instinctively knew that it was his long-lost sister Elsie.

The room seemed to hold its breath as the siblings clung to each other, their hearts and memories intertwining after years of separation. Tears flowed freely, speaking volumes where words fell short. Walter felt a sense of completion, a missing piece of his life's puzzle falling perfectly into place.

Introductions unfolded in a harmonious symphony of voices as Walter was introduced to Elsie's children. There was an undeniable aura of excitement and curiosity as the family gathered around the table, creating an atmosphere that exuded warmth and an unwavering sense of acceptance.

Joe, the mastermind behind this heartfelt reunion, observed with a contented smile as Walter and Elsie began reconnecting, bridging the chasm of lost time. The tantalizing menu was checked with great interest, accompanied by an ambience teeming with laughter and the shared tales of yesteryears. As the evening progressed, dishes were passed around, stories recounted, and the clinking of cutlery became a symphony interwoven with the echoes of heartfelt laughter. The Curry House bore witness to a momentous occasion… a long-awaited reunion of siblings, an ode to family, love, and the enduring resilience of relationships that stand the test of time.

When everyone had eaten their fill, a gentle lull settled over the gathering. Memories fluttered through their minds like autumn leaves, each whispering tales of bygone days, painting a bittersweet symphony of emotions. Walter's heart swelled with the realization of the profound impact of human connections, the fleeting encounters, the enduring friendships, and the joyous reunion with family. Each thread wove seamlessly into the rich tapestry of his life, an iridescent mosaic of shared moments and newfound belonging.

Amidst the shared reflections, Walter pondered the unforeseen twists his life had taken, the fateful encounter with Joe, the unexpected reunion with Elsie, and the jubilant celebration that tied up loose ends. These once-distant dreams now rested as vibrant chapters within the story of his existence, illuminating his path with newfound hope and healing.

As the clock struck midnight, a hushed anticipation enveloped the gathering. They circled together, hands entwined, and the soulful strains of "For Auld Lang Syne" reverberated through the air. The haunting melody was accompanied, as it should be, by the soul-stirring sounds of the bagpipes a poignant tribute to cherished memories, enduring connections, and the promise of a new beginning.

The End.